The Flower Arranger at All Saints

THE
FLOWER ARRANGER
AT ALL SAINTS

Lis Howell

Carroll & Graf Publishers
New York

Carroll & Graf Publishers
An imprint of Avalon Publishing Group, Inc.
245 W. 17th Street, 11th Floor
New York, NY 10011-5300
www.carrollandgraf.com

AVALON
publishing group incorporated

First published in the UK by Constable,
an imprint of Constable & Robinson Ltd 2007

First Carroll & Graf edition 2007

Copyright © Lis Howell 2007

ISBN-13: 978-0-78671-913-6
ISBN-10: 0-7867-1913-3

Printed and bound in the United States of America

To my mum, Jessica Edna Baynes,
the best-read person I know, who
made us all go to Sunday School!

1

Easter Eve

Lighten our darkness, we beseech thee, O Lord . . .
From the third Collect at Evening Prayer

The cold evening light flooded through the Gothic windows of the flower vestry at All Saints Church. Phyllis Drysdale was bending over the bucket of arum lilies, which were just opening on their stiff green stems, but she looked round to catch the glow. Outside, the sun was starting to set beyond the North Country fells in a final burst of chilly gold, as if to say, 'Look what you'll be missing!' Within half an hour it would disappear behind Tarnfield Scar.

'Goodbye, Phyllis,' the Reverend Nick Melling called from the church. 'Will you be all right working here by yourself? It's nearly six o'clock.'

It would soon be dark, but there were only the lilies left to do. They were to be the crowning glory of the big Easter Sunday arrangement at the altar, after the bleak flowerless days of Lent.

'Yes, of course I will. Thank you, Nick.'

She disliked calling him Nick. Phyllis was old enough to find diminutives too familiar, except for babies or pets. But Nick Melling, the new parish priest, was in his early thirties and insisted on informality.

Phyllis shivered.

She was used to working in the cold. But Easter was very early this year, in March, and it seemed especially icy in the flower vestry, which was at right angles to the main church, about twelve feet square, with windows facing east and west on each side, and a big stone sink in the corner. All Saints had been built more than a century and a half earlier. In the 1980s someone had added metal shelves to the flower vestry's stone walls but they were now bent and scratched, packed with plastic urns and huge lumps of oasis foam, and the wires, scissors and secateurs needed for the job.

A piece of rusty chicken wire stuck out and jabbed Phyllis's elbow through her cardigan as she straightened up.

'Ouch!' she gasped.

You needed to be careful. Some of this stuff was dangerous. She groped around for her toolbox on the floor. The sun was still there in the west, but through the opposite east-facing windows of the vestry it was already night. With her fingers wet and aching from cutting and wiring, Phyllis thought it was a good job her arthritis wasn't so bad in her left hand. Her right was pretty useless but at least she could still manage. Oh, the spiteful trials of age! She was tired now. She would put the lilies in place; then it would certainly be time to go home.

Tarnfield village was always quiet at this time of the evening, especially on a Saturday during a bank holiday weekend. No one was at the Chinese takeaway yet, the Lo-cost supermarket was almost empty, and the last bus had gone. It was getting colder. Phyllis loved Easter when it came in April, but she thought March was a mean month, showering you with bitter little raindrops or slicing you with icy blasts of wind, just when you thought it was warming up. Still, she was pleased with the flowers. There were lilies, forsythia and flag iris and tons of daffodils – though of course they wouldn't mix with the others. Daffs were poisonous to other flowers.

Poison. The thought stopped her rummaging through her tools. Phyllis was worried. She was one of those rare people who feel uncomfortable with gossip. The back-biting which was so much a part of parish life worried her. It seemed there was nobody she could talk to about the information that was wriggling away in her brain like the nasty little caterpillars they sometimes found in the chrysanthemums at Harvest Festival.

She heard the porch door at the back of the church creak and swing open, and Suzy Spencer shouted, 'Are you there, Phyllis?' Carrying the lilies, Phyllis nudged open the vestry door. She caught sight of Suzy's cropped bright highlights in the final shaft of silvery sun through the rose window.

'Yes, Suzy, I'm fine. I'm just doing the lilies now. I'm so glad we splashed out on the arums. There's no need to stay. I know you're busy, you get away . . .'

'Oh, thanks, Phyllis. I've got to get the kids on the six fifteen train to their dad's . . .'

'I understand, dear. You ought to hurry.'

Suzy raised her hand in a wave and disappeared. She was an unlikely helper, Phyllis thought. Two children, a job 'in media' and a husband, if he *was* her husband, who was obviously living somewhere else. And surprisingly it had been Phyllis's dear friend, the late Mary Clark, who'd recruited Suzy Spencer.

'Not really our type,' Mary had said briskly to Phyllis, 'but she was hanging round the church and she seemed to need something to do.' Phyllis was surprised at Mary's interest. Mary had been conventional – and judgemental sometimes. There was no doubt Suzy's lifestyle as a harassed working mum had clashed with Mary's perfect housekeeping standards.

Suzy often missed the meetings of the flower arrangers' group. At the last gathering, one or two of the others had taken the chance to bitch about her, something Mary had done constantly before she died. Phyllis had said nothing, but it had made her feel awkward. Yvonne Wait, a smart single woman in her forties with a bell of glossy dark hair, had groaned, 'I see Suzy Spencer isn't here again. I don't see why she can't be a bit more organized. Anyone would think having two children meant your brain was on hold!' Yvonne was an administrator at the local hospital.

Phyllis had said quietly, 'Well, she does work as well, you know . . .'

'Oh, I really don't agree with working mothers,' tall, faded fair-haired Jane Simpson had added regally. Jane lived in Tarnfield House, and had one grown-up son who'd spent most of his adolescence at boarding school. Phyllis had sighed. She could remember when Jane had been just Jane Strickland, a girl from the village, with secret pretensions. Phyllis had never really liked 'Lady' Jane, with good reason. But she was far too mild-mannered to let the past intrude.

Monica Bell from Bell's Wood Yard had tried to change the subject. 'Well, whatever you think of Suzy Spencer, we need her energy. No one else here can get up the ladders to put those floral swags on the pillars.' Monica, small and stocky, was always practical. Her husband Frank had fixed great hooks into the church masonry to hold trailing displays of flowers and, like Frank himself, they were big, solid and just a bit awkward. It was a great relief to Monica that Suzy Smith was agile enough to get up the ladder to them. Monica was too heavy, Jane was too grand, Yvonne was too smartly dressed, and poor Phyllis was limited by her arthritis.

How difficult it was getting church people to work together without all sorts of personality clashes, Phyllis thought. It had been different when Mary was alive. She had been Phyllis's best friend since they were children in Tarnfield, but she had died just over a year ago. Mary Clark had virtually run the church, whipping everyone into shape, and her death had left a big hole in Phyllis's life – no, in the life of Tarnfield. Mary's husband Robert tried hard to help, but he had never been as committed to All Saints as Mary, and he was wrapped up in his own grief. He was a quiet man, five years younger than Mary, too young to be one of those people Phyllis considered 'their' generation, the last generation really to have any sense of old-fashioned values, so he failed to fill the gap for her. Phyllis had always been rather shy of men. They could be so temperamental, she thought, remembering her own

10

past. And now she had the Bible study group to deal with. Oh dear. Mary had always coped with it all before.

Phyllis went back into the flower vestry to get her scissors, and blinked in the growing gloom. Just this last armful of lilies to do, and then she could get home to the bungalow. But where did I put my final Bible study list? she wondered. Oh, why am I so absent-minded? I never imagined Mary would go before me, she thought yet again. Phyllis had been the older one with the weak heart, the one who barely survived rheumatic fever in childhood, the 'old maid' with endless complaints. Yet Mary, efficient and capable, had died, and Phyllis was left. God certainly moved in mysterious ways.

As she thought the word 'moved', Phyllis sensed there was someone behind the vestry door, in the church, but she stifled the idea.

'Look to the west,' she told herself, 'and turn your back on those dark east windows.'

Outside, the fells were a dusky skirting board to the setting sun, but its dying brightness still filtered into the pointed lead-lighted windows. Phyllis thought of Psalm 121, *I will lift up mine eyes unto the hills, from whence cometh my help*, and tried to ignore her sense of disquiet. Such a pity Nick Melling hated the psalms so much. He'd replaced them at the Family Service with songs to guitar, which Phyllis found fatuous. Mary might have talked him out of such silliness. But he wouldn't listen to anyone else, and he was stubbornly enthusiastic. Phyllis sighed.

There was a rustle behind her again, but she ignored it. She didn't want to grope for the light switch. Electric light so finalized the day. Ah, here was the Bible study group list.

Phyllis looked through it: apart from the women who did flower arranging too, there were the three men to add. Clever but sad Robert Clark who was Mary's widower; grumpy and crude old Tom Strickland, the veteran churchwarden; and super smooth Alan Robie who lived with his 'friend' in Church Cottage.

Oh, and of course there was also Daisy Arthur. Phyllis

sighed. Daisy was still just a girl, who'd come back to the village after university. Phyllis put the list in her pocket thoughtfully. Apart from Daisy and Suzy Spencer, it was mainly old faithfuls, which was a shame. Phyllis had felt particularly hurt at being snubbed by the new church-warden and his wife, Kevin and Janice Jones. They were young marrieds who lived in Tarn Acres, the new houses behind the church. They maintained that they couldn't come to the group because their children were so tiny, but Phyllis suspected that they secretly sneered at traditional scripture study. Janice was a straightforward local girl, but Kevin Jones was a Yorkshireman with a round shaved head who wore black T-shirts with slogans on. He was very chummy with the new vicar, whom he called Nick the Vic. Best not to think about that, Phyllis told herself. There was a nagging suspicion at the back of her mind that both Nick Melling and Kevin Jones would be quite happy to get rid of the traditions she was trying so hard to maintain.

But some people appreciated her efforts, and, surpris-ingly, spiky-haired Suzy Spencer was one of them, despite Mary's misgivings. Suzy was a neighbour of Kevin and Janice Jones in the 'executive homes' in Tarn Acres. She had turned out to be kind and helpful, but . . . Phyllis sighed. It wasn't just her casual appearance, or the time she'd used a four-letter-word in church. Perpetually on the go, Suzy had a favourite saying, 'If a job's worth doing it's worth doing badly,' which she would repeat with a laugh whenever her flower arrangements collapsed, which was often. Most people at All Saints took it all more seriously.

The rustling in the main church was growing.

'Who's there?' Phyllis shouted. Her voice trilled from the flower vestry as crackly as the dried thistles they had sprayed gold one Christmas. The rustling stopped.

'Who's there?' she said again, trying to sound author-itative. The words echoed like a church mouse's squeak.

I will have to go into the dark and see, she thought. Propelled by a sense of both duty and foreboding, still clutching her scissors and the last few lilies, she opened the flower vestry door and moved in between the pews to the church nave.

It was the last voluntary move she made.

Robert Clark suddenly noticed that the sun was setting behind him and he stopped digging. He wasn't quite sure why he was turning the earth over anyway. But the garden had always been his wife's territory and, like so many other things, he felt he had to keep it going as Mary had left it. Carefully, he knocked the clumps of soil from his spade, took it to the shed, wiped it, shut and locked the door, and walked round to the front of his house so he could leave his heavy shoes in the vestibule. He sighed. The front garden fence was in need of attention.

'Evening, Robert.'

He turned to see Alan Robie from Church Cottage out for his evening walk. 'Just my daily constitutional,' Alan boomed. Alan played the role of middle-class countryman to perfection, with his pipe and tweed jacket. Robert found it rather touching. Everyone knew Alan was gay.

'Evening, Alan. I expect you'll be at church tomorrow?'

'Oh yes. Never miss Easter Sunday, you know. Just hope Nick Melling isn't going to astound us all with his guitar playing again. Not my cup of tea.'

'But Stevie likes it, doesn't he?'

At the mention of his partner, Alan assumed a paternal look. 'Younger people, you know. I suppose they have to be catered for. By the way, Robert, are you joining the Bible study group again?'

'Oh yes, I think so!'

'Jolly good!'

Robert watched Alan walk purposefully down the lane from The Briars. He smiled, but Alan's remark rankled slightly. I don't think of myself as old, he thought. But perhaps that's how other people see me. And of course Mary was older than me, which might explain it.

Inside, he took off his boots and straightened out the

hems of his brown corduroy trousers, hung his gardening hat on the convenient peg, and ran his fingers through his hair, where he'd perspired under the tweed cap. He still had a lot of hair, not all of it grey. Mary sometimes used to kiss him on the top of his head. He put the kettle on. It was fourteen months and two weeks since she had died, and he missed her more now than ever. Hadn't C.S. Lewis written something about how, when shock and grief end, the power of memory kicks in?

It was Easter Saturday. Tomorrow would be the biggest day in the Church's calendar and he would be there, singing in the choir as he had done for ten years, smiling and pretending he was coping. Christ is risen, he thought. But Mary is dead. It was now, when all the activity was over, that he really hurt. He'd been distraught when her cancer had been diagnosed, but then they had fought it so hard it had energized them both. Mary wasn't the sort of person to give in. But astonishingly, she had lost. Her death had been a sort of outrage, a massive event, which had its own grim momentum. Now, there was nothing.

He sat alone at his scrubbed wooden kitchen table, with Mary's china collection in the dresser and the copper-bottomed pans he never used hanging on the wall. He was drinking his tea, aware it was getting dark. What could he do to fill in the next hour? At seven thirty he would go to the Plough for a pint. He remembered how, when they'd married, Mary had said, 'You must do your writing while I make dinner.'

That had been the plan, but he'd given up his attempts to be a novelist. Being a teacher suited him better. Mary had occasionally hinted at her disappointment, but they had rubbed along happily, just the two of them. In those days, women over thirty didn't usually start families and Mary had been thirty-four when they married. When she suggested that it was too late for children, he had agreed. And generally, their marriage had been good. It had its ups – and one very big down – but in the end they had each other and that had been enough.

What am I to do with myself? he thought. There was

nothing for it but to go on, living the life Mary had chosen for them. She had loved Tarnfield, and she'd encouraged Robert to apply for his job at Norbridge College. She'd seized the chance to move back to the village where she had been brought up. As a girl, Mary had been 'someone' in Tarnfield – the local doctor's daughter. When her childhood home, The Briars, had come up for sale she'd rushed to make an offer and all their available resources had been spent on the deposit and mortgage. It was a lovely detached Edwardian house, double-fronted with two bay windows, and a fanlight over the door. It was at the end of a little unmetalled cul-de-sac. Even with Mary's salary from the part-time job which she'd taken in the office at Bell's Wood Yard, there was no money left for anything else. The house had been their world. Keeping it going was a huge drain on Robert's resources. But he couldn't imagine any other way of life.

Tomorrow he had been invited to Easter Sunday lunch with Monica and Frank Bell, nice people of this parish, though Frank never darkened the church's door except to do odd jobs. With a little glow of pleasure at having something to do, Robert remembered he needed to iron a shirt.

He went upstairs, pausing in the loo and afterwards looking at himself in the mirror. Short brown hair, grey at the sides. A nice average face. Sad eyes. I'm becoming an old fogey, he thought, with my outdated interest in the church, and my clean living and my silent misery, guaranteed never to embarrass anyone. The thought of sex worried him a little, but he was never the sort to resort to glossy mags, or the internet, or lap-dancing clubs in Manchester. He was aware of all that of course and he was sad that his sex life was over. But he also knew from experience that in times of trouble that was the first urge to go. When it pounced back sometimes, he sublimated it in grief for Mary, his only lover for twenty-five years. He imagined that people thought a middle-aged churchgoing couple had none of that. But they were wrong, and once again he longed for the smell and touch of her.

He always did the ironing in the little spare bedroom at the front of the house. There was still enough light from the setting sun to mean he could stand there in the darkness for a moment, looking out up the lane to the main road which wound like a grey tarmac ribbon down the hill. As he watched, he saw a car coming towards the village.

To his surprise, instead of passing the end of the lane, it trundled round the corner and came straight towards The Briars. Robert knew exactly what was going to happen, and there was nothing he could do but watch. The car slowed down as the lane flattened out, but then it continued on towards his low front-garden fence. There was the crack of contact, a silence, then the sound of falling timber. As he turned to run down the stairs, Robert recognized the driver. He groaned. It was Suzy Spencer, the woman his efficient wife had labelled the local flake.

2

Easter Eve, earlier

*We acknowledge and bewail our manifold sins and
wickedness.*
From the Confession at Holy Communion

A few hours earlier, Easter Saturday had become the day
from hell for Suzy and the rest of the Spencers, or at least
those of the family who still lived in Tarnfield. Nigel
Spencer had escaped three months earlier to live with his
PA in a smart new apartment in Newcastle. He had left his
wife and their two children in the picturesque village he
had chosen when he uprooted them from London and
moved the family 'up North' for his job in advertising.

'I don't want to go to Daddy's,' squealed six-year-old
Molly. 'It's my best friend's party today.'

'Well, we can't all go to everything, sweetie.' Suzy
smiled through clenched teeth. 'Daddy's meeting you and
Jake off the six o'clock train. He's taking you roller-blading
tomorrow, and he's booked Pizza City.'

'I don't like pizza any more.'

'Molly, that's ridiculous. I'm not listening to this. Where
are your roller-blades?' Suzy Spencer yelled up the stairs:
'Jake? Have you packed?'

'Yeah.'

'What about your clean jeans?'

'They're still wet. I'm going to wear these ones.'

'With the bum down to your knees? No you're not. Are
you taking your sax?'

'Yeah, I want to practise.'

Well, that was a turn-up for the books. Jake's enthusiasm for music was a surprise, since neither Suzy nor Nigel could play a note. It was great that he was taking the sax over to Newcastle. The kids didn't realize how lucky they were to be getting out of the village for Easter, Suzy thought, despite all the upheaval.

She suspected Nigel had been disappointed with Tarnfield from the start. He'd chosen it because it was pretty; the houses in Tarn Acres were smart but relatively cheap; and now that Suzy was forced to be a part-time freelance TV producer, she could drive the children to school in Norbridge. But Nigel's knowledge of country life had come from reading a leisurewear catalogue and he couldn't cope with a place where you needed to be third generation in order to understand the bus timetable. Country life could be very stressful, the Spencers had discovered. The Lo-cost supermarket shut at eight, and the cinema and video shop were miles away. Without a car you'd be lost. There was toughness about Tarnfield too. It hadn't always been a cosy place to live and it had a ferocious history. The sheltering dark sandstone walls of the church, rebuilt in Victorian times on a site a thousand years old, cuddled the Plough Inn protectively from marauding Scots. The High Street formed a backbone against which everything else clustered.

One winter had been enough. It had been no surprise in the spring when the telltale signs of another of Nigel's 'flings' appeared – late working, weekend conferences, new bright-coloured underpants. They'd been living in the village for eighteen months when he said he couldn't stand it any more and decamped. Just after Christmas, in a weekend of tears and hysteria – some of it genuine – Suzy closed the door behind him with relief.

And now here she was, stuck in a close-knit northern village where she had no friends, working for three days a week as an assistant producer at Tynedale TV, getting the odd bit of work for Granada in Manchester, looking after Jake and Molly, but with no social life of her own. And for the first time since she'd left university years before, she had no idea where life was taking her.

'I want to go to Sunday School tomorrow,' wailed Molly, surprisingly.

'That's funny. Half the time you don't want to go when you can!'

'But we're making an Easter garden tomorrow with Daisy.'

Daisy Arthur was one of their neighbours in Tarn Acres who also ran the Sunday School at All Saints. She was a pretty but earnest girl who had come home to Tarnfield after uni, with sleek light brown hair and a taste for bright colours. Molly was at the age when she thought all teachers were wonderful, and Mummy had become boringly familiar.

'Well, tough. You're going to your father's.' Sometimes Suzy cracked with the effort of persuading the children to love their defecting dad. 'Jake . . . hurry up!'

Jake had been experimenting with fierce sulking because he wanted to spend Easter Monday on a car trip down the M6 to a paint-balling centre near Preston with some of the older village lads.

'No. Out of the question,' Suzy had said. 'That's just the sort of long journey that could end in a nasty accident on the motorway.'

'Dad wouldn't say that. You only say that because you're a crap driver yourself.'

He had stormed off to his room where the sound of loud incoherent music started to bounce off the walls. It was cosmetic anger: Jake was an easy-going boy and usually he and his mother got on well. But Suzy was irritated because she knew he was right. She *was* a bad driver. And she felt bad about banning his expedition. Was she projecting her own failings on to him and his mates? Would Nigel have said, 'Yeah great, go for it'?

Then, infuriatingly, the washing machine flooded the kitchen. And just when Suzy was trying to mop up, one of her neighbours knocked on the door, ostensibly to ask her to join the 'Ban the Wheelie Bins' campaign. Barbara

Piefield had been born in one of the Tarnfield labourers' cottages and she and her husband had upgraded to Tarn Acres as soon as it was built. Keeping the neighbourhood 'up' was Babs's life's work. She viewed Suzy with a mixture of curiosity and suspicion, but she liked to gossip. Though she wasn't a churchgoer herself, she loved all the speculation and controversy surrounding Nick Melling, the new vicar, and his intentions. No one was really sure which way All Saints would go now – high church or happy clappy – but most people in the village had an opinion about it, even if they never went near the place.

Babs sat and chatted and wouldn't go home, so it was three o'clock before Suzy phoned the washing machine engineer on the 24/7 hotline.

'Ooh, Tarnfield. The earliest we can possibly get there is Monday week sometime between eight o'clock and one o'clock.'

'So I have to take the day off work?'

'It's not our problem' hovered unsaid.

'God, this place!' Suzy swore to herself, not for the first time.

And yet . . . if she was fair, it hadn't been too awful. After some enquiries – and a few raised eyebrows from the earth mother brigade – she had arranged for Sharon Strickland to come and look after Molly for a few hours after school when she was working. And two of the 'school gate mums' from Norbridge had invited her for coffee. But going to see them meant a twenty-minute drive. Tarnfield was tiny by comparison to the nearest town, and in the village almost everyone was connected to everyone else through birth or marriage. Getting to know people was like trying to catch up with a soap opera – except that this drama had been running for at least fifty years, to the same participating audience. It wasn't the life Suzy had expected for herself and her children – and it was alien and frustrating at times – but even so, when the larks sang like celestial smudges in the screensaver blue sky, or the smell of woodfires curled round the village on autumn evenings, she felt it wasn't all bad.

One lonely Thursday shortly after moving to the village, she had visited All Saints. She had been brought up as an Anglican so it was one of the few things in Tarnfield that felt familiar. She went in and sat down in a pew. There was a quiet beauty to the church and a sense of its being lovingly cared for. After the chaos of an aggressive marriage and frantic family life, the peace brought tears to her eyes. Then she had heard voices, and suddenly Mary Clark had waylaid her, assuring her of a warm welcome at services. Mary had been insistent, in a bossy, efficient, no-excuses kind of way, and Suzy had felt obliged to go back the next Sunday.

It wasn't such a bad idea. Going to church meant she could escape from Nigel's weekend blues for a few hours. Suzy sensed that Mary Clark didn't approve of her, but Mary dutifully chivvied her into getting the children involved. Molly went to Sunday School and even Jake had been persuaded to take part in some sort of male bonding, clearing the churchyard undergrowth with lads wielding serious metal implements. But that had been nearly two years ago. The super-competent Mary Clark was dead now. This was Suzy's second Easter in Tarnfield and, despite the church, she felt like an outsider.

By five o'clock on this Easter Saturday, she was still mopping up the water on the kitchen floor with old towels. She needed to hurry. She wanted to call in at All Saints on her way to the station to check that Phyllis Drysdale was managing with the Easter lily display, despite her arthritis. The train to Newcastle passed through Tarnfield Junction at six fifteen. If the kids weren't on it Nigel would go mad. He had been working all day – on yet another crucial deal, of course. But he had insisted the children come to him for Saturday night when his girlfriend would meet them off the train. They would stay for Easter Sunday and come home that evening, leaving him and his partner to Easter Monday in peace. It was all organized to suit him, and to avoid Suzy meeting his current 'squeeze'. Sod him! Suzy thought.

By now she had given up on clean jeans for Jake but

there would be hell if Molly forgot her roller-blades. Taking them blading on Easter Sunday was something Nigel had promised weeks ago. She imagined that the girlfriend would look gorgeous in lycra leggings.

'But Mum,' Molly was whining, 'I can't find the bag for them.'

'Just grab them, and get in the car. I'll find a plastic bag in the boot.'

'I can't carry them, not with Flowerbabe as well.' Molly had recently taken to carting a grotesque baby doll around with her.

'Jake, take Molly's roller-blades. Don't argue. Do it now!'

They scrambled into the car with seconds to spare and Suzy swung it into the village. It took her about three minutes to call into All Saints and check that Phyllis was fine, and then she started uphill to the station. It meant driving past Tarnfield Scar, with its sudden dramatic cliffs cutting down to the Tarn river, and then on to a higher valley which dissected the slab of the Pennines and followed the Tarn east. At Tarnfield Junction the kids tumbled out in a state of panic and sudden diffidence. It was getting dark.

'Here's the ticket money. Pay the guard on the train. You've seen me do it.'

'OK, Mum don't fuss.' But as well as giving her his usual perfunctory hug, Jake had kissed her.

'You'll be fine,' she murmured, sensing his nervousness. 'You love blading and Dad will have got you fab Easter eggs. Save me some chocs. And I'll meet you here tomorrow. Look after Molly. It's only a half-hour journey.'

Through the carriage window she could see the comforting outlines of women who'd been shopping. And there was a ticket collector on this train, patrolling up and down. Jake was thirteen and Molly was six, hardly a baby. It was quite safe. But as the train heaved noisily away towards the blackness of the eastern plateau she felt a moment of panic.

Then it was quiet and still again, and she trudged slowly back to the car. She called Nigel on her mobile and tried not to react to his terse office-bound interrogation. Yes, the kids were on the train, they had everything they needed. Why does he treat me like some sort of inadequate? she thought. Perhaps because his girlfriend doesn't need to lose pounds, and I bet her roots don't show. It was funny how Nigel's women 'on the side' were always cool, dark and willowy. She thought that people tended to go for the same type, yet his lovers – and she knew there had been quite a few – couldn't be more different from her. It made her feel frumpy and unattractive.

Well, tonight she had her freedom. She was going to open a bottle of white wine, ring her friend Rachel Cohen in London and talk for about an hour without anyone shouting 'Mum' at her. And then she'd watch a film. It would be fine without the kids – though even thinking about them made her strain to hear the distant growling of the train levering its way over the hills. It was silent. They'd gone.

In the car she started to think what news she would have to tell Rache. They'd been best friends since starting work together in Manchester. They always had a giggle about Suzy's attempts at flower arranging. She remembered how Mary Clark had approached her one Sunday, as if it were an honour.

'We could really do with some help, especially for festivals, now Phyllis's hand is getting worse,' Mary had said. 'So can we count on you for Harvest?'

And Suzy had actually enjoyed making the huge hedges of chrysanthemums and autumn leaves. Mary and Phyllis had been to a decoration wholesaler's in Leeds and come back with mounds of additional stuff – bright red and orange varnished berries, and some really vicious-looking reeds and rushes with wire spines.

'They'll stiffen up the displays,' Mary had said, and Phyllis had twittered, 'Oh, like "All Things Bright and Beautiful" . . . You know, *the tall trees in the greenwood, the meadows where we play, the rushes by the water, we gather every day.*'

'You should have seen me struggling with the lungwort and hellebore,' Suzy told Rachel.

'Try antibiotics,' her friend answered.

Suzy took the turn down towards Tarnfield a little too sharply. Something shot from under the dashboard on to the floor. It was one of Molly's blades. Oh bugger, she thought. Bugger, bugger, bugger. She tried to reach down with her left hand but it had fallen under the clutch pedal. With her scrabbling, she failed to change gear, and took the corner back into the village far too quickly. She tugged on the handbrake and the car careened right. There was nowhere to pull over, even if she could brake, so she turned the wheel, crossed the carriageway, and the car shuddered into Briar Lane.

'Please God, let it stop,' she prayed, but even as she did she knew God had bigger things on Her mind. The car rolled down the lane and hit the late Mrs Mary Clark's garden fence.

'Oh fuck,' said Suzy as her chest gently bounced off the steering wheel and the sound of splintering woodwork rippled through the clear, still evening.

That wasn't the only noise in Tarnfield. Up at the church, someone slammed the door of the flower vestry on the dark east side. A glance up and down the alleyway leading on to the High Street revealed no one in sight. The door was locked swiftly, and the figure slipped away into the village.

3

Easter Eve, continued

Defend us from all perils and dangers of this night.
From the third Collect at Evening Prayer

'Time for a sundowner,' said Alan Robie in his best plummy voice, as he opened the cottage door. He'd been for a Saturday evening stroll around Tarnfield and had been standing at the end of the High Street, looking down with satisfaction to the cottage he shared with his partner Stevie. This evening, his sense of security was greater than ever. He was so glad to be living here. He enjoyed village life, playing a full part in the parish as a member of the Parochial Church Council and the Bible study group, and helping the good lady flower arrangers from time to time with the heavier decorations. For years previously, his only recreation had been as a leading light in the amateur dramatic society in Norbridge, the town where he had practised law for thirty years. Being homosexual wasn't what people expected from their family solicitor and he'd spent his time miserably lusting after the bereaved or newly divorced, knowing it was highly unprofessional.

Each summer his one spurt of activity had been at the Edinburgh Festival. One evening, watching a dire modern version of *She Stoops to Conquer* in 1920s dress, he had been taken by the lithe figure of Stephen Nesbit. Later, in the harsh light of the Assembly Rooms bar, Stephen had looked every one of his thirty-three years, but Alan found his lined and tired face as much a turn-on as the choirboy looks he'd expected. He wanted to rescue Stephen from his life as an emotional victim and disappointed thespian.

Within months of their meeting, Alan had taken over their lives, going for early retirement and buying the house in Tarnfield, bringing Stephen to live with him. They'd been there for five years, turning the place from a dreary nineteenth-century labourer's cottage into an amalgam of styles and ideas which should have been ridiculous but wasn't. Stephen was definitely into fabrics, with curtains and flounces on everything. Alan was much more macho, wanting stainless steel kitchen units and white roller blinds. But thanks to their ability to buy the very best of everything, the mixture worked. Alan's inheritance had come at just the right time.

Stephen came to stand next to him by the french windows, which looked over their Tuscan-style patio. At the back, the eastern fells rose steeply, so that the light was fading as they watched.

'It should be a nice day tomorrow,' Stephen said.

They were going to visit some lesbian friends down in North Lancashire. Stephen was particularly excited. Though he loved the cottage and could cope with Tarnfield, he liked the emotional thrills and spills of gay politics and needed his fix of the bigger picture. But Alan was the boss. Stephen snuggled up to him in a puppyish way. One of the delights of their relationship was its private code. They allowed themselves no affectionate gestures outside the cottage, but inside it was an erotic dream, the conventional Alan besotted by the camp, risqué, streetwise Stevie.

'People can suspect what they like,' Alan had said. 'But why should they know?' Coming out wasn't his style.

'We'll get away in time after the service tomorrow, won't we?' Stephen said in his sweetest voice. He didn't mind the churchgoing – in fact he'd recently taken a new interest – but he didn't want Alan hanging round puffing his pipe, talking to the other middle-aged men for ages about the current gossip. Their friends would be annoyed if they kept them waiting again, as they had done when the former vicar had had his breakdown and Alan had gone into Mr Reliable mode, taking over the crisis and spending hours sorting things out.

'Yes, of course.' Alan had his own reason for getting Stephen out of church. Nicholas Melling, the new vicar, was a good-looking lad, though he was taking his role too seriously. He was too febrile for Alan's taste, which veered towards a 'bit of rough'. Stephen on the other hand seemed entranced by the Reverend Nick. He simpered at everything he said, and had started to play his keyboard again, badly, in the hope that they might do a 'jam session' sometime. Alan was suspicious of all this modernity at All Saints. He sighed.

Stevie had gone to get the gin-and-tonics. Alan loved habit and routine. This was what they always did on Saturday evenings. And tomorrow it would be Choral Eucharist for Easter Day, then the trip south, which they made every three months to catch up on the news. He liked Stevie's old friends from the gay scene, but was always glad to get back on the road to Tarnfield.

Steve returned to his side and Alan put his hand affectionately on his right buttock. If they weren't out to dinner or seeing a film on Saturday nights, they usually went to bed and ate supper later in their dressing gowns, watching telly. Standing together, Alan felt the pure happiness which life with Stevie brought him, even with the occasional tearful rows and tantrums.

'It's a pity that Sammi and Wendy invited us tomorrow, you know,' Alan said, 'because the Bells asked me if we'd like to go there. I'm not sure if they realize . . .'

Oh, dream on, thought Stevie. Sometimes a reality check was needed. Everyone here knows about us. They're just too polite to say anything. Well, perhaps polite was the wrong word for some of them . . .

'But I've had a few nasty looks from Tom Strickland.'

'Don't be paranoid, Stevie. Tom Strickland is all bark and no bite.' Alan's voice was husky with affection. 'And you're all right here. No one in Tarnfield will harm you.'

He turned towards his lover protectively. This will take

his mind off Tom Strickland, he thought, as the sun finally went down. He put his arms round Stevie's smaller, slighter figure.

'Oh Al, I do love you,' whispered Stevie. 'I'd die if you ever left me alone again.'

Across the Green in their council semi, Tom Strickland and his wife were settling down for their favourite Saturday night entertainment. He lowered himself into his chair, and wiped the back of his hand under his large, mottled nose. His big frame was hunched now, and he slumped rather than sat in front of the TV while he fiddled with the remote. He and Vera liked their Saturday night telly. They weren't highbrows, Tom thought, but at least he was a churchwarden.

Mind you, his influence mattered less now. He frowned at the screen. He had been right-hand man to the former vicar. But the Reverend George Pattinson had had a break-down of some sort and been sent on extensive sick leave by the Bishop, which was disappointing in someone who was officer material. That was why the Bishop had asked his curate, Nick Melling, to run the show.

Tom Strickland shook his head. In his opinion, Nick Melling had some very weird ideas. Tom liked his clergy-men to be warm, jolly and upper crust. George Pattinson had been just right. All this modern first-name stuff, clap-ping and guitar songs in church, was going too far, he thought. Of course Phyllis Drysdale tried to keep tradition going but she was an irritating old bat who was willing to compromise. Tom was firmly conventional.

It was a pity that Mary Clark had pegged it. He'd admired Mary for years. She'd have put Nick Melling in his place. Why she'd married that wet bloke Clark, he'd never understood. Robert Clark was another person who was trying hard not to fall out with the new vicar, but Tom thought that was a waste of time. He even suspected that Nick Melling might be a queer, like that nancy-boy Stevie Nesbit who lived with Alan Robie. And Alan seemed such a decent bloke too. Disgusting. What was the church coming to?

It needed sorting out. But as an ex-squaddie, I've never minded doing things that bothered other folk, Tom said to himself. He decided to have a couple of beers at home till his favourite show was over, and then walk the dog up Tarnfield Fell to a snug little pub he knew, where he could have a few shorts. He smiled as he got the right channel and the TV programme flowered into life. He had every confidence the church would get back to normal soon. He chuckled grimly and raised his pint pot to his lips.

I'd go out again, except I don't want to bump into Tom Strickland, mused 'Lady' Jane Simpson as the locals mockingly called her. And I do wish Phyllis Drysdale had taken my advice, she thought irritably. Surely there was no need for all those arum lilies? The daffodils would have been tasteful enough, and Jane had been loath to contribute extra money to the flower-arranging fund. She took off her rather worn Burberry mackintosh and beige cashmere beret, then shook out her greying blonde hair – which she highlighted herself every two months – and went into the front room of Tarnfield House to turn on the electric fire and try to get the place warm.

The room badly needed decorating, but she wasn't sure if they could afford it. Jeff had never been much good at DIY, and now he was over seventy there would be no chance of his even trying! She looked away from the growing patch of damp above the deep cornice.

Standing in the gloom, gazing out of the big Victorian bay window, she saw her husband going across to the Plough. He never bothered to say goodbye these days. Heavy and bad-tempered, Jeff Simpson was an unhappy man. Jane sighed. His family had been in business in Tarnfield for over a century but Jeff had been forced to sell up. It still rankled. The Simpsons had once been the equivalent of the local gentry – trade of course, but 'well-to-do'. Things were different now.

And worry over their son Russell didn't help. He had refused to get any qualifications and worked in Newcastle in some sort of meaningless modern job to do with marketing and 'clients'. Jane knew he was constantly asking for handouts, and spent money like water. Jeff and Russ had never really been close, perhaps because Jeff had been so much older when Russ was born. At one time it had been vital to provide an heir, but now she wondered if there would be anything left for Russell to inherit. Not that he showed any sign of producing progeny in turn. He was far too busy drinking, clubbing and driving down rural roads at breakneck speed with his pal Matthew Bell from Bell's Wood Yard.

The electric fire was making little impression on the big, dank room. I'll walk over to The Briars and see Robert Clark, Jane decided, though she would have to avoid Tom Strickland on one of his evening prowls. She preferred not to remember that she and Tom were distantly related though it had served her purpose once before. She glanced at the carriage clock on the mantelpiece, then the noise of a pick-up truck hurtling past made her look out of the window. Frank Bell, driving like a maniac, she thought. Monica Bell was nice enough but the Bell men were rough diamonds and it was a shame Russell was so friendly with Matthew. What he needed was a nice girlfriend.

Walking would keep her warm. She pulled on her beret and Burberry again, and set off, in the opposite direction to the Bells' pick-up.

Half an hour later, outside the large modern house next door to their wood business, Frank and Monica Bell were unloading the shopping from Tesco's in Carlisle in the growing darkness. Monica had been to Carlisle in the Volvo. She was going to do a big family roast on Easter Sunday, and she'd invited Robert Clark as well as the rest of the family. Monica Bell liked her food. She had put on weight over the last year or two, but her hair was still brown and curly, and thanks to her hysterectomy she'd seen the menopause off a few years earlier. Monica thought looks were an overrated asset. She had health and strength, and a good husband. What more could you want in your fifties?

She was keeping her fingers crossed that Matthew would be prepared to stay at home for Easter Sunday lunch, and not escape in his boy racer car with his best mate, Russ Simpson from Tarnfield House. She'd bought nineteen-year-old Matthew's favourite Tesco trifle and some extra drinks. There were a lot of bags to cart into the house. Her husband Frank had been out, she noticed, because he was on the doorstep wearing his wellies when she backed the car into the drive. He was really balding now, and he looked rather miserable, like a hungry vulture.

'You were a long time,' he said crossly. So that was his problem! Frank liked to know where she was.

'Yes, it was busy,' she answered. 'Where've you been?'

'Delivering some shelving to the church. I didn't go in, though. Didn't want to bump into Phyllis Drysdale. She might have asked me to be in the Bible study group. Or arrange flowers!'

Monica laughed. 'She really annoys you, doesn't she?'

'You can say that again. She wasn't so bad when Mary Clark was alive. But she's become even more of a nag now. You'd think she'd have learnt I'm not the Bible-bashing type.'

'I know.'

Monica had been through this, hundreds of times. Frank had no objection to her churchgoing but he would have nothing to do with it himself. Except of course to be indispensable as handyman and supplier, and so entitled to express his view all the time. Her husband was one of those men, she thought shrewdly, who crave attention but had been brought up to believe that 'putting yourself forward' was a cardinal sin. Frank pretended to be sensible, but underneath he was inclined to let his heart rule his head. It was a good job she was so practical.

'Well, never mind, Frank. Maybe Phyllis will stop trying

to persuade you eventually. She's got me roped in for the Bible study group though, not to mention the flowers. Tell you what, you can do a good Christian thing anyway and help me unload the shopping.'

Frank Bell made a grumbling noise, and then started heaving bags into the house. Funny, thought Monica. He was usually quite good-tempered. But something was eating him tonight. She hoped he'd cheer up for Easter Day.

At 6 Tarn Acres, Kevin and Janice Jones were bathing their toddler daughter and the baby and feeling excited about the Easter Festival. Kevin was getting the children a bit too worked up, his wife thought, as bath water slopped on to the carpet and Zoe, aged three, shrieked with hysterical laughter. Janice felt her sweatshirt getting drenched. She was red-faced and perspiring, conscious of her excess weight as she crouched by the bath. She had been working hard. The Easter eggs had all been hidden round the house for the hunt after church the next day and, as 'born again' Christians, she and Kevin were looking forward to Easter Day.

'What's Nick got planned for the service?' Janice asked her husband.

'Well, there's the Easter Anthem and I suppose we'll have to sit through the usual old rubbish. But he's talking about some of the Songs of Fellowship stuff during communion, on guitar. That should shake them up a bit.'

'Good thing,' said Janice heartily. But her mum, who farmed just outside the village, would be there on Easter morning. She wouldn't appreciate the music. Her mother had always been a bit unhappy about Kevin's brand of Christianity. He wasn't a Tarnfield boy, of course, which didn't help. Janice had met Kevin at college in Yorkshire. He'd been her first and only boyfriend and she had loved him from the day of their first date. He's my husband, Janice thought, and I've got to support him. He for God only, me for God in him, like John Milton said. And that was all there was to it.

'Did you get the baby shampoo when you went up to Lo-cost?' she asked him.

'I think we'd better use our shampoo, love, with lots of water added. They'd run out when I got there.'

'Oh.'

Their children splashed happily, unaware of the shadow that had crossed their mother's face. She had seen plenty of baby shampoo on the shelves a few days earlier. If Kevin hadn't got any, why had he been away so long?

So Tarnfield was settling into its Saturday night routine. But in the church, Phyllis Drysdale was dying, her eyes fixed on the thing piercing her left hand.

4

Later Easter Eve into Easter Day

It is better, if the will of God be so, that ye suffer for well-
doing, than for evil-doing.
From the Epistle for Easter Even, 1 Peter 3:17

In The Briars, Suzy Spencer sat with her head in her hands
at the kitchen table. To his own surprise, Robert Clark had
found it quite easy to deal with his gatecrasher. He'd been
amused to hear the expletives punctuating the clear Tarnfield evening and, far from being distraught and flaky as
he'd feared, she seemed to be coping well.

'I'm OK, really I am. I'm just so sorry.'

'Well, at least you missed the variegated holly bush.
That was Mary's favourite.'

'I'm glad about that. But your fence will need completely replacing.'

Robert found he was smiling. Now with the fence to be
repaired, there would be something to do in the two long
weeks left before college started again. Apart from his
Thursday evening creative writing class, there was nothing
in his diary. And sorting out this mess would be more
interesting than marking assignments.

Suzy stared at him. 'You think it's funny?'

'As a matter of fact, I do. I watched you come down the
hill. I could see the panic on your face. I didn't recognize
you at first. But then you stopped. Or the fence stopped
you, to be accurate!'

'God, it was awful! The car just kept rolling. I turned the

34

ignition off but it had its own momentum. I hadn't a clue what to do!'

It was good of him to take it so well, Suzy thought. Mary Clark would have made a huge fuss.

'Would you like coffee?' he asked. 'It might help you get over the shock. I assume you'll want to drive home. The car doesn't seem too damaged.'

'Coffee would be nice. That's another stupid thing, not being in the RAC or AA or anything. That was something Nigel used to sort out. But as long as the car goes, I don't care. I've got to drive to work on Tuesday.'

'What is it you do exactly?'

'I'm a part-time producer on daytime TV. It's the sort of job that makes people at dinner parties treat you as a moron. Or a dangerous dumber-downer.'

'And are you?'

'Absolutely not! Bondage and body piercing are the real issues of our time!'

Robert wasn't sure if she was making fun of him or herself. He put the kettle on.

'I'd better drink up and get away,' she said. 'It may be getting dark, but if the car's stuck there for more than half an hour the whole village will know about it.'

'They will anyway, Mrs Spencer.'

'Actually, it's Ms,' Suzy said. 'But people don't use titles in my job. Anyway, Ms is much more appropriate now my husband's buggered off to Newcastle to live with his PA.' He might as well know, she thought. It would mean another raised eyebrow, but there was no point in him thinking that a man was going to appear any minute, give him a cheque, and carry her off home.

'I'm sorry.'

'I'm not, not very anyway,' she said. 'And my problems aren't in your league. Nigel's still alive, more's the pity!'

Ouch. How gross! The shock was making her gabble. To get over her faux pas, she added, 'I came to Mary's funeral, you know. You must have been devastated. She was an amazing woman.'

'Yes, she was.'

'She got my daughter Molly into Sunday School. And she persuaded Jake to do some gardening. She was certainly a forceful lady. I wasn't really her cup of tea of course, but she talked me into going to church.' I'm trying too hard, Suzy thought, he must know his wife never really took to me! I always wondered why she was so keen to get me into the congregation at All Saints.

Robert passed the coffee and an overloaded plate of biscuits. He looked at the woman sitting in his kitchen. She wore flared jeans with patches on, and her hair could only be described as two-tone. She had one long earring, but the other had been a casualty of the accident. Or maybe not. Maybe she'd forgotten it anyway. He'd heard Mary saying Suzy's house was a tip, toys and books everywhere, and the TV on in the afternoon.

'I'm sure Mary liked you,' he said, looking away.

'Oh, come on! Of course she didn't. She hated daytime telly. I certainly wasn't her sort. Mind you, I respected her. She was pretty formidable and she certainly got me organized.' Where was this stuff coming from? Why couldn't she just make soothing noises like everyone else?

Robert looked back at her. This was a very different approach from the usual condolences. But Suzy had reddened. She said, 'I'm sorry. I've had a bugger of a day. I didn't mean to be rude . . .'

'It's OK, you really don't have to be tactful with me,' he said quietly. 'Actually I get sick of everyone pussyfooting around.' He smiled. They both knew Mary had criticized Suzy roundly behind her back and he suddenly felt there was no point in pretending. And Suzy looked so crestfallen at her indiscretion. 'Look,' he said, 'I know my wife could be very bossy sometimes. Just because you love someone doesn't mean you're blind to their faults. Anyway, people are bigger than the sum of their parts.' It was such a change to be able to tell the truth. One of the problems of a community like Tarnfield was the conspiracy of kindness – everyone subscribed to the same story. Mary Clark was universally agreed to have been wonderfully efficient and the backbone of the church, and that was all there was to say. The real Mary had got lost in the myth.

Suzy's eyes widened in surprise – and relief. She hated trying to say the right thing. And why was talking to the bereaved so hard? Especially to someone like him, who looked you in the eye and smiled. Social lies required complicity, but he wasn't going to help her utter platitudes. What is going on here? she thought. One minute I'm yelling rude words and my car is covered in planks, and the next I'm sitting here talking to this man like a confidant. Yet she was touched by Robert's openness, and his realistic love for his wife. If only she felt like that about Nigel. But she never thought of him as bigger than the sum of his parts. His parts were always running the show, anyway.

There was a sudden sharp ring from the doorbell. Robert said, 'Excuse me,' and got up and left her. She could hear him welcoming a woman with a posh voice, and explaining to her about the fence. Jane Simpson, she thought. She heard the bustle and smelt the perfume before the grand entrance.

'Dear me, Mrs Spencer, what a state the garden is in! How awful! Poor you, Robert!' Jane Simpson turned imperiously away from Suzy to monopolize Robert's attention. 'I came round to talk to you about Phyllis Drysdale's Bible study group. I think Nick would prefer an Alpha course, which would be so nice with the meals and the entertaining and so on. I think Phyllis is such a nuisance, really. I'm sure Mary would have made her move with the times.'

Robert smiled. It was amazing how his dead wife could be invoked to endorse almost everything. He opened a kitchen drawer and took out a printed card with his details and handed it to Suzy.

'Let me know about the insurance.'

'Of course,' Suzy said, and looked at the card. He was so efficient it was painful. He and Mary Clark must have been an awesome combination. Mr and Mrs Perfect.

'Thanks,' she added, standing up. 'I'd better be going.'

Robert took her to the door in silence. He seemed pre-occupied. He must want to get back to Jane Simpson, Suzy thought, she's more his type. Her eye caught the coat rack in the stained glass vestibule with Robert's mac and anorak hanging on coat hangers, surmounted by two tweed hats. He's rather an old fart, she decided. For a nanosecond in the kitchen the coffee, the good humour and that hint of sensitivity had fooled her.

The car looked all right except for a dent on the bonnet. Suzy turned the ignition key and put it into reverse and, after coughing a bit, it heaved itself out of the rut made by the fence's foundations and chugged normally. She felt much better inside her own car, surrounded by the kids' mess, back in her own world. The whole encounter had been disturbing. Of course, she had had a shock – so no wonder she had chattered on like that. But hadn't she been a bit insensitive? Then again, why lie to him? That wasn't her style, and he wasn't stupid. And it didn't really matter anyway. She and Robert Clark were unlikely ever to do more than nod to each other at church. But still . . . Suzy made a face at herself in the driving mirror. Trust me to open my big mouth, she thought.

As she drove past Phyllis Drysdale's bungalow she thought how odd it was that the lights weren't on. It was completely dark. It would be great if poor old Phyllis had finished the church flowers and was out having a good time. Phyllis was a kindly person despite her stuffy manner. A few weeks earlier, Suzy had been let down by Sharon Strickland for babysitting, and Phyllis had offered to take Molly to the bungalow to see her new kitten.

'We've called the pussy cat Flowerbabe,' Molly said ecstatically.

Calling the cat after Molly's hideous doll had been an even greater act of kindness than the childminding, Suzy thought. Tonight, she hoped Phyllis was visiting someone nice in Tarnfield, but she couldn't imagine who that could be. She put the dark bungalow behind her, accelerated, and drove on, down the hill towards that waiting bottle of wine.

Suzy passed a silver convertible without noticing. Yvonne Wait, dark and glamorous, was at the wheel, driving home from her weekend shift at Norbridge General. She observed Suzy Spencer's car and Suzy's face creased in concentration, and smiled to herself. As usual Suzy had been too harassed to see what was going on around her, unlike Yvonne, who had just spotted Kevin Jones outside Lo-cost. That had amused her. Kevin hadn't clocked Yvonne driving past and, if Yvonne was right, he'd been in rather a compromising situation. Interesting! Yvonne liked knowing things about her neighbours. You never knew when these things would come in handy.

Yvonne parked in the garage she'd had built next to her detached Georgian house. It was good to be home. It had been a busy day at the hospital, where she had had the misfortune to be working on Saturday reception because of the Easter holidays. As usual people had been bloody stupid. The public was ghastly at the best of times. To crown it all, a stupid old man with a minor burn had complained just because Yvonne had raised her voice, which had led to an idiot foreign doctor gabbling on at her in pidgin English for about ten minutes just when her shift was about to end. And Yvonne had reasons for wanting to get home early tonight.

Her elegant house was at the end of the High Street. It had been her parents' house and her father had used it as his dental surgery too. It was one of the most beautiful buildings in Tarnfield, the only significant one left from the place's heyday. Now all that was gone, and decade by decade Tarnfield had shrunk to become an agricultural village, though the parish church had retained its importance.

Opening the thick black front door with its shiny brass fittings, she found a note on the mat from old Phyllis Drysdale about her bloody silly Bible study group. Still,

Yvonne had her reasons for attending. She decided to read it before winding down with a drink.

Phyllis wrote in shaky longhand, thanking Yvonne and listing the other people. The usual suspects, Yvonne thought contemptuously, pretty much the same people who helped with the flowers plus a few dreary men. There was dowdy Monica Bell from the wood yard – a tedious woman who thought she was indispensable, but who had gone to seed in her fifties, or so Yvonne thought, crossing her own long, shapely legs. With the callousness of the naturally beautiful she could afford to be contemptuous of Monica. Then there was 'Lady' Jane Simpson of Tarnfield House, whose faded grandeur never failed to amuse Yvonne – who had made her own very sensible financial provisions for the future. Property, that was the secret. She had no time for people like Jane Simpson who lived beyond their means and let their houses go to pot. Oh, little Daisy Arthur was joining them. Daisy was pretty in a girlie way, but with no real style. Inconsequential, really. Tom Strickland was a dirty old man who had once accosted Yvonne in the alley behind the church. He fancied his chances but she hadn't been interested despite his showing off about the other women he'd bedded. Then there were those two silly queens, Alan and Stevie, from Church Cottage. Though they might prove productive . . . And of course there was Robert Clark, the not-so-merry widower. Now there was potential if only he would smarten himself up. And toughen up too. All this grief was ridiculous, especially when most people knew Mary Clark had been a bossy bitch.

So the Bible study group might come in useful. Not to mention the odd bit of flower arranging. Yvonne liked to know everything that was going on, and people gossiped as they trimmed and wired. Oh, here was one surprise – Suzy Spencer, whom she'd just passed in the car. Suzy was well known for being a complete mess, at least according to Mary Clark, with those two kids and the tasty husband who'd done a runner. No wonder. So she was going to the Bible study group too. Interesting.

All very promising! But tonight Yvonne had other things on her mind. In an hour, her married lover would arrive. As a key administrator at the hospital he was rather a catch – and very useful. He'd packed his wife off on holiday to Spain for Easter, staying at home on the grounds of extra work, which left him and Yvonne the night to themselves. She went into her marble bathroom and started to run the steaming hot water. Five minutes later she stepped into the bath and lay there, Junoesque, while the foam frothed around her. She sipped at her cold glass of Sancerre.

Smiling to herself, Yvonne shut her eyes and let the warmth of the water lap round the most intimate bits of her luscious body.

A few minutes later, Daisy Arthur parked her car outside her mother's house in Tarn Acres where she had lived since coming home from college nearly two years ago, and dashed inside.

'I've got an hour before I get out,' she called to her mum, who was preparing for a nice evening watching TV and finishing some quilting.

'Where are you off to, Daisy?'

'I'm going round to see Nick the Vic. I'm sure he'll be interested in what I've planned for tomorrow's Sunday School lesson.'

Nancy Arthur sighed. She'd worried that Tarnfield would be too boring for her daughter once she left college. But though Daisy was supposed to be looking for a job somewhere more exciting, she seemed to find the village completely absorbing.

It was the church. Mrs Arthur didn't like Daisy being so involved, but there was nothing she could do about it. Daisy was working at Lo-cost, Tarnfield's only shop, and showing little sign of moving on. A boyfriend would change all that, her mother thought, but there was no one on the scene. Daisy had never really found anyone to live up to her father. She'd been his favourite, and they had been close, until a heart attack had caused his premature death while she was at university.

If I didn't have ME I'd be more help to her, Nancy Arthur thought. But as it is, I've got chronic fatigue and I'm marooned here. And it's not as if I really belong in Tarnfield; although I've lived here for thirty years, I hardly get hundreds of invitations. Nancy rarely went further than the garden gate and since Daisy had come home, there was even less need to go out. Her daughter was a little bit over-protective but Nancy had her visits from the district nurse, as well as Babs Piefield who was in the Neighbours' Support Scheme and who visited frequently. Sometimes a little too frequently, thought Nancy wearily. But Babs always had plenty of information to pass on. Thanks to her, Nancy knew all about the changes at All Saints.

Her daughter didn't tell her much. Did she have a crush on that new vicar chap? It would be just like Daisy to be wasting her chances on some lost cause. Mrs Arthur sighed. Daisy was her third child, her baby and her only girl. She was clever and intense, but with none of her brothers' drive. I just hope she pulls her socks up and gets out of this village before it claims her for life, Nancy Arthur thought anxiously.

Robert Clark woke far too early on Easter Sunday. He hadn't slept well. He had gone to bed irritated with Jane Simpson for wasting hours at The Briars moaning about Phyllis Drysdale's flower arrangements. Of course there was a history there. The two women had been rivals for years. He would have preferred to go on chatting to Suzy Spencer – there had been times since Mary's death when he'd found himself watching daytime TV and he'd been intrigued. He would have liked to ask her more about it. He felt concerned about the cool way he had seen her out of The Briars, but once Jane turned up, it had been impossible to go on talking to Suzy.

Another lonely day stretched before him, but at seven

thirty when he was dozing, the phone's ringing wakened him. It was Tom Strickland, in his role as the senior churchwarden.

'Robert? That you? I'm at the church. Can you get over here?'

'Yes, of course. What's up?'

'It's Phyllis. When I opened up for eight o'clock communion I found her in the chancel. I think she's had a heart attack. She was stone cold dead but there's blood everywhere. I've rung the ambulance. And the police are coming.'

'I'm on my way. Have you told Nick?'

'Aye, for all the good it'll do. He's not here yet.'

Robert levered himself out of bed and pulled his clothes towards him. 'Tom,' he said, 'if she died of a heart attack, where's the blood from?'

'She'd cut her hand with some flower-arranging thing. A long green wiry decoration. Nasty. It's gone right through the skin. How soon can you be here?'

'In five minutes, Tom.'

'Well, brace yourself for a shock.'

It's all right, Robert thought. I've seen death at its most ghastly so I can cope with this. He knew Phyllis had a weak heart, she told everyone so, and though this was sudden, he wasn't entirely surprised. He hoped for her sake it had been quick. Poor Phyllis. She was annoying at times, but she had been Mary's best friend. And a lot of people would miss her. Nick Melling won't cope, he said to himself; he's not good on personal pain. He'd been hopeless when Mary died. Then Robert went out into the cool morning, glanced at his ruined fence, and opened the garage.

The sound of his car engine starting shattered the early morning silence of Easter Day.

5

Easter Sunday

Therefore let us keep the feast.
From the Easter Anthem

Monica Bell of Bell's Wood Yard looked at the chaos in her living room. She rubbed her temples under her brisk brown curly hair, and thought she had better get on with it.

'Oh well,' she sighed to herself. On a whim, she'd invited as many people as she could for lunch, and now people were sitting on anything they could find, including a coffee table which was straining under Alan Robie's well-upholstered weight. The general invitation had seemed the only decent thing to do after the shock. She'd phoned her daughter and told them the family meal was off, and her son Matthew had disappeared, saying he'd grab a sandwich with his mate Russell. So much for everything she'd planned, including inviting Robert Clark to eat Easter Sunday lunch with them. He was a quiet chap, no trouble to entertain, and she felt sorry for him, living alone at The Briars.

But inviting Robert was one thing – having a dozen church members there, twitching with the shock of Phyllis's death, was another. Still, Monica was glad she'd invited them on the spur of the moment. Someone had to do something, though Frank hadn't seemed best pleased; in fact he'd been a bit moody since the night before. But now, Monica saw, he was doling out sherry and gin-and-tonics like they were going out of fashion, and he was going to carve the joint with his usual verve, once it had cooled down. She could add the ham she'd got for tea, so there'd be enough for everyone.

That morning, when Frank had dropped her off at All Saints for the ten o'clock service, Robert Clark and Tom Strickland – who was even grumpier than usual – were standing at the door turning people away. The ambulance and the doctor had finally gone, and the service had been cancelled. Nick Melling had talked to the police, separately and with the air of a pained professional – and had disappeared quickly back to the vicarage.

Then Suzy Spencer had come over.

'Oh, how awful. Poor Phyllis! I hope she wasn't alone in there suffering for too long. I feel so guilty. I'd been going to help her, but I had to cry off because I needed to get the kids to the station.'

Tom Strickland had said gruffly, 'You two are both flower arrangers, aren't you?'

Monica Bell shrugged. 'I'm not very artistic, you know. You've done a lot more lately, haven't you, Suzy?'

'Well, I help when I can. Why do you ask?'

'Because Phyllis's flower-arranging kit is all over the place,' Tom grunted. 'It needs sorting out. The police have been and said we can tidy up. It's a pity she had to have a seizure in the church. But there's nowt suspicious.'

'Of course not,' said Monica, shocked.

Robert Clark came over from explaining the cancelled service to an irritated family. Tom Strickland nudged him to one side and said quietly, 'I don't think we should tell people about that thing in Phyllis's hand. I took it out.'

'What? Why did you do that, Tom?'

'We don't want people asking questions about health and safety or first aid arrangements in the church, do we? The police think she had a clutcher and that's what happened.' His thin, sharp face was inches away from Robert's and his hand was on Robert's lapel.

'I don't think you should have touched it.'

'Well, I did. My view is, least said soonest mended. All right? I mean it was only a stupid bit of decoration.'

'What was?' asked Suzy Spencer, moving forward to be helpful.

'Phyllis had something in her hand,' Robert said quietly.

Tom looked even more cross. 'It was nothing. A decoration. She must have cut her hand on it.'

'But we weren't using decorations. It's Easter. We planned to use fresh flowers. And greenery.'

By then a knot of anxious people had formed around Monica Bell, who said impulsively, 'Come over to our house, we've all had a shock. Pass the word on. I'll do us a quick buffet lunch. Ask Nick as well, Tom.'

'All right,' he said gracelessly, realizing that if he put a move on, he could pop home first and tell his wife Vera not to defrost their 'Roast Ready Meal'. He stomped off.

'Terrible!' Alan Robie was booming as he walked over to join them. 'This really is unpleasant for everyone. You said something about lunch, Monica?'

'But there's nothing we can do,' Stevie Nesbit added anxiously, trotting behind him. 'We're due in Lancaster at one o'clock.'

'On the contrary, I think we need to caucus. If Monica's kind enough to invite us at this difficult time, I really think we should be there. Now, Robert, what are we telling people?' Alan led Robert to one side.

'You'll come to lunch as well, Suzy?' Monica asked.

'Thanks, Mrs Bell. I'd love to.' But Suzy was surprised. Monica was usually wrapped up in her family and the wood yard business. She had never spoken much to Suzy, who always thought the Bells had written her off as a weird townie. Monica had been one of Mary Clark's coterie too. But still, it was a kind gesture, and Suzy was aware that she felt a little bit winded. A sudden death always does this, she thought. How awful, that she had passed Phyllis Drysdale's bungalow last night, and hoped that the older woman was out having fun! And all the time she was in the church, dying. Robert Clark touched her lightly on the arm.

'Perhaps you could help, like Tom Strickland suggested?' he said softly. 'There's a terrible mess in the church and it's all flower-arranging stuff. We need to tidy it away.'

'OK,' said Suzy tentatively. She followed Robert cautiously into the church.

He was right, it was a mess. Phyllis had used a modern plastic toolbox for her flower-arranging materials and this was up-ended, with the hinge shattered and all the contents strewn around the aisle. There were thin wires for winding and fastening, two or three rolls of shiny coloured ribbon which had uncoiled like bright snakes, reels of different sorts of sticky tape, and thin strips of green foam which were adhesive on one side only, for holding small sprigs in place. A large piece of oasis foam still oozed water slowly on to the tiled floor, and the metal plinth with a round shelf on top, which was used for the big flower arrangements, had fallen down on its side.

'I recognize some of this kit,' Robert said, 'but I've no idea what all of it is for.'

Suzy picked up the secateurs.

'Oh, it's hard work. It's not just a question of standing and putting some daisies in a vase while looking elegant, especially in a church where you need big displays. You have to hack and chop and twist things. Then wire them against their will. It's quite exacting. Not that I really know much about it. Everything I can do, I learnt from Mary and Phyllis.'

And now they're both dead. Suzy shivered, and glanced at Robert. The same thing had occurred to him, it seemed. He had found a black plastic bag and was putting the crushed lilies in it.

'Who do you think will do the flower arranging now?' he asked.

'I don't know. There's Monica and me. Then there's Yvonne Wait. She always contributes her own display, although she doesn't work in the team as such.'

Robert looked up sharply. 'Yvonne Wait, who works at the hospital? I didn't realize she helped.'

'Oh yes, she's very good. But she usually turns up with

something she's already done and then adds the finishing touches in here. Jane Simpson from Tarnfield House did some stuff at Christmas . . .'

Suzy paused, remembering Jane's holly, tortured around a candlestick which she must have told them ten times was a family heirloom. She couldn't imagine Jane taking charge.

'Oh, and of course there's young Daisy Arthur, who runs the Sunday School. She and the younger children once made a lovely scene representing "All Things Bright and Beautiful".'

'*The purple-headed mountain, the river running by . . .*'

'That's right. We used fake reeds and a mirror for the river. The reeds were too sharp for the kids, so Daisy asked Mary to put them in.'

'Yes, I remember. It was really effective.'

'Daisy might do more flower arranging now –' she paused – 'but Nick Melling doesn't really like flowers in church. Too many middle class people with time on their hands and money to waste. And you don't have to be Freud to know that Daisy Arthur has a big-time crush on Nick.'

'It would be a shame if no one did it. What about you?'

'Me? You must be joking. Mary Clark would turn in . . .' Suzy tailed off, then grimaced.

'It's all right. I'd rather people said the wrong thing, than said nothing. That's far worse. Anyway, why not you?'

'I suppose I could. I'm not really the type, but I could have a go sometimes.'

What am I thinking of? Suzy thought. Me, head flower arranger? Successor to Mrs Perfect? Robert was gathering up crushed stems. She said, 'The paramedics must have trampled all over this stuff.'

'It was a mess even before they arrived.'

'But Phyllis was always so tidy. And I still don't understand about the decoration.'

'Tom Strickland said she'd cut herself with it. Perhaps that brought on the heart attack.'

'Phyllis? Cut herself? You must be joking.'

Robert thought, if Tom Strickland has moved the decoration, it wouldn't do any good to talk about it. No one else had noticed anything amiss. An elderly woman with a heart condition had cut herself flower arranging and had suffered a heart attack. That was all there was to it.

'We'll never know, will we? Best not to speculate.'

Suzy shrugged, stooped, and picked up a small sharp pair of scissors with a serrated blade. The metal caught the light, but she noticed that the point was dulled. She peered at it. There was a brownish stain on the tip. Odd, she thought. Mary and Phyllis had been scrupulously careful about wiping and drying tools after use. 'Rust,' Mary would say as if talking about the plague. 'Rust must be avoided.' One of Phyllis's cloths was lying over a pew end, so Suzy picked it up and wiped the scissors till they were shiny, before putting them back in the damaged box.

'I'll put this in the flower vestry. I suppose it'll belong to whoever inherits Phyllis's stuff. She didn't have any family, did she?'

Robert studied the knot he was tying in the plastic bag. 'I can't say,' he answered shortly.

I'll shut up then, thought Suzy, feeling dismissed. She couldn't see what was so undiplomatic about asking what would happen to Phyllis's belongings. It was a shame because she'd started to enjoy talking to Robert Clark. Again. She closed the box, and wiped her hands on her trousers before running them through her spiky blonde hair. She realized there was slime from the crushed lily stems on her face, and mud on her jumper. Gorgeous, she thought. Exactly the sort of neat, tidy person Mr Perfect would admire! Perhaps it was a good job their conversation had come abruptly to an end.

Behind them she heard voices. Nick Melling and Tom Strickland had both come back into the church. Nick sounded even more forced, his professional clergyman's voice a few notes higher, and his tone even more strained than usual.

'Thank you, I'm fine now, Tom, and I'll certainly be, yeah, brill for lunch. It was just shock. I mean how often does one come in for eight o'clock communion and find a dead person in the church?'

'I was the one that found her. And I didn't faint,' Tom grumbled.

'Oh, yes, of course. I don't mean that I found her. It was just a form of words.' Nick Melling's bright tone sank under the weight of patience he needed for the less educated members of his flock. 'And by the way, Tom, I didn't faint either. I just needed to sit down, and to have a moment of, kinda private prayer. That's why I went back to the vicarage with the police. After all, you and Robert were in here.'

'Good thing too,' rasped Tom Strickland. He thought Nick Melling was a lazy sod on top of everything else. He stamped into the choir vestry at the back of the chancel, where they kept the Parish Council paperwork.

Robert turned back to Suzy. 'Do you want a lift to the Bells' for lunch?' he asked.

'No thanks, I'd like the walk,' she answered coldly. If he was going to keep putting her in her place, he could sod off! Then she felt guilty. Her car had demolished his fence only the day before and he'd been very good about it. She turned to say something softer, but Robert had disappeared after Tom Strickland and the vicar.

The full electric lights were on now, pricking the gloom, and outside the day was a monochrome grey. The light through the stained glass windows was dulled and the church was uniformly dim and exposed, all mystery gone. She looked towards the altar, which was dressed in white for Easter, the most important day of the year. But even from where she was standing she could see that the altar cloth had been pulled sideways to expose the plain trestle beneath. There was a streak of blood across the front of the cloth. How awful! Phyllis must have grabbed at it after cutting her hand.

But it just didn't figure, she thought. Then she told herself not to imagine things. What had happened was a horrible accident – that was all. And if she was going to get to the Bells' on foot, it was time to leave the church and to get moving.

She tore her eyes away from the sparkling white brocade, but the dark stain lingered like a rip at the back of her eyes.

6

Lunch on Easter Sunday

Thou dost put into our minds good desires, so . . . we may
bring the same to good effect.
From the Collect for Easter Day

Half an hour later, Monica Bell called, 'Now would everyone come into the dining room? Lunch is ready,' and was
relieved to see that, when Alan Robie stood up, the coffee
table was undamaged.

'Where's the vicar?' she whispered to Frank as she
passed him carrying a big bowl of coleslaw.

'In the cloakroom, looking down on the unemployed.'

'Oh Frank, don't be disgusting.'

'Well, I don't suppose he knows what to do with his
willy. Is he gay, d'you think?'

'I don't know! Daisy Arthur's after him . . . and of course
there's Yvonne . . .' Monica raised her eyebrow to Frank
and he smiled.

'She'll find this one has hard nuts to crack.'

'Frank!'

Their eyes met with the friendliness of thirty years of
marriage. The Bells had hardly spent a night apart, except
for ten years earlier when Monica had been in hospital. But
as Frank went back to the kitchen to get the garlic bread
out of the Aga, his wife felt a shiver of concern. She
couldn't put her finger on it, but Frank had been pre-
occupied since the previous evening. Thank goodness he
seemed to be his old self again now.

Suzy found herself talking to her neighbour from Tarn Acres, Janice Jones.

'My mum's minding the children for me for an hour. She's really upset. She's known Phyllis Drysdale for years.'

'I didn't know you were from Tarnfield!' Though I should have done from the accent, Suzy thought.

'Kevin, my husband, isn't. He's from Bradford. But my mum farms locally.'

'Really? It seems that everyone's related to everyone else round here.'

'Yes,' said Janice seriously. 'It's nice. Though sometimes Kevin feels a bit left out of it. But I think it's good that the children have got their grandma nearby.'

I wonder, Suzy thought. From what she had seen, Kevin Jones was a self-righteous young man who probably felt he was doing Tarnfield a favour by living there. She couldn't imagine him enjoying having his mother-in-law on the doorstep. He had once cornered Suzy, his shaved head down like a charging bull, when she was putting out the rubbish early one Thursday for the bin-men, and asked her if she felt the congregation at All Saints really knew the Lord.

'Janice and I have had a personal experience of the living Jesus,' he had said. 'We know he's with us even when we're doing things like hoovering and tidying the garden.' So that's where I've gone wrong, thought Suzy; I really ought to try more weeding.

'Does your mother go to All Saints?' Suzy asked. She was surprised to see Janice's plump, healthy face crinkle a bit.

'Oh yes, well, not every week now. She used to get on very well with the old vicar before he had his heart attack or whatever it was, and opted out. Everyone looked up to Mr Pattinson. But of course he wasn't as . . . well, he wasn't as . . . committed as Nick.'

'What do you mean?'

'Kevin says that Nick's been quite disturbed by the lack of real witness at All Saints. Christianity isn't about singing in the choir and flower arranging, you know. There has to be a real sense of the Spirit. Nick's worried that we'll never get more people into All Saints while the old guard are in control. People like the Clarks and Phyllis Drysdale.'

'Well, you seem to be on a winning streak,' Suzy said drily. Janice looked at her rather blankly.

'Excuse me.' Suzy wanted to escape. 'I must go to the loo.'

The Bells' house was large and modern, with four bedrooms, a big double garage and a conservatory. Frank had developed the next-door wood yard shrewdly, with a factory shop outlet selling all sorts of do-it-yourself stuff. And he'd been at the forefront of the fashion for wooden floors. There was probably more parquet in Tarnfield than any other village in the north of England, Suzy thought. But it wasn't all good news for the Bells. Their nineteen-year-old son Matthew had failed his exams at Norbridge College the summer before and hadn't worked since. Suzy knew he spent most of his time driving round like a maniac with the Simpsons' son, but he wasn't above encouraging the local adolescents so he could bask in hero worship. She suspected it was Matthew Bell who was behind Jake's pleas to go paint-balling on Easter Monday.

There was a cloakroom downstairs but, to get well away from Janice, Suzy went upstairs to the lavish bathroom. On the landing, she was surprised to find it was fully carpeted and her feet slipped softly along. She used the toilet and was just about to clatter downstairs when, over the banisters, she saw the top of Robert Clark's head. He had a lot of hair, and it was still surprisingly brown. And he had quite broad shoulders too, she noticed.

Then she realized there was someone else in the hall. Robert was pinned at the bottom of the stairs.

'Well, hello, Robert,' said Yvonne Wait. 'I've wanted to get you on your own for the last hour. What's going to happen about Phyllis's bungalow?'

'You know as much as I do, Yvonne.'

'Oh, come on! I wondered if she might have told you anything . . .'

'Why should she?'

'Because she was Mary's little lamb, that's why.'

Suzy saw Robert's head move stiffly. He was cornered. 'I don't know anything about it.'

'Oh, really? You'd better keep me informed, Robert. And if there's anything you can do to help my case . . .'

Yvonne was standing very close to Robert now. It made Suzy uncomfortable. Yvonne laughed, a deep sexy sound. She said something that sounded like, 'After all, I know all about Mary's insisting . . .'

'You should mind your own business, Yvonne.'

'It is my business. Literally.' Yvonne put her beautifully manicured hand, with its square shiny nails, on Robert's shoulder. Then she bent forward intimately and whispered something more. Robert stood, motionless for a moment.

What's this all about? Suzy thought. What's going on between them?

Yvonne left him and swung her shiny cap of hair into the Bells' sitting room; Robert came up the stairs two at a time. Suzy wondered for a moment how she could avoid him, but it was too late. He pulled up sharply in front of her.

'Oh, hello again . . .' He glanced down into the hall. He's wondering if I was listening, Suzy thought.

'I've just been admiring the Bells' lovely bathroom.' Suzy smiled. 'I've always wanted to try a two speed bidet. Now I'm flush with success!'

It sounded asinine. But Robert laughed. 'You know, you're such a breath of fresh air!'

'Wait to say that till you've been in the loo!'

Robert laughed louder, and she moved over to let him pass. It's happening again, she thought. I'm finding myself liking him. But I mustn't forget how he snubbed me in the church earlier.

And what exactly *was* going on between him and the ghastly Yvonne Wait?

For two years Suzy had managed to steer clear of too much involvement in Tarnfield. It had been partly her circumstances, but also partly her choice. She had been lonely but she had told herself it wasn't her world.

Phyllis's death changed that. Over the last few months Suzy had really come to like Phyllis, and at the back of her mind something about the situation was niggling her. Perhaps the answer lay with the people in Monica Bell's dining room.

And for once, she had nothing to go home to.

7

Easter Sunday lunch, continued

Mortify therefore your members which are upon the earth;
fornication, uncleanness, inordinate affection, evil
concupiscence, and covetousness . . .
From the Epistle for Easter Day, Colossians 3:5

An hour later, and much better informed, Suzy had begun to enjoy herself. The local dynasties were slipping into place. A sly remark of Frank Bell's revealed that Jane Simpson was born Jane Strickland, who had married shrewdly. She kept that hidden! Jeff Simpson's family had been proprietors of the once lucrative Tarnfield cattle auction mart. Well, well, well! And Monica told her that Daisy Arthur's father and mother had kept the village shop, while Alan Robie's great aunt had lived nearby and had left him all her money.

Chatting to Alan revealed that Janice Jones's mother was a wealthy local farmer whose sheep dotted the fells as far as the eye could see, while Yvonne Wait's father had been the village dentist for forty years. And everyone she spoke to assumed Suzy knew that the former vicar George Pattinson had come from an extensive Tarnfield family, and that the Piefields had been farm labourers and vociferous Nonconformists for generations.

Only the Spencers and Stevie Nesbit seemed to have no connections, and there was no likelihood of Stevie siring a bar sinister, Suzy thought, watching him mince over to talk to Nick Melling.

It was all very enlightening. Suzy had no commitments

until she needed to pick up the children at six, so she offered to stay and help wash up. And then she remembered guiltily – we're only here because Phyllis is dead. At that moment, Monica came into the sitting room and looked round.

'Now it's just us left,' she said. 'Jane, Yvonne, Suzy, Daisy, Tom, Robert, Alan and Steve, and me. And Nick of course.' She bowed her head in the direction of the former curate, now acting vicar, who smiled winningly. 'Nick, I think the question is, do we go on with the Bible study group a week on Tuesday? Or should we cancel it?'

'No!' Everyone looked surprised at Yvonne Wait's outburst. 'I mean, Phyllis went to all this trouble to set up the group, I think we should go on.'

'But really,' Jane Simpson laughed in a light, braying fashion which put Suzy's teeth on edge, 'don't we all feel that the Bible study group is a bit pointless now? I'm sure Nick doesn't really want us to do it, do you, Nick?'

The Reverend Nick Melling ran his fingers through his coxcomb of thick blond hair. 'This is a difficult one, Monica. Bible study is vital. But I think Phyllis's idea of taking a text and talking around it isn't what we want to do any more.'

Suzy looked up and caught Robert Clark's eye. He was half amused and half annoyed, she could tell. When she had been to the Bible study groups she'd enjoyed Robert's contributions. Phyllis had told her that Robert had studied theology as a mature student, just for the interest. But she sensed that Nick Melling didn't like too much competition. For a moment she had a mad picture in her mind's eye of Robert Clark and Nick Melling holding a God-calling contest, like the ancient Hebrew prophet Elijah versus the pagan prophets of Baal. She would want Robert to win, despite Nick's film star looks.

'Well, we'll go ahead with the group then, shall we?' said Monica. 'But we need a new secretary.'

'I'll do it,' said Yvonne. There was a wriggle of interest that passed through all the listeners like a tiny, seated Mexican wave. Yvonne Wait, volunteering! I wonder what she really wants out of this, thought Suzy. She remembered the shiny nails and that bobbing, snaky motion of Yvonne's head as she leant towards Robert, trapped in the stair well. Yuk.

Yvonne was still talking. 'But of course, we'll have to hold it in the vicarage, Nick. My house isn't big enough.' Suzy saw Monica raise her eyebrows ever so slightly.

'Oh. Well, I suppose we could.' Nick looked slightly peeved. More work for him!

'That's agreed then.' Monica heaved herself from the sofa, and started to clear up. Suzy stood alongside her in the kitchen and helped load the plates into the dishwasher. Monica seemed surprised not only that Suzy was doing it, but that she was doing it efficiently. So what had Mary Clark said about me? Suzy thought. That I was some sort of slut? Together they scraped and stacked.

Suzy said casually, 'It's helpful of Yvonne to take over the Bible study group, isn't it?' Monica worked at a smear of caked mayonnaise. 'Helpful? Pull the other one!'

'So why would she do it?'

'Because she's got an eye for the main chance. For a start, she's tried it on with every man in the village.' Monica scrubbed at a clean plate. 'She even had a go at my husband once.'

She paused, waiting for Suzy's reaction. Suzy laughed and Monica relaxed.

'You watch, Suzy. She's got an ulterior motive. She's got a finger in every pie round here. She inherited that lovely Georgian town house from her father's family and property is her sideline.'

'So was her father a local man?'

'Oh yes. Who else would be a dentist out here? His mother was a Drysdale. Like Phyllis.'

Suzy thought again about the conversation she had overheard from the landing. She was about to ask what it might mean, but Monica was still talking: '. . . of course Phyllis had no family. Robert will sort out her effects, as she and Mary were so close. He's pretty organized as you'd expect from someone who lived with Mary Pattinson for twenty-five years.'

I can see that, thought Suzy, remembering the tweed hats, and the anorak neatly hung on a hanger, in the vestibule at The Briars. Not like my hallway, with Jake's bike and a box of muddy garden toys and the doll's buggy for Flowerbabe –

'Oh no,' she said, nearly dropping one of Monica's Indian Tree plates. 'Flowerbabe! Phyllis's kitten.'

'What? Did she have a cat?'

'Yes, she only got it a few weeks ago. It'll be trapped in the bungalow. We need to go and get it. Does anyone have a key?'

'I'm sure Robert will. What shall we do about it? Matthew has allergies so I can't have it here.'

There was a significant pause, then Suzy heard herself say, 'I'll take it home with me. Molly will love it.'

I must be mad, she thought. The last thing I need, as well as two kids and a career, is a kitten. Perhaps somebody else could rescue it? But Alan Robie was still eating trifle in the dining room, and pontificating on Choral Evensong to Nick Melling. Daisy Arthur was sitting alongside them, looking mesmerized over a cold cup of coffee. Tom Strickland was in the kitchen helping himself to more of the Bells' beer. Jane Simpson was walking around the garden talking plants with Frank.

And through the door into the sitting room Suzy saw Stevie Nesbit, his hands between his knees as he perched uncomfortably on the big stuffed sofa, with Yvonne Wait berating him. What's she up to now? Suzy thought. Yvonne looked like a harpy.

'I can take you up to Phyllis's house.' Robert had appeared.

'Thanks. That would be kind.'

But in his car on the way to the bungalow, Suzy felt uncomfortable. Perhaps when she had asked about who would inherit Phyllis's belongings, she had hit a nerve? Maybe her estate was an issue and he hadn't meant to shut her up, he just genuinely couldn't give her an answer. And he must know she had overheard Yvonne in the hall.

She took a deep breath and said, 'Look, I didn't mean to listen, but I heard Yvonne talking to you earlier . . .'

The car jumped slightly. 'And you want to know what it was about?'

'Yes,' she said simply. 'I'm curious.'

He liked her frankness. Perhaps he owed her an explanation. He had been a bit short with her earlier. And he had the feeling that despite her chatty manner Suzy Spencer was quite discreet. You couldn't talk people into appearing on TV if you weren't, he thought. And something else occurred to him. How much had Suzy really heard? It might be better to offer her a satisfactory explanation than to have her conjecturing. Whatever his wife might have said about her, Suzy wasn't stupid.

She prompted him. 'Monica told me that Yvonne and Phyllis were related.'

'Yes. Everyone knew that. But only Mary and I knew how close they really were.'

'Close enough for Yvonne to think she should get everything? Even the flower-arranging box?' She smiled. 'Is that why you shut me up in the church?'

'I didn't mean to be rude.'

'Don't worry – after the crass things I've said to you I can't afford to be touchy. So why is that a problem?'

'Because if Phyllis has made a will, Yvonne could be bypassed. That's why she's worried.'

'And she was hoping you could tell her?'

He shivered. 'Yes.'

So that was the explanation. Suzy remembered what Monica had said about Yvonne and property. That was her 'sideline'. She hadn't thought about it before, but Phyllis's old-fashioned blue and white bungalow with its jerry-built porch, peeling paint and large English country garden was on a prime site, just under the brow of the hill where The Briars stood. For someone with an eye for these things it would be well worth having.

'I see! So Yvonne's sitting pretty. Or she hopes she is.

And that's why she was quizzing you . . .' She paused, remembering. She might as well get it all cleared up. 'And there was something else Yvonne said, about Mary. Insisting on something.'

There was a long pause while Robert stared intently out of the windscreen.

'Oh, that. It was about Mary trying to get Phyllis to make things clear.'

Really? But he sounded unsure. And why had Yvonne stressed it so much? There been a touch of predatory sexuality in her movement. Suddenly Robert swung his car to an abrupt halt outside Phyllis's house and turned to face her.

'Look, I don't know why I'm telling you this – probably because, like me, you're not from this bloody village. But Yvonne Wait is one of the nastiest people I've ever met in my life. Just don't let her get her hooks into you as well as everyone else round here.'

'Thanks, but I'm in media. I'm used to nasty people. And anyway, I'm a woman. It's men she seems to go for.'

Robert laughed sharply. 'Oh, you thought there was something going on between Yvonne and me. Well, that's not her game. And if it was, I wouldn't be playing.'

Good, Suzy thought, but she suddenly felt embarrassed that it should matter to her. If Robert Clark and Yvonne Wait were bonking like rabbits why should she care? She jumped out of the car and raced up the path to the sound of mewling inside the house.

'We'd better go in,' said Robert. He slowly opened the door into the dim, empty bungalow. Suzy followed him inside.

'But I can't think why you suddenly want to do this!' Alan Robie's voice was still deep and powerful, but all hint of amateur theatricals was gone. This was real drama. They had only been back from Monica Bell's lunch party for ten minutes, and Stevie had started this!

'That's not fair, Alan.' Steve Nesbit's voice had taken

on a whiney tone, less cute kid than moaning brat. 'You've been saying for weeks that if we sold off the orchard then we could afford to build an extension over the garage. Then we could have more people to stay, do more things –'

'Stevie, that's not true! It came up once, in conversation. Anyway, is that what you really want?' This wasn't just a discussion about selling land. This cut to something much deeper.

For Alan, as a boy, coming to stay with his Aunt May Robie in Tarnfield had been one of the highlights of his summer holidays and their mutual affection had continued into his teens and adulthood. She'd been a butch, bad-tempered woman who'd lived alone in a smallholding she had acquired after being a Land Army girl in the war. The Robies originally hailed from the Border country and May Robie had been accepted in Tarnfield despite her eccentricity. It wasn't unusual for tough women to manage the land. It was tolerated *faute de mieux*. May Robie had worn men's clothes and done men's work well. When she died, the money she had left had been enough to set Alan and Steve up together and provide for the best of everything.

Alan wondered sometimes if, as a teenager, he had sensed in her the homosexual gene he suspected in himself, and there was no doubt Aunt May had provided him with some sort of hope when his conventional family and respectable friends had talked about 'queers'. Interestingly, he felt more secure in Tarnfield than in the town, which was why he'd brought Steve there to live. Like Aunt May, he felt he was respected in his own right. He knew everyone and everyone knew him. It was a sort of damage limitation exercise. The last thing he wanted was more room, so Stevie could invite his gay friends to stay and draw undesirable attention to their set-up.

'We don't need an extension to Church Cottage,' he said. 'It was just casual chat, that's all.'

But there was no such thing as casual conversation with Yvonne Wait, he reminded himself, and he was furious that he had given her a chance to approach them both together, with her seductive offer. Only a few weeks earlier, she'd cornered them after one of Phyllis's Bible study groups and mentioned buying the orchard. She'd been crafty, of course. She could see Steve's delight at the idea. And she'd had the cheek to suggest that they could extend their cottage with the money, as if it was any of her business what they would do! But she was pretty shrewd about property and she could see another bedroom would make all the difference to Church Cottage. Stevie's face had lit up at her words.

Alan was wary of Yvonne, as he was of most women. An eligible bachelor, he had frequently been approached by middle-aged women when he was practising as a small-town solicitor with a secret life. They were the biggest threat to his safety. If he rebuffed them too brusquely they might start spreading rumours. If he encouraged them, he was promising them something he couldn't deliver. It was best to avoid women, unless they were safely married like Monica Bell. In the amateur dramatic society he had hinted at a sad ongoing affair to keep them at bay, but he had never been sure how convinced people had been.

He had first fallen foul of Yvonne five years earlier. She'd had her eyes on Auntie May's place. She'd got the wrong end of the stick, though, when she'd hailed Alan in the Plough. He'd been having a drink, mulling over what to do. Yvonne had sidled up to him at the bar, all glossy hair and perfume, perfect make-up over yellowing skin, Alan's worst nightmare. She'd introduced herself.

'Your aunt was one of my father's patients. Fascinating old lady! I hear the place is on the market. Private sale, is it?'

'Yes. The farmer next door wants to buy it.'

She had put her manicured hand on his arm. 'I might be able to rustle up an extra grand or two, and outbid him. And it would give us a chance to get to know each other better.'

Ugh, Alan had thought. He'd offered the property to his neighbours in good faith and he wasn't going to let them down. He'd ignored her approach, but at his peril. For the last five years, he'd felt she was out to get the better of him, somehow or other.

And he was right, of course. Now, only a few minutes after getting home from lunch at the Bells', on a day when someone had tragically died, all Stevie wanted to talk about was selling the orchard! Yvonne Wait had been getting at him again. Why wouldn't the woman let go?

'But Alan, you said that the orchard was just a load of extra work. You know you did. And Yvonne says she only wants to build a small bungalow on it, something for when she retires.'

Alan had a disturbing thought. 'What's she been saying to you, Stevie?'

'Nothing!' Steve jumped up from the sofa where they'd been sitting with Alan's boringly predictable G&Ts. It would be fab, Stevie thought, if they could have a cocktail or an alcopop or something different. I get tired of living like an extra in *Salad Days*, he grumbled to himself. Of course, that wasn't entirely fair. Alan wasn't really living in the past; there was the state-of-the-art home entertainment system and the new Apple Mac to disprove that. But just sometimes Stevie felt his partner needed shaking up.

He went to the window and looked out at the Tuscan patio. He had to admit it was really lovely. How else would he ever get the chance to live in such luxury? He could get irritated with Alan on occasions, but without him he would be in a bedsit in Brixton, pretending to be part of the London gay scene whilst getting older and more raddled every year. It still tempted him of course . . . and that was the cause of all his problems.

Oh, that ghastly woman, he thought. Why did she have to find him in the sitting room at the Bells'? He'd been trying to avoid Tom Strickland, who was prowling round looking for more drink, and she'd pinned him to the sofa. He'd agreed to help her, of course. He'd been sure Alan would want to sell, once they'd talked about it again. He could usually persuade Alan to do anything. But this time he was being so stubborn.

Alan said, 'Has Yvonne Wait been bullying you?'

'No!'

For the first time since coming home, Stevie suddenly felt really frightened. If he couldn't persuade Alan, then perhaps Yvonne would really do what she had threatened. It didn't bear thinking about. The bitch! The cow!

'Alan, I really want you to do this,' Stevie said. 'Please. For me! That money would *sooo* come in handy. And we could have such a wonderful life here. The only thing I've ever wanted, you know, is just a tiny bit more company.' He sidled to Alan's side, perched down beside him and put his hand on his partner's thigh. 'Please, Alan,' he whispered.

'It's not what I want to do, Stevie.' Alan felt a frisson of sexual arousal. He adored Stevie but sometimes the boy had to be checked. The idea that there was endless money, that the orchard could be sold and the house extended just like that, had to be nipped in the bud. Stevie had to come to terms with Tarnfield life as it was. Alan was the boss. He braced himself for the inevitable but exciting tantrum.

'I can't believe it,' Stevie wailed, standing up again. 'You say you love me and you want to make my life happy after all the horrors of the past. But you won't even do this one little thing for me.'

'Selling the orchard is hardly one little thing. And even if I did there's no guarantee that I'd use the money to extend the house. So calm down.'

'I can't calm down. You don't love me at all. And you don't understand.' Stevie began to cry, huge sobs making his neat body shudder.

'Oh, pull yourself together.' Alan got up masterfully and put his hands on his partner's shoulders. 'Sometimes, Stevie, you just have to do things my way.'

'No, I don't!' Stevie screamed.

'This is ridiculous! Don't get hysterical. You know you just have to ask me and we can go and see your friends anywhere! We don't need the gay scene descending on Tarnfield all the time. This isn't Camden Town. It's quiet, and conventional. And because we live a quiet life, people here like and respect us.'

'They don't like you. They sneer at you. And they hate me!' Stevie yelled. 'You're so cruel to me. I'm caged up here!'

'Stevie! That's not fair.'

'Fair? I'll tell you what's not fair. Treating me like a slave isn't fair.' Stevie picked up Alan's drink and threw it on to the pale beige carpet. It was a calculated gesture. His rages in the past had usually led to delicious making-up sessions when Alan became much more malleable.

But this was much more extreme than Alan had expected and Stevie suddenly knew he had overstepped the mark. Alan withdrew his hands and stared at him coldly.

'That's an awful thing to do, Stephen. Pick that glass up now!'

There was only one other way to get Alan eating out of the palm of his hand, Stevie thought. 'I hate this place!' he screamed. 'There's only one person here who understands me. And it isn't you!'

'What on earth do you mean?'

Stevie shook Alan away. 'I need someone who really cares. I'm going to talk to Nick Melling.'

8

Easter Sunday afternoon

Not with the old leaven, nor with the leaven of malice and
wickedness, but with the unleavened bread of sincerity
and truth.

From the Easter Anthem

In Phyllis's bungalow, Suzy followed Robert into the cool
dark kitchen at the back. She scooped some special kitten
food out of a tin left on the counter, and ran some fresh
water for Flowerbabe.

'Everything's in reasonable order,' Robert said.

Suzy shuddered. 'It feels very odd,' she said, 'being here
without Phyllis.'

'Yes. And the whole place is so reminiscent of her, isn't
it?' Phyllis's dark crowded kitchen was cluttered. There
was a teapot and tea cosy, and a few jars of tired pasta on
the work surfaces. And everywhere there were little piles
of mixed paperclips, elastic bands, very old coupons and
pencil stubs.

Robert said, 'I'm sorry I wasn't kinder to Phyllis after
Mary died.' The thought had been on his mind all day, but
he felt better now he had said it out loud, and safe saying
it to Suzy. He perched at the kitchen table and watched the
kitten wolfing its food.

'I don't think you can blame yourself,' said Suzy. 'You
must have been pretty devastated.'

'Well, that's true. But I knew it was coming. The trouble
was, you know, that Mary and I were too wrapped up in
each other. I couldn't see beyond my own pain, so

I couldn't accept that other people were in pain too. If I had, Phyllis might have confided in me more, and I could have helped her.'

'In what way?'

'Well, I'm sure her heart condition was made worse by all this stress at the church. If I hadn't just gone on, doing my own thing and letting the church politics wash over me, maybe I could have given her more support.'

It was funny, Suzy thought, how Robert was circumspect when it came to All Saints. He was very knowledgeable and very involved, but he was clearly wary of a conflict with Nick Melling. He had offered no opinions, nor had he said anything about the former vicar George Pattinson, though Mary had been such a pillar of the parish.

'So what really is happening at All Saints?' Suzy asked. 'I can see that Nick has new ideas. But that's inevitable, isn't it?'

'Yes and no.' Robert sighed. 'No one minds new things. It's just that no one really knows what Nick wants or how far he'll go to get it. Kevin Jones is trying to steer him into evangelicalism and probably succeeding. But Steve Nesbit and Alan Robie think he's a repressed gay and would like to see him as one of those Anglo-Catholic types.'

'All dressed up in a lacy surplice. He'd look really cute!'

'But that would horrify Tom Strickland who can't stand him anyway because he's young and posh. Talking of which, Jane Simpson just dislikes anything to do with Phyllis, so she supports anything new that Nick brings in. Overall it's uncomfortable and messy. And on top of all that, Nick's awful at dealing with people. I found that out when Mary died.'

'Why did Jane Simpson dislike Phyllis?'

'Oh, years ago Phyllis was engaged to Jeffrey and he dumped her for Jane. Jane feels guilty, I suppose. Or perhaps she feels jealous in some obscure way. That would be more like Jane.'

Suzy laughed 'You've got them all off to a T,' she said. And I wonder what he really thinks of me? she thought.

She said nothing, and the silence was surprisingly companionable. The kitten seemed to be intent on eating five times its own weight. There was time to carry on talking.

'Was Phyllis attractive?'

'Oh, yes, in a fluffy sort of way. Of course she was a few years older than Mary. But she was nice-looking. Old-fashioned but sweet.'

'Why were she and Mary such good friends?'

'They were brought up together, practically. And later, Mary went to secretarial college when Phyllis was doing her teacher training. Then Phyllis came back to Tarnfield to care for her mother.'

'Funny . . .' said Suzy, and stopped. Robert looked at her. It was one of those moments, she thought, when she could either be honest about what she was thinking, or she could fudge.

'What were you going to say?'

'I was thinking that of the two of them Mary seemed much more like a teacher, much more authoritative. I was always surprised that Mary only worked part-time at Bell's. She was such a capable woman, with no children, and she was a brilliant organizer. So why didn't she . . . well . . . do more?'

It occurred to him that it didn't matter what he said to Suzy Spencer. He hadn't realized how much dissimulation he had been going through, with everyone watching him and dissecting his grief, monitoring his recovery, waiting to pounce on symptoms of disloyalty, keeping Mary's memory going. But none of them had really understood his wife. She had been marvellous in many ways, but not in everything, and he was tired, now, of the hagiography.

Suzy said, 'I hope you don't mind me asking?'

'No, I don't.' To my own surprise, thought Robert. He paused, and said, 'My wife was an outstanding woman. She was really clever and an amazing motivator. But she never achieved her true potential.' He paused again.

'What held her back?'

'She had a very bad experience in her teens and in some ways she never got over it. I always felt that I helped and encouraged her. But she was handicapped by her past. No one here would ever know how insecure Mary could be.'

He turned away and fussed with the tin of cat food. He could hardly believe he was confiding in this unlikely woman. But telling the truth didn't make him love his wife less. He wasn't stupid. He knew that Mary had been bossy and judgemental sometimes. But that made no difference to his devotion. And unlike everybody else, he knew the real reason why Mary was like that.

I see, Suzy was thinking. So mild, unassuming 'backroom boy' Robert Clark was the strong one in the Robert and Mary story. Like everyone in Tarnfield she had assumed that he and his wife lived this perfect life, with every pillowcase ironed and fish knife polished. But she had always thought that Robert was just Mary's sidekick in this ideal home experience.

But they'd all been wrong. It was on the tip of her tongue to ask what awful thing had happened to Mary, but she could see that would be going too far. Anyway, the kitten was reeling slightly, its tummy practically on the floor and its legs splaying out.

'I'd better take Flowerbabe home,' she said. 'Would you give me another lift back? There'll be a lot to take, as well as the kitten.'

Robert smiled. 'Of course. Let's get the stuff together.'

He started to collect up the tins of food, and Suzy turned to rinse the cat's dishes in Phyllis's sink. Her eye caught the cork noticeboard above the draining board.

Robert came over to stand beside her. In very large letters on a piece of paper which Phyllis had pinned to the board, they read: *Must ring Geo re meeting Sun night.*

'I wonder what that's about?' Suzy said. 'Looks like she was leaving herself a really urgent note! Who's Geo?'

Robert was silent for a moment, looking at the paper.

'George Pattinson maybe? He'd disappeared from Tarnfield but they'd known each other for years.'

'Well, she won't be making any meeting with him tonight, if that's what she meant. Will anyone have told him what's happened?'

'Probably not,' said Robert quietly. 'George Pattinson has kept himself pretty much to himself since he left All Saints.'

He had gone cold again. He was staring past her, out of Phyllis's kitchen window and into her cottage garden where the winter flowering jasmine looked like scrambled egg thrown along the leafless hedge. Suzy looked over his shoulder. From Phyllis's kitchen, you could see The Briars on the crest of the hill. The bungalow was practically at the bottom of his garden. If Yvonne inherited this, Suzy thought, she'd probably build it into three storeys and block his view, just out of spite.

'I think you need to call him,' she said. 'Perhaps he'll be waiting to see Phyllis tonight.'

Robert pulled himself back from the bare branches of the laburnum.

'Would you mind doing it?' he asked. 'I'll give you George's number.'

She was about to ask why, but Robert avoided her eyes. His face looked closed and hard, just as it had in the church when she asked about Phyllis's belongings.

'OK,' she said, filling the silence. 'But we'd better get this kitten back to my house. I've got to pick my kids up at Tarnfield Junction. Not to mention a load of hand washing I've got to do, because my machine's buggered. If you take me back now, I'll call George Pattinson on my mobile while you drive . . .'

In the car, Robert put on the radio and the local traffic news reported yet another motorway accident, with four people dead. It was a bank holiday phenomenon.

'That's just the sort of thing that terrifies me about Jake,' Suzy said. 'He wanted to go to Preston paint-balling tomorrow with some local lads. I think one of them was Matthew Bell. Anyway I said no. It's a long journey and I'm terrified of an accident.'

'You're right. Matthew Bell drives like a maniac. And

he's encouraged by Russell Simpson. Russell used to be a nice lad till he hit puberty. But from what I've seen of Jake, he'd be bored sick with that mob after an hour in a car with them.'

Suzy felt relieved. She had worried about depriving Jake of fun, or having him appeal to his father who might take his side. Nigel tended to opt in and out of childcare, and to want to be popular. But Robert is a teacher, she told herself, so he must have some knowledge of young people. She glanced at him out of the corner of her eye. She'd imagined him teaching Jane Austen and Matthew Arnold to ladies at evening class, but that was just his Tarnfield persona. He probably taught science fiction to iconoclastic adolescents. She should have learnt by now that not everyone from the village was like Phyllis.

'I suppose there'll be an inquest into Phyllis's death?' she asked.

'Yes, but it will be straightforward. Poor Phyllis had a heart attack in the church.'

Suzy frowned, but this time she said nothing. She didn't want to disagree, but straightforward wasn't the right word, she thought. She couldn't pin it down, but there was something wrong about the picture. Suzy had a very visual imagination. She tried to see in her mind's eye how Phyllis could have stabbed herself with a flower-arranging decoration. It just didn't look right.

The kitten started to wriggle. I must do as I offered and ring George Pattinson straight away, she thought. He might be waiting for Phyllis to call. She fumbled with the phone.

The former priest of All Saints sounded a hundred and ten when she spoke to him and a hundred and twenty after he had heard of Phyllis's death. In a shaky voice he thanked her, and then he surprised her by saying, 'You're the new woman, aren't you, the one with the two children? From Tarn Acres?'

'Yes, that's me, Mr Pattinson. I'm glad you remember me. I only joined the church about two years ago. Mrs Clark brought me in.'

'Yes, I remember,' said George Pattinson at the other end of what was a very bad connection. Robert was looking straight ahead; the kitten had woken up fully and was trying to claw its way inside Suzy's jacket.

'I wonder,' said the tinny voice at the other end of the line, 'would you be kind enough to keep in touch with me this week over the funeral arrangements? I don't tend to be in much contact with All Saints. Don't want to tread on Nick's toes, things like that. I'd appreciate it if you let me know.'

'Of course,' said Suzy, surprised.

'Thank you so much,' said Mr Pattinson in a tired, formal voice, and hung up.

'Funny that,' Suzy said as she clicked the phone off. 'He doesn't seem to be in touch with anyone much from All Saints now. He sounded terrible. When I came to Tarnfield he was really looked up to, by everyone.'

Robert concentrated on parking.

'I mean, he was such a big name locally, the Reverend George Pattinson.' Suzy stopped. 'Oh . . .' What had Monica Bell said? Any man would have to be efficient who lived with Mary Pattinson. Not Mary Clark. Mary Pattinson.

'Hey, were your Mary and the old vicar related too?' she asked. 'Like Yvonne and Phyllis? I mean, everyone's related to everyone round here, aren't they?'

'Yes.' Robert was straining to look over his shoulder. He's making a meal out of getting into this parking space, Suzy thought. He said, 'They were related. Distantly. The Pattinsons are a big family.' At that moment Flowerbabe chose to make a bid for freedom and leapt on to Suzy's shoulder. By the time she had untangled cat and sleeve, Robert was opening the door for her.

'Thanks, I'll keep in touch,' she said, struggling out of the car. 'We've still got that broken fence to sort out.'

'Oh, there's no rush on that.'

'That's good. Thanks.' She levered herself out of the car, but couldn't wave to him because her arms were full of the kitten and its accessories, so she flapped her elbows up and down, grinned, and turned up her path. He couldn't help laughing back with her, but he knew they had ended on a strained note again.

Robert got into the car and sat for a minute, both angry and surprised at himself. He had handled that badly because the call to George Pattinson had shaken him. He had been thinking of asking Suzy if she wanted to use his washing machine, seeing hers had broken down. His machine was empty most of the time, and she had a lot to do. He had genuinely wanted to help her. But the moment had passed. And now the evening stretched ahead of him, bleaker than ever after all the activity of the day.

Oh Mary, he thought, why was life with you always so complicated? I loved you so much, but sometimes I think I never really knew what made you tick.

For a second he rested his head on the steering wheel. Then, resolutely, he sat up, restarted the engine and turned towards The Briars.

9

Easter Sunday evening

Give grace, O heavenly Father, to all Bishops and Curates,
that they may both by their life and doctrine set forth
thy true and lively Word.
From the Prayer for the Church Militant, Holy Communion

Nick Melling looked at the two staring, expectant faces opposite him and felt cornered. It really wasn't fair, he thought. How could anyone cope with Kevin Jones and Daisy Arthur at the same time in the same room? There were times when too much support was burdensome.

'I know any death is sad, Nick,' Kevin was saying forcefully, sitting on the edge of the overstuffed armchair in what had been the Pattinsons' elegant front room. When Nick moved in after George disappeared on sick leave, he had planned to use it as a quiet sitting room where he could help souls in need, coming to him for words of wisdom and spiritual insight that would change their lives. Instead he'd found that what most people wanted was to sit there and talk about church politics, or slag off their fellow men.

'Any death is sad,' Kevin said again in his slow, uncompromising Yorkshire voice, 'but we've got a great chance to shake this place up a bit. I mean all that traditionalist rubbish must go now! Phyllis Drysdale kept that lot going. We should act quickly. No time to lose.'

Daisy Arthur looked at Nick with huge bovine eyes. She was undoubtedly very pretty, but the fact that her mouth was always slightly open and her jaw moving spoiled the effect. There was something feverish about Daisy these days, Nick thought. She'd seemed bright and enthusiastic when he'd first met her. But over the last year she'd become more volatile and even Nick was aware that it had something to do with him. He hadn't encouraged her. But there weren't many young graduates in Tarnfield, and he was slightly uncomfortable about the way he'd given her so much eye contact in the early days. Of course I was rather lonely, he told himself, and she was so enthusiastic, whereas so many other people in Tarnfield had an undermining tendency to question things. He remembered Suzy Spencer clasping his hand at the church door after his searching Ascension Day sermon and whispering worriedly, 'You don't believe all that, do you?' Awful woman. At least Daisy showed some respect. Too much perhaps, but that was better.

'Oh Nick,' she said, breathing heavily, 'do you think Kevin's right? Could this be your chance to get things changed here?'

Nick looked back at her, trying not to engage those big brown eyes. After one Harvest Festival, he'd talked to her about updating her thinking. She had organized the little children to make up a flower arrangement based on a schmaltzy Victorian hymn and it really wasn't modern enough. She'd hung on his every word, and then gone to Newcastle to some of the more evangelical bookshops and churches. At Christmas, she had run a cartoon characters' nativity service, with Scooby Doo in the stable. It had been chaotic, and perhaps rather hard to relate to a Christian message. Not to mention the mess. He sighed.

It was very difficult, Nick thought. He wanted a church full of attractive young families, a sort of breakfast TV-targeted religion, and he didn't know how to deal with the elderly or the difficult. But his trendy new congregation had to include genuine spirituality. And that had to emanate from him. He was in charge now, and he was just what the church needed: young, intelligent, committed, good-looking. Everyone thought so. Especially the Bishop: Nick had a lot to live up to.

'Of course we can't say that Phyllis's death was a blessing exactly,' Kevin continued, though he sounded doubtful. 'But it does mean we can sweep clean.'

Oh dear, Nick thought. Kevin's enthusiasm was sometimes a little inept. The day had been so stressful. Though he was grateful to Monica for lunch, he could have done with some space. And then he'd needed a lift home, which Daisy provided, and Kevin had turned up. So he was stuck with them. At least they were his fans, but that had a downside too.

Not for the first time, Nick wondered what God was doing, testing him with Tarnfield.

The responsibility of a full pastoral role had come too soon, he felt. George Pattinson had been a larger-than-life vicar, blooming with the confidence of late middle age, a local star. Nick had been his curate for a year when George had suffered his breakdown. Nick hadn't been told what it was all about, but within weeks of his illness George had been reduced to an old man. The Bishop of Norbridge had breezed in and out, there had been high-level talks behind closed doors in the study, and George had disappeared on extended sick leave which looked like being permanent.

Now George Pattinson and his wife Joan had gone from the Tarnfield scene, to live in a bungalow belonging to his family on farmland miles away. And Nick was suddenly in charge, with instructions from the Bishop to leave George alone to recover.

Nick had stayed on at the vicarage. He'd been promised support from the Rural Dean and the Archdeacon, both of whom had been to visit. But they made no secret of the fact that they thought this was an amazing opportunity for a vaunted young curate like Nick to make his mark. An Oxford graduate just turned thirty, who'd done a couple of years in public relations before responding to the call, Nick had been hailed, literally, as the answer to the Bishop's prayers. Perhaps now, he rather regretted being labelled as the coming man. He suspected it made other clergymen less supportive. So he found it impossible to tell anyone that he might be out of his depth. After all, the Bishop had told everyone that he was a gifted young priest!

But somehow his parishioners hadn't noticed. In fact, Nick could go as far as to say they seemed ungrateful. In the trendy urban parish where he'd done most of his training, his role had commanded a respect that was missing in Tarnfield. People here might be bucolic and conventional but they were somehow sophisticated when it came to getting their own way. They seemed to want to outwit his initiatives rather than defer to him. He deplored the fact that so much of the Anglicanism in Tarnfield was based on habit and tradition and family pressure. And comfort. Nick didn't do comfort, though at this moment he felt bizarrely in need of it himself.

'Of course, Phyllis's death is a tragedy, Kevin,' he said severely. 'And yes, of course it means things will change. But we should move slowly, this week at least. There will be the funeral to organize, to start with.'

A nightmare, Nick thought. I can't stand funerals. I have real difficulty dealing with the distress of the bereaved. At least Phyllis hasn't left a husband. Nick shuddered, remembering how hard he had found it to talk to Robert Clark when his wife had died. Everything he had said had seemed trite and juvenile. Mind you, he consoled himself, that event had derailed even the much-respected George Pattinson. He'd been at his peak then, but Mary's death had been one of the few times when he hadn't seemed able to cope. Odd, Nick thought.

'I guess they'll cancel the Bible study group now,' Kevin laughed brusquely. 'I can't stand those sorts of things. I don't reckon we want an Alpha course either. We need a home prayer group.' He looked at Daisy with fierce intensity. 'Don't you agree, Daisy?'

'Oh, Kevin, I'm not sure. I think we should study the Bible, I really do. But it should be all about what Nick wants.' She stared at Nick again. And then, with the intelligence Nick had sensed in her when they'd first met, she said, 'Phyllis wasn't the problem. She was just keeping things going because that was what Mary did. The problem really is the fellow travellers.'

'What d'you mean, Phyllis wasn't the problem? Without her, all that stuff will fall apart.' Kevin sounded more aggressive than ever. It was as if Phyllis's death solved everything.

'Will it? I doubt it.' Daisy was looking down at her hands now, and was slightly pink. 'Phyllis wasn't just a silly old biddy, you know. Oh no. She was quite shrewd. She . . .'

Daisy stopped and looked up again into Nick's eyes. I wonder what she was going to say, Nick thought, and yet again he was surprised. Then Daisy's lips parted and her breath came noisily. 'Sorry, Nick. But I've known Phyllis all my life, ever since Mum sent me to Sunday School just to get me out of the house! It will be strange without her.'

'Of course.' Nick tried to sound soothing and smiled at her. Daisy beamed back, all sadness dispelled by his smile, then resumed chewing the cud.

'Well, I still say we make plans now.' Kevin wasn't giving up. He wanted them to move quickly, to have a plan of action. In a few more minutes he would have to go home and report all this to Janice. Her mother had threatened to call round that afternoon, and by coming to see Nick, Kevin had hoped to miss her. Nobody could complain if he was at the vicarage for an hour or two, but he couldn't push his luck and avoid the kids' tea as well.

He glanced sideways at Daisy. She was so beautiful, he thought. It was obvious to him that the Holy Spirit was acting through her. Sometimes he felt Janice's faith was watered down now she was back, living so near her mum. And she'd gone really plump over the last year, too.

'Maybe you're right, Kevin,' Nick Melling said. 'Perhaps this is the cue for more change.'

Kevin sat back, satisfied. 'I'm not saying we should ride roughshod over everyone, Nick. But we need to put out the right signals pretty quickly. You're not going to let them go ahead with the Bible study group next week, are you?'

'Well . . .' Nick paused. 'As I said, Kevin, I don't want to do anything drastic before the funeral.'

'OK, if that's how you feel.' Kevin shook his big bullet head as if more in sorrow than in anger. 'I hope this will be the last one, though. Those Bible study evenings just give people like Robert Clark a chance to show off.'

That was true, Nick Melling thought. When it came to Bible study, Robert Clark sometimes talked with as much authority as a vicar, which was very irritating.

'On reflection, I think you're absolutely right there, Kevin. The group should be stopped. Perhaps it should be cancelled after the next meeting.' And that would have the added benefit of ousting the infuriating Yvonne Wait who, for some strange reason of her own, had offered to organize the group.

'Good thinking, Nick. Go for it! And you need to think about why we have a choir, next. All those people in fancy dress standing at the front of the church as if they were holier than everyone else. Not to mention all the flowers. Like a funeral parlour. Gives the wrong message. But I'll leave that to you to mull over. I'm off now.'

Kevin beamed and stood up, but Nick was concerned to see that Daisy remained seated. He really did not want to find himself alone with her in the sitting room. He dreaded the thought that she might assume some level of intimacy, and he couldn't face that.

'I'll see you out, Kevin. And Daisy, I think I need some time to think about all this now. I'll see you a week on Tuesday of course, at the Bible group.'

'Oh, yes, Nick. Perhaps we could talk then about the Whit Sunday Festival I'd like to do? With the kids?'

That was another worry, Nick thought. Tarnfield always made a big fuss of Whitsun, in that North Country way. Daisy had been talking about some sort of event, and had hinted that perhaps something more evangelical should happen, a sort of mission type of service. While Nick was keen to be seen as the man who pulled All Saints kicking and screaming into the modern world – a hero priest who turned the parish around – he balked at the thought of anything too emotional. And it would be a lot of work, too. He really shouldn't take too much on!

The doorbell rang. It sounded as if someone was keeping a finger on it until the door was opened. Nick leapt up to answer, hoping to be rescued, and found Stevie Nesbit on his doorstep. His heart sank.

'Ah, Stevie, do come in. Kevin and Daisy are just leaving.'

Kevin gave Stevie a contemptuous glance and the merest nod, and then watched Daisy Arthur walk lightly over the gravel sweep of the vicarage drive. She glanced back, but her look wasn't for him. She gazed at the vicarage with an expression of pure longing; Kevin clenched his fists in frustration and prepared to go back home to toddlers' teatime and the stress of making conversation with his mother-in-law.

Still, he thought with some satisfaction, at least one obstacle was out of the way. Before long, All Saints would be the sort of church he would be proud to belong to. It was vital that the Lord's will was done, and he, Kevin Jones, was the man to do it. With that thought, and the sight of Daisy Arthur's shapely bottom in her low-cut trousers as she bent over to open her car door, Kevin felt sustained.

10

The Thursday in Easter Week

*. . . for I work a work in your days, a work which ye shall
in no wise believe . . .*
From the Epistle for Tuesday in Easter Week, Acts 13:41

On the Thursday of Easter Week, Suzy Spencer took Jake
to a music workshop in Norbridge. These holiday activities
were always difficult for her to organize. She'd left Molly
with Sharon Strickland, Tom's daughter, her regular babysitter and mother's help.

It was surprising, she thought, how kids in the Tarnfield
area had to be ferried everywhere. The country was supposed to be so healthy, but she reckoned many rural children were more car-bound and got less fresh air than in the
towns. But to express this view would be heresy in Tarnfield of course.

There were quite a few children in the village, and a lot
of them got dragged along to All Saints Sunday School.
Suzy remembered her mother telling her that Sunday
School attendance in years gone by had everything to do
with parental need for privacy and much less to do with
the promotion of religion. 'Most babies were conceived on
Sunday afternoon,' her mum had laughed. 'Ask your
grandma!' So much for good old-fashioned Christian
values, Suzy thought. Now, the morning Sunday School
was more of a social event for the village children. Molly
seemed to like it, and Daisy Arthur was doing a good job,
though she needed some help. But she seemed to like

taking it all on her own shoulders. The Scooby Doo nativity had been hysterical, and in need of a good producer, Suzy thought.

She wondered what they were going to do for Whitsun now Phyllis was dead. They'd planned a sort of minor flower festival with swags of *Viburnum opulus*, whitebeam foliage, gladioli and delphiniums – if Phyllis's Magic Moon was out early – curving down the pillars of the church. Suzy liked doing swags. They were big and bold enough not to need the attention to detail. It was detail that had made Mary and Phyllis such great flower arrangers. No chance of that now. Suzy was nothing like as knowledgeable or thorough as the older women had been.

But it occurred to her that perhaps she and Daisy could get together and do something with flowers that involved the kids. Maybe the children could make great big paper flames to represent the Holy Spirit burning on the heads of the disciples at Pentecost, and they could build easily obtainable bright commercial flowers into it – sunflowers perhaps, or gerberas. It would look amazingly dramatic, and get the kids' work into the main church. Molly would love messing around with orange paper and gold and silver foil. She would suggest it at the Bible study group. And there were the children who sang in the choir. They could help too. She would ask Robert Clark about that; he was a chorister.

Yet again she wondered what was happening to her. This wasn't in the script. She had talked about it to her friend Rachel on Saturday night, after she had demolished Robert's fence. It seemed light years away now.

Rachel had made her feel better. 'I don't see why you shouldn't do these churchy things. It's about the community, isn't it? I don't suppose my mum asks herself detailed questions about the relevance of the Torah when she goes to play bridge at the Schul.'

'But Judaism's different, Rache. You get born into it once. You don't have to get born again. I find all this upfront evangelical stuff embarrassing.'

'Well, are you a Christian or not?'

'I don't really know. In fact I don't think I believe much at all. I just like going to church. I like the singing and the building and the sense of peace.'

'Well, shouldn't that be enough?'

'No, not according to some of the people round here.' She thought of Kevin Jones lurking around the dustbins, waiting to pounce and test her on her faith when she put out the rubbish.

'Oh, they're just the extremists,' Rachel said. 'I think you should go for it! You chose to go and live in some Cumbrian Clochemerle, so you might as well make the most of it. You either need to get involved in this church or to get back into full-time work. You know you're missing it.'

'Yes and no. I'm not really missing being a line producer on *Living Lies*.'

Suzy's final assignment in London had been working on a programme where people revealed that they had been living in a parallel universe, usually to the horror of their nearest and dearest. For a while Rachel had worked there too, as a researcher. Rachel liked to make serious documentaries about social issues, but when times were tough she would freelance anywhere. She and Suzy had been friends for years, since they started as Granada trainees. They were both from Greater Manchester, though Rachel was from a wealthy Jewish family in Didsbury while Suzy had been brought up in Broadheath.

'So tell me about these village people,' Rachel had demanded.

'Well, there's Phyllis Drysdale. She was best pals with Mary Clark who died of cancer and who ran the show. It was Mary who roped me in. I went to see the church, and she and the vicar were there.'

Looking back, Suzy felt uncomfortable about her first visit to All Saints. She was sure Mary had been there with George Pattinson, but he had melted away. Now that she knew about the routine at the church, she had wondered several times what they had actually been doing there on a Thursday afternoon. She hadn't noticed them at first, and suddenly Mary had loomed at the end of her pew.

Suzy shook her head to clear it, and continued, 'Then there's Yvonne Wait who works at the hospital; very smart and brisk. Jane Simpson is a duchess type from Tarnfield House, and the Bells are local business people; they're all right.'

'Any men?' Rachel asked.

'Not in the sense you mean. But there's Tom Strickland, who's a gruff ex-squaddie in his sixties, and there are two gay guys. One's so "out" it's not true and the other's a pipe-smoking closet queen. They're a scream. Then there's Daisy, our token young person . . .'

She stopped suddenly. There was another man, of course. 'And there's also Robert Clark. Mary's widower.'

'Uho . . . come on, Suzy! What's the subtext here?'

'There isn't one. I told you about him earlier. He's the one whose fence I ran into.'

'You said nothing about him! Why did you leave mentioning him till last?'

'No reason.'

'Oh yes? You usually wreck people's property and then stop thinking about them?'

'Oh Rache, get lost! You are so annoying. I swear to you that he's just an old fart. He wears hats and teaches poetry. And sings in the church choir. Give me a break.'

'OK . . . though the words "protest" and "too much" spring to mind, methinks.'

'Go to hell. Or better, come up here for a weekend! I'll go mad if I don't see you soon. I must be halfway there already, if I'm doing flower arranging and chatting up widowers.'

Rachel had laughed. Now, though, Suzy felt more unsettled. Everything had changed so much since Saturday. Phyllis would be cremated the following Monday. Daisy had told her that there'd been a post mortem, which had confirmed that she had suffered a massive heart attack. Poor Phyllis, Suzy thought.

She sat in the car park outside Norbridge Community College, and waited. Jake had forbidden her to listen to his contribution, and anyway the woodwind session was running late because one of the other kids had split the reed on his sax. Jake had been unpleasantly triumphalist.

'He's a plonker anyway,' he said to Suzy. 'My teacher says he's really disorganized. No wonder he's got a broken reed!'

'Don't be nasty, Jake. There's no guarantee you're going to do so well yourself.'

'Oh no? The teacher says I'm really good. You watch this space, Mum.'

She was delighted for him really. Neither Jake nor Molly was a neat or tidy kid. But when it came to taking care of the saxophone Jake really tried hard. There'd be no chance of him having a broken reed.

Broken reed. The phrase seemed familiar, like something from the Bible. She had the idea it was a byword for unreliability – wasn't that what Jake's teacher was getting at?

Suzy sat bolt upright in the driver's seat. She had suddenly realized what had been worrying her about Phyllis's accident. Yet again, the scenario everyone else had so glibly accepted just wouldn't work in Suzy's head.

How come a decoration had cut Phyllis's left hand? And what sort of fake flower would do that? There was only one thing that fitted the bill. But why would Phyllis have been using that? It made no sense. And not only would it have been totally uncharacteristic for Phyllis to cut herself – it was physically impossible.

But shouldn't the experts have spotted this? Wouldn't the police have seen it? Or Phyllis's doctor? Wouldn't the pathologist have come up with a sensible explanation? So what was the official line?

Robert Clark was arranging the funeral. He would know.

It would be at least half an hour before Jake would be finished at the workshop. Suzy locked the car and walked quickly over to the college's reception before she could change her mind.

'I know it's the holidays, but is Mr Clark in?'

'Yes. He does evening class on Thursdays. Creative Writing. Who shall I say it is?'

'Oh . . . just say Suzy Spencer. About the church.' She felt stupid, and turned to read some leaflets about further education.

'He's coming down,' the woman said.

Suzy felt her stomach turn over. Am I being ridiculous? she thought. Probably, but what's new! She turned to see Robert walking down the corridor. He looked taller and more casually dressed, more at home. This is Robert's world, she thought. Tarnfield was Mary's. He's different here.

'Hi,' he said. 'Good to see you. What's this about? Problems with the kitten?'

'No. The kitten's fine. Look, Robert, you'll probably think I'm mad but is there somewhere we can sit?'

'Just here in reception if you like. In a minute it will probably fill up with Spanish for Beginners, but it's free for the moment.'

He ushered her to a bench just around the corner from the receptionist. I must put this calmly and sensibly, Suzy thought, or he'll think I'm crazy. After all, his wife gave me a pretty bad press. Why should he trust me? Just because we've had one or two decent conversations doesn't mean we're bosom buddies. But if I can't talk to Robert, who can I talk to in Tarnfield? And I have to talk to someone.

She took a deep breath.

'I'm here because it's Jake's music day – one of those holiday workshops. He plays the sax. But something he said made me think. That flower-arranging decoration Tom found through Phyllis's hand – what did it look like?'

'He said it was long and wiry. And green.'

'I knew it! It was a fake reed, wasn't it? Mary bought them for the Harvest display the year before last. And where was Phyllis cut?'

'Through the skin between her thumb and forefinger.'

'Which hand?'

'Her left.'

Suzy gave a little cry, part horror, part satisfaction. 'Exactly! It just doesn't add up. For a start, Phyllis wasn't going to use the reeds. There was no reason for her to get them out.'

'She may have had some reason which we don't know about –'

'No! She always planned everything thoroughly, just like Mary. But even if she changed her mind, she couldn't have done it.'

'Why not?'

'Because she had terrible arthritis in her right hand. She couldn't use it. And her left hand couldn't injure itself!'

'What are you getting at?'

'Don't you see? Someone else must have done it. Those reeds were tough and spiky, but not tough enough to pierce a hand by accident. What did the police say? Or the coroner?'

Robert was silent. Then he said, 'The pathologist didn't see the reed, Suzy. Neither did the police. At the time it didn't seem important, but Tom pulled it out.'

'Oh no! Why did he do that?'

'I don't know. Nick was in a state, and I was trying to deal with him at the time. Tom said something about not wanting a fuss about health and safety in the church. So all the pathologist saw was a cut to Phyllis's hand.'

'And what did he say?'

'He was harassed and didn't chat for long. There'd been that accident on the motorway over the weekend where four people were killed. He said there was no doubt Phyllis died of a heart attack and I could apply for the death certificate.'

'Did you mention the reed?'

'I didn't have to. He said it was crystal clear that Phyllis had cut herself on something and had a coronary. The cut itself wasn't the cause of death, though it might have brought it on.'

They sat there in silence.

Then Suzy said, 'I think someone else cut her deliberately. But why do it? And why choose a reed? I think it's a symbolic thing. You know a lot about the Bible, Robert. Doesn't it ring a bell with you?'

'Perhaps. There's something about broken reeds. In Isaiah, I think. I don't know off the top of my head. I'll have to look it up.'

'You don't think I'm being stupid?'

He was silent, thinking. Then he said, 'No.' He paused. 'I knew it was odd. I should have realized at the time. But I just wanted as little trouble as possible.' He grimaced. 'That's always been my mistake.'

'I tried to ignore it too. But it's the only explanation.'

'You may be right. I'm sorry I snapped at you in the church.'

'It doesn't matter. I'm just glad that you understand now.' She looked at her watch and jumped up. 'Look, I'll have to go and get Jake. If you find that Bible reference will you email me? I've got a sick feeling about this. There's one thing daytime TV has in common with Christianity . . .'

'What?'

'You learn how evil people can be.'

Later that evening, the Reverend George Pattinson sat by the window of the bleak box of a bungalow where he now lived, and shuffled some papers in his hand. One of them was a handwritten note from Phyllis Drysdale.

Dear George, it said, *Forgive me for bothering you when I know all you want is peace and calm after the misery of the last year. But I need your help. An old colleague has some very disturbing information about someone. I can't go to Nick Melling about it. I need to talk to you. Sunday night perhaps? Yours, Phyllis.*

But she was dead now. George Pattinson was an experienced clergyman. He realized that Phyllis Drysdale had been scared. And he hadn't been able to do anything to help her. His hands shook. He knew about wickedness.

And he knew there was something deeply disturbing going on in Tarnfield.

But he was out of it now. He took Phyllis's note, and pushed it under the Bible on his desk. Out of sight, out of mind.

11

The Friday in Easter Week

We commend to thy fatherly goodness all those, who are any ways afflicted or distressed in mind, body, or estate.
From the Prayer for all Sorts and Conditions of Men

Friday evening was always a crabby time at Tarnfield House, because Russell Simpson never came home for the start of the weekend. He usually arrived at midday on Saturday when he would be hung over.

When her son had been born, Jane Simpson thought her life was complete. She had hated pregnancy and in fairness it hadn't been easy, the sickness and the later toxaemia adding to her sense of being bloated and cow-like, hardly the slim Twiggy type who had caught Jeffrey's eye. But she had longed for a child after nearly two decades of marriage. The treatment she'd gone for, discreetly, in Carlisle and Newcastle, revealed no reason for her infertility. Jeff of course wouldn't consider any tests. On top of that, there had been the pressure from Jeff's mother who subjected her to verbal and visual examination every other Sunday. After a few years, Mrs Simpson senior resigned herself to not being a grandmother, but the resentment was always there.

Then, six months before Jane's forty-third birthday, Russell's astonishing arrival had put them all in their place and silenced twenty years of remarks about Jane not being quite good enough. Russell had been a handsome baby and a lovable little boy. He was adored by his mother and his grandmother, putting his father's nose slightly out of joint.

The Friday after Easter, Jeff said, 'Where's Russ?' grumpily, looking down at his dinner plate where two dry lamb chops nestled against some chips and frozen peas. And of course there was the fancy tomato and bit of lettuce Jane put on all their meals. Garnish, she called it.

'He called from work, darling. He's staying in Newcastle tonight.'

'How's he coping without a car?' Russell's motor was in the garage again, after yet another 'bump'. 'Couldn't you go and pick him up?'

'Oh Jeff, he doesn't want to be tied to our apron strings at his age.'

'He doesn't mind being tied to our wallets though, does he? Correction. I mean my wallet.'

Jane sighed. Until this exchange, she and Jeffrey had sat in silence, as usual, at the kitchen table. Recently she had become less and less interested in preparing meals as she had once done, getting out the best china and lighting the candles in the dining room. Her roasts, steak and kidney puddings, interesting pastas and occasional forays into oriental cuisine had become rare events. Jeff was always grumbling about indigestion, and his weight. Over the last six months he seemed to have become an old man. Of course he was over seventy now. And he was angrier than ever with his son who wasn't here – yet again.

Russell was nearly twenty now, and supposedly working. He certainly had a job in some sort of agency in Newcastle. But he was part of a gang of young people intent on drinking their way through as much fun as possible. When Jane asked him where he had been he would say, 'Oh, I dossed down at Marcus's place,' or Jed's place. Or at Louise's. Or Charlotte's. Gender didn't seem to matter in Russell's world where male and female alike hung out in pubs and clubs any day of the week, taking a 'disco nap' sometimes before clubbing until dawn. Newcastle upon Tyne wasn't famous for its extensive upper middle class. But there was a small, tight group of young people from the outer suburbs and the Northumberland gentry, who stormed the city nightly from their jobs in ad agencies, PR companies, solicitors' offices and media, and joined the students having a great time in the new Northern metroland. It was all totally alien to his father.

Jeff Simpson was ten years older than Jane. He'd put his youth behind him swiftly when his own father died, and he inherited the ownership of the cattle market. The Simpsons had been agricultural brokers of some sort since the eighteenth century and Jeff had been brought up to think of himself as wealthy and established. He liked life's luxuries, and thought of them as his due. In return, he knew he would settle down and become a mainstay of the rural hierarchy.

But he had seen things change massively during his middle age. The auction mart had slowly run down, until he had sold off the land to a wholesale supermarket chain. He had retired to live on the proceeds. But after the shareholders and other family members were paid off, he and Jane were left with a finite sum of money, which was being whittled down much more quickly than he'd anticipated.

Though there was a reason for that, which Jane knew nothing about.

He looked at her across the kitchen table, in her new cashmere cardigan and her silly shoes designed for a woman half her age, and felt both disgusted and ashamed.

Dressed up like a dog's dinner, he thought to himself. She must think I'm made of money.

But he knew in his heart that was unfair. Jane had always felt under pressure to live up to the Simpson image. Waiting for the pain to start, the moment he swallowed a mouthful of his over-grilled lamb chop, he wondered what would have happened if he had married Phyllis Drysdale. Now she was gone, he let himself indulge in regret, though he hadn't thought much about her for the last thirty-five years.

Jeff had met Phyllis at a family wedding, and she had seemed like the ideal wife for a young county chap. She was soft and curvy and sweet. He was attracted to her fragility and he encouraged her to be fluffy and scatter-brained. She accepted his teasing bantering and played down the fact she had trained as a teacher. Sometimes they'd gone out with Mary Pattinson and other boys in a foursome, but Mary definitely wasn't Jeffrey's type. He liked his women to know their place. His engagement to Phyllis had lasted two years.

Then, one evening in the Plough, he had seen Jane behind the bar. She had just left school and was barmaiding there for the summer before going to Carlisle to work in a small clothes shop. She had white-blonde hair, which framed her face in a perfect Mary Quant bob, a flat chest with tiny pointed breasts, slim hips and incredibly long legs right up to a perfect little bum. She wore the shortest skirts Tarnfield had ever seen, pop-art tops, and eyes made up like a panda. But she wasn't tarty. Even then, she affected a 'far back' accent and upper class style, along with the doll-like behaviour of a mannequin. Her with-it image was the vehicle for a girl who wanted to be conventionally successful. If Susan George could date Prince Charles, then Jane Strickland could catch Jeff Simpson.

Jeff sensed all that, and he had to have her.

It had taken him five years to persuade his mother, shake off Phyllis and get Jane up the aisle, by which time he was over thirty and his new fiancée had become twice as snooty as he was. She'd moved on to Jaeger and Country Casuals, and was thinking of herself as the local aristocracy. Jeff bought Tarnfield House outright, and looked forward to having a brood of successful children and a lovely lady wife who was an ornament to local society.

But ornaments are costly. And when a son finally did arrive there was a lot to pay for. Russell had been born when money was already tight, but Jane had wanted the best for him. He'd been a bottomless pit as far as funds were concerned, with boarding school fees and all the extras. When Russ left school at eighteen with no qualifications, things didn't improve. Now his friendship with

Frank Bell's ne'er-do-well son made matters worse. Matthew Bell had money to burn.

Jeffrey was jealous of the Bells' success. Frank and Monica were years younger than the Simpsons, and Jeff thought of them as Tarnfield's nouveau riche with their smart new four-bedroom house. How had they got planning permission? Jeffrey wouldn't have been surprised to find that Frank was involved in some sort of financial funny business – he'd had his fingers burnt by Frank in the past. Of course Monica tried to keep Frank straight. She wasn't an ornament to anything, and she certainly looked her age, but she was a big help to Frank. Jane, on the other hand, knew nothing about business, cared less, and spent too much on appearances. You couldn't win with women, Jeff thought.

But he knew he had to carry the can for their money problems. He'd always overspent on things that didn't last – flashy meals out, cruises, dodgy investments, cars, big holidays. He'd assumed the family business would last forever and he hadn't really been interested in modernizing. And he'd always been susceptible to women. His affair with Yvonne Wait had been the last of his many ill-judged sexual adventures. He wasn't sure whether or not Jane had ever guessed. Of course it was all over now. Yvonne had made it clear he was too old and she had other fish to fry, but, even so, she never quite let go, as his bank statements testified.

'I'm off for a pint,' he said, pushing his plate away with the oven chips untouched.

'All right, darling, I'll see you later.' Jane stood up to collect the dishes. One of her gripes was that they couldn't afford a dishwasher. It wasn't so much the machine, as getting in a builder to adapt some part of Tarnfield House's kitchen, which had been untouched for twenty years. She sighed elaborately as a shorthand way of conveying this to Jeff, who ignored it as he always did. Then she shivered. Jeff was mean about the heating, but then of course, she thought irritably, he would be warm as toast in the fug of the pub. As usual in the evening, Jane would huddle in the living room in front of the electric fire and watch TV.

But at least tonight, she could call Nick Melling and Robert Clark to find out what was happening at All Saints. It was Phyllis's funeral on Monday, and she wanted to know how they were handling it. Now she was older and grander, part of Jane's role as a Simpson of Tarnfield House was to take an essential part in the life of the local church. There, at least, she felt important.

Jeff left her surrounded by the debris of his dinner and grabbed his jacket. It hadn't mattered when they married that Jane was a real dumb blonde, whereas Phyllis had just played at it. But the genes came out in the children, he reflected. Russell had inherited his mother's brains and materialism, sadly. For the last ten years it had been one wrecked piece of equipment after another. Bikes, computers, cars. And there had been the fines too; parking tickets, clamps, non-payment of fares, you name it. Jeff was pretty sure his son took recreational drugs, and he thought grimly that the constant demands for money, which got up Jeff's nose, went up his son's too. Of course his mother had spoilt him. Jane still believed that her sweet little boy, darling of the church choir, was inside him somewhere. But Jeff actually disliked his son now. Life was pretty grim, he reflected. If only Yvonne would lessen her grip, that would be something. But she never would.

He sighed. Why did he never have any luck? He should pull himself together to tackle Yvonne Wait. He wasn't too old yet to muster a bit of strength and deal with her. All he needed was the chance and a bit of Dutch courage. He slammed the door behind him and tramped across the Green towards the Plough.

12

The Friday in Easter Week, continued

That it may please thee to strengthen such as do stand;
and to comfort and help the weak-hearted.
From the Litany

All day Friday, Suzy had been on edge without really knowing why. Jake, still high from his success at the music day, had been infuriating, teasing Molly until she had hysterics because he had hidden her doll in the shed. Flowerbabe the kitten needed to be renamed, but not without more tears from Molly who wanted both the doll and the kitten to be called Flowerbabe because it was her 'all-time favourite name'.

'It's too confusing, sweet pea. And anyway, Flowerbabe isn't really a sensible name for a cat.'

'What about Flowerbabe One and Flowerbabe Two,' Jake had suggested helpfully. 'You know, like Spiderman One and Spiderman Two. Or better still,' he was on a movie theme now, 'what about calling that doll Golum? If we cut its hair off it would be Golum's body double. My precious, my . . .' He advanced on Molly doing the sinister voice from the *Lord of the Rings* classic until Molly screamed and Suzy had to intervene.

'Be quiet, both of you! Oh, for heaven's sake, Jake, are you still on the internet? I've told you a million times not to use it before six o'clock. And you should turn it off when you've finished and not waste electricity.'

'That's not logical. Either I shouldn't use the internet,

or I should switch off when I do. Now, decide which you mean.'

'Jake, you're trying my patience.'

'Well, I'm just wondering why you're so keen to get on the computer, Mum. You've been on your email three times already today. Are we expecting a message?'

'It's none of your business!'

'Oooh, Moll, look at Mum! She's gone all pink. What's going on here?'

Nothing, thought Suzy, nothing at all, as she logged on. Well, to be honest, she was hoping to hear from Robert Clark. It was pure curiosity, of course. Was she right about the Bible references? After confiding in him the day before, she had felt embarrassed by the time she got home. Had she overreacted?

But that night she had been unable to sleep. Surely, she thought, I'm just using too much imagination? But Phyllis and Mary had been so careful with their flower-arranging implements that the idea of Phyllis having a stupid accident just didn't wash – not with an out-of-season decoration, in the wrong hand, in the wrong part of the church.

'Let's have a funeral for Flowerbabe,' Jake was yelping at his sister. 'Let's bury her in the garden. Then we can pretend she's a zombie and she can rise from the grave to suck our blood. Like this . . .' He picked up the doll and pretended to sink his teeth into the plastic neck. Molly started screaming again.

'OK.' Suzy got up from the computer. 'We're all going out in the car. I need to go and see the old vicar. You can come for the ride, and on the way back we'll get a film for tonight. Something for us all, Jake.' The last time Jake had chosen a movie it had starred zombies and had *not* been family viewing.

'Yeah! I'm in the front, you're in the back, little baby Moll,' Jake yelled, getting Molly worked up again, but at least he agreed to come.

In the car, Suzy put on one of their comedy CDs and they all laughed their way through Tarnfield, out into the open country. It was a high grey afternoon, with a cool wind butting the daffodils planted on the outskirts of the village, and new lambs huddling for shelter like scraps of dirty washing blown on to the sage green fell sides. George Pattinson's new address had been printed on the back of an old All Saints Parish Newsletter, wishing him well. Rereading it, Suzy had thought how perfunctory it sounded after his years of service.

Joan Pattinson looked grey when she opened the door, but managed an impression of her former warmth. She was a quiet, unassuming woman, Suzy recalled. It had been her husband who got all the attention.

'Hi, Mrs Pattinson, I'm Suzy Spencer, from Tarn Acres in Tarnfield. Your husband asked me to call and let him know about Phyllis Drysdale's funeral.'

'Oh yes. You'd better come in.'

'Thanks, but I can't stop. I've got the kids with me. It's the Easter holidays.'

At the mention of the children Joan Pattinson's face brightened. 'Well, why don't they come in too? I've got some orange squash, and some home-made chocolate cake. I baked it for George but he wasn't very interested. You go in to see him. I'll call the children.' She let Suzy pass, down the dark hallway.

In the small sitting room cramped with furniture from a much bigger and more elegant home, George Pattinson sat staring into space. Next to him was a huge desk crowded with books and papers. The Pattinsons had left half their stuff in the vicarage, but here there was hardly room to turn round. Why such a come-down? Suzy thought. Surely somebody like George Pattinson would be better prepared for his retirement?

'Hello, Mr Pattinson. It's Suzy Spencer. We talked on the phone on Sunday. I suppose you already know, but Phyllis Drysdale's funeral is next Monday. It's at two o'clock.'

'Ah, thank you. Sit down, Mrs Spencer. I wanted to speak to someone who knew Phyllis.' His voice retained some of its warmth and authority, but his right hand twitched and scrabbled at the desk as if he was searching for something.

Suzy said, 'I wouldn't say I knew Phyllis that well. Not like you did. And Mrs Clark too; you were all friends, weren't you?'

George Pattinson trembled, as if cold. 'Yes, yes, we were all friends. Great friends. But I hadn't seen Phyllis for months. I don't keep in touch with many people from the parish. It's always difficult with a new man, and the Bishop specifically asked me not to get involved.'

'But Phyllis wanted to speak to you, didn't she? We found a note pinned to her noticeboard saying she was hoping to meet you last Sunday.'

George Pattinson started to grope again among the mess on his desk, his right hand working away amongst his papers while he looked straight ahead at Suzy. Suddenly, jerkily, he pushed a note at her.

'I want you to take this away.'

'What is it?'

'It's the letter Phyllis wrote to me. I'm too ill to deal with it. She knew I really couldn't do anything about All Saints. It's not my church any more. I lost it.'

Strange terminology, Suzy thought, taking the piece of paper. She unfolded and read it, and felt disturbed. 'But this sounds like she was really worried about something. Did she give you a clue about what it was?'

'No.' Suddenly George Pattinson sat up in his chair. 'But Phyllis wasn't as silly as some people thought. If she was worried about something, then it would have been worth it.' He slumped again. 'I can't deal with it. You'd better pass it on to Nick Melling.'

'But she asks you not to do that in this note. What about Robert Clark? He's dealing with her effects.'

George Pattinson turned to stare out of the window. 'Or Robert. Yes.' He shut his eyes and his head drooped.

I'd better go, Suzy thought. She stood up, but he didn't react, so she tiptoed out.

The whole thing was odd, Suzy thought as she started the car with the kids back on board. Why did nobody else from All Saints keep in contact with the man who had been their much-loved vicar? She headed for Asda on the edge of Carlisle. The children seemed happy enough after their cake and juice, and she had time to think.

Was the strange letter Phyllis had written to George linked to her death?

As soon as they got home, she logged on and went into her Hotmail account again. There was one new message, and it was from rclarkthebriars@aol.com. It was titled Bible References. Suzy hit the key and waited to see whether or not she had been right about the reed.

Robert had slept badly again on Thursday night. At seven o'clock in the morning there was no point in trying to get back to sleep, so he got up, brewed himself a pot of tea, and went into the spare bedroom which he and Mary had made into his study.

He'd been thinking about Suzy Spencer's theory. Initially he'd been shocked; then, as the evening had gone on, he'd been more inclined to dismiss her ideas. After all, Mary frequently said Suzy was unreliable. But that hadn't been Robert's impression. Suzy might be harassed, stressed and inclined to drive into other people's fences, but she was also bright and capable. Just because she affected a self-deprecating manner and clearly didn't care what Tarnfield thought of her, didn't mean she was imperceptive. By morning he was feeling very concerned about what she had said.

His study was a large, bright room with a bay window and lined with bookshelves. The obvious place to look was Cruden's Concordance, the traditional index to words in the Authorized Version of the Bible. He took the concordance down from the shelf, along with his old Bible, and started to flick through it. There was a reference to a 'bruised' reed. In fact, there were two. Robert took a deep breath, and read both passages, slowly and carefully.

They were in the second book of Kings and in the book of Isaiah, and referred to the same event. Judah was being attacked by the Assyrians from the north. The King of Judah, Hezekiah, had paid them off with all the treasure in his possession, but they were still taking his kingdom bit by bit, and in 701BC they were camped at a town called Lachish. Like all small countries, Judah needed an ally. With any luck, the Pharaoh of Egypt would come to their rescue.

Of course, thought Robert. My enemy's enemy is my friend. But the Assyrians sent the Rabshakeh, an Assyrian envoy, to undermine the King of Judah with some scary propaganda. You can't rely on the Pharaoh, the Rabshakeh said. He's just like a reed, which you lean on like a stick, but it breaks and cuts your hand.

To make certain, Robert found his copy of the Revised Standard Version. At 2 Kings 18:21, he read, *Egypt, that broken reed*. So that was the version Suzy had remembered. He took another Bible from the shelf. This was the New International Version, a more modern translation. This version said, *Look now, you are depending on Egypt, that splintered reed of a staff, which pierces a man's hand and wounds him if he leans on it!*

Robert needed to think this through. He'd often found that by doing mundane things he freed his brain to roam, and answers came. He went downstairs and made more tea, even though the pot was still warm. Then he put some washing in the machine. He got dressed, and, as he'd planned, drove to the supermarket, which took a couple of hours. He came home later, unpacked the car and heated up some soup for lunch. He listened to the news. But Phyllis's injury was always in his mind, and he couldn't work it out.

Had someone mutilated Phyllis to show that, like Pharaoh, she had proved untrustworthy? But it didn't ring true. Phyllis didn't let people down. She annoyed them, nagged them, frustrated them, but she was never untrustworthy. He looked at the passage again in the RSV. *You are now relying on Egypt, that broken reed of a staff, which will pierce the hand of any man who leans on it.*

So Phyllis was the leaner. But whom had she been

relying on? Who was the 'broken reed'? And who would want to send her that message in such a horrible way? It didn't make sense. The perpetrator was certainly saying something. But what?

He drank yet more tea. Then he sat down at the computer and composed a long email. *Dear Suzy,* he began, *It looks as though you were right . . .*

After the children had gone to bed, Suzy read Robert's email again, with the Bible references itemized. But Robert hadn't seen Phyllis's letter to George Pattinson. It gave her the creeps to look at it, but she took it out of her shoulder bag and unfolded it.

An old colleague has some very disturbing information about someone. I can't go to Nick Melling about it . . .

When Suzy researched guests for TV shows, she sometimes needed to go over and over their stories, cutting through the skin of self-justification and supposition which had grown over the truth. So what did they really have here? Phyllis had been alone in the church. Someone had inserted a broken reed in her hand. In the Bible, as Robert had pointed out, the reed symbolized a false friend. So Phyllis, like King Hezekiah, had relied on someone untrustworthy.

Perhaps the person who hurt her had been saying, 'You're wrong. Your informant is unreliable.' Perhaps a vicious way of ramming this home would be to force a reed through Phyllis's hand and say, 'Look, that's what your information is worth.' Perhaps that person had then left her, bleeding, but with no idea that she would die.

Suzy looked at the keyboard and pressed Reply.

Dear Robert, Do you remember how I found those scissors in church, with that rusty stain on? I think that was blood. I think someone jabbed them through Phyllis's skin, then stuck the reed in. There's no way this was opportunism. You know what Mary and Phyllis were like. Dangerous objects had to be put away in the toolbox. And those reeds were sharp. Mary insisted that they had to be safely stored in a plastic bag on the shelf. Whoever did this knew how Phyllis and Mary operated . . .

Suzy reread what she had written. But what comes next? she thought. What are we going to do about it?

She took a deep breath, and then she wrote, *I went to see George Pattinson today. He showed me a note from Phyllis saying she'd found out something disturbing about someone at All Saints. George doesn't want to deal with it. So that just leaves us. I think the letter and the mutilation may be connected. And it must be to do with someone in the parish . . .*

13

The Monday after Low Sunday

Earth to earth, ashes to ashes, dust to dust . . .
At the Burial of the Dead

'Of course I wasn't surprised.' Babs Piefield took another sip of tea and looked over the cup at Nancy Arthur. 'I mean, she goes to work, and has two children, and gets involved with all this church activity, so what do you expect? The repairman had come all the way from Newcastle, and she wasn't in! Good job I spotted him!'

Poor Suzy Spencer, Nancy Arthur thought, shifting wearily in her chair. No wonder she'd forgotten about the washing machine engineer. That afternoon it was Phyllis Drysdale's funeral and Suzy was there along with almost everyone in Tarnfield. Except Nancy Arthur and Babs Piefield.

Nancy thought, I may be housebound with ME, but I'm not an idiot. She was well aware that Babs was visiting because she didn't want to be just an 'extra' at the funeral. Babs was always very keen to stress that she wasn't a churchgoer. Her family was 'chapel' anyway. But that didn't stop her wanting to come round and gossip; and at the Arthurs' there was a chance of getting information from the horse's mouth. But Babs must have realized by now that Daisy didn't talk at home to her mother about church matters, even a dramatic death. Daisy suspected her mother disapproved of how much she was getting involved at All Saints.

And she was right, Nancy thought. I do.

Babs was still rattling on about Suzy Spencer. 'I mean, it's so difficult to get tradesmen out here. Of course I went straight over and said, "I'm sorry, she's not there."'

'Did you tell him that Suzy was at a funeral?'

'Oh no, I didn't think it was my job to explain her whereabouts.'

Typical, Nancy thought. Far be it from Babs to get someone else out of a hole.

'Talking of the church,' Babs was saying, 'Janice Jones told me that the good-looking young vicar chap is determined to push through a lot of new ideas. But he's getting on people's nerves. I don't blame him, though. I mean, he's got to modernize. It's the only way to attract people.'

'Is it? Would that attract you?'

'Me? Oh no! I mean, you don't have to go to church to be a Christian, do you?'

Nancy sighed. I don't know what you have to do to be a Christian, she thought wearily, but she suspected that Babs had a long way to go. She found her eyes were closing. Nancy preferred to have visitors in the morning when she was more alert. She liked to have all the tea things prepared, and to have the energy to tidy up, herself. There was no way she wanted Babs prowling round her cupboards.

'Shall I wash up, then?' Babs said.

'No, thanks. I may be an invalid but I can manage.'

Suit yourself, Babs Piefield thought. Nancy had always been fussy about her kitchen. Of course she had everything money could buy, including a big dishwasher and two refrigerators. Babs sniffed. The Arthurs had all sorts of equipment, some of it left over from when they'd run the village shop. Roger Arthur had come from Leeds, but his father had been an agricultural salesman who'd travelled in the Tarnfield area. When the shop had come up for sale, Roger had taken it on and developed it. But then he'd had a stroke, and died in his fifties a few years ago. Afterwards, Nancy had gone down with one ailment after another, and then she'd got this weird ME. Yuppie flu, they called it, but that was odd because Nancy wasn't a yuppie. And this certainly wasn't flu. Babs sometimes thought the ME was just an excuse for Nancy to sit at home in comfort. Not everyone could afford a leather chesterfield suite and parquet floors with Persian rugs on top.

Babs had never heard Nancy talk about her own family. There was some story about them cutting Nancy off when she married Roger, but they'd obviously not been short of a bob or two. There were some lovely old pieces in Nancy's lounge, which Babs guessed were pretty expensive. Nancy's eldest boy was some sort of accountant and the younger one was a lawyer. They'd done very well for themselves, Babs thought, despite losing their father, and their mother going down with this strange illness. Babs's own son had left home and joined the navy. She rarely saw him.

'Are you sure that you wouldn't feel better if you just tried to make another pot of tea?' Babs would have loved another cuppa, and she was convinced that if Nancy made a bit more effort generally, things would click back into place. She was always suggesting that Nancy 'just try' something else. Nancy passed her hand over her brow. It was pointless trying to explain myalgic encephalomyelitis to Babs. They'd been friendly for over twenty years, but Nancy had never held a serious conversation with her neighbour. There were so many things Nancy knew she couldn't explain to Babs.

Nancy sighed. 'I'm really feeling a bit weary. Perhaps it would be better if I had a lie-down.' ME was awful, Nancy thought, but at least she had her family. She suspected that Babs needed the visits more than she did, but at this point she just wanted her to go home. Babs showed no sign of moving. She was still there ten minutes later when the car drew up outside and Daisy came bouncing down the path.

'Hello, Mrs Piefield,' Daisy said cheerily. 'You OK, Mum?' She was smiling, and her cheeks were pink. A flicker of anxiety passed over Nancy Arthur's face. Her daughter's determined brightness sometimes worried her.

'I'm fine, love. How was the funeral?'

'OK. The church was packed. Nick was very good. I didn't stay long at the wake.' There had been funeral baked meats at the Plough, organized by Robert Clark with Phyllis's solicitor.

Nancy grimaced and heaved herself towards the door. 'I really would like a rest now, Babs, especially as Daisy's back.' She laboriously turned and, using the wall to support herself, she walked into the hall and saw Babs out. It still took Babs five minutes of more chatting before she could detach herself from the doorstep. Then Nancy dragged herself back inside. At the door into the living room, she paused and watched her daughter. Daisy was sitting in the armchair, her head in her hands.

'I did love Phyllis, Mum,' she murmured. Nancy went over to her and stood beside her, cradling her head against her bosom.

'I know you did, sweetie. After all, she taught you at Sunday School and gave you all that advice about university.'

Daisy had started to cry, big gasping sobs.

'Keep calm, Daisy,' Nancy said softly. 'It's all right.'

The doorbell rang. Daisy wiped her eyes on a tissue, and just as suddenly resumed her bright manner. She got up and looked through the window.

'Oh, it's Yvonne at the door. I'll go. I'm sorry, Mum. I just lost it for a moment. I'll be fine.'

I doubt it, if Yvonne Wait is calling on us, Nancy thought grimly.

It was funny, Suzy thought. Before moving to Tarnfield she had hardly been to a funeral in her life, but in the last eighteen months she had been to three. First had been Rachel Cohen's father's, an orthodox Jewish affair at the Burial Grounds in North London. It had been very moving, but very different from the next one, which was Mary's Church of England service. That had begun with George Pattinson intoning the ringing words 'I am the

Resurrection and the Life.' It had sent shivers up her spine.

Today had been Phyllis's turn.

Nick Melling started off reasonably well, though he had none of the presence of George Pattinson, and his voice warbled and varied from deep and meaningful to light and over-familiar. Nick's sermon was as uneven as his tone. He tried to say nice things about Phyllis but couldn't resist referring to her as a 'regular churchgoer' and a 'stalwart of All Saints' as if these things were strange old-fashioned habits like using a tea cosy or a china po.

Suzy had felt very alone. She found herself wondering if anyone else had thought about the reed in Phyllis's hand. She hadn't wanted to talk to any of the All Saints regulars, so she sat at the back. She had seen Robert in the distance, but he had been far too involved to speak to her. It had all made her feel very uneasy and distracted.

Walking home down Tarn Acres, she saw Yvonne Wait pull up in her smart silver convertible and then stride ahead of her to the Arthurs' house. Yvonne was wearing an extremely smart black trouser suit and crisp white blouse, which made Suzy feel hot and lumpy in her jumper, jacket, long skirt and boots.

She jumped when someone tapped her on her shoulder.

'Mrs Spencer! You missed the washing machine man. I told him you weren't in!' Babs Piefield yelped triumphantly.

'Oh no! Sod it!' said Suzy.

While Babs's mouth was still open, she managed to use the moment to say, 'Thanks for letting me know,' and escape. Inside the house Molly came running to meet her. Jake had agreed to mind his sister for once, and to Suzy's delight they seemed to have got on well.

'How's Flowerbabe the kitten?' Suzy asked. In the end she had given in, and the cat had retained its name.

'She's fine. Look, we've made her a house out of this cardboard box.' Jake smiled sheepishly. 'It's quite good, isn't it, Mum? Would you like a cup of tea?'

Suzy felt tears coming into her eyes. Poor Phyllis, she

thought, how awful to think that she's dead. And now the kitten she loved is here with us, people she didn't really know. She went up to Jake and Molly and put her arms around them both and hugged them. Whatever ugliness was lurking in Tarnfield, Suzy had shut the door on it. For now.

In the Arthurs' house, Nancy was staring Yvonne Wait squarely in the face.

'We're not selling the land behind the shop, Yvonne,' Nancy said, 'so just come to terms with it.'

Yvonne looked past her to Daisy. 'We'll see about that,' she said.

14

The Tuesday after Low Sunday

Jesus came and stood in the midst, and saith unto them,
Peace be unto you.
From the Gospel for Low Sunday, John 20:19

Why am I doing this? Suzy asked herself the next evening as she walked up the gravel path to the vicarage. It was dusk, and the house was in darkness. In the Pattinsons' time there had always been a lamp on in the porch and the hint of buttery light behind the curtains, but Nick Melling had no idea of hospitality. The house was so clean and neat it seemed sterile, and overall it now gave the impression of being grey and cold.

Nick opened the door, and ahead, in the Pattinsons' lounge, Suzy could see Monica Bell, Alan Robie and Tom Strickland. Yvonne hadn't arrived yet and to Suzy's surprise Kevin Jones was in the kitchen with Daisy, making the coffee.

'I thought we'd start with a drink as Yvonne is going to be a bit late,' Nick said. There was tension in the air, Suzy thought. Usually they started the meeting with a prayer, and had coffee at the end, but this evening everything was being done out of sequence.

Nick got up to answer the door again and Suzy sat down on the long sofa, by Monica. It was odd, she thought, how the same room with the same people could be comfortable and welcoming on one occasion and seem hostile the next. There was no fire in the raked grate, and the overhead bulb was bleak instead of the soft light of

Joan Pattinson's table lamps. Robert Clark was the next to arrive, and Suzy saw to her surprise that he was wearing jeans. Not such an old fart, she thought. He sat down next to her and smiled.

'No sign of Yvonne?' he said to Nick, who shook his head.

'Not yet. She phoned to say she was going to be late.'

Nick Melling took the upright chair in the middle of the circle and Suzy realized that all the seats had been angled to face him. He coughed. 'Daisy, Kevin, is the coffee ready?' He had the air of someone about to make an important announcement.

'Yes, here we are.' Daisy put the tray on to the coffee table in the middle, and sat down on the floor at his feet. Nick shifted and looked embarrassed, but was clearly not going to be put off by her devoted upturned face.

'Look, everyone.' Nick addressed the group. 'Welcome. But before we start, I think we really ought to take this opportunity to discuss just how we want All Saints to progress. Kevin has come to join us tonight because he and I have been talking and we think, er . . .' His voice tailed off.

'We think,' Kevin continued gruffly, 'that now Phyllis is dead and buried, we need to make changes. That's right, isn't it, Nick?'

'It is indeed,' Nick said, looking serious and failing to meet anyone's eyes.

'What changes?' said Alan Robie, his voice even deeper with anxiety.

'I think we need to, er, get real,' said Nick. 'You know, if the church is to survive we need new blood. There are families in Tarnfield who never come near us. We need to think of ways to bring them in. Perhaps the Bible study group and the other things we usually do aren't, you know, the most attractive methods.'

'But isn't this a matter for the Parochial Church Council?' queried Alan.

'Well, of course, but so many of you sit on the PCC and also come to the Bible study group that Kevin and

I thought this might be the time to, well, informally broach some new ideas.'

'Like what?' said Tom Strickland brusquely.

'Like getting rid of the flowers. And the choir. And this group,' said Kevin. 'What we need is to scrap all this traditional stuff and go for a new approach. We need a home study group with music and modern prayers. I've got this CD with new choruses on it here. We should be playing it before we start. I've brought my portable disc player –'

'Hang on . . .' Tom Strickland started to bark. Monica Bell said loudly at the same time, 'This is a bit sudden.' And Alan Robie boomed, 'But look here . . .'

The whole group seemed to erupt, and at that moment the doorbell rang again.

'That will be Yvonne,' Nick said, leaping to his feet and escaping. Kevin Jones had advanced to his ghetto blaster and the sound of loud rap-style music cut through the babbling. Suzy caught Robert's eye and for a moment, to her amazement, she thought he was trying not to laugh.

Into the hubbub came Yvonne, looking even more glamorous than usual, her hair shining under the light. She was wearing a dressy outfit with a flouncing skirt and high-heeled shoes, with pointed toes and an ankle bracelet.

'What on earth is going on?' she demanded in her bossiest voice.

'Do sit down, Yvonne,' Nick shouted over the noise. 'And perhaps we could turn that down for a moment, Kevin?'

Kevin shrugged and obliged, but the pulsating beat went on in the background. For a minute Suzy wondered how the words 'bitch' and 'white trash' could be incorporated into religious music, but the lyrics were being growled so she couldn't hear them.

'Are you really saying you want to get rid of the choir and the flower arranging?' Monica said in a baffled voice.

'You can't be serious. This is a bad mistake,' rumbled Alan Robie. There was sudden quiet except for the beat of strangled music. Nick Melling looked tortured. He glanced at Kevin for reassurance.

Then to Suzy's astonishment Robert Clark said quietly, 'I think you have a point, Nick. The church certainly has to move on.' He stopped and waited, then added, 'But let's not be too hasty. Lots of people like the traditional things. Maybe we could compromise.'

'Compromise?' Kevin Jones looked as if he would like to vomit.

'Yes, why not, Kevin? Let's have a new, vibrant, unconventional service, say once a month to see how it goes. And let's talk about ways to incorporate tradition and progress . . .'

Suzy glanced at Nick Melling. 'That's right,' she said. '*I'm* new to All Saints, so it *does* attract some people. And I think I'm up to date, with a teenage son and a little girl. But there are some things about tradition that I like.'

'So you're in favour of compromise too?' Robert suggested.

Suzy took her cue from him. 'Absolutely. In fact I was going to suggest that Daisy and I got together. We could get the children to make some flower decorations for Whitsun. Doing Sunday School is such hard work for you by yourself, Daisy.'

Daisy Arthur's face lit up. 'Oh Nick, could we?' she breathed. 'A Whitsun Festival is just what I would like! It could be a real mission!'

Nick Melling looked confused. They had hijacked him. But he was the vicar! This was not on the agenda. He had psyched himself up for the moment when he would confront all these people with their fixed ideas and argumentative notions, but here they were, twisting his words and taking Daisy, his biggest supporter, with them. He felt outmanoeuvred by a bunch of country bumpkins. He could see that Kevin Jones was furious too. He'd been all geared up for battle and the wind had been taken out of his sails.

'It's not good enough, Daisy,' Kevin said angrily. 'You're

giving in. You talked about fellow travellers. That's all these folk are!' He made an expansive gesture with his right hand and unfortunately caught Yvonne Wait on the leg with his wrist.

'How dare you!' she squealed. 'This is insulting.'

'It's only a discussion, Yvonne,' Robert said mildly.

'Yes, that's right,' Suzy chimed in. 'We've got to take everyone's views into account, and Kevin has made some very good points.' Kevin Jones shook his big, bullet head, as if he couldn't believe what he was hearing. He's disappointed, Suzy thought. He wanted a fight.

'I like the idea of the Whitsun flowers,' said the ever pragmatic Monica Bell. 'I could get Frank to put some trellising up against the pillars and you could do something really effective, Daisy. Remember when you did "All Things Bright and Beautiful"? That was lovely!'

'It's a wonderful idea,' said Daisy breathlessly. 'Just what you want, Nick. Something contemporary and exciting, with families involved instead of a load of middle-aged worthies!'

'Steady on,' said Robert good-humouredly, and he caught Suzy's eye. He knows what I used to think of him, she thought. She smiled back.

Yvonne exploded. 'I'm not a middle-aged worthy! I think these are bullying tactics!'

'That's rich, coming from you,' Kevin Jones murmured under his breath. He looked up like a rogue elephant assessing the chances of a charge. Here at last was someone to attack. His big head swayed from side to side and his little eyes glinted.

'I *beg* your pardon!' Yvonne tossed her beautifully coiffured head and crossed her long elegant legs with a tinkle of anklet as it slipped over her silky stockings. 'What did you say? I heard you saying something?'

'I said, that's rich coming from you,' Kevin growled.

'What on earth do you mean?'

There was an aching silence in the group. Suzy fought to

116

stop glancing at Robert. No one wanted to support Kevin's rudeness, but no one wanted to back Yvonne either.

'You don't give a toss about real faith.' Kevin said. 'You only want to organize the Bible study group so you can be Lady Muck and find out what's going on. Flowers! Organ music! It's all just superficial.'

'That's outrageous!' Yvonne had a high colour. In her way she looked rather magnificent, Suzy thought. She dominated the floor. 'I took on Bible study and flower arranging in good faith. I have the interests of All Saints at heart. Just because I like the lovely things in the church and want to save them from the philistines . . .'

'Now, now, people . . .' thundered Alan Robie, looking desperate.

'Please . . .' Nick Melling's voice was squeaky and plaintive. 'Please, Kevin, Yvonne, calm down. Daisy, do stop crying.'

'Calm down! You say calm down!' Kevin was shouting now. 'You've got to sort this lot out, Nick. I thought you had Vision. I thought you were really going to get rid of the sort of sad people who just come to church because they've nowhere else to go. You've got to get your act together, mate. And as for you . . .' He turned to face Yvonne. 'You're just the sort of person who's keeping the church in the past. I don't know why you're involved but I'm willing to bet you've got your own motives. And the rest of you aren't much better. Snobs!'

He lurched past her to grab his CD player, and bowled out of the room on his short legs. Nick Melling went after him calling, 'Kevin, just wait a moment . . .'

Then the ring of the doorbell cut the air. Kevin waited, his chest heaving with anger, while Nick let in the latecomer.

'Oh dear, I'm so sorry I'm late,' twittered Jane Simpson. 'Russell came home unexpectedly and I needed to get him something out of the freezer. Have we started? I've prepared a reading, like you suggested, Yvonne. *Consider the lilies of the field*. Such a pretty story, don't you think?

117

Solomon in all his glory was not arrayed like one of these.' She beamed graciously at the mesmerized group.

The door slammed. Kevin Jones had left in disgust.

When Suzy got home at ten o'clock she was drained. The group had settled down after the row, as if embarrassed with itself, and, after some desultory discussion of the parables, Monica had very practically turned the subject back to the idea of a Whitsun Flower Festival. There had been gentle progress towards accepting Suzy's proposal, and even Yvonne, grudgingly, had been brought round, especially when it was suggested that she could have a starring role as organizer. Nick had been quietly acquiescent as long as he hadn't been asked to do anything. Nobody had mentioned Kevin Jones again.

Suzy made herself a cup of tea and opened a packet of chocolate digestives. Then she walked over to the computer and turned it on. She went upstairs and changed into her pyjamas and fleecy dressing gown, came down and poured more tea, and sat at the keyboard. There was no harm in seeing if there were any emails. She logged on and waited for the screen to resolve.

And there it was. Her heart did a little dance and she took a deep breath. It wasn't really significant – was it? – that Robert Clark had gone straight home from the Bible study group and emailed her? She clicked on 'Message from rclarkthebriars@aol.com' and read:

Dear Suzy,
Thank you for your support tonight. I think the Whitsun Flower Festival by the children of Tarnfield is a wonderful idea.

Of course we still need to talk about what happened to Phyllis. It's even more sinister now, isn't it, when you realize what a rift has been brewing in the church!

Are you around tomorrow night? I remember you said your washing machine was broken. Why not bring a load over to my house? Molly and Jake can come too and I can help Jake

*with his poetry module. You said he was having trouble
with it.
Robert.*

Without waiting to think about it, Suzy wrote, *Thanks.
We'll be there . . .*

Then she formed a new message. *Dear Rachel*, she wrote,
You won't believe what's happening to me . . .

15

The Tuesday into the Wednesday
after Low Sunday

*That it may please thee to forgive our enemies, persecutors
and slanderers.*
From the Litany

When she left the vicarage after the Bible study group,
Yvonne Wait was still fuming. She didn't really give a toss
about a Whitsun Flower Festival and she was furious on
two counts. First, Kevin Jones had rumbled her. It was true
that she'd had her own reasons for keeping the Bible study
group going. People tended to give themselves away when
they prayed and discussed the Bible!

But secondly, she was even more enraged by his allegation that she was sad and middle-aged. Yvonne prided
herself on her sleek looks and smart clothes. She liked to
sit near Monica who wore frumpy cardigans and crim-
plene trousers. It was even more fun to show up Jane
Simpson with her pathetic attempts to combine some
faded designer rag with the latest M&S classic. I despise
them all, Yvonne thought. But I loathe Kevin Jones most of
all. He mustn't think he can get away with this. She smiled
grimly. I can make life pretty uncomfortable for Mr Bullet
Head and his mumsy little wife.

And she had other fish to fry, too . . .

'Alan!' she called loudly as he tried to sneak past her to
his car. 'I need to have a word.'

Alan Robie sidled up to her, wearing his 'I'm really too
important' face. 'Yes, Yvonne? Can I help?'

'I don't know about that. I just wanted to find out where you were with that orchard sale.'

'Orchard sale? Oh, I don't think that's on the cards. Must dash . . .'

'Hasn't your little playmate talked to you about it?'

'If you mean Stevie, yes, he has. But there's nothing doing, Yvonne.'

'Oh, isn't there? I must talk to Stevie again. I thought he was rather keen . . .'

'What the devil has it got to do with you, Yvonne?'

'Oh, stop talking to me like something out of Oscar Wilde. I can see right through your act. You'd better go home and have a heart-to-heart with your boyfriend. Call me, but it had better be soon . . .'

She didn't wait for more. Monica Bell was saying good-bye to Nick at the vicarage door, which meant that she would have to walk past Yvonne's car.

'Goodnight, Monica,' Yvonne called gaily.

'Goodnight, Yvonne.' Monica sounded wary.

'And give my love to Frank, won't you? I was at the Arthurs' the other day, by the way, admiring their parquet. Nice job! In every sense.'

Yvonne's tinkly laugh met with a blank stare from Monica, who turned and plodded away, looking older and frumpier than ever.

'Nighty-night, Jane,' called Yvonne to the last person to leave the vicarage. 'Remember me to Jeff. Oh, and how's Russell? He's the image of you, isn't he?'

She was starting to feel better. But there was still the most important thing left to do. She just had to work out which bit of the information in her head to use. When she got home she poured herself a small glass of Grand Marnier, added tinkling ice, and curled up on her new cream sofa. She kicked her shoes off and they skittered across the beautiful blond ash floorboards. It wasn't going to take much to get her own back. She just had to think of something . . .

*   *   *

Early the next morning she drove her convertible down Tarn Acres and stopped to deliver a pretty lilac-coloured envelope to the Joneses' house. Yvonne liked lilac stationery. It was her trademark, she thought. It fell on to the mat as Janice and Kevin were having their Crunchy Wheat Nuts and Janice was trying to feed the baby, who was making a real mess.

'What was that?' she said.

'Post,' Kevin mumbled. He was in a bad mood this morning because of the debacle at the Bible study group. He hadn't slept. It had taken him ages to get Nick Melling on side and now things were falling apart. But at least he'd put the wind up Yvonne Wait. If she abandoned her stupid idea about organizing the boring Bible study group it would soon collapse. None of the other old fogeys wanted to do it, lazy sods. He grunted. If Janice wanted to fetch the post she could do it herself.

Janice wiped the rim of the spoon over the excess on the baby's face and fed it back in. 'All right, I'll go,' she said. She put the dish of baby food on the table and went into the hall.

'Oh, how nice,' she said. 'It's a hand-delivered card!' She was rather excited. The Joneses didn't get many invitations or notes. She ripped it open and read it eagerly. Then she sat down heavily at the kitchen table, and pushed it silently at her husband.

Kevin stopped eating and picked up the card. He read:

Dear Janice and Kevin,
Just to say I'm sorry for getting so cross at the Bible study group last night. I'd had a very tiring day at the hospital. I'm sure we all said things we didn't mean.
I think the idea about the Whitsun Flower Festival is a really lovely one and I am sure, Kevin, that you and Daisy will continue to co-operate really well together, but this time alongside the rest of us rather than the two of you on your own. I do realize that you and Daisy have been getting

together in the evenings to talk about changes at All Saints but I just want you to know that I do believe we can work together.

You and Janice must bring your little family to tea with me one day soon.

All the best, Yvonne xx

Kevin Jones got up from the kitchen table and crumpled the note in his big fist. Then he stuffed it in the rubbish bin under the sink. Janice said nothing. When he'd gone to work, she got the note out, smoothed off the bits of Crunchy Nut and read it again. Daisy Arthur, she thought. It wasn't a complete surprise.

That night, for the first time ever, she turned away from Kevin when he put his arm around her. Kevin rolled over and tried to let thoughts of Daisy console him. But it didn't work. In the dark, he could hear his wife's miserable little sobs.

So how did Yvonne know? he thought to himself. Then he remembered. On Easter Saturday night he'd gone up to the supermarket to get some baby shampoo. He'd hoped to see Daisy. He'd hung around inside until the last person in the queue had been served, then he realized Daisy wasn't at her till. He'd been so disappointed he'd forgotten about the shampoo and mooched off. The light had been on in All Saints because Phyllis Drysdale had been in there, arranging the flowers. Silly old bag . . . but of course she was dead now. Kevin didn't want to think about that.

Then he'd met Daisy in the darkening village street, just past Lo-cost. It had been a piece of luck. She'd been outside checking the lemonade delivery. He remembered, now, that Yvonne's shiny grey car had bounced past them, over the cobbles but with hardly a sound, as he and Daisy had been talking. Perhaps he'd even put his hand on her arm. That's what Yvonne had seen. Alan Robie strode past too and raised his walking stick, like the local squire.

But he wasn't the sort to gossip. Not like Yvonne Wait, who's a world class bitch, Kevin thought to himself in the dark.

Suzy sorted out the more disgusting items of washing, like Jake's socks and underpants, and left them in the basket, then she rammed the respectable stuff in a plastic bag. She didn't want Mr Perfect seeing the stains and skidmarks, but she was grateful to him for taking on the rest. Molly's school tracksuit was practically walking to the machine by itself and she was short of jumpers.

To her surprise, Jake was quite keen to go to The Briars. 'Mr Clark might have some new software,' he said. 'That'll be great. Much quicker.'

They set off after dark, which made Molly quite excitable. Robert was surprisingly relaxed and easy-going with the children. He had some juice and biscuits available, and suggested that Jake sit at the computer with a list of websites that were used at the college. Suzy heard Jake chortle. Robert had probably had the sense to find him something mildly vulgar. Molly settled down on the sofa with some valuable-looking children's books which had belonged to Mary. Suzy had worried that there would be nothing in the staid 'solicitor Regency' style of The Briars that might appeal to a six-year-old. But the books went down well.

It was the first time Suzy had been anywhere but the kitchen and hallway. Robert's front room was decorated in blue, with some pretty watercolours, and a big old-fashioned three-piece suite around the original fireplace. What an ordered life the Clarks had lived, Suzy thought, though her eye was caught by a jug of Mary's variegated holly, dried and forgotten since some Christmas past. Robert was living in a time warp.

He showed her the washing machine in a utility room off the big, farmhouse-style kitchen. When she'd loaded it, she joined him at the table. He had laid out some papers and a couple of heavy books, and looked absorbed.

'I've been doing some work on the reference to the broken reed,' he said. 'It's in Kings, and Isaiah. There were several Isaiahs, you know. The one who was writing about the reed story was the first one, Isaiah of Jerusalem.'

'How many were there?'

'At least three. All their wit and wisdom was collected in the book of Isaiah. They were the political advisers of their time. But the first one was probably the most significant.'

'Why?'

'Well, he was one of the first prophets to write about political morality. Isaiah believed the Assyrians threatened Jerusalem because the Jews hadn't been living decent lives. The Assyrians had already beaten Pharaoh, though the Jews didn't know that then.'

'The Assyrians sound like tough nuts.'

'Oh, they were. Look at this book. It shows the siege of Lachish. That's where the Assyrians were camped at the time the bruised reed propaganda was being used. It must be the first example of PR spin, mustn't it? There are really elaborate carvings of the whole thing. It was a huge event at the time.'

'Lachish! Oh, I've heard of that. It's a frieze in the British Museum, isn't it, some sort of stone bas-relief. I've been there with my Jewish friend . . .'

'It looks amazing.' Robert pushed an illustration towards her.

'That's it! It's quite significant in Hebrew history. You should see the frieze. It's a pity you couldn't come with me and Rachel.'

'That would be nice,' Robert said.

Suzy felt the blush creeping up her neck. Shit, she thought, what have I said? Pull yourself together, she told herself, and get back on the subject. 'So the person who attacked Phyllis would need to know this Bible reference and also to know that we had the reed decorations in the vestry?'

'Yes. That really does narrow it down, doesn't it?

Monica, Yvonne, Daisy, Jane, Tom, Alan, Kevin and Nick. Oh, and Stevie, I suppose.'

'My money is on Yvonne,' Suzy said. 'She's a bully, and could be used to doing medical things, you know, injecting people and so on. I don't suppose she'd think twice about sticking something into a feeble person like Phyllis.'

'But why would she do it?'

'To make sure she got her hands on the bungalow? Or . . .' Suzy groped in her bag for the letter Phyllis had written to George Pattinson and handed it to Robert. 'Perhaps it was something to do with this, like I said?'

Robert read the note silently, then got up and put the kettle on.

'It's plausible, given Yvonne's character,' he said. 'Phyllis might have found out something damaging about her. But would Yvonne have cared? You know, I can't understand why she'd go to these lengths. She was all too likely to try and intimidate Phyllis. But why stick a decoration through her hand?'

'Yes, Yvonne isn't the sort to go in for ironic messages, is she? When I heard her at the Bells', quizzing you about Phyllis's will, she was being pretty direct. Though there was another thing, wasn't there . . .?' Suzy looked quizzically at Robert. There was still something about that conversation which wasn't properly explained . . . 'Oh yes, it was about Mary insisting on something . . .'

Robert was pouring out the coffee. 'I told you, it was about Phyllis making a will. Milk and sugar?'

'Just milk, thanks. So if we agree that sticking a reed in someone's hand is too subtle for Yvonne, who did it?'

'Well, Alan and Stevie both have colourful pasts,' Robert said, coming back to the table. 'Perhaps Phyllis had learnt something about them. Or maybe she'd found out about some suspect deal Frank Bell was involved in. Or discovered something about the Simpsons. Jeff has always been a hopeless businessman.'

'But it sounds as if the information came from someone who wasn't local.'

'Well, everyone's been out of Tarnfield at some point.'

'Tom Strickland?'

'He was a soldier for years and there could be all sorts of things lurking in his past. And we mustn't forget Nick Melling, just because he's a clergyman. He had every reason to try and shut Phyllis up. She was an obstacle to his new ideas, plus she might well have discovered something compromising about him.'

'Yes. And Kevin Jones or Daisy Arthur might have wanted Phyllis kept quiet. We saw last night how passionate these people can get. They've both got real evangelical passion. Kevin seems like a fanatic.'

'But we shouldn't be too hard on him,' Robert replied. 'He's a computer expert who's found religion, and it means everything to him. Imagine if you had a really personal experience of God talking to you! No wonder he thinks all those things we love about the good old C of E are superficial.'

'But he can be aggressive. As can Tom for that matter. And Alan's pretty forceful sometimes.'

Robert deepened his voice, and in an uncanny imitation of Alan Robie he boomed, 'I say, old boy, what are we telling people?'

Suzy spluttered over her coffee and laughed. 'That's very good.'

'Well, I'm a pompous old fart too, aren't I?'

'No! You're not!' Their eyes met and again Suzy found the blush creeping over her neck. Then Robert took a deep breath. He was suddenly serious.

'Of course there's someone else you should consider, Suzy.'

'Who's that?'

'It's me.'

'You? Why on earth would you want to hurt and frighten Phyllis? She was your wife's best friend.'

'Yes. Which means she knew an awful lot about us. And not all of it was good, you know . . .'

Suzy stared at him. Suddenly she saw someone quite different sitting there. Robert no longer looked like Mr Perfect, in his neat tidy house with his neat tidy marriage.

For the first time, she saw something haunted in his face. His look was almost pleading and she had to glance down at the books in front of her. There's something here that I don't understand, she thought.

Then, in the heavy silence, she went over things. There had definitely been something intimate about the way he'd talked to Yvonne Wait, huddled in the Bells' stairwell. She only had his word for it that he hadn't been involved with her. He could have been having an affair with her before Mary died. Phyllis could have found out and been about to tell George Pattinson.

Or perhaps Yvonne had dumped him, which was why he hated her so much, and why she had a hold over him?

Or maybe the hate was just a bluff? Robert had said nothing about Phyllis's will since their visit to the bungalow. How hard had he tried to find it? Or had he been keen to overlook it and let Yvonne inherit?

And there was certainly something odd about the way Robert and George Pattinson no longer communicated. He had been the parish priest and one of his dead wife's closest associates, after all. Had George suspected Robert and Yvonne? Was that why George and Mary had been so close?

What do I really know about Robert Clark? Suzy thought. Is he trying to help me or to warn me off?

Her head started to spin with the whirr of the washing machine on its final cycle. She could feel Robert's eyes willing her to glance up, to lock with his, and to give him permission to talk. I'm not going to do it, she thought. I'm not going to make the eye contact. This has all suddenly become too disturbing.

'Mummy!' Molly's voice, with its six years of accumulated outrage, broke the moment. 'Where are you? What are you doing? I want to show you this book.'

Suzy jumped with relief. 'Come here, sweet pea, and show me.'

Molly was holding a book called *The Language of Flowers*.

It was full of illustrations of Edwardian children, with poems and pictures of flowers.

'Red roses for love,' Suzy read. 'That's pretty, isn't it, Molly?' She ran her finger down the page. 'In this book, all the plants are listed with the things they're supposed to stand for. It's got "reed" here. It represents inconstancy. That's interesting.' She could look at Robert now. Molly had broken the spell. 'Perhaps that reed gave us the same message on different levels.'

'Perhaps it did.' Robert shifted in his chair. He seemed his normal, sensible self again. He smiled at her. But she didn't smile back. As they sat, looking at each other in silence, the washing machine in the scullery screamed to a halt. I have to get out of here, Suzy thought.

'We ought to go now,' she said. She stood up unsteadily and went into the utility room. The damp washing clung and twisted round her hands as she hurried to stuff it into the bag. 'Thanks so much, Robert. It's been a real help to get this done.' She stood there awkwardly.

'You're not going?'

'Yes, I think so. It's past Molly's bedtime.'

'But what about your theory about the reed?'

'Perhaps it's better not to poke around any further, like you said in the first place. You're only looking into it because I asked you to.'

He looked bemused at her sudden change. Then he felt a warm but cowardly sense of relief. He had been about to confide in her, and the feeling had been astonishing, challenging. For over thirty years he had only really talked to one person and she was dead. It seemed suddenly ludicrous that he had wanted to open up to Suzy Spencer, of all people. His heart had been pounding and his palms were coated with sweat. But the moment had passed, thank God.

'And about the fence,' she was saying, 'I'll get an estimate from Frank Bell and put the insurance company on to it.'

I've got to get out of this house, she thought. Whatever the truth is, there's something going on here which gives me the creeps. I've made a mistake. I need to keep my distance from people in Tarnfield. It's not my type of place. There's too much going on under the surface. I'm an open, urban person. Village life isn't for me.

It took a further five minutes to disengage Jake from the computer and Molly from the *Girls' Own Annual 1958*, but all that time Suzy avoided Robert's eyes.

'Goodbye,' she said at the door. 'And thanks.'

He listened as she marshalled the children into the car with squeaks from Molly and Jake's broken-voiced growl. Then she started the car and pulled away.

So that's that, he thought. He went back into the kitchen, closed the books and tidied the papers. There was no need to think about Phyllis's hand again. Or talk to Suzy Spencer either. It had all been a wild-goose chase. Thank goodness he hadn't given into the awful temptation to tell her things that no one should ever know. The danger was over, but only just. He felt relieved, but also empty and rather cold. He would make a cup of tea and go to bed.

Suzy drove the short distance to Tarn Acres. The garage was full of Nigel's stuff, so she parked in the road and struggled to unload a sleepy Molly in her arms. There was a sudden burst of headlights behind her, and Daisy Arthur overtook her and pulled up.

'Hi,' she said. 'I've been following you since you came out of The Briars Lane.'

God, Suzy thought, you could do nothing in Tarnfield without being spotted. But at least it was Daisy who had seen her, not Yvonne, who would have said something snide. Daisy didn't comment, but leant forward and brushed Molly's cheek with her lips. 'She's sweet,' she whispered. 'See you on Sunday, Mrs Spencer. Goodnight.'

'Goodnight,' Suzy said. She had been thinking of dropping All Saints Church. But seeing Daisy reminded her of how much Molly enjoyed the Sunday School. And where else was there to go? I'm trapped in Tarnfield, Suzy thought as she bundled the children up the stairs. I might as well carry on as I did, before I thought I'd found a friend in Robert, Mr Perfect, who could be as guilty as anyone.

Later, when they were settled, Jake reading and Molly sleeping, she sat up, wide awake. I didn't want it to be like this, she thought. I was very near to really liking Robert and I think he liked me too. She put the light out, but she couldn't sleep. A kaleidoscope of pictures invaded her mind – the Assyrians at the siege of Lachish with their long dreadlocks and spears, the dead lilies crushed underfoot in the church, Flowerbabe mewling in the bungalow, Isaiah ranting to the Israelites, and Yvonne murmuring under the stairs, 'I know Mary insisted, I know Mary insisted . . .'

Uneasy dreams wearied her until morning.

16

The Thursday after Low Sunday

To be true and just in all my dealing.
From the Catechism

Frank Bell backed the pick-up to the door of the wood yard factory shop and parked neatly outside. He liked the practical side of the work, and still enjoyed the feel of the various grains of wood under his hands. In the back of the truck was some wood-chip shelving he'd been going to use for the flower vestry at the church. The old metal shelves were dangerous, he reckoned. He'd already delivered some on Easter Saturday but everything had ground to a halt with Phyllis's death. Now he thought it was time to get on with the job.

He was whistling as he walked into the shop. It was really a small warehouse with a till which was manned sporadically by him, his wife, their son when he felt like it, and one of the kids from the council estate. Mary Clark had taken her turn too when she'd been alive, but Frank had always thought Mary a bit too grand for the check-out. She'd worked two days a week on the admin side of the business, helping Monica with orders and deliveries. She'd been good, but not dedicated. Mary's real commitment had been to All Saints.

Frank had always found her rather distant, and he liked Robert, but he had little in common with either of them. The Clarks had been a closed couple, Frank thought. Not like himself and Monica who tended to keep 'open house'.

Monica was a good old stick. Maybe not a great looker but the backbone of the business.

The office was upstairs, in a sort of gallery above the shop floor. Frank had built it himself. Cheerily, he went up the stairs two by two.

'Is the kettle on, love?' he called to his wife. He could see her hunched over some paperwork. She didn't reply. He walked in, still whistling.

'Monica . . .' he said. His wife looked back at him, her face pale and crumpled. 'What is it? Is it Matthew?'

'No, it's not Matthew. It's you.'

'Me? What've I done?'

'Don't look at me like that, Frank. I've spent the day going through the books.'

'So . . .?'

'Don't get shirty with me. It's about Tarn Acres.'

'Tarn Acres? What's going on there? We haven't done anything at Tarn Acres since it was built ten years ago!'

'Exactly. Ten years ago. So why did those houses have parquet floors? Upstairs and down? It wasn't even fashionable then, except for really posh places. I always wondered. Those floors were far too expensive, even for executive homes.'

'Well, that was what they asked for. I got a contract.'

'I know you did, Frank, but it doesn't make sense. Who was the developer? Who stumped up all this money they paid us? Because whoever it was must've lost a fortune on the flooring.'

'That's not my problem, Monica –'

'Oh yes it is. We made a lot of money on that, Frank. Far more than I realized. I've looked back at the accounts –'

'I swear to you, Monica, we didn't do a thing that wasn't on the level. If they wanted parquet floors, who was I to question it?'

'I'd have questioned it if I'd realized. This happened when I was in hospital, didn't it? And it was the year I wasn't well and you got that shifty accountant from Newcastle to do the books. I wasn't on the ball. But it stinks, Frank.'

'What's made you dig this up now?'

'Something Yvonne Wait said last night.'

Frank groaned and sat down in the chair at his desk opposite his wife. 'Oh God . . .' he said. 'Why did she do that?'

'For fun, I expect, because she was miffed. You'd better tell me what she knows, Frank. And then we can sort her out.'

Frank sat down heavily in front of his angry wife.

'It was Jeff Simpson,' he said. 'He was on the board of the development company that built Tarn Acres. Tarnfield Homes. And he'd been knocking off Yvonne for years. Then when you took ill, she turned her attention to me.' Monica nodded, lips pursed. 'You knew that, love, I told you . . .'

Yes, thought Monica, but only after Babs Piefield did first. 'Go on, Frank,' she said drily.

'Yvonne wanted new floors in her house. She was ahead of the trend. Everyone else was still into fitted carpets. I gave her a quote and she said it was too high. I forgot about it and then one night when I got back from visiting you in hospital she was waiting for me. I invited her in of course . . .'

Frank paused for a moment, and remembered Yvonne's perfume in the warmth of his living room, her shiny hair and the touch of her hand on his arm. They'd got down to it, just the once, on the sofa. It hadn't really been worth it, Frank thought, and he'd made it clear to Yvonne as she lit a cigarette afterwards that it would never happen again. He'd lived in terror of Monica coming home from hospital and smelling the smoke. Ever since she'd been pregnant with Matthew she could smell cigarette smoke a mile away, and he knew if she ever found out she would never forgive him. That's why he'd been a pushover for Yvonne's deal.

'Yvonne told me that she could get me a contract to install parquet floors throughout the new houses they were building in Tarn Acres. And in return, would I give her a hundred per cent discount on new floors for her house? So I did . . .'

'And how did she swing this? Putting pressure on poor Jeff Simpson?'

Frank lowered his head. 'I suppose so,' he mumbled.

'Oh, Frank, how could you have been so stupid?'

'It wasn't stupid!' Frank replied, angry now. 'If Tarnfield Homes, or whatever it was called, chose to ask Bell's to do the flooring, why not?'

'Because we all know Jeff Simpson has always been strapped for cash. And at some point people might want to look closer at some of his business dealings. They might want to investigate Tarnfield Homes. There were other directors on the board, I assume? You wouldn't need to run the Bank of England to see that Bell's were paid way over the odds for flooring that was totally unnecessary. These things can come back to haunt you, you know. And there's Yvonne . . .'

'Well, she's hardly likely to blab, is she?' Frank huffed.

'Oh Frank, use the little bit of brain you've got! She's only got to go to the chairman of Tarnfield Homes or whatever it is now, and let the cat out of the bag, and we've had it. She's pally with people like the Ridleys and the Armstrongs who run local businesses. If she talks, we could be sued. Or at the very least accused of bad practice. She's got us where she wants us. The only reason she hasn't called this in before is because she's had other schemes going on.'

'Like what?'

'Oh, think about it, Frank. I've overheard her trying to get Alan Robie's orchard, and before that she had a go at Nancy Arthur. When Nancy and Roger sold the shop, they kept the land behind it and Yvonne was after that too. And she "persuaded" poor George Pattinson to let her have that pasture which his family owned on the North Road. She's lethal, Frank.'

Then Monica thought for a moment. 'Of course, these schemes might not be coming off. Maybe that's why she's decided to start dropping hints about our floors in Tarn Acres.'

She looked at her husband shrewdly. 'Is it something to do with this that was eating you on Easter Saturday night? Had she said something to you too?'

'No!'

'You'd better tell me, Frank.'

'Oh, if you must know, it was that ruddy Phyllis Drysdale. I saw her when I went up to the church with the two-by-fours for the shelves. She was just going in and she looked worried. I asked her what was wrong and she gave me a funny look and said she needed to talk to someone about some information she had.'

'Did you think Phyllis had found out about the floors? If Yvonne's suddenly decided to talk about it, she might be making sly remarks to everyone.'

Frank looked at her. It was all a bit too complicated for him. But he was sure of one thing – it was better that Phyllis was dead than asking questions, and it was a pity Yvonne couldn't join her.

'Monica, now we've twigged all this, what are we going to do about it?'

'I don't know yet. But I'll think of something. And I'll tell you one thing, Frank: we're not going into this on our own. The Simpsons have got as much to lose as us. I'm going to call them. This afternoon.'

Monica got up. As far as she was concerned the discussion was over. Frank had been a bloody idiot but the situation could probably be remedied. Still, she could hardly bear to look at him as she walked out. With her shopkeeper's instincts she had heard the bell ring in the warehouse as her husband had been talking. There was a client downstairs and, despite all this, there had to be business as usual at Bell's.

She was walking down the little staircase when Frank came flying after her.

'Don't do that, Monica. Don't call the Simpsons about it,' he called.

What if Yvonne told Jeff about me, and that sad bit of

nookie we had on the sofa? he thought. If she did, Jeff might tell Monica.

She looked back at him, anger and contempt mixed in her eyes. Monica loved Frank, but he could be such a fool. With a curt nod of her head in the direction of the shop floor, she indicated that they had a customer who had heard him.

'Shit,' mumbled Frank, and he went back into the office.

'Hi, Monica,' said Suzy Spencer. 'I need an estimate for repairing Robert Clark's fence.' Everyone in Tarnfield knew she had knocked it down, thanks to Jane Simpson.

Monica smiled at her, but then glanced warily up the stairs towards the office. How odd for the Bells to be bickering, Suzy thought. And about the Simpsons too. I didn't even know they were friendly.

'We should be getting together soon, Monica, to discuss the Whitsun Flower Festival,' Suzy said cheerily. But Monica merely nodded, and then turned away to pull out a big catalogue. She avoided Suzy's eyes.

So what's up with the Bells? Suzy wondered.

In the vicarage, Stevie Nesbit was sitting looking at Nick Melling in despair.

'Please, Stevie.' Nick's face was twisted with anxiety. 'If you won't tell me why you are so worried, there's little I can do.' Nick was deeply confused. Despite all his training, he found it very difficult to deal with real people and the complications they brought with them. He was great on the theory. He'd read all the right books and even contributed a chapter to a compilation of essays on sex and spirituality. But when it came down to meeting human misery on his settee, he was at a loss.

This was the second visit from Stevie. The first time, Stevie had just wanted to rant about how Alan didn't love him, and there had been an embarrassing moment when Stevie had reached out his hand to Nick, and Nick had recoiled before taking it and replacing it on Stevie's lap.

Nick was acutely aware of his own attractiveness and it had occurred to him that Stevie might be nurturing ideas of a closer relationship. Nick Melling had spent a long time thinking about his own sexuality. In his late teens he'd had girlfriends like everyone else. But in his twenties the thought of marriage had terrified him. In his original profession of not-terribly-successful public relations guru, he had worked on the image of the gorgeous, inaccessible bachelor until he had woken up to the fact that he hadn't had a sexual relationship for over a year. He was becoming estranged from people generally, he realized one Saturday morning when cleaning the classic Boxster down at the local car wash. He'd called an old friend from Oxford, and gone to stay the next weekend. They'd been to an inspirational church service aimed at young, bright academics, and in the evening a couple of friends had joined them and they had sat in front of the fire, while the grey rain pattered outside, talking about religion.

Nick had taken a few more days off work. In the dreamy atmosphere, with an autumn mist coming from the river and brown leaves curling round his feet, he'd felt that the Church was calling him. He'd attended both an evangelical meeting, and a baroque Choral Eucharist with smells and bells. Charismatic young priests held the stage at each service. He had felt a vocation, at once. The Church of England was right for him, he thought – it really didn't matter which branch. And until now Nick had been a hit wherever he'd gone, culminating in his captivation of his current Bishop who thought he was marvellous.

With the realization that he was a success had come his determination to put sex and marriage on the back burner until he was settled in a parish of his own.

Of course that had come more quickly than it should, with George Pattinson's mysterious illness. Nick sighed. He had thought of George as a 'character', a vicar from central casting who stood for the past while he, the bright young curate, was the symbol of the future. But now, he wondered if there was more to George's success than that. Until his breakdown, George had seemed able to handle anything Tarnfield could throw at him and, as Nick was learning, quite a lot could be chucked your way. Like Stevie Nesbit's problems.

He had hoped Stevie wouldn't come back. But here he was.

'Please, Stevie. Everything you tell me is in total confidence. I can see you're very unhappy.' They had tried prayer but Stevie had just cried. Nick was running out of technique.

'If we can't get any progress towards closure on this I think we will just have to leave it in the Lord's hands.'

Somewhere in his conscience Nick recognized that this was a cop-out, but he was stumped. Stevie gave a cry of genuine pain.

'No, I couldn't bear it if you abandoned me too.' He turned his big, blue, only slightly wrinkled eyes to Nick who looked away in embarrassment.

'All right, all right, Nick,' he whimpered. 'I'll tell you. Yvonne Wait is blackmailing me.' Even in his distress, Stevie couldn't resist peeping up to see the effect of his words.

'I beg your pardon?' Please let me have misheard, Nick thought, but he knew he hadn't. I'm really out of my depth here, he thought. Stevie was calm now he had made the decision to talk. His voice sounded deeper, more masculine.

'Every year or so, I go back to London. I tell Alan it's to do voice-overs, or perhaps help a friend with a drama workshop. And usually that's true. Except that I also take the opportunity to visit some of my former gay haunts. It's a few days' break that I really need, but Alan would never understand.' He paused to get Nick's sympathy.

'And the trouble is, Nick, that you can never be absolutely sure about HIV. So, after my last trip I took a test. I did it locally, and the GP was absolutely discreet. But somehow, Yvonne found out about it. It had to go to the hospital to be processed, I suppose, and she has some sort of means of finding things out.'

'And she's threatening to tell Alan?'

'Absolutely. She wants me to persuade him to sell some land to her – the orchard, to be precise. But he won't sell, so she's putting more and more pressure on me. If he finds out he'll throw me out. And if he does that I don't know what will become of me.' Stevie's voice was rising again.

Nick Melling stood up and walked around the room. He had absolutely no idea how to deal with this. He was shocked about Yvonne, but not entirely surprised. And he was also angry with himself because his prevailing feeling was disgust. He had always been fastidious. The thought of what Stevie got up to, in those clubs, revolted him.

'Was the test positive?'

'What? Oh, no. But that isn't the point, is it? Just taking a test means I've been unfaithful.'

What a mess, Nick Melling thought. 'Is it out of the question to tell Alan?' he said suddenly.

'I couldn't possibly.' Stevie was crying noisily now, with no consideration for how he looked. 'It's all that ghastly woman's fault,' he sobbed. 'I could kill her.'

17

Rogation and Ascension

Be ye doers of the word, and not hearers only, deceiving
your own selves.
From the Epistle for Rogation Sunday, James 1:22

In the North of England, like everywhere else in Britain,
Easter is felt to be the beginning of spring weather – but
sometimes this seems like a southern assumption which
has been imposed on the cold wet soggy farmland and
scratchy bare fells. Like Phyllis, Suzy felt that it was a time
of broken promises, dishwater sunlight which drained
away to leave steel skies, and lukewarm patches which
were swept away whenever the wintry wind roistered
round the corner.

It had been a fortnight after Easter when Suzy had been
in Lo-cost, chatting about the weather, and she had heard
a woman who looked like an older version of Janice Jones
laugh and say, 'Well, ne'er cast a clout till May is out.' Well,
these days you could cast your cloths and prance round
Carlisle with your belly button showing in January, thanks
to central heating and alcohol. But Suzy knew what
Janice's mother had been getting at. It still wasn't remotely
warm despite some deceptive days. There was a sprinkling
of blossom, but from a distance the tough bits of cream
petal on the trees looked like stones from the shale-covered
paths that had been scattered into the branches. There was
no sense that summer was anything more than a Techni-
color memory, and it seemed certain that anyone who

stripped off so much as a liberty-bodice would go down with pneumonia.

It was a busy period at Tynedale TV. Jake and Molly were back at school. Sharon Strickland was babysitting and Suzy was commuting from Monday to Thursday. On the long drives Suzy found she couldn't help going back over things, even though she tried to distract herself for the sake of her own security. She knew she had run away from Robert because there was something there she couldn't face. But no amount of radio or CD playing could stop the sudden memory of the bloodstained altar cloth or the crushed lilies snapping garishly into her mind like unwanted porn on a PC screen. She was compelled to look. She unpicked and re-sorted all the details in her mind again and again. However much she tried to explain it, she was still sure someone had wounded Phyllis's hand before she died. And she was doubly sure Robert Clark had been about to tell her something.

At the weekends she found herself looking up Church festivals on the internet. So Easter was originally the festival of the fertility goddess Eostre. The original church in Britain, the Celtic Church of St Columba, had celebrated Christ's Resurrection on a different date from everyone else in the world. At the Synod of Whitby, the British had turned their backs on their ascetic, independent saints and turned to the warm sun of the south and to Rome, adopting the Roman Catholic way of calculating the date of the festival.

When was the Synod of Whitby? She looked that up too. It was in AD 664. So the North of England had been the hub of the universe in the seventh century! It had to be something to do with access from the coast. No one in his or her right mind would voluntarily attempt something like Tarnfield Scar on foot, especially in sandals and a monk's habit.

On that day when Suzy had come out of the super-market into a blast of vicious wind and rain, she found Janice waiting for her mum, her puffy anorak pulled up round her head, her hands in woolly gloves clasped around the handle of her toddler's buggy.

'Your mum's still at the till,' Suzy told her.

Janice had nodded, and said suddenly, 'But she can follow me on. I'll walk up to Tarn Acres with you.'

Suzy was surprised. She hadn't spoken to Janice since the lunch at the Bells'. She looked at her. The face that the younger woman turned into the biting wind was not just wet from the fine, insistent rain, but also with a sheen of tears. Janice walked as if on a route march, pushing the buggy and saying nothing. But she clearly wanted to talk.

'Would you like to come in for a cup of tea?' Suzy asked.

'I can't. Mam's on her way up. She's furious anyway today. Have you heard the latest, Suzy?'

'What?'

'Rogation Sunday. Nick Melling isn't doing anything about it and it's causing a lot of trouble with the older folk. I think Mam'll be falling out with Kevin over it. As if there wasn't enough trouble between us at the moment!'

'Rogation Sunday?' Suzy didn't want to admit her ignorance, and anyway the wind was whipping through her tweed coat.

'I agree the Church has to move with the times . . .' Janice said, tossing her head. For a moment she seemed strong and healthy again, rather than the pasty-faced young woman Suzy had found snivelling outside the supermarket, '. . . but try telling that to my mother. Anyway, Nick says there'll be no beating the bounds this year. It was missed last year because Mr Pattinson was taken ill. So now Nick says there's no point in reviving it.'

'Beating the bounds? You mean walking around the parish?'

'Yes, of course.'

Suzy couldn't imagine Nick Melling wanting to trample through the mud and over the dry-stone walls of outlying Tarnfield with no audience except a couple of dour farming families and a few sheep. It would have been different if he could have worn resplendent robes and blessed a shipping fleet for a crowd of bronzed Mediterranean males. But in Cumbria, during one of the coldest Aprils on record . . . Suzy smiled grimly.

She glanced sideways at Janice, who was making no effort now to stop the tears dripping down her face. She sniffed, and then absorbed the stream with her woolly glove which had a grey matted look. In the buggy her little girl arched her back and took a deep breath, preparing for a scream.

'Why not pop in tomorrow for a coffee?' Suzy said. 'Molly would love to play with the baby.'

She had been aware for about a week, without being able to put her finger on it, that there was something wrong between Janice and Kevin, and vaguely conscious that it had something to do with the debacle at the Bible reading group. They hadn't been seen walking down to the shop together, and on the few occasions she had bumped into Kevin he had lacked his usual self-satisfied expression.

'I can't,' Janice said bluntly. She would have sounded ungracious if she hadn't been so obviously unhappy. She had wanted some company, Suzy was sure, but she was too gauche to know how to ask. 'Kevin likes me to be in on a Saturday. And Nick sometimes comes to see us. Kevin would be angry if I wasn't in when he came. Anyway, I'll have to go. Here's Mam.'

A beaten-up Land Rover was rounding the corner and heaving its way up Tarn Acres. Janice moved off, pushing the buggy like an offensive weapon, jabbing it into her path. She didn't even wave back at Suzy. Poor Janice, Suzy thought, caught between two strong personalities like her mother and Kevin Jones.

Suzy had gone home intending to do some work, but found herself wondering about Rogation. It didn't take long to look it up on the net. It was a service to do with prayer, which seemed to have become a calling for God's support for the natural word, and covered everything from a sort of rural England Green approach, to praying to be spared from huge calamities like tsunamis. There were three Rogation Days in the Church of England, the Monday, Tuesday and Wednesday before Ascension Day. Sick of looking at the screen, she went and found the old Prayer Book she'd been given when she was confirmed. She found the readings for Rogation Sunday quite easily, though for a brief moment she wished she could call Robert Clark and ask him to explain it all for her. Why should 'beating the bounds' be a Rogation thing? It was in three weeks' time, the fifth Sunday after Easter.

And four days later came Ascension Day, forty days after Easter. Suzy remembered trying to get Nick Melling to explain to her exactly what he believed about Jesus ascending into heaven. But he had brushed her away, horrified that she should find the concept difficult. Well, she wouldn't challenge him again this year. Nick Melling seemed to have trouble enough on his hands without Suzy's contribution.

But she still liked to go to church. She had attended on a couple of the Sundays after Easter, and chatted to Monica and even to Jane Simpson, but she failed to pick up any gossip about whether Phyllis's bungalow would be inherited by Yvonne. Yvonne was looking pretty sleek, and was taking an executive interest in the preparations for the Whitsun Flower Festival, which were going well. It wasn't to be the major evangelical event Daisy had envisaged, but everyone had agreed on a compromise. Nick Melling had actually consented to big floral displays on the church pillars, thanks to pressure from Daisy, and flyers had been sent round the Church of England school in Norbridge and the surrounding hamlets. It was rumoured that the choir had been practising a modern anthem, and that Stevie Nesbit was going to play the keyboard with Nick Melling on guitar.

Suzy collared Kevin when she saw him washing his car outside the house.

'I need someone to help me decorate the church. It needs to be someone fit, who's capable of getting the swags up there.'

'What about Frank Bell?' Kevin said churlishly.

'Frank would normally do it, but Monica says he's got work over in Hexham at the moment which is keeping him busy.'

'What exactly are you making?'

'Big, bright, modern decorations to symbolize the Holy Spirit. The kids are finishing them off on Whit Saturday afternoon. It's good outreach. Bring your two along. We could really do with you and Janice.'

After a minute Kevin said grudgingly, 'All right.'

Suzy took a risk. 'You asked me for Sharon Strickland's phone number, don't you remember, so you could get her to babysit when you went out? I didn't have it on me then, but I've got it here. D'you want it?'

He could hardly say no. After a pause he said grumpily, 'Might as well.'

'If you ask her to sit this Saturday, tell me how she gets on.' She added innocently, 'I wouldn't like to recommend her without getting some feedback. Not with something as important as babysitting.' Kevin paused, then grunted. Good, Suzy thought. At least she'd put him in a position where he felt he ought to take his wife out, if only because now he had to report back on the babysitter!

A week later, Sharon mentioned that she'd been asked to mind the kids next door, and the following Saturday Suzy saw the Joneses walking hand in hand, pushing the buggy, to the Plough at lunchtime. What is happening to me, watching the neighbours? she thought. I'm getting as bad as Babs Piefield! But at least some sort of harmony had been restored, although Janice's mother had announced she was leaving All Saints if the church wasn't prepared to 'beat the bounds' next year.

And during all of this, no one had said anything more about Phyllis Drysdale. Suzy had gone through it all in one of her increasingly long and dependent conversations with Rachel.

'Isn't there anyone at all that you can talk to in Tarnfield?' Rachel had asked.

'No, not really. Robert Clark was the nearest but . . .'

146

'But what?'

'I don't know. We were talking everything over and suddenly I had the impression he wanted to tell me more.'

'So?'

'I don't know, Rachel. It gave me the creeps. It was as if he wanted to confess. What if it was Robert who used the reed to hurt Phyllis?'

'Then why would he encourage you to investigate? Perhaps he wanted to spill the beans about something else.'

'But what sort of beans?'

'Runners, to get you so worried. Though from what you've said, he doesn't seem the type to mutilate elderly ladies.'

'No, but there was something going on. I could see it in his eyes.'

'That's because you were too close. Serves you right!'

But despite her manner, Rachel sounded worried. She offered to come up and stay with Suzy for a long weekend as soon as she could.

'That would be great, Rache. Let's hope I'm not insane by then.'

'You'll know, when you start sticking flowers up people's bottoms. Or whatever it is that turns you lot on up there.'

'It was her hand, Rachel. And it wasn't funny.'

'OK, OK, I just had a good taste failure. Look, you sound quite low. Why don't you return the compliment and come to me at the start of the summer holidays? Bring the kids. They could go to a couple of museums . . .'

For a moment Rachel's words reminded Suzy of how she had invited Robert to come with them and see the Lachish frieze in the British Museum. That was a forlorn hope now.

She sighed. 'That would be lovely, Rachel. I haven't got a summer holiday sorted. I'm still waiting to find out what Nigel wants. How's work?'

'Slow. I'm back on *Living Lies*. Funnily enough, next week it's people who have a secret religious faith. You know, like finding out your son's a Scientologist or something. There's more of it about than you'd think. Religion causes a lot of trouble, doesn't it?'

Too right, Suzy thought. It could even be fatal.

18

Whitsuntide weekend

Give peace in our time, O Lord.
Because there is none other that fighteth for us,
but only thou, O God.
Versicle and response at Morning and Evening Prayer

The best way to deal with spring in the North is to lower your expectations. It comes a lot later than you expect, but it does come – and it's amazing. There's nothing to excite and delight like the first, astonishingly reliable warmth after the endless wet blanket of winter. The tentative waking of the countryside, and the idea that cold shivers aren't inevitable every time you open the door, start to suggest that summer might actually happen. In Tarnfield in May, the light speckles of stone-coloured blossom dotting the fields were slowly becoming full-blown lacy drifts, and the grass was coming through, lush and green.

Suzy started pegging the washing out for the first time that year. The wet sheets billowed against her in the wind and she felt like generations of women, fighting and using the breeze to get the clothes dry. It was seven weeks after Easter, the traditional Whit weekend.

This year the religious festival had fallen a week earlier than the official Spring Bank Holiday, and the half-term holiday for the schools. When Suzy was small the bank holiday in May had always been called Whitsun and was a church and state holiday – and a nightmare to plan for because it was such a movable feast. Now the state holiday was fixed, and more evangelical Christians called the religious festival Pentecost, but Suzy preferred the old name. As a child she'd been taken to see the Whit walks in the Lancashire cotton towns where all the children wore white.

'Whit' came from *hwita*, the old English for white, referring to the white garments worn by newly baptized church members. The festival commemorated the time that the disciples of Jesus had received the Holy Spirit in the form of flames. It was the way the early Church had come to terms with the fact that Jesus himself was gone, but his influence lingered, and even grew. It fascinated Suzy to think about the way the early Christians had been literally inflamed with the excitement of their new philosophy.

Pity Nick Melling wasn't as inspiring. She found his sermons simplistic and patronizing. She thought about Nick's rivalry with Robert Clark. It was over five weeks since she had spoken to Robert and she would have liked to laugh with him at some of Nick's banality. And rather than forgetting Phyllis's death, she had pushed it out of her mind only to find it came back to her while she slept. In one dream, she had found a note from Phyllis in her own kitchen, asking who had cut her hand. Suzy had woken, sweating and scared. She had been fond of Phyllis and she remembered what Robert had said about wishing he had been kinder to her. There had been real regret in his voice. Would a man who had bullied and mutilated an elderly woman say that?

When Suzy finished pegging out the clothes she decided to make an apple pie. She was going through a domestic phase. A few weeks earlier, the producer of the series she was working on had told her they'd be coming off the air from May to September because the network was doing a special series on the national scourge of obesity instead.

'It's a good time to do it. People might try and get fit for summer,' she had said. 'Some women can't even *see* their bikini line!'

Suzy had laughed, hollowly. It had been months since she'd even bothered to shave her legs. But a hiatus in her job was a depressing thought. At least for the time being, though, money wasn't too much of a crisis. Nigel had been paying the mortgage since the move to Tarnfield, and she could keep living expenses down. But it meant Suzy was relying on the village for interest. She had managed to compartmentalize the worry about Phyllis and to get caught up in the Whitsun Festival, to her own surprise. And she had already started to plan some half-term activities too, for next week. As long as Jake didn't keep lobbying to go joyriding with Matthew Bell, and Molly stayed pally with her new best friend, there was a chance the half-term break might be bearable.

After sorting out the washing, and making the pastry, feeling like a good old-fashioned mum, she looked at her watch. It was five o'clock and there had been no message to say where Jake was. He should be home from school. With relief, she heard his key in the door.

'What time do you call this to come home?' Suzy said, half pleased, half annoyed. She could hear her mother's voice, shrill with relief, coming out of her own mouth. Jake was usually good about getting home from school, especially when she was at work and Sharon Strickland was holding the fort. Suzy had been getting on well with her son lately.

'I went to Mr Clark's. I thought you wouldn't mind.'

'Robert Clark's?' Suzy was taken off guard. 'Well, I don't know whether I mind or not. The point is, you didn't tell me. Why did you go there?'

'I saw him when I got off the bus. Actually . . .' Jake looked a little bit sheepish, 'I asked him if I could go and use his computer, 'cos he's got some good software. And I wanted to ask him about this stuff I've got to do on some poet. Yeah, Geoffrey Chaucer. It's quite rude as a matter of fact.' He guffawed in a particularly irritating way.

'You asked him! Oh, Jake, I wish you hadn't.'

'Why not? A couple of weeks ago he was your new best mate!'

The pastry was sticking to the rolling pin. It was going to be a mess and already had a grey look. These bursts of domesticity usually coincided with some disappointment in her career, but this time that wasn't all. She was unsure what had brought it on. She paused, her fingers coated with sticky mess.

'You'd better get changed, Jake, and help me tidy the living room. Daisy's coming over to discuss the finishing touches for Sunday's decorations.'

The next day, Daisy and Suzy – and anyone else who wanted to help – would be dressing the church with the children's efforts at paper flame making. They would add in the sunflowers, gerberas and thick bunches of anemones that Suzy and Monica had bought, for the swags down the big Gothic columns. They had worked well together recently, though Monica had seemed preoccupied. She was under some sort of family pressure, Suzy thought. The first time she called in at Suzy's house to talk about the Whit-sun decorations, she spent most of her time looking at the parquet floor. Then, quite suddenly, she had lightened up and now seemed almost her old self.

Suzy put her apology for a pie in the oven and shouted, 'Supper's at seven. Now, you two, get clearing up because Daisy will be here any minute.'

When Suzy opened the door, Molly ran to Daisy who picked her up and swung her round. Daisy was looking particularly attractive that evening. She had been over twice before to help with the decorations. Suzy liked Daisy and realized she was bright, though there was something febrile about her that was unsettling. Suzy put it down to religious fervour mixed with unrequited love. Whenever Nick Melling was mentioned Daisy would blush, and if Suzy ever mentioned church gossip she became defensive. She was a Melling loyalist, but her creed went deeper than a crush on the vicar. At one point, when they were cutting up huge swathes of orange wallpaper, Suzy had asked Daisy what she really believed.

'It's very simple,' Daisy had said. 'Jesus is the Way, the Truth and the Life. There's no way to the Father but through him, and the Bible is his word.'

'So do you believe everything in the Bible?'

'Absolutely. Of course there are some interpretations that vary. But if it's the Word of God then it has to be accessible to everyone, doesn't it? So it must mean what it says.'

'But what about people who are born into Hindu or Muslim communities? Or Jews. Or African bush tribes. Aren't they at a huge disadvantage? Why would God make it easy for someone in Tarnfield to believe and hard for someone in Africa?'

'Africa has the fastest growing Christian population, Suzy. And knowing Jesus is so easy, being in another culture isn't that much of a barrier. Haven't you heard of those Chinese drug addicts who could be converted and speak in tongues within hours of hearing the Word?'

Drug addiction could do funny things to the brain, thought Suzy.

Daisy went on decisively, 'I'm much more worried about people who have the chance to learn about Jesus, but go on to reject Him.' She shuddered. I wonder if she thinks they'll burn in hell? Suzy thought.

'Where did you go to university, Daisy? And what did you do?'

'I went to London. And I started reading English and then changed. It meant I was a bit older than the others.'

'I did English too!'

The doorbell rang again, and Suzy heard Jake bounding downstairs. I hope it's not Matthew Bell, she thought. Matthew's influence over Jake was growing. Suzy thought it was pathetic, but Matthew seemed to take on all the pubescent males in Tarnfield to ensure a constant supply of admiring passengers in his boy racer car while Russell Simpson was in Newcastle. Suzy was on the verge of a downright ban on the Bellmobile, but so far circumstances had been in her favour and Jake hadn't been able to join Matthew on his sprees.

She was relieved to hear Jake say, 'Oh, please come in. It's for you, Mum.'

It wasn't Matthew Bell – but it was only marginally better. It was Yvonne Wait.

Yvonne smiled her Cheshire cat smile. 'Hello, Suzy. Hello, Daisy! Nancy said I'd find you here. I want to talk to you about something. But it can wait a few minutes.' She stood there, waiting to be invited to sit down, looking round with interest at Suzy's furnishings.

Then her eye caught the Whitsun decorations. 'Mmm. So is this what you're doing for Sunday? Oh well. How's it going?'

'Fine, thanks.' Suzy resented Yvonne's superior managerial air. Daisy tried to hold up the yards of orange wallpaper.

Yvonne looked unimpressed. 'Very loud, isn't it! Last year I did something rather smart with clivia and witch hazel and a few sprays of pussy willow. Still, I suppose for children . . .'

She sighed, flopped on to Suzy's sofa, then extricated Flowerbabe's catnip toy from under her bottom and chucked it on the floor. Suzy thought, she's settling in. I'd better offer her something.

'Since it's getting on for supper time, how about a drink?' she suggested. 'White wine?'

'I don't mind if I do,' Yvonne smirked. 'I don't suppose you have Sancerre, do you?'

'Just Pinot Grigio.'

'That would be lovely,' said Daisy, surprisingly. 'What a great idea!'

Suzy hoped the wine would give Daisy a bit more confidence. She poured three generous glasses. It was a few days since she'd had a drink herself, and it went straight to her head. She wondered why Yvonne had turned up. Perhaps she thinks she's got something on me now, like she has on Robert Clark, and on Stevie Nesbit too, she thought. Suzy remembered how Stevie had been pinned to the couch in the Bells' living room with Yvonne hovering over him. Yuk.

But what could Yvonne possibly have on her? One of the advantages of telling everybody all your shortcomings, Suzy thought, was that you had no reputation to protect. Unlike poor Mary Clark, Mrs Perfect.

Then it suddenly occurred to her that perhaps Yvonne's power over Robert wasn't to do with him, but to do with Mary. For nearly two months, Suzy had let herself suspect that Robert had been having an affair with Yvonne after all. But looking at the woman as she sat there, sipping wine and sneering at the efforts she and Daisy were making, Suzy felt that couldn't be true. The man who had talked so frankly about his love for his wife was hardly likely to be having a relationship with the village witch. Not every man was like Nigel.

Suzy thought for a moment and then said casually, 'It must have been very different at All Saints when Mary Clark was alive?'

'Too right,' Yvonne said languidly.

'More wine?' Suzy offered.

'Oh, why not,' said Yvonne graciously. 'This isn't too bad for plonk.' Suzy bit her tongue and offered Yvonne a generous top-up. Yvonne knocked a good half of it back.

'How did you get things done with Mary in charge?'

'Oh, with difficulty!' Yvonne purred happily. It was always fun to indulge in a little character assassination before supper. 'No one else got a look-in. Mary Clark had the whole parish sewn up. Flowers, Bible study, choir . . . She was Superwoman. Looked like the back of a bus of course, though I have to say she did have the occasional smart outfit, not like poor Monica, or Jane with her glad rags. Or should I say, sad rags!' Yvonne laughed like sandpaper on glass. It put Suzy's teeth on edge.

'I thought Mary was very kind,' Daisy said breathily. 'She and Phyllis used to run the Sunday School when I was little.'

'Oh God, yes. Mary would love brainwashing the kiddies. They couldn't answer back!' Yvonne laughed again.

'Telling people about Jesus isn't brainwashing,' Daisy said, with a sudden burst of bravery. Then she seemed to cave in a little. 'But like Kevin says, I don't think Mary or Robert had a real experience of the Lord. I mean, they were good people and churchgoers and everything but Kevin says he doesn't know if they had real commitment.'

'Oh, for goodness' sake,' whinnied Yvonne, 'that's ridiculous, Daisy. You shouldn't listen to Kevin Jones. All this "born again" stuff is just embarrassing nonsense.'

'But if you haven't got real religious commitment, then why work so hard for the church?' Suzy asked.

It was a question she regularly put to herself. Why do I do this? The only answer she could find was that Tarnfield wasn't exactly full of alternative entertainment. But that wasn't all. There was something about being involved with All Saints that satisfied her more than it irritated her, though it irritated her too, for sure. But I certainly haven't got Daisy or Kevin's faith, she thought.

'Well, I do it because I just love to see the church looking beautiful,' said Yvonne. 'And of course a well-kept, well-run church is an asset to any community. Heaven knows what would happen to property values round here if the church was turned into a tile warehouse or something.' She shuddered.

'But what about Mary Clark? If, as Daisy says, she wasn't "born again", why was she so keen?'

'Oh, Suzy,' Yvonne took a final gulp from her glass and turned her eyes to heaven, 'don't you know?'

'Know what?'

Daisy stood up suddenly and dropped the scissors. 'Don't do this, Yvonne,' she said tensely. 'You really shouldn't say things about people behind their backs. You've no proof.'

'But there you are!' Yvonne stood up too, as if in triumph. 'The very fact that you know exactly what I'm going to say, Daisy, means it's common knowledge. Why shouldn't Suzy know too?'

'Because it's wrong to spread rumours.'

'Oh, don't be such a silly little cow.' Yvonne's laugh was scornful this time. 'It was so obvious anyway. Obvious to everyone except Robert of course. Though in the end, even he could see – once I mentioned it, of course.'

'What was obvious, Yvonne?' Suzy asked.

156

'Even an incomer like you should have seen the signs!' She laughed with a scoffing sort of sound. 'Mary Clark and George Pattinson were having an affair!'

'You mustn't say things like that, Yvonne. You don't know.'

'Daisy, you'd be amazed what I know. Which, as a matter of fact, is why I came to find you tonight. I really do need to talk to you. Now, preferably.'

Yvonne was totally assured and in command. She gave Daisy a long, knowing look. Then she said, 'Thanks for the wine, Suzy. We'd better go. Daisy and I have things to discuss. And it seems as if you've finished with those paper things.' She looked down at the decorations, and sniffed. Daisy started to gather her belongings together. 'I'll get there a bit early tomorrow,' she said apologetically to Suzy. 'I'll leave Lo-cost at lunchtime and take some stuff from the shop, for the children.'

Suzy could hardly wait to shut the door on them before sinking into the sofa. So that was what it was all about. Mary Clark and George Pattinson had been having an affair. No wonder the vicar had had a breakdown when Mary died. So that was why he had been consigned to extended sick leave, and alienated from his former flock. She drained her own glass. Well, well, well. That explained what they'd been doing in the church that Thursday afternoon. But she didn't have time to think any more about it. Jake came thundering down the stairs.

'Yuk,' he said. 'What's that disgusting stink?' Oh God. Now he'd pointed it out, there was no mistaking it. Yvonne's lingering perfume was mingling with the smell of burning pie.

After dinner Suzy flung the sticky mess into the dustbin and opened a carton of ice cream instead. She let Jake have three helpings because her mind was somewhere else. George and Mary? Had that been what Robert was going to tell her that evening at The Briars? That his wife had been bonking the vicar? Perhaps all Robert had wanted to do was tell Suzy what everyone else knew, that George

Pattinson and Mary had been some sort of unspoken 'item'.

So why would he want her to know? Perhaps because, as Yvonne said, it was 'common knowledge'. So if she and Robert were supposed to be working together to find out who'd injured Phyllis, Suzy needed to know too.

Then something else struck Suzy. If Mary's infidelity was as well known as Yvonne said, Phyllis would have known about it for ages. There would be no reason for Robert to suddenly attack her.

While Jake and Molly watched telly, she sat at the computer.

Dear Robert, she began, *I'm sorry I haven't been in contact for a while. And I never really thanked you for letting me use your washing machine. Can we meet?*

19

Whit Saturday

Yea, the time cometh, that whosoever killeth you will think that he doeth God service.
From the Gospel for the Sunday after Ascension, John 16:2

This was the third time Suzy and Robert had faced each other over his kitchen table. Molly had gone to Carlisle for Saturday morning, with her new best friend's parents, and Jake was playing football. Robert had phoned Suzy in response to her email and suddenly it had seemed quite clear that she should go and see him straight away.

She took a deep breath and said, 'I've been avoiding you, because I thought you might have been the person who injured Phyllis. But now I realize that was stupid, and I'm sorry.'

'It's not stupid. After all, I told you I might be a suspect.'

'I know you did. But you wanted me to be sure it *wasn't* you.'

'Yes. You were bound to think of me at some point so I thought I'd bring it up and we could talk it through. There were things I thought you needed to know. But then . . .'

'I freaked. I thought you were going to confess!'

'I was, in a sense. But I wasn't going to confess, Suzy. I was going to confide.'

'You don't need to. You see, Yvonne Wait came to see me yesterday. And after a very large glass of wine, she told me all about it.'

Robert suddenly leapt up from the table, and then leant his hands on it and stared down at Suzy. But he wasn't frightening. Of the two of them, he looked the more worried.

'What did Yvonne tell you?'

'Please don't ask me to repeat it. But Yvonne said everyone in Tarnfield knew.'

'Suzy, what are you talking about?'

Suzy gulped. 'Mary and George Pattinson. Of course I should have been able to work it out for myself. That would explain why Mary was so keen to befriend me, wouldn't it?'

'What do you mean?'

'I wasn't Mary's type at all, was I? But perhaps she wanted to divert any suspicions I might have had after finding her with George in the church. Why else would she be so pleased to take somebody like me under her wing?'

And by telling everyone you were a flake, she could ensure that anything you said would be taken with a pinch of salt, Robert thought. Except Suzy's not a flake at all. Oh Mary. You were so clever and so scared.

And you're clever too, Suzy, but actually you've got it wrong.

He groaned and slumped down at the table. 'So you thought my wife and George Pattinson were having an affair! Oh Suzy, if only it was that simple!'

For goodness' sake, Yvonne Wait thought. It was Saturday morning and the church looked a complete mess. There was orange paper and foil all over the pews, and there were the huge paper sunflowers for the centrepiece of the first swag, ready and waiting. Only half an hour previously, Yvonne had had a phone call asking her to go down to the church to help put up the first of the decorations.

She'd been surprised to be roped in at such a late stage, but nobody else at All Saints was particularly capable, she thought. It had been the responsibility of others to actually get the stuff put up. But, as usual, people had fallen short of her expectations. It was a good job she was practical *and* creative. She looked with satisfaction at the arrangement of *Pieris floribunda* with guelder roses and eucalyptus that she'd ordered from the florists in Carlisle and brought to the church the day before. Nobody needed to know she hadn't made it, and anyway she'd virtually designed it.

Suzy Spencer's efforts were much tackier. It wouldn't take long to put these things on the pillar, and if she did the first one then the others could just follow her example. At least the ladder was here, propped ready. Yvonne was wearing her flounced skirt, but she'd been sensible enough to put on her flat ballerina slippers. The bracelet, a gift from her friend the hospital administrator, moved seductively around her left ankle. Nobody is here to look up my skirt, she thought, so I might as well get on with it.

Gripping the sunflowers in her left hand, Yvonne started up the ladder. It wasn't very high, just about fifteen feet, up to the hook coming out of the pillar where they always hung the Christmas holly and ivy. It was quite a good idea, this Whitsun effort, she thought, though she would never give Suzy Spencer the satisfaction of hearing her say it. Suzy was getting a bit too prominent at All Saints. It had been fine when Mary Clark had been telling everyone how hopeless Suzy was, but now Suzy seemed to be coming into her own. That wasn't a good development. Yvonne wanted to manage everything, because that way she could keep her finger on the pulse of what was going on in the village, and her victims nicely under control.

She slotted the sunflower bouquet neatly over the hook, and then slowly climbed down. This was really quite easy. She couldn't think what all the fuss was about.

Next, she grasped the streamers of wallpaper and foil that represented the flames. She began to climb the ladder again. At the top, it was rather more difficult. The stiff cardboard flames had to go upward, and the flowing loose pieces of wallpaper had to hang down. It was quite a struggle to get them into place. Yvonne worked hard, the pink tip of her tongue protruding. She pulled at one of the streamers and felt the ladder sway suddenly.

'Oops!' she said aloud. 'Better be careful.' Out of the corner of her eye she caught a movement beneath her. 'Oh, there you are,' she called to the person below. 'I'm glad you've managed to get yourself here after calling me out. That's right, hold the ladder . . .'

But strangely, the ladder was swaying even more now.

'Hold on to it, you fool!' Yvonne shouted. But the ladder, with a scraping noise, was slipping sideways off the pillar. For a second it seemed to right itself, but that only caused it to gain more momentum as it hovered and then swung widely into space.

Yvonne looked down in horror. She could swear that the person at the bottom of the ladder was actually pulling it away from the pillar. And laughing. With a sickening lurch, the ladder swayed backwards, forwards, then backwards again to bring Yvonne crashing down. She had no time to scream before the back of her head cracked on the stone of the chancel steps.

Alan Robie had popped home after a quick pre-prandial snifter at the Plough, to find Church Cottage in chaos. Instead of the Provençal tablecloth meeting his eyes, with a carafe of white wine, and the freshly baked quiche he had expected to smell as he came in the door, there was flour all over the counter. An egg was smashed on the floor. There was a coffee mug half full of cold scummy brown liquid, and an empty glass with the dregs of what smelt like brandy on the table. Nigel Slater, Stevie's favourite cookery writer, was tipped up on the floor.

'Stevie!' he called. 'Where are you?'

There was no answer. My God, Alan thought, has the boy run off? Stevie hadn't been himself for the last few weeks. He knew Stevie had been to see Nick Melling at least twice, and although the older man had been consumed with jealousy, he had used all his reserves to prevent himself quizzing his lover when he returned. He had always kept his jealousy under control. Alan Robie was nobody's fool. He knew quite well that when Stevie went back to Town, he made the occasional trip to clubs like Heaven or Chariots. Stevie was always so much more loving and imaginative when he came back. And Alan got a buzz from the fact that Stevie had been down in the fleshpots but still returned to Tarnfield.

'Stevie!' he called again, feeling the claw of fear in his throat. 'Stevie?' But there was no reply. Alan pushed his feet back into his green wellingtons. He was going to have to find him. But just as he reached the back door of the cottage, it swung inwards, and Stevie stood there, his eyes swollen with tears, his hands hunched into his tight-fitting safari jacket. He looked frozen.

'Stevie . . . What's wrong?'

'Oh Alan.' Stevie stumbled forward and into his lover's arms. 'Oh Alan, I've got to tell you, but you'll never forgive me . . .'

'Whatever it is, I will. Trust me. Where have you been?'

'In the church, Alan. I've been in All Saints. And I've seen something terrible.'

Suzy was late back for lunch after being at Robert's. It was raining and she drove home quickly. She had to brake sharply to avoid Stevie Nesbit who was crossing the road from the church, but it didn't really register. She was in a hurry. She was planning to start preparing for the decorating party at two o'clock so she didn't have much time. But a few minutes later, as she gulped her hot minestrone and cut the crusts off Molly's cheese sandwiches, she was still thinking about what Robert had said to her that morning.

'I can understand why people thought Mary and George were having an affair. That's why they've turned their backs on George now. And why they treat me with kid gloves. They pretend Mary was a saint for my benefit. But people don't know the real story . . .' He had stopped.

Suzy nodded. A few years earlier she would have bad-gered Robert until he told her everything, but she had learnt that waiting was best. It was a professional tech-nique she had perfected on *Living Lies*. And she was older and wiser now. If people told you things before they were ready, they might hate you for forcing the issue. And she didn't want Robert to hate her.

She said quietly, 'But if you won't tell me what the real story is, how can I be sure you didn't hurt Phyllis?'

'You can't. But it wasn't me. Trust me.'

'Why can't you tell me? You were going to, last time.'

'But it would have been wrong. I was tempted, just to make myself feel better. But it reflects badly on someone else. And it would have put pressure on you.'

I suppose that's right, Suzy thought. Knowing secrets isn't comfortable, unless you're like Yvonne, using other people's problems to feather your own nest.

'So what are you asking me to do, Robert?'

'I want you to go on working with me. For Phyllis's sake I want to find out who put that reed through her hand.'

Suzy had sipped her coffee. This time, she didn't break the eye contact. Trust is like faith, she thought. You either have it or you don't. And now I do.

'OK,' she said. 'I'll take your word for it. Let's talk next week, after the Whitsun Festival. If that goes well, there'll be a different atmosphere at All Saints.'

'That'll be the day!' Robert had laughed.

He'd seemed enormously relieved. And she felt better too. She had hurried home soon afterwards, still curious but quite calm. Robert will tell me in time what this is all about, she thought. I have to forget Yvonne's bitchy remarks and be patient until he's ready.

That afternoon, the rest of the regulars were due at the church at two thirty. Frank Bell had offered to drop a ladder off early in the morning on his way to Hexham. Daisy was going early to prepare, and the Joneses had agreed to come, as had Monica. It would be a real com-munity effort, Suzy thought.

But she was wrong. At a quarter to two the phone rang. It was Daisy and she was hysterical.

'Suzy,' she wailed. 'There's been a horrible accident. Yvonne's fallen off a ladder and I think she's dead. And Suzy . . . she looks really weird!'

20

Whit Saturday afternoon, continued

*Suffer us not, at our last hour, for any pains of death to fall
from thee.*
From the Burial of the Dead

Daisy had called Nick Melling, and Robert too. Robert ran
to his car and drove at top speed to All Saints. He found
her cowering at the back of the church, shivering with
shock. He put his jacket around her and walked up the
aisle to the chancel. Yvonne Wait was on her back, her head
surrounded by a halo of congealed blood. But the horror
was not just that Yvonne was dead. She was lying there,
wide-eyed, and virtually bald-headed. Her beautiful
glossy hair had been cropped to within half an inch of
her skull.

Robert had been dialling 999 on his mobile as he
approached her. 'Ambulance. And police,' he said.

He could hear Daisy crying now, and Suzy Spencer's
voice. 'Don't look,' he said, 'it's pretty nasty.' But Suzy was
beside him.

'Good God!' she said. 'What's happened to her hair?' It
was a professional-looking job, which changed Yvonne's
appearance completely.

'It's gone.' Robert said grimly. He felt an urge to be sick,
and turned away. Suzy was tougher than he'd thought.

'I've seen a few horror scenes,' she said matter-of-factly.
'I started out as a local news reporter. Traffic accidents,
things like that. But this is weird, like Daisy said . . .' She
felt nauseous now, but made herself concentrate.

'Daisy called you too?'

'Yes. The rest of us were supposed to meet here at two thirty, but Daisy had the afternoon off from Lo-cost and got here first. Yvonne must have decided she could do better than the rest of us, and turned up this morning by herself. How long has she been dead?'

'At least a few hours by the look of it. Was Yvonne supposed to be part of the group?'

'Oh no, she hadn't offered to help. That's what's strange about this. I was due to meet Daisy, Monica and the Joneses. Not Yvonne.'

A trailing mass of orange and gold paper lay half hidden by Yvonne's body.

'Hang on,' Suzy went on. 'What's this greenery?' To one side, there was a sprinkling of green leaves. 'We weren't going to use any foliage with the swags. What's this doing here?'

She was about to scoop up the leaves when Robert said, 'Don't touch it, Suzy . . .'

'Why?'

'Look . . .'

Suzy peered at the foliage, dark against the grey and white tiles of the chancel. 'What am I supposed to be looking at?'

'I think it's a pattern,' Robert said. 'It's not just random. Come over and see it from here.'

Suzy walked over to stand beside him. 'God! I think you're right,' she whispered.

They stood looking at the leaves. 'It doesn't make sense. 133116,' he said.

'Or eighteen W small B. Something like that. It's really peculiar.'

They had neither of them noticed that Daisy had come to join them. 'Oh no, it's awful,' she started saying, again and again. Her eyes were wide with horror.

'You're in shock,' Suzy said. 'Come on, Daisy, let's go to the vicarage. Poor Yvonne has had a terrible accident, but we can do nothing for her now.'

'But her hair!' wailed Daisy.

'I know, I know, but she might have had it cut this morning . . . we don't know.'

'She wouldn't have done that!' Daisy sobbed. She went forward as if compelled to look closer, and slipped on the chancel steps. Robert rushed forward to catch her, but her feet scattered the leaves as he did so. Suzy shot him a glance as he held the shuddering Daisy close to him.

'Well, whatever the hellebore was saying, it's gone now,' she said.

'Hellebore?'

'Yes, those serrated green leaves. It's dried hellebore. I know because it was one of Phyllis's favourites for the sort of displays she and Mary used to do. It was far too fiddly for me, but they loved it. There was usually some in a jug in the vestry . . .'

She felt she was gabbling, overcompensating for the silence of the church and the horror of Yvonne's staring, unresponsive eyes. I may be resilient, she thought, but I'm not that tough. This is awful.

The sound of the ambulance and the arrival of a pale Nick Melling interrupted her chattering. Nick had waited until the police were on the scene before coming into the church himself. He seemed to Suzy to be distracted, yet at the same time determined. He moved to stand near his parishioners, but avoided their eyes and said nothing, waiting for the officials to set some sort of process in motion.

He really needs to brace himself for all this, Suzy thought. It's awful for all of us, but Nick is the most disturbed. Some people can cope even though it's grim, like Robert. Some people go to pieces like Daisy. And some people positively enjoy the drama, like Alan Robie. Though why is Alan here? He wasn't supposed to be involved in the decorating.

'Robert! Nick!' Alan's deep brown voice and heavy foot-fall preceded the emergency services as they stood at the back of the church and took stock. 'What is it, this time?' he boomed. 'Good Lord, it's Yvonne. She must have fallen.'

'Thanks, everyone, please move back,' said the chief paramedic. The policemen who followed him seemed huge and official, out of place in the church but bringing their own brand of gravitas. The larger of the two went to speak quietly to Nick, who was wearing his clerical collar, and drew him aside. The other policeman came over to Daisy, Suzy and Robert.

'Who found her?' he asked.

'It was me,' Daisy whispered. She was shaking again, under Robert's jacket.

'Let's go to the back and I'll take some details,' said the officer. 'Then we need to get you something to take for the shock.' Daisy was crying again, making no attempt to wipe her eyes. The policeman guided her by the arm, down the nave to the last pew, and Robert and Suzy followed them like some grim wedding party. They glanced at each other.

'Phyllis?' said Robert.

'We should mention it,' said Suzy firmly. 'This isn't a coincidence. Think about the hair.'

Robert shuddered. He was very pale. 'It's the same thing, isn't it?' he said. 'A message. But what?'

The policeman motioned them into the pew.

It was five o'clock that evening before Suzy got home. She felt dirty and tired. In her hurry to get out earlier, she had failed to locate Sharon Strickland, so had called Babs Piefield, who had dashed around to mind Molly. Babs was waiting all agog to hear the details, but Suzy just wanted to be alone with her children.

'There was an accident in the church,' she said bleakly. 'Yvonne Wait fell off a ladder and was killed.'

'That's what people have been saying!' said Babs, who had spent most of the afternoon on Suzy's phone.

Though she knew it was silly, Suzy felt guilty. If she hadn't suggested the Whitsun Flower Festival, this wouldn't have happened. She had felt confused and light-headed by the time the police had questioned her. She and Robert had been separated to give statements at the vicarage, and he had gone by the time the police had finished with her. She had tried hard to explain to the officer that she thought there was a link between this death and poor Phyllis Drysdale's. The policeman had seemed unmoved.

'You say her hair was cut off?' he asked. 'How do you know she hadn't had a haircut earlier in the day? There wasn't a trace of hair near her.' Suzy had felt silly and then tearful, which annoyed her. She suspected that the policeman thought she was making a fuss about nothing.

When the children had settled down and were laughing at some comedy film, she called Robert.

'I told the man from Mid Cumbria police about Phyllis and the reed,' she said. 'He seemed to think I was a bit loopy.'

'I mentioned it too. The chap I was talking to said they'd take it into account. He *did* seem to think that two deaths in the same church in seven weeks was a bit surprising.'

'But I couldn't get them to take me seriously about Yvonne's hair. He kept saying that she could have had it cut before the accident. Whoever cut it off had cleared up really well around her.'

'Did you mention the pattern of hellebore leaves?'

'No. I was going to, but he already seemed to think that I was raving mad. And after all, we don't know that there was a message. It could have been a coincidence.'

'But it wasn't, was it, Suzy? Hang on . . . there's something I want to look up . . .'

Suzy waited. She heard Robert's footsteps and thought of him walking around his house, alone. He must be as shocked and upset as I am, she thought. More so, probably, given that he'd known Yvonne for so long. Maybe he hated her, but that was very different from wanting her dead. But at least this time I can't suspect him, she realized with relief. Yvonne had probably died in the morning, when they were meeting. Or later, in which case Robert wouldn't have had time to get to the church, kill Yvonne, and go home again, in between drinking coffee and getting back to All Saints in response to Daisy's call. It was impossible, even if he had a motive for killing her. But then who didn't? Everyone in Tarnfield loathed Yvonne.

She heard him come back to the phone.

'I've just been looking in that old *Language of Flowers* book, Suzy. And I've found hellebore.'

'You have? What does it signify?'

'You won't believe it. It's calumny. Scandal and calumny.'

'Exactly what Yvonne stood for in Tarnfield!'

'Yes. So it must have been deliberate. And there was definitely writing in the leaves. But why?'

'Who can say? All we know for certain is that there's someone very weird and very dangerous out there. Come over to Tarn Acres, Robert. We need a drink.'

21

Whit Saturday, continued

We beseech thee, leave us not comfortless.
From the Collect for the Sunday after Ascension Day

Monica Bell stood in her front room, the phone frozen in her hand. Jane Simpson's strained vowels rang in her head.

'I could see the police cars and the ambulance from my window,' Jane said. 'I called Nick Melling and there was no reply. So I went down the drive and saw Tom Strickland going past in a hurry. Nick had summoned him, apparently. And he told me. Yvonne had fallen off the ladder in the church, and been killed outright. I was astonished. I mean, that wasn't what we planned, was it?' Jane's brain seemed to be turning like a rusty old mangle. Monica could almost hear the process.

'Of course not!' Monica was shocked.

Three weeks earlier, Monica had arranged a discreet lunch party. The Bells and the Simpsons didn't meet much socially, and the atmosphere had been strained at first. Monica needed to tread carefully. She wanted to discuss what to do about Yvonne. Jane appeared to have no idea that her husband had been Yvonne's lover, so they couldn't be too open about her scurrilous influence over him! Yet despite her apparent naivety, there seemed to be an unscrupulous side to Jane. Once she grasped the situation she was far more uncompromising than the rest of the group.

But at first, Jane had wittered on, making conversation

about Monica's new three-piece suite. She had obviously been impressed by the pristine condition of the Bells' modern house, but was ever-so-slightly condescending about the lack of family heirlooms. Monica's idea of good china was John Lewis's best, and her curtains were from Marks & Spencer's Home Range, so she was way behind when it came to competing with the Simpson family Spode and cut glass. But her dishwasher was state-of-the-art.

The two men had assumed chumminess, with Jeff Simpson trying not to be too grand. He was wearing a blazer, and cream trousers with a razor-like crease. Frank wore a bottle-green fleece and crumpled jeans. Monica had a bright aubergine polo shirt underneath a shapeless mustard jumper, while Jane wore a rather dated two-piece in beige cashmere, and very high-heeled shoes. The only thing we really have in common, Monica had thought grimly, is that the vile Yvonne Wait is persecuting us.

A white wine from Tesco, and then the claret that Jeff had brought from the cellar at Tarnfield House, followed generous gin-and-tonics. The roast was good. Jeff began to relax and even enjoy himself. His tummy seemed to be calmer, and it was rather nice to have gravy and Yorkshire puds, he thought. Not a lettuce leaf or cut tomato in sight. By the time they had all finished sticky toffee pudding – from the supermarket, Jeff noticed, but never mind – the atmosphere was almost cheerful.

With coffee and liqueurs – God only knew how Jeff would drive home! – Monica thought the time was right to broach the subject of Yvonne. She was just about to start when her son's cheeky face appeared around the door.

'Mum, Dad, hi!' Matthew beamed. 'Can I borrow your motor? I'm low on gas.'

'Well, bloody well fill it up yourself, lad,' growled Frank. 'And round here, we call it petrol. You're not in America. You're in Cumbria.'

'Yeah, tough shit,' Matthew grimaced. 'Hi, Jane, hi, Jeff.' Jeff Simpson tried to look comfortable with their hosts' nineteen-year-old son, while Jane simpered at him. Matthew breezed on: 'I'm just going to see if your Russ is up for a trip to Carlisle before he goes back to Newcastle tonight. D'you reckon he'd like a spin?'

'Oh, I'm sure he would,' twittered Jane. She was clearly a little bit tiddly and, despite being very arch, she seemed slightly flirtatious.

Matthew gave her a grin like a split melon. 'I'll go and get him then,' he said, and disappeared.

'That lad!' Frank snarled. 'He's a menace. I don't know where he gets it from.'

'Russell's the same,' Jeff added. 'I don't know where he gets it from either.'

Monica was suddenly aware of a silence. Better move swiftly on, she thought. 'Look, everyone,' she said, taking another after-dinner mint, 'what are we going to do about Yvonne Wait?'

'What do you mean?' asked Jeff, eyes narrowing aggressively.

'That's what I really wanted to talk to you about. She's been having a go at Frank and me about those floors over in Tarn Acres. Jeff, it's no good protesting, we all know that Yvonne pressured both of you two men into doing a deal for over-expensive parquet, and in return, Frank was stupid enough to do her floors for her. Be quiet, Frank . . .'

Both Jeff and her husband had started to splutter.

'But does it matter?' said Jane. 'It was a long time ago. And they are lovely floors. I just wish we could have had them at Tarnfield House. But Jeff prefers wall-to-wall carpet, don't you, dear?' Her husband ignored her, but his face took on a social grimace. 'Anyway . . .' Jane went on, her brain grinding slowly but thoroughly, 'why did Yvonne pressurize you?'

'She could be very persuasive,' Monica said quickly.

'She talked me into it,' said Jeff at the same time.

'Oh,' said Jane, slowly. 'So why is it a problem now?'

'Because she's started to talk to people about it,' Monica explained patiently. 'She referred to it after that awful Bible study meeting. And she didn't keep her voice down either. I think she might be going to make an issue of it.'

'Won't that land her in it too?' asked Jeff, with a superior little laugh.

'Why should it?' Monica sounded sharp but shrewd. 'If she tells the board at Tarnfield Homes, they don't need to know she had her own floors done for free. All she has to do is to ask them why they paid so much, and hint that there was a carve-up between the two of you, and we're done for. You know what she's like. It would be a quiet word in the ear of Malcolm Ridley at some county cocktail party. She's got her fingers in everything.'

'She's got to be stopped!' Jeff Simpson suddenly stood up. His pretence at urbanity was over.

'That's why we're here,' Monica had said calmly. 'Of course she's got to be stopped. The question is, how?'

All four looked at each other. Then Jane said, 'It's a pity she doesn't drop dead. Like stupid Phyllis.' The words sounded spiteful rather than sinister.

'She's hardly likely to drop dead,' said her husband ruefully. 'The trouble is that no one's tough enough to tackle her head on. Bullies usually cave in when you play the same game.'

'There must be some way we can threaten her,' said Monica.

'Why bother?' said Jane in her prissiest voice. 'One of you men should just tell her you'll smash her face in.' Monica spluttered into her coffee, but the words seemed to energize Frank.

'I think you should leave it to me,' he said suddenly. 'I'll tackle her. You're right, Jane. I should have been tougher about this sooner. I feel responsible for this mess, and I'll sort it out.' He flexed his big, workman's hands. 'But we have to pledge to cover each other's backs.'

'Sounds good to me,' Jeff had said. It sounded good to Monica, too. Although the alcohol had helped, she knew Frank meant what he said. She felt a weight lift from her shoulders and, for the first time in ages, she was proud of her husband.

'What will you do, Frank?' she asked.

'I'll speak to her, face to face. There's no point being

subtle with a woman like that. I'll tell her we had a deal and that if she thinks about ratting on it, I'll be round there taking up her tongue and groove quicker than you can say laminate!'

He sounded full of confidence. It may have been the Bailey's Irish Cream, but suddenly Frank was twitching to sort Yvonne out. And this time, he told himself, if she went to Monica and told her about the pathetic shag they'd had on the sofa, he'd just deny it. But, with luck, he could warn her off before it came to that. It would do everyone a favour. It just meant that Jeff and Jane had to back him up. If Yvonne thought she could divide and rule they'd be worse off. The Simpsons and the Bells had to stick together. This lunch of Monica's had been a bloody good idea. He'd had his reservations but as usual Monica was right.

'But you two have got to tell us everything, understood?' he said. 'If she tries to approach you, or make contact in any way, report it to me. OK?'

They had all nodded, and Monica had poured out more coffee and liqueurs. It seemed as if everything was going to be all right. Frank might be a bit hasty sometimes, she thought, but when it came down to it, he really was tough enough to take action. And she'd be there to ensure he kept it all under control.

But three weeks later, listening to Jane, Monica suddenly thought that it wasn't under control at all. What had Frank done? Jane had blithely assumed Frank was capable of murder. Would other people think so too? Was her husband capable of killing? Frank got angry and he lacked judgement sometimes. There had always been a self-justifying side to him, and he'd been the one who'd got involved in the dodgy deal in the first place. Monica felt ill. Frank had told her he was going to the church that morning, to deliver a ladder for putting up the Whitsun decorations. And now Yvonne was dead, having fallen off the blasted thing. Monica gabbled her goodbyes to Jane and ran to her impeccable downstairs cloakroom, where she was sick.

22

Whitsun Eve

Almighty God . . . who desireth not the death of a sinner but
rather that he may turn from his wickedness and live . . .
From the Absolution at Morning and Evening Prayer

'OK,' said Suzy, handing Robert a glass of wine, 'so we
think there was a message in the greenery, but we don't
know what it said.'

'Exactly. Have you got any paper?'

'Of course I have. I'm a journalist, aren't I? Here's some
A4 and a pencil.'

'Thanks. I thought it might help if we wrote down what
we think we saw in the leaves.' Robert took the pen and
wrote 133116. 'I can't see any sense in that,' he said.

Suzy went and knelt on the floor beside his chair. It was
a strange sensation, being so close to him. In the modern
living space at Tarn Acres, with her soft lamps and battered sofa with the colourful throw, this seemed more like
a puzzle to be solved than a clue to a violent crime.

'The way you've written it, it looks like a weird mobile
phone number.'

'Well, perhaps that's it,' said Robert excitedly.

'Yeah, right. Yvonne lies dying and writes a phone number in hellebore leaves, which have magically appeared
from the vestry. I don't think so, Robert. Anyway, it didn't
look like that to me. It looked like this . . .' She took the pen
from Robert and wrote 18Wb below his letters. 'But I must
admit that makes even less sense,' she said. 'Anyway, it

wasn't a full 8 I saw. Or at least, it was an 8 which was broken up a bit.'

'But hang on a minute,' Robert added, 'if you saw one thing and I saw another, let's write yours on top of mine and see what it looks like. For example, how big were the figures you saw? Given that we both saw the same thing, let's try to keep the letters the same size. Look . . .' He wrote 133116 once again on the paper.

'OK. But it will just be a muddle.' Laughing, Suzy took the pen and put a 1 directly on top of Robert's writing, then a larger 8 which she superimposed on Robert's first 3.

'That's a point,' he said thoughtfully. 'The bottom of my first 3 wasn't really so clear. The second 3 was really plain to me, but I'm really not sure about the first one . . .'

'But if they don't have to be numbers,' Suzy said thoughtfully, 'perhaps the first 1 is really an I. And look – your bottomless 3 and my topless 8 make something which is more like an S.'

Then she added her W on top of his following 11, followed by her small B and his 6, which could go either way. They both looked at the result. It was still meaningless.

'But it's not quite what I saw,' said Suzy. She got up and went over to the desk where Molly had left her pink pencil case. Inside she found an eraser. She came back to Robert's chair, and took the paper. Then she rubbed out the third stroke of her W and straightened it out to look like a backwards N.

'That's it,' she said. 'That's what I saw. Still just a mess.'

But Robert said nothing. He stared at the page. Then he took a sip from his wine. 'Suzy,' he said slowly, 'have you got a Bible?'

'Yes, somewhere. It's not exactly bedtime reading in this house.'

'I want to check something.'

'OK.' Suzy got up and went over to the bookshelves by the computer, and rummaged till she located Jake's battered Good News Bible stuck behind his Geography files.

'I think,' Robert said very carefully to her back, 'that this refers to a book, chapter and verse in the Old Testament.'

'What?' Suzy turned around, the Bible in her hand.

'Look, Suzy. IS3V16. Does that look like what you saw?'

Suzy squinted at the paper. It was like looking at a map, not knowing which was sea and which was land, and then suddenly seeing the shape of a familiar coastline and everything falling into place.

'Yes, I can! You're right. Isaiah, chapter 3, verse 16. Oh God, Robert, this is creepy. Isaiah again. Like with Phyllis.'

'Read the verse. What does it say?'

Suzy felt she was taking an age flicking through the pages. Then she found the place. As she read, her scalp prickled. '*The Lord said, "Look how proud the women of Jerusalem are! They walk along with their noses in the air. They are always flirting. They take dainty little steps, and the bracelets on their ankles jingle . . ."* Oh God, Robert!'

'This is it, Suzy. Remember Yvonne's ankle bracelet? This is a real message, left by the person who found her dead.'

'Listen.' Suzy read on. 'It gets weirder: *A day is coming when the Lord will take away from the women of Jerusalem everything they are so proud of,* and then in verse 24: *instead of having beautiful hair, they will be bald.* Oh my God.'

'That explains her hair being cut.'

'Yes. It couldn't be a better description. There's no way Yvonne would have had her hair hacked short at the front like that. She had mounds of glossy hair and loved flicking it about. But why pick Isaiah?'

Robert stood up and put the paper on the table. 'The Old Testament is about blame and the New Testament is about forgiveness. Quite different. We're dealing with someone who has a special relationship with the Old Testament here. We must call the police and tell them. This is really important. Either Yvonne fell and someone cut her hair off afterwards and left us this message –'

'Or,' Suzy broke in, 'the person who left the message pulled Yvonne off the ladder. What are the chances of Yvonne falling backwards like that? Pretty remote, I would say. We're dealing with someone really violent here, Robert.'

'That's what we need to tell the police. Should we do it straight away or on Monday? I think we should do it now.'

'But what are we going to say? Guess what, officer, there's an Isaiah freak on the loose? Come on, Rob, it sounds ridiculous. If you were the police, what would you do? Pull in all the flower arrangers from All Saints and give them a Bible study quiz?'

'I suppose you're right.' Robert came back to the chair and sat down. She could feel his confusion. The village had been his life for twenty-five years. Which of his friends or neighbours did this? she wondered. Which of *my* friends or neighbours did it, for that matter?

'Who has a key for the church?' she asked.

'Lots of people. I still have Mary's keys. The Bells do because Frank does so much DIY there. Jane Simpson does, on the grounds that Tarnfield House is opposite All Saints and she can keep an eye on the place. Alan does because he likes to be important. Kevin does because he's a churchwarden like Tom, who also has keys. Actually, almost everyone does. When you drove home from my house this morning did you see anyone around the church?'

'I don't know. You don't think about it, do you? We're all in and out of All Saints at the weekend. Choir practice, flower arranging, kids' activities. Frank Bell was going early to drop off the ladder, but I assume he'd done it by the time I went past. Mind you . . .' Suzy forced her mind back to the drive from Robert's. She had been so wrapped up in what he had said about Mary that she had driven on autopilot.

'There was someone . . .' she said slowly. 'I'm pretty

sure. I'm trying to remember.' She bit her lower lip in concentration. 'It was Stevie Nesbit. He looked as if he'd just come out of All Saints. I wasn't really thinking about it, though. I was thinking about you.'

The words were out of her mouth before she could stop them, but Robert didn't seem to register what she had said. 'Stevie . . .' he said thoughtfully. 'He very rarely goes into the church. I mean, when there aren't services. What on earth would he have been doing?'

'I don't know,' Suzy shuddered. 'But then again, perhaps he had an appointment with Yvonne. I remember seeing her hectoring him, when we were at the Bells' for lunch. Maybe he pulled the ladder away.'

'But he's hardly a Bible expert, is he?'

'How do you know? He's an accomplished actor and very knowledgeable about drama. The girlie voice and cute boy act are misleading. He could easily know about the Bible. I hope it's not him . . .'

'I hope it's not *anyone* we know,' said Robert, 'but it must be. And wasn't it a bit of a coincidence that Alan Robie turned up at the church this afternoon?'

'I suppose it was. Do you want me to tell the police I saw him?'

'Yes. No. Oh, I don't know. I can't see Stevie as a murderer. Hysterical, volatile, but not evil. The only evil person in Tarnfield was Yvonne. We're in a difficult position, Suzy. I think we need to have a conversation with Alan and Stevie.'

'But when?'

'It's late, but I'm going to go and see them now.'

23

Whitsun Eve, continued

Endue thy ministers with righteousness.
Versicle at Morning and Evening Prayer

'How are you feeling?' Alan Robie bent over the figure of
his lover, who was lying on the double bed. Stevie had a
rug over him, and struggled to sit up. 'Here's some tea,'
said Alan. 'Did the sleeping pill help?'

'Absolutely. Thank you, Alan.'

'It was the least I could do. You were in a terrible state.
And I know you haven't been sleeping lately anyway.
You're completely overwrought, Stevie.'

'I know. Oh God, I know.' Stevie started to cry again.
Alan shook him roughly but affectionately by the
shoulders.

'Stevie, I went to the church after I put you to bed. You
were right, Yvonne Wait was dead. She'd fallen from a
ladder. It was obviously an accident. Except . . .' Truthful-
ness got in the way of Alan's need to be reassuring.

'Except what?' Stevie's voice was even higher with
stress.

'Her hair. It had been cut off at the front. Even I could
tell it wasn't the sort of style Yvonne would have liked,
and I know sod-all about women's fashions.'

'Oh God, that's awful. It means someone got at her. But
it happened before I went in, I swear it. I could see the
ladder on the ground and her body on the steps by
the altar but I didn't go near it, I tell you, Alan. It
wasn't me.'

'So why don't you think it was an accident?'

'Because there was someone else there. And they certainly weren't calling for an ambulance or giving her mouth-to-mouth resuscitation.'

'Are you sure?'

'Yes. I could hear them. They were rummaging in the little room to the side of the church.'

'The flower vestry?'

'Where they keep all the urns and vases and stuff like that. I sat down at the back because I needed to think. Things have been getting so on top of me. I'd gone to the vicarage but Nick wasn't in.'

'That's odd. He's usually around on a Saturday morning.'

'Well, he wasn't this time. I took your keys and went to the church in case he'd gone there, thinking that at least I would get some peace inside. You know that I was an altar boy when I was a kid. Anyway, I tried praying, and then I noticed the ladder. I sat up and then I could see something crumpled at the top of the aisle. I walked to the end of the pew and I recognized Yvonne lying there. I just turned and ran home. Suzy Spencer nearly killed me as she came round the corner. Her driving is lethal.'

Even in his misery, Stevie couldn't keep the catty edge from his voice. Good, thought Alan, he's getting back to normal.

'But why were you so upset in the first place, Stevie? You can tell me, you know.'

'No! No, I can't.'

'Yes you can. I love you, Stevie, and there's nothing worse than knowing you're in a state, with nothing I can do. I can't think of anything that would make me love you less. You've got to tell me.'

'But you'd never forgive me.'

'How d'you know? For goodness' sake, the way you're talking is making it far worse for both of us. You haven't remortgaged your share of the house, have you?'

'No!'

'Or fallen in love with someone else?'

'No!'

'Or gone back on cocaine?'

'No!' But there was an edge of doubt in Stevie's voice. Alan looked at him. 'Well,' he said, 'only once or twice.'

'In London?'

'Yes.'

Stevie started to whimper like a small boy. Alan sat on the bed and put his arms round him. 'Listen, Stevie, I know what you're like. That's why I love you. I know that when you go back to London, you play the field a bit. That's your nature. I'm not like that. I'm doggedly faithful. But that's not because I'm virtuous. It's because I'm made that way. It costs me nothing to be monogamous. But I know that it's a huge effort for you.'

'You do?'

'Of course I do! I can't say I like it, but I can live with it. And I hope and pray that as time goes on you won't need the other things so much. But if you need them now, that's OK. I'll live. So you'd better trust me, Stevie, and tell me the truth.'

Stevie started to talk, haltingly at first and then with increased fluency. When he got to the bit about Yvonne Wait blackmailing him, Alan stood up so sharply that the mattress bounced.

'That awful woman!' he said. 'I can't believe she fell. It would be too much like good luck. Whoever pulled that ladder from under her did a lot of people a favour.' Then he sat down again. 'Forgive me, Stevie, that was a rotten, unchristian thing to say.'

'You should be forgiving me. I was so scared that she would tell you about my HIV test that I was prepared to try anything to get you to sell the orchard.'

'You must have been desperate.'

'Yes, but not desperate enough to kill her. I swear it, Alan. Do you believe me?'

'Of course I do, Stevie.' Alan smiled, and for the first time Stevie closed his eyes, genuinely relieved. Alan stroked his brow and said again: 'Of course I believe you.'

But would anyone else? Alan shuddered. Even he couldn't be absolutely certain. Stevie was capable of fierce attacks of temper. He wouldn't kill Yvonne deliberately, but Alan could imagine him kicking the ladder from under her in fury. He felt fear, mixed with anger. His life, which at last had been turning out the way he wanted it, was suddenly under threat. He felt like berating the God he'd believed in all his life.

Was it too much to ask, he wanted to rail, for two harmless old queens to have a peaceful existence? You created us this way, he said under his breath to some paternalistic force he sensed somewhere above the bedroom ceiling. He thought of the collect for Ash Wednesday. *Almighty and everlasting God, who hatest nothing that thou hast made . . .* So why make it so hard for us, Lord? Why do people like the Bells and the Simpsons have an easy life and get away with so much, when I have to pay such a price for wanting the domestic peace they take for granted?

Then he stopped himself, and took a deep breath. He thought of Christ on the cross. A bit of recitative from the *Messiah* came into his head again. It was from Psalm 69: *He looked for some to have pity on him, but there was no man, neither found he any to comfort him.* No one has suffered like you, Lord, have suffered, he reminded himself. It was true. This was nothing by comparison with the torture of crucifixion. Giving your life for your friends was what Christianity was all about. Stevie was his lover and he would protect him at all costs.

Early on Saturday evening, Nick Melling came out of the Arthurs' house and could not stop himself from pausing in the driveway and closing his eyes. It had been an appalling strain. Daisy had been in bed, which had created far too intimate an atmosphere, particularly as her mother was too tired to lever herself upstairs to chaperone.

Mrs Arthur slept in what was the front living room – an arrangement that had made Nick feel uncomfortable on his rare visits to Daisy's. As soon as he crossed the threshold at 8 Tarn Acres, he felt as if he was being lured into some female lair, though at least Nancy Arthur had taste – unlike most people in Tarnfield, he thought. This time, as he went up the stairs with leaden footsteps, Nancy had stood watching him anxiously from the hall, with that awful voyeuse Babs Piefield gawping behind her, mouth open in excitement.

Daisy's pink frilly bedroom had come as a shock. Her posters and cuddly toys had unnerved him, though he'd reminded himself that Daisy was only in her twenties and had used this bedroom since her teens. But the whole environment was at odds with the mission he had steeled himself to accomplish – giving Daisy the spiritual strength to survive the ordeal of finding Yvonne dead. Why couldn't she have been sitting in an easy chair, with coffee and biscuits to hand and a reassuring log fire in the grate? Or if she *had* to be in bed, why wasn't it the crisp white virginal room he had imagined in the past, with Daisy propped up as a sort of Victorian nun, waiting to receive his blessing? It was hard to operate with Piglet and My Little Pony looking back at him. And Daisy had been so hysterical. She'd actually tried to pull him towards her at one point. It had been ghastly. He had been reduced to suggesting counselling, which wasn't what he had planned. He had wanted to give Daisy all the support she needed himself, not turn to secular agencies. After all, he was 'a gifted young priest'; the Bishop said so. So why was this all too much?

Nick opened his eyes, taking in the little crescent of neat executive homes which he had come to hate. He had walked to Tarn Acres. He had a small car in the garage, but he despised it after the Boxster. When he felt confident, as he had earlier that afternoon, he was capable of dealing with Tarnfield on foot. He could even imagine himself as the benign, much-loved parish priest, nodding and smiling at grateful parishioners as he walked through the streets like an East End father. But when he felt defeated, which was so often the case in the village, all he wanted was to get back into the carapace of his sports car and hide from everyone.

As he expected, he'd hardly walked a few yards when he heard the sound of someone running after him. It was Kevin Jones.

'Nick! I saw you coming out of Daisy's. We really need to talk, don't we?'

Nick tried to smile. Why couldn't these people leave him alone? Couldn't they see that he was under strain too? More strain than they were, actually. On top of everything, he had to go through all these tedious, wretched visits, and mouth all these trite sentences, and all the time he was screaming to be on his own so that he could put his thoughts in order. It was too cruel.

'Oh, hi, Kevin. I was lost in thought. To be honest, I really need to get back to the vicarage and, er, get some stuff together . . .'

'Oh, I know, it's a bit frantic, isn't it? But we do need to talk, and Janice put the kettle on as soon as she saw you. A nice cuppa's just what you need.'

Kevin smiled the smile of the totally self-centred, and pulled Nick around by the arm. 'We've got some nice ginger cake from Asda, too,' he chuckled. Nick felt physically sick.

In the bland living room of the Joneses' house, ignoring the residue of toys and books on the patchy beige shag-pile carpet, Nick tried to calm his pulse and restrain his impatience while Kevin bombarded him with questions.

'Yes, the Bishop is coming to see me. Tonight,' he answered. 'The question is whether we need to have some sort of rededication after a violent death in the church.'

'I think all that is so much bollocks,' said Kevin forcefully. 'It's awful that Yvonne fell off a ladder but Jesus is everywhere, Nick, and if he can be at wars and scenes of carnage, then he can still be at All Saints.'

Nick had come to terms with the all-seeing mysterious omnipotence of God a long time ago. Some things couldn't be explained. For example, as he heard Kevin talking somewhere just outside his consciousness, he wondered why some people were gifted and some people stupid. But, like all these things, it wasn't for him to say. It was God's will. He sighed, closed his eyes, and opened them to find Kevin's excited face inches away from his own, breathing sickly ginger cake fumes at him.

'This is our chance, Nick. We can sweep through now and get rid of all that pointless ceremonial stuff. You've got to do it, man. We don't know how the Lord works, but we've got to take the chances he gives us. And in the end nothing is bigger than your Vision.'

Not for the first time, Nick regretted confiding in Kevin. During a moment of lonely soul-searching six months earlier, he'd been interrupted by Kevin at the vicarage door. Nick had invited him in and told him about how he envisaged All Saints developing – how he wanted it to become an invigorated parish with a whole new tradition, which he, Nick Melling would orchestrate.

'Yes!' Kevin had said ecstatically. 'Let's make it a place for young families with real commitment. Not a shrine to Tarnfield toadies!'

Now, the Vision seemed a scary thing. There had been a few times since the discovery of her body when Nick had wondered if Yvonne's death was a ghastly sort of mistake, an anomaly in God's plan, an indication that he wasn't handling things well at All Saints. But as he looked back into Kevin's eyes, he suddenly thought – yes, he's right. I must stop reverting to all my old, sentimental, half-baked ideas about death. God is God and in His wisdom He allowed Yvonne to die. Just because Kevin is fat, unattractive and gauche doesn't mean he isn't right. He believes in me. He sees this as an opportunity, which it is. And God sends His messages in many ways – maybe Kevin Jones is the Lord's despatch rider! I must stop indulging in regret and agonizing over things. Nick gulped his tea and stood up, feeling new strength.

'Thank you, Kevin,' he said. 'You're right. Today marks

a new stage in the spiritual development of Tarnfield. And I'm its leader.'

'Good on yer, Nick. I knew you'd come through it!'

The Bishop of Norbridge graced Tarnfield vicarage with his presence that evening. He was hugely relieved to find that Nick Melling was coping. In fact, he was doing better than that. He was on fire with keenness! The Bishop acknowledged that it was, of course, dreadful that someone had been killed in the church. It was an accident, but it was very nasty nevertheless, and it could have really upset someone less intelligent and less, well, *classy*, than Melling. His main worry had been that he would find that Nick was out of his depth, or much worse, wanting to resign, but thank God that wasn't the case.

True, it did seem a little extreme to be talking about clearing the church of traditionalists and starting again. But the Bishop flattered himself that he knew his man. As always with bright young enthusiasts, pragmatism would temper all that ardour and he was sure Nick wouldn't feel quite so polemical in the morning. And the main thing was – Melling was still functioning, and not looking for expensive or time-consuming support!

As he went out to his car, the Bishop smiled to himself. Ghastly things will happen in the best-run parishes, he thought, but with luck this could be weathered. His Lordship didn't want any more crises at All Saints after that business with old George Pattinson. Fortunately Pattinson was out of the way now. This latest incident was just a bit of bad luck, irrelevant to the real job of the vicar.

So, hopefully, there was nothing to worry about. Melling was a good chap, just as he'd always said. And he should know – after all, they'd been to the same college!

Inside the vicarage, after midnight, Nick started to make a list. Now Phyllis and Yvonne were dead, who else from All Saints had to go?

24

Whitsun Eve into Whit Sunday

The end of all things is at hand; be ye therefore sober and watch unto prayer.
From the Epistle for the Sunday after Ascension Day, 1 Peter 4:7

'I've been waiting for you for over an hour.' Monica Bell was sitting in the living room when Frank came home on Saturday evening. 'Why didn't you phone?'

''Cos I took the old truck, and you know there's no hands-free phone in there. Keep your hair on!'

'Oh God!' Monica was thinking of Yvonne Wait. Despite police discretion, most of the village knew by now that she had been found dead with her hair cropped.

'What's wrong?' Frank advanced on his wife, who had collapsed on to the sofa and was holding her head in her hands. This wasn't like Monica. He was used to a bit of shrewish telling-off, but he had rarely seen her look despairing.

'Haven't you heard?' she mumbled.

'Heard what?' But Monica didn't answer. Instead, she looked up at him, her face white and her eyes red-rimmed. Her happiness and security depended on what Frank would say next. If he knew nothing about Yvonne's death, he would go on quizzing her and it would be clear to anyone that he was innocent. But if he didn't . . .

Frank looked at his wife, and tried to read what was in her face. This strained, silent woman wasn't his Monica.

'Is this about Yvonne Wait?' he said forcefully. 'Because she's not going to be a threat to us any more!'

Instead of his words reassuring her, he saw his wife open her mouth in a soundless scream. Then she gagged, and recovered herself to say, 'How did you know Yvonne Wait was dead?'

'Good God. I didn't. What happened?'

'You know fine well, Frank Bell.' Monica groaned. It seemed like the end of the world for her. She stood up sharply and pushed past him out of the living room. He heard her feet pounding up the stairs, then the slam of the bedroom door.

At the same time, Jane Simpson felt that the atmosphere in Tarnfield House had changed for the better. Jeff had been out playing golf, and when he came home at four o'clock, feeling rather mellow after a good lunch at the nineteenth hole, she rushed into the hall where he was hanging up his Barbour in the dark cupboard under the stairs, and told him all about Yvonne's death.

'. . . and the ambulance has only just gone,' she panted. 'I could see it out of the window. The police are there and they've been questioning Suzy Spencer and Robert Clark, and little Daisy Arthur. But no one's said anything about Frank.'

'Frank?' Jeff had driven home automatically, enjoying a cigar in the car where Jane couldn't complain about the smell, listening to his Sinatra CD. As he slewed the Volvo round the country roads, he knew that things were taking a turn for the better. True, Russell was still a nightmare, but it had been at least three months since any major problem, and Jeff felt he could cope with being ignored by his son, as long as he didn't have to dole out any more money.

He had been thinking about Frank Bell, too. He had come to feel a grudging admiration for him since their summit lunch meeting. Perhaps it had been some sort of fellow feeling, but he had sensed that Frank had 'poked' Yvonne too, as he put it to himself. Ten years ago he'd have been mad with jealousy, but now it made Jeff feel

191

tougher all round. Frank wasn't the only one with new resolve.

So, when he heard the news from his breathless wife, for at least two minutes he kept his head in the cupboard before backing out into the hall and facing her.

'You mean people think Yvonne fell?'

'Absolutely. I've spoken to Monica . . .'

'What did she say?' Jeff asked sharply.

'Well . . .' Jane looked thoughtful. 'She didn't say anything really. I said I didn't think that had been the plan.'

'What hadn't been the plan?'

'To get rid of Yvonne by pushing her off a ladder.'

'For God's sake, woman! D'you know what you're saying?'

But as he shouted at her, Jeff was thinking, perhaps the silly cow is right. Perhaps everyone really does think Frank did it. He straightened up, and as he stood there he felt a wave of what he could only describe as peace. Yvonne was dead, and he wasn't in the frame.

'Frank must be braver than we thought,' he said reflectively.

There was a long silence while Jane waited for him to speak. It had always been Jeff who decided on Simpson family policy, and Jane who implemented it. Then his wife saw something she hadn't seen for weeks, not since lunch at the Bells'. Jeff was smiling. And not the usual sneer but a real grin. For someone whose idea of affection was 'pulling your leg', a sort of teasing abusive banter, a proper smile from Jeff was a rare and welcome thing.

'I think this calls for a celebration,' he said. 'There's a bottle of bubbly in the cellar, Janey. You go and get it while I visit the little boys' room, and then I'll get the glasses.'

Jane could hear him whistling 'My Way' as he went up the stairs. I think I'll do Chicken Supreme and defrost some Black Forest cheesecake, she thought. And tonight, we'll eat in the dining room.

She went into the kitchen and took a recipe book off the shelf. It was sticky with dust and grease. I should try harder, she thought. She'd forgotten how nice it was to see

Jeff smile. She put the book down on the table and pushed all the usual rubbish to one side – the circulars, the free newspaper and some junk mail. And then she remembered that a letter had come for Russell that morning, with rather girlie writing. Perhaps things were changing there too, she wondered. Life would certainly be improving if Jeff was cheering up and Russell getting himself a girlfriend!

Jane started humming like her husband as she read over her favourite recipe, only her tune wasn't 'My Way': it was something by Dusty Springfield, half forgotten. After a minute, she thought she had better put Russell's letter somewhere he'd be bound to see it.

Such a pretty colour, she had murmured happily to herself as she propped the lilac envelope on the dresser.

It was later that night that Robert Clark found himself in Church Cottage, a glass of whisky in his hand. In front of him, Alan Robie was at his theatrical best, oozing bonhomie, leaning forward from time to time to rearrange the artificial logs in his gas flame-effect fire, which was surrounded by marble gleaming so white that it could never have been within yards of any real smoke.

'So you're saying that you think Yvonne's death might not have been an accident? Oh really, old boy . . .'

'I know it sounds ridiculous, Alan. But you and I both know that someone had been tampering with the body. Yvonne Wait would never have had her hair cut down to the roots at the front like that. Look, I might as well be honest with you. Stevie was seen coming out of the church this morning.'

'By whom?'

'Never mind who saw him –'

'It was Suzy Spencer, wasn't it?'

'It doesn't matter, Alan. Look, I like Stevie and I respect you. But you should know that the police will be investigating this death properly. They aren't going to believe this was an accident too.'

'What do you mean, "too"?'

'Oh, come on, Alan. Don't you think it's weird that Phyllis and Yvonne have both died in the church?'

'You think the two deaths are linked?' Suddenly Alan leant forward, and his voice sounded low, sensible and natural. 'You think that if Yvonne was attacked, then Phyllis might have been attacked as well? By the same person?'

'That's exactly what I think.'

Alan leant back in his Liberty chintz winged chair. This changed everything. Stevie was certainly a suspect when it came to Yvonne, but there was no way he could be implicated in Phyllis's death. He hardly knew the woman.

'All right,' he said quietly, all hint of drama gone from his voice. 'I'll tell you the truth. Yvonne was blackmailing Stevie. And Stevie did go into the church this morning. But it was purely coincidental. And he had nothing to do with Phyllis Drysdale.'

'But you would say that, wouldn't you?'

'Because Stevie's my partner? I know Stevie like the back of my hand. I know he's flighty and unfaithful and camp and sometimes a bit ridiculous. And of course I can't be sure. But I don't think he attacked Yvonne. Even though he can be a fool at times.'

There was a yelp from the doorway. Alan leapt to his feet. Stevie was standing there, fully dressed. He turned into the little porch, and grabbed his Barbour from the peg. Alan was after him in seconds. He grabbed his own anorak and followed Stevie outside.

'Stevie!' he shouted. 'Come back . . .' But the heavy rain which had been rehearsing all day was now coming down in sheets. Alan's cry was lost in the wind and wetness. 'Wait for me!' he shouted over his shoulder to Robert. He sounded more exasperated than worried. 'I'll bring him back.'

Robert heard the sound of a car starting up. He had the feeling that these flounce-outs were a familiar part of the Church Cottage routine. He settled into the sofa, and waited for a while, confident that Alan would be back with

Stevie in tow. All that would be needed was a grovelling apology.

But after fifteen minutes, nobody had returned to Church Cottage. It was nearly midnight. This is ridiculous, Robert thought, I want to go and tell Suzy what's happened. Alan couldn't expect him to wait forever.

He slammed the front door shut behind him and walked into the wind and rain up the hill, past the church, and round the corner to the dark half moon of houses which was Tarn Acres. There was still a light on in Suzy's hall. He knocked softly on the glass panel of her door. She came running from the kitchen, in a pair of pyjamas and a bulky dressing gown. He felt a sudden delight at her enthusiasm and a need to be with her, inside in the warmth, away from the stinging rain and the darkness. 'It's me, Rob,' he said when the door opened a crack. It was years since he'd called himself that.

'Oh, thank goodness. I was worried about you. Coffee? Whisky? Tea?'

'Tea,' he said, sitting down and feeling suddenly tired. The thought of hot, comforting tea was just right.

'What did Alan say?'

He told her, in between sipping the welcome drink. Suzy sat opposite him, leaning forward, her eyes on him. When he'd finished, she said, 'I think you're right. I don't think Stevie did it either.'

She was interrupted by a hollow banging sound. Suzy jumped up and ran into the hallway. Robert followed her. The peremptory pounding on the front door was punctuated by the doorbell ringing two or three times.

'Bloody hell, that'll wake the kids,' Suzy hissed. She opened the door. Alan stood on the doorstep, hatless and soaked to the skin. She stood back to let him in, then pushed him into the living room where she could close the door and keep the sound in. He was already talking.

'You locked me out, Clark! I've been looking everywhere for Stevie and I can't find him.'

'I thought you had your keys with you because you took the car!'

'I didn't take the car, you fool. Stevie did. I've been running around the village like a madman trying to find him, but he's gone.'

Robert said quietly, 'But surely he'll come back when he's calmed down? What you said wasn't so bad. He'll see that. He's got a brain.'

'He might have a brain,' Alan shook his head and slumped on to Suzy's sofa like a big wet dog, 'but he hasn't got a driving licence.'

25

Whit Sunday

*Grant us by the same Spirit to have a right judgement
in all things.*
From the Collect for Whit Sunday

There had been a light on all night at All Saints vicarage. Nick Melling had been pacing the floors with a growing sense of excitement. At seven o'clock in the morning – taut with tiredness, his heart skipping into his mouth every time he heard a noise, adrenalin racing – he marched briskly out of the house. In one hand was a flapping poster, in the other a box of drawing pins. He hardly noticed how fresh and clean everywhere looked after the lashing rain of the night before. The sky was already porcelain blue, with that sense of fragility that comes with the perfect English spring dawn. The churchyard was lush and green with spots of colour from the aubretia and the late tulips, and in the distance the dark fells were clearly drawn against the bowl of the sky like dramatic slashes from a charcoal pencil. Nick marched to the door of the church and, feeling like Martin Luther, he pinned his notice at eye level. *Whitsun services are cancelled owing to an accident in the church. Nick Melling will lead a short service of prayers for Pentecost at noon.*

And that was it. No more compromise, no more commit-tees, no more conciliation. There would be a proper spirit-ual leader in the community for the first time in generations. He had the Bishop's backing and that was all he needed, plus of course his God-given Vision. Keyed up by action, Nick felt he could cope with the final task he had to perform before the revitalization of All Saints would be properly under way – the announcement of his new executive role to his flock.

Of course, technically, the Parochial Church Council could vote against his initiatives and these days no vicar was supposed to be in total control. But Nick suspected that nobody at All Saints knew enough about church law to stand in his way, except perhaps Robert Clark. And as far as Nick was concerned, Robert Clark was one of the big-headed obstructive people who had to go. So a confrontation would be no bad thing, now he was strong enough to survive it. If God had dispensed with Mary and George, and Phyllis and Yvonne, there were no limits to what He would do to see Tarnfield transformed.

It wasn't too early, he thought, to pop in on the Jones family for breakfast. They'd probably be delighted to see him. Then he could hop over to the Arthurs' to find out how Daisy was and make up for the rather messy way he'd left things yesterday, which already seemed light-years away. That was in the past. The old, muddled, unfocused Nick Melling had been replaced overnight by this new man.

Janice Jones was astonished to hear her doorbell at seven thirty on Whit Sunday morning, and even more surprised to find the vicar on her doorstep. He looked alarmingly bright and cheerful, pink-faced and scrubbed. She was still in her dressing gown.

'Oh hello . . . we're just having breakfast.'

She was aware that Kevin was standing on the landing in his vest and boxer shorts. She couldn't call him down until he'd had a chance to get dressed. There was nothing for it but to ask Nick into the kitchen diner, where the baby was splattering mush all over the high chair, and three-year-old Zoe was watching lurid TV cartoons at a high decibel level.

'Coffee would be wonderful, thank you, Janice – instant is fine.'

What else does he think we have? Janice thought. She

put the kettle on and waited for Kevin to burst into the room. He'd be desperate to know why Nick was here. Nick started an attempt to talk playfully to Zoe, who didn't turn her eyes from the screen. Janice watched him. Nick had never shown the children any attention before. He seemed to find it hard to make jokes or light conversation. He wasn't good at it, she thought, for all his plans to turn All Saints into a vibrant church full of young couples and bright healthy kids. It went against the grain with Janice, but since Nick had chosen to ignore Rogation, there were times when she thought Kevin had got it wrong. He shouldn't have insisted that Nick clear the church of the over-fifties who had kept it going so long. At least they could tickle a baby under the chin, or push a buggy for you without looking as if they were committing a style crime.

'Nick!' Kevin came thundering downstairs in his tracksuit. 'Great to see you! I take it you've abandoned the eight o'clock communion service because of Yvonne? Good thing too. There's really no point just for a group of old farts. This could be a turning point, you know.'

'Absolutely!' Nick leant over his steaming mug of dark grey coffee, trying to ignore the fact that it smelt metallic, the cheapest brand the supermarket had to offer. It was remarkable that Kevin had hit exactly on the point. He told himself to overcome any snobbish feelings. They were hangovers from his past. Jesus had chosen dim-witted fishermen and venal tax collectors. None of them were any better than Kevin Jones, IT expert and blunt Yorkshireman.

'Kevin, today is the start of a new era. You were right all along. We must revitalize All Saints and turn it into a strong, vibrant, young parish. And the greatest of these is young! We have the Bishop's blessing and all that remains now is to get out there and do it.'

Janice was reminded of when the baby caught a nasty cold last winter. She'd been pink, flushed and overactive for a few hours, so Janice hadn't realized that it was feverishness – and not rude health! Into her mind came an old phrase of her mother's about things ending in tears. Far be it from her to interrupt two knowledgeable men like Nick and Kevin while they were discussing church matters, but then she thought of her mum again, and wondered where all this would leave the regular Tarnfield churchgoers.

'So what will you do?' she asked.

'Do?' Her husband looked at her with a mixture of astonishment and irritation. 'You know, love. We've talked about it. First thing, Nick's got to send a note round telling people that changes are afoot. He's got to tell them directly that there'll be no more flowers, no more stupid "holier than thou" people in choir robes, no more old-fashioned hymns, just one big, happy family service at ten o'clock every Sunday. Right, Nick?'

'Absolutely!' Nick repeated, even more emphatically. It would be a lot easier to have just one service. For a start, he would only have to prepare one sermon, and he could abandon the lectionary and the readings if he wanted to. In fact the whole style of the service would be up to him. It wouldn't be Anglicanism as everyone knew it, but it would be better, simpler, more meaningful, more focused on a real leader.

There was only one flaw in Kevin's proposal and that was the idea of sending a note round to people. That would mean more work, and Nick really didn't have time for that.

'I'll make a notice sheet and you can give it to people at the back of the church,' he said. 'I think that will be enough. There's a PCC meeting the week after next and they can discuss it there. I know a lot of people will think I'm a bastard,' he said joyously, 'but I don't care what they think. We need a Vision.'

And a lot of people will be really hurt, Janice thought.

'Perhaps you should talk to folk first?' she suggested tentatively.

'Like who? Robert know-it-all Clark? Or Lady Jane Simpson?' Kevin jeered.

'Well . . .' Janice paused, but she wasn't beaten. Kevin

had never really appreciated her doggedness. Janice Jones might not be the most glamorous woman around, but she was her mother's daughter underneath and she was tougher than most people thought. 'Don't you think you should at least talk to the other churchwarden – Tom Strickland?' she said.

Kevin and Nick both stared at her, open-mouthed. Nick looked bemused, as if he had forgotten that Tom existed. Kevin chuckled, recovering himself.

'Don't be daft. Tom won't kick up too much of a fuss. He used to act as if he was George Pattinson's right-hand man, but when George disappeared from the parish Tom stayed, didn't he? He'll toe the line. I mean, he needs the church more than the church needs him. What else has he got in life? Watching telly with Vera?' He chortled into his coffee mug, making slurping noises.

'I think Janice might have a point, though, Kevin,' Nick said, with a charmingly deferential nod in her direction. Janice blushed agonizingly, feeling annoyed with herself. In fact, Nick was thinking, she had a very good point, though perhaps she hadn't realized it. The last thing he needed was for someone like Strickland to make a fuss and complain to the Bishop. His Lordship would ignore any pleas from mere members of the congregation, Nick was sure of that, because it was far more important to retain the loyalty of a gifted young priest than to appease the moans of the middle-aged. But a churchwarden – well, that would mean messy resignations and, worse still, it would look as if he, Nick Melling, couldn't carry people with him. He sighed. This was going to be more complicated than he'd thought.

He had already calculated that he would lose more worshippers than he would gain, at least initially. That would mean fewer people giving money to the church. But he'd decided that one way of meeting any financial shortfall would be by pressurizing the Jones family to give more. After all, Janice came from a pretty wealthy local dynasty. They might not be very upmarket, but they did have money. And he himself had some rich and ageing relatives. A small legacy could possibly be made over to the parish to plug the gap. If he could get more bums on seats, the sort of young shapely bums he wanted, the takings would inevitably go up.

He went through a mental checklist.

Jane Simpson would stay. She liked being someone important in the church and had no intellectual pretensions. Neither had Monica Bell, but he thought she might be angry enough to leave on principle. Alan Robie would go, of course, making a big fuss about traditional values, but at least that would mean the grubby gay Nesbit was out of the way. Daisy would stay, and perhaps bring some of her lively young friends in, which would be rather nice. Suzy Spencer would have to go. She was the right demographic, but she had the wrong attitude. She had tried to talk to him a few times about her lack of real faith, but what could he say to that? If she had no faith, what was she doing in the church? She was an irritating know-all too, not as knowledgeable as Robert Clark, but she would dredge up her secondary school RE lessons and presume to quiz him. Of course she wasn't Oxbridge, but she could still be rather challenging. And that was tiring. If his parishioners couldn't be his educational equals, then it was best if they were dumb and devoted.

But Tom Strickland was dumb and difficult. Even in his enthusiasm Nick recognized that some people who would remain on his electoral roll were pretty needy types. Was Tom one of those? He wasn't sure. But he had to agree with Janice – who wasn't very bright either, but who had common sense – that it would be a good idea to keep Tom on board.

Either that or pray that he too could be removed like Phyllis and Yvonne.

During the pause, Kevin had been picking his nose, waiting for words of wisdom from Nick.

'Kevin, could you come with me to see if Tom's at home, as there's no eight o'clock service?'

'Yeah. Why not? I'll leave you to clean up, love – you don't mind, do you?'

Janice nodded. She followed Nick and her husband to the front door. As they were standing on the step, Sharon Strickland came running round the corner. She was wearing her usual denim miniskirt and shabby Ugg boots with an old parka jacket flung on top and a very grimy scarf, and was hurtling uncharacteristically through Tarn Acres.

'Sharon!' Kevin called in a hearty way. 'Hiya! We were just coming round to your house to see your dad!'

She stopped at his gate. 'You were? Well, you'd 'ave a job. He's in the Mid Cumbria. Half dead!'

26

Whit Sunday, continued

That it may please thee to preserve all that travel by land
or by water.
From the Litany

Suzy Spencer had slept only sporadically. But she'd managed to get her head down at about six o'clock, only to be woken two hours later by Jake leaning over her and prodding her, saying someone was banging at the door. For a confused minute she thought it must be Alan again, back from searching for Stevie. She told Jake to get dressed, and pulled on her jeans and a jumper. She ran downstairs and struggled, still half asleep, to open the door. Sharon Strickland was on the step.

'Hi, Suzy. I couldn't use my key 'cos you had the chain on. I came to say I can't help with the kids today. We've got to go the Mid Cumbria Hospital straight away.'

Sharon might be a churchwarden's daughter but she rarely went near All Saints. It was nothing to do with belief, more that it interfered with her Saturday night routine of having five pints and at least as many 'shots' in Carlisle before crashing at her boyfriend's. But even she had become caught up in the Whitsun preparations, and had offered to come and help.

'Start again, Sharon,' Suzy said. 'I'm a bit befuddled. So what's happened now?' She moved blearily towards the stimulus of a cup of coffee. Sharon followed her into the kitchen area.

'I know the service is off, 'cos of Yvonne. But I thought

you might still need me. And I can't come. 'Cos of me dad,' Sharon said patiently. 'He's in intensive care. Some bugger ran him down last night. He's got a fractured skull and broken ribs and a broken leg and he's in concussion. So I can't help out this morning.'

'My God, that's awful! Have you been over to see him?'

'Nah, me mam tried last night in a taxi. But they took the back roads and there were so much standing water at Tarn Ford they turned back. Then it were so late she came home. So we're going this morning.'

Suzy stopped with the kettle in her hand. 'How awful for your dad! Poor Tom. It was a really wet night. Was he on foot?'

'Yeah. He won't drink and drive. Someone saw the dog barking by the side of the road and rang police. If he'd been left there all night in that rain, he'd 'ave bin dead by morning.'

'Do the police know who did it?'

'Nah. Anyhow, don't bother wi' coffee or owt for me. I'd best get back.' She smiled, a beautiful smile that transformed her podgy face. Fleetingly, Suzy was reminded of someone else. 'Me dad'll be fine. He's tough.'

'Well, give him my regards,' said Suzy. 'And let me know if there's anything I can do. I mean it, Sharon. If your mum needs a lift . . .'

Sharon's smile turned to a cheeky grin. 'Lady Jane is taking us to the hospital. She's family. I'll see meself out, Suzy. Tara.'

'Bye, Sharon. And thanks for letting me know.'

Sharon beamed back at her, and bounced up the hall to the door. Suzy went on drying the mug for her coffee. Like everyone in Tarnfield, she knew that Tom Strickland drank, and that he didn't always go to the Plough. Sometimes he walked half a mile to the Scar Head, a drab stone-built alehouse that crouched down at the side of the road. It was reputed to hold lock-ins until midnight and beyond on Saturday nights. Tom must have been run over walking home, Suzy thought. And on such a wretched night . . . a bad night for anyone to have been out driving a car.

Particularly someone without a licence.

She went over to the phone and looked at it. It was Sunday morning and it was early, but not that early. She knew the number for The Briars off by heart. She dialled and waited for a reply.

'Hi, Rob,' she said. 'Did Stevie turn up last night?' She closed her eyes when he said no, he hadn't heard from Alan. 'Then I should tell you that Tom Strickland's in intensive care. He's been knocked down by a hit-and-run driver.'

'What? And you think that it might have been Stevie?'

'Yes. Don't you?'

'Looks like it. I'll call Alan now.'

An hour later, Robert, Suzy and Alan were back in her living room. Alan was white-faced, and wearing a thick grey fleece over a black corduroy shirt and trousers. He still couldn't stop himself shivering. Suzy handed him some tea.

'So there's been no sign of Stevie?' she said. Alan shook his head. For a moment she thought he was going to cry, but he pulled himself together.

'There's no answer on his mobile, and nothing on the voicemail at the house.' Even as he said this, he brightened. The thought of the answering machine seemed to cheer him up. Who knows, at this very moment Stevie might be calling Church Cottage, or even coming home? Alan made to rise out of his seat as if there was good news. Then he remembered there wasn't, and crumpled back on the sofa.

'Alan,' Robert said softly, 'Stevie's disappearance is going to make him look guilty as hell. If the police find out that he was in the church and now he's gone . . .'

'Don't you think I haven't thought of that?' Alan exploded angrily. 'And now that Tom Strickland's been injured, you've landed poor Stevie with the blame for that too!'

Suzy caught Robert's eye. Alan saw the glance and slumped.

'Oh God, I don't know.' He rolled his large head around as if there was a monster weight on his shoulders. 'Look, it could have been anyone. The hit-and-run driver probably didn't even see Tom till it was too late. You know what he was like, skulking along those back roads full of drink. It was usually a wonder he got to eight o'clock communion on a Sunday morning, and sometimes he smelt the worse for wear then!'

Robert nodded. 'But it looks bad for Stevie. He went to the church yesterday, and now he's done a runner.'

'It wasn't Stevie who pulled Yvonne off that ladder! I've been thinking about it all night and I'm sure it wasn't him. Anyway, he told me there was someone else in the church, in the flower vestry.'

Suddenly he leapt to his feet.

'I'm going home now. Stevie's probably back there as we speak, with his tail between his legs. And I appreciate your concern about Tom Strickland's accident. But I'm sure that's nothing to do with us either. When Stevie gets back, we'll go to the police like you said, and tell them everything we know about Yvonne. Don't worry. It will be OK.'

He smiled, a false dawn stretching across his face.

'You'll let us know as soon as you hear from him?'

'Of course.' Alan looked awful, white and taut, but with a crazed pink wet-lipped grin. He left them with an exaggerated wave, and slammed the front door behind him before walking jauntily up the path. Suzy wondered how long his grotesque optimism would last.

'What do you think?' she said quietly to Robert.

'I think it's highly likely that Stevie Nesbit hit Tom in the dark. This is a quiet part of the county. There aren't that many cars about on the back roads and we know Stevie was in a state.'

'I wonder where he went. Sharon said that the Tarn

flooded at the ford. Her mother tried to get through that way by taxi last night, but had to turn back.'

'He could have gone down to the motorway but my guess is that he stayed round here, and maybe slept in the car. He'll come back today. There isn't much potential for a drama if he stays away, is there?'

'What about the police?'

'I suppose they'll be making inquiries. They must be treating it as suspicious.'

Suzy shivered. She was finding it impossible to keep warm. The heating was on full. She went and stood with her bottom on the radiator and her arms folded across her chest.

'I need something reassuring to do. What's Nick suggesting about the church services today?'

'There's a sign up saying they're cancelled but that there's a service of prayers for Pentecost at twelve o'clock. Do you want to go?'

'I suppose I ought to face it. Oh, I really don't know.'

'Can't Jake mind Molly? Why don't I take you down in my car? We have to go back into All Saints sometime. I don't have that much confidence in Nick Melling, but at least he's opened the church.'

Suzy was reluctant, but she didn't want All Saints to become a no-go area. It would look different now Yvonne's body had gone, and she had to admit that Nick Melling had shown some guts in going ahead with a service.

'I'll get my jacket,' she said.

The children seemed fine, unaffected by the crisis around them. Molly had been disappointed about the Whitsun service, but she seemed to understand that something sad and grown-up had happened which didn't really concern her, and now she was happily working on her book of stickers. Jake was doing homework. He'd grumbled about it before Alan came, and had made a plea to go out in Matthew Bell's old banger again, but Suzy had vetoed that. Then he'd sulked, but now he seemed to have recovered. Even so, for the first time Suzy wished

Nigel was nearer than Newcastle. She was a little bit shaky this morning and some parental solidarity would have been nice.

But the kids would be fine on their own for half an hour. She followed Robert to his car.

27

Whitsun Eve into Whit Sunday, continued

*It was ordained for the mutual society, help, and comfort
that the one ought to have of the other, both in prosperity
and in adversity.*
From the Solemnization of Matrimony

On Saturday night, for the first time in thirty years of
marriage, Frank Bell had slept in the guest room. It made
him uncomfortable in more ways than one. Bloody Yvonne
Wait, he thought. She was almost as much trouble dead
as alive.

Monica had refused to speak to him, and he had been
able to hear her snuffling through the bedroom door. At
about eight o'clock, when he finally realized she wasn't
coming downstairs, he'd defrosted a luxury fish pie, eaten
it and left the dirty plate in the sink. He'd just been
deliberating about whether or not to go down to the
Plough when the phone rang. It was Jeff Simpson, and he
was pissed.

'Frank!' He sounded conspiratorial. 'Sounds like we're
off the hook, old man. Any idea how it happened?' There
was something in the wet, slightly slurping, and prurient
tone to his voice that made Frank stop before he replied.

'You mean Yvonne?'

'What else, sonny? Bit of amazing luck!' The word lingered fatly in the air.

'I wouldn't say that . . .' Frank thought that in all
decency a woman's death shouldn't be called lucky. Even
if it was.

'Not luck, eh? More good management, Frankie? I say, and I know I shouldn't, well done you!'

'What d'you mean?'

'Don't be coy, old chap. I always thought you had the steel to get things done. And no silly scruples.'

What's he on about? Frank thought. Then he understood. He's accusing me of pulling the stupid bitch off the ladder! This could be bloody dangerous! But his worry at Jeff's allegation evaporated almost immediately at the warmth of the flattery in the older man's voice.

Jeff was saying: 'So we can breathe a sigh of relief, can't we? How about popping over for a snifter with me and Janey?'

'No, Jeff, much as I'd love to, Monica and I are having an early night.'

'Yes, well . . .' Jeff laughed heartily. 'I suspect you're rather done in. Want to rest on your laurels, eh?'

'Something like that,' Frank said, and echoed the hearty laughter. If snobby old Jeff Simpson wanted to treat him like a local hero, then why not? He put the phone down and pounded upstairs.

'Monica, love,' he said through the bedroom door, 'can't you come down now? Jeff Simpson has just been on the phone. You'll never guess what he said.'

But Monica didn't have to guess. She had picked up the extension in the bedroom and heard the whole conversation. She lay on the bed, her knuckles rammed in her eye sockets to try and blank out the pictures behind the lids. Eventually she heaved herself up and took two of the over-the-counter sleeping tablets she rarely needed, from the drawer in the bedside table. Then she scrubbed herself clean in the en-suite bathroom, got into bed and pulled the duvet over her head. For an hour, she listened to the rain pounding on the windows, waiting to sleep.

Before the relative relief of drifting restlessly, she decided that in the morning she would get up at daybreak and drive to her daughter's in Carlisle. She needed to distance herself from Frank. She wouldn't rouse Matthew, who'd either be comatose or still out with his mates. She'd leave a message for him on his mobile, and then she would wait for Frank to phone and talk to her. She was angry as well as frightened.

She had her son and daughter to think of. Frank was just the sort of idiot to say something stupid. And if that happened, she'd be implicated if she tried to help him. If she were to be prosecuted for being an accessory, what would happen to Matthew? Or to her daughter Joanne, who was married to a builder whose attachment to her wasn't entirely based on deep romantic love? If she tried to quiz Frank now, it would be all bluster and defensiveness, and he would immediately look to her to bail him out. But this was far, far worse than the things she'd sorted out for him in the past. She wasn't going to do it again.

It was the worst night of Monica Bell's life. How could Frank screw everything up like this? The man's vanity was unbelievable, virtually confessing to Jeff Simpson like that, because he felt flattered. Jeff might be a crap businessman but he was a manipulative bastard. It would suit him to divert suspicion on to Frank.

At six o'clock in the morning she crept downstairs, and slipped outside.

Frank heard the door close in his sleep. He woke suddenly and pounded downstairs after her, his feet still in their socks from the night before, slipping on the wood flooring in the hallway. 'Monica!' he shouted. But she had gone.

Frank didn't know what to do. What had happened? Had someone told Monica about his one bonk with Yvonne Wait? But who? There was nobody who knew for certain – though some people like Babs Pie-face had guessed. Anyway, he would just deny it again. Why was Monica so worked up? He knew his wife would have taken her mobile, and he guessed she was on her way to their daughter's. Monica was a good old stick, but she did go over the top sometimes. It was stupid, her getting so aerated. Yvonne Wait was dead and it looked like an accident. So they were all in the clear. That was all that mattered.

I'll call her when she's had time to calm down, he thought. In the meantime I'll have a fry-up.

An hour later, he wondered why Matthew hadn't come downstairs. It was very early, but the smell of bacon usually got him out of his pit. He went upstairs, and knocked on his son's door. There was no reply. He gingerly put his head round. There was never any knowing what Matthew might be up to in his bedroom. But instead of the orgiastic scenes he expected, Matthew's room was empty and his bed undisturbed. Oh well, Frank, thought. His son was out on the razz again. He was probably at the Simpsons', with Russell.

He knew he should call Monica but he put it off. Women! He smiled as he pottered around the house till midday, when he went to the Plough for a pint. Jeff Simpson greeted him like a long-lost friend and immediately ordered a malt whisky for him. Frank smirked back. But then he noticed that the barman seemed less friendly than usual. A couple from Manchester who came up at weekends waved to him enthusiastically as they always did, but the real locals couldn't meet his eye. Frank was aware that people edged away from him at the bar. What's Jeff been hinting? he thought.

And for the first time the reality of his situation hit him. Thanks to Jeff's big mouth, his friends and neighbours suspected that he had killed Yvonne. They might all have wanted to be rid of her, but they stopped short of congratulating him. Not everyone thought he was a hero. And killing her was a damn sight worse than screwing her.

He thought of Monica's white, terrified face. That explained it. She wasn't outraged, she was scared. This wasn't jealousy; it was fear. A bit of boasting had put him in the frame in the eyes of the whole of Tarnfield. Bloody Nora! He knocked back the scotch. Then he strode out to his car, revved it like a boy racer, and set off towards Carlisle in search of his wife.

He put his foot down on the accelerator and left Tarn-field Scar behind him, its outcrop of granite cutting the blue sky like a hunchback.

Nick Melling faced his small congregation. He thought the fact that so few regulars had turned up was a sign things were moving in the right direction. Monica Bell wasn't there, nor Alan Robie and his little friend. Tom Strickland was in hospital reaping the consequences of his Saturday night drinking. Jane Simpson had been roped in to face her Strickland family responsibilities – a well-deserved smack in the face! There was no Daisy because she was still recovering. No Yvonne, because she was dead!

But there was an encouraging sprinkling of young couples who wanted to ensure their children got into the Church of England school in Norbridge. Nick never questioned their commitment, because they were just the sort of people the church needed, he told himself. And of course there were a few elderly people who came to church once in a while and who wanted to see the scene of the drama, but they were of no consequence.

But unfortunately there was also Robert Clark, with Suzy Spencer. Seeing them sitting there, together, reinforced Nick's determination. They weren't the sort of people he wanted at All Saints. They weren't committed to his Vision and they weren't young enough, or sexy enough, for the image of his parish. They would have to go. He would alienate them so much they would have no option. It was easy, really. It wouldn't be his fault.

Nick kept his sermon to a minimum. A tragedy had occurred, he told them, the day before the traditional date when the Church remembered the arrival of God's Holy Spirit. But that was just a tradition. The Holy Spirit was always with us, in ways we least expected. A death, however tragic and surprising, didn't alter that. He would lead prayers for Yvonne Wait, he announced, and people should try to remember her good points, but God's witness came to us through good times and bad, in happiness and in tragedy, in good people and bad people. His message was coming to us now. This death meant change.

Suzy tried not to look at Robert, but she knew him well enough now to realize that he was appalled by the way Nick was using Yvonne's death. She felt his body shifting in the pew, and he folded his arms and stared ahead. After they prayed for Yvonne, Nick asked them to pray for the future of the parish, and for the strength to see what might be needed to revitalize the place. This might be an opportunity, he said, to discover where All Saints really should be in the modern world.

Robert exhaled noticeably, and somewhere at the back of the church Kevin Jones said a loud and triumphant 'Amen'. When they stood up to go, Robert whispered to Suzy: 'I'm sorry we came. This isn't good.'

Kevin was standing at the door as they filed out. 'Have one of these,' he said, pushing a piece of paper at them. He was giving them out to everyone who was leaving. Suzy looked down at hers.

Dear Parishioner, she read: *There is never a good moment to bring in changes which may upset people, but perhaps Pentecost is as good a time as any, whatever personal tragedy, we may have witnessed this week* . . . She looked up at Kevin, who was grinning.

'Things have to move on, y'know,' he gloated. 'There'll be a PCC meeting, but I reckon Nick's pretty set on this . . .'

Robert had taken the paper and walked out. Suzy followed him. It didn't seem worth arguing with Kevin, who looked sleek with success. They said nothing until they were in the car; then Suzy asked: 'Have you read this? He's getting rid of the choir. And the Bible study group. What's going on?'

'Well, after a year of not knowing what sort of Anglican he is, he's finally decided. Kevin Jones has won, we've lost.'

'But can he do this?'

'Well, in theory we could fight him on the PCC. But I don't know, Suzy.' Robert put his head down on the steering wheel. Then he looked up. 'It's all a bit too much. I suppose we could try and persuade him not to be so extreme. And we can write to the Bishop. But this hardly seems the moment to start a battle.' He sounded weary.

They said nothing on the short drive to Tarn Acres. Suzy felt slightly sick as she got out of the car. I really can't take much more of this, she thought. I don't need to be here in this awful place, where everything that should be normal, sane and comforting is slightly mad. She had considered inviting Robert for lunch, but now she changed her mind. She wanted to cuddle the kids, hug Jake's big gangly limbs and feel Molly's squirmy little body clinging to her legs. She would ring her mum in Manchester and tell her they were coming down next week for the half-term holiday.

Outside the car, the North Country sky looked huge and mottled. It was clouding over. Tarnfield was cold and hostile. And Robert with his strange secret seemed like a lost soul, too far away for her to reach. Perhaps she should get away from the place altogether.

'I've left my mac on your banisters,' Robert said bleakly.

'Oh. You'd better come and get it.'

Well, she thought, he could go home as soon as he'd picked up his coat. And she would decide about whether to jettison all her plans and get herself and her children out of the village for good. She felt that Tarnfield was, literally, God-forsaken. She could go to her mum's, to Rachel's, anywhere. But she didn't want to stay here.

28

Whit Sunday, continued

O Merciful God, grant that the old Adam in this child
may be so buried . . .
From the Public Baptism of Infants

Suzy's key in the door met no resistance. Barbara Piefield,
who was wearing a smug look, opened it for her on the
other side.

'Hello! You're back. Your son knocked on my door and
asked me to babysit Molly till you came back.'

'What?'

'Jake. Your son. He's gone out. He left you a note.'

Suzy brushed past her into the dining area. On the table
was a note in Jake's messy handwriting. *Dear Mum, Have
done my homework. I thought you wouldn't mind. Back at
5 o'clock Jake.*

What was going on? Suzy took a deep breath, and tried
to steady her voice. 'That's really kind of you, Babs. But we
mustn't keep you any longer.'

'No?' Babs was looking Robert up and down.

'Really. Thank you. I'll see you out. It's been very kind
of you, especially at lunchtime.'

Babs smiled appraisingly at Robert, who smiled back but
said nothing.

'Well, I'll be off then. Bye-bye, Molly.'

Molly looked up from her crayons and gave Babs Piefield an insecure smile. When the front door shut behind
her, Molly ran and buried her head in Suzy's stomach.

'Are you all right, Molly?' Suzy asked.

'Yes, Mummy, but I don't feel hungry.'

'Where did Jake go?'

'That big boy came for him. Matthew Bell.'

'I thought so. Oh no!' Suzy whispered. Then she made an effort to sound breezy. 'Come on, Molly, you can have some chocolate biscuits before lunch just for once. I'm sure you're hungry enough for them.'

Molly looked as if she might cry. Suzy checked herself. She mustn't leave Molly straight away, though she was desperate to run to Jake's bedroom to see if his mobile phone was there. As soon as her daughter was munching her biscuit, Suzy pounded upstairs. The phone was on the charger beside her son's unmade bed. She felt an upsurge of fury and helplessness. Jake was out of contact. How could he do this to her?

And where was Nigel when she needed him? Then she steadied herself and sat on the bed. Jake had behaved stupidly but by and large he was good. He would be back at five o'clock and she would give him the bollocking of his life. But there was absolutely nothing she could do till he came home. And she had Molly to consider. She had to stay here and wait.

She looked at Jake's radio alarm clock. It was ten past one. He would be back in three hours and fifty minutes. Panic rose in her throat again, but she swallowed it, stood up, and started to go downstairs. As she stood on the landing, she stopped. She could hear the sound of giggling from the kitchen. She listened. Robert was talking to Molly, doing something that was making her shriek with laughter, all her insecurity gone. Suzy hurried down to join them, worried for a minute if Robert was tickling her or doing something unsuitable. He was a childless middle-aged man, after all. But he had been drawing in Molly's colouring book and she saw a caricature of herself – spiky yellow hair and baggy trousers, coat and scarf flailing.

'It's you, Mummy,' Molly yelped delightedly. Robert smiled at her, his face clear and open after all the tension of the morning. Suzy smiled back. She was glad now that he was here. Unlike Babs, there was no sign of judgement in Robert's look.

'Jake will be fine,' he said.

She glanced towards Molly. 'I'm sure he will.' There was no point in upsetting her.

'I mean it, Suzy. Once Jake's done this once, he won't want to do it again. Matthew Bell is a bit brainless. That's why he courts all these younger boys. He needs hero worship, and from what I've seen of Jake he's too independent to go along with that.'

'God, I hope you're right. Thanks for saying it, anyway, Robert. And there's nothing I can do except stay here in case Jake comes back. Would you like lunch with us? I've got a nut roast in the freezer. Not very Tarnfield, I know, but it's the best I can do.'

'That would be great.'

'You know, I was wondering on the way back from church about just getting the kids, throwing some clothes in a case, and getting out of here. I could go to Mum's. Or Rachel's . . .'

'No!' Robert made Molly jump and look up at him. He softened his tone. He was surprised himself at the strength of his voice, and his feeling of sudden anxiety. In the warmth of Suzy' s brightly coloured kitchen, with Molly's paints and crayons all over the counter, and the untidy heaps of utensils and books and magazines, he felt that the unpredictable coldness of late spring in Tarnfield had been kept at bay. With Mary, Tarnfield had always dictated their moods and Mary had called the tune. But in Suzy's house it was different.

They both worked hard on restoring a normal atmosphere, for Molly's sake. There was little he or Suzy could say in front of her about the Tarnfield deaths, or even Nick Melling's sudden extremism. Instead, they talked about what she was doing at school, and her friends in the village, and how the kitten was getting on. After lunch, Molly sleepily watched one of her DVDs while he and Suzy sat at the table over their coffee.

'I'm glad you didn't decamp to your mum's.' Robert felt

his heart beating uncomfortably. He wanted to say this, but he was unsure why.

Suzy raised her eyebrow. 'But I have no feelings for Tarnfield, except fear now. I think I'd rather get away than stay here in the hope of finding out who's behind these deaths. I'm not like Mary, with a vested interest in the place.'

'You're not like Mary at all,' he said. The remark hung in the air like the steam from the mugs. Then it disappeared. Suzy hadn't responded, and he was glad.

'Are you completely unconcerned about the person who did it? The flower arranger?' he asked.

'Well . . .' Suzy wasn't sure. She had put Yvonne's death to the back of her mind since Jake's disappearance, but suddenly her dead face appeared in front of Suzy's eyes. She shook her head, but it wouldn't go away. And what about the Bible message in the leaves? They had both seen it.

'OK,' she said, 'let's give it one last try. Who do you think killed Yvonne? And what do you think the hellebore message was really about?'

Robert said softly: 'It has to be someone who knows about the flowers.'

'But that could be anyone. Even Stevie.'

'Or someone like Frank who isn't a churchgoer but who knows where everything is kept. He must have gone to the church yesterday to deliver the ladder. People of his age used to learn passages from Isaiah by heart at school. You know, the bit about "He was despised and rejected of men." It was supposed to be a foretelling of the coming of Jesus.'

'And was it?'

'Well, some people say it's about Isaiah himself. And the virgin bearing a child – well, that could be about Isaiah's own young wife. People think he had three sons. Believe it or not, one was called Immanuel – "God with us"!'

'But I thought Immanuel was the name for Jesus!'

'It depends on whether you think Isaiah was referring to his own eldest son, or to the Son of God to come. That's why Isaiah is so important to Christians, particularly as a justification for Jews to be converted – you know, it can be read as their own prophet foretelling the coming of Jesus. Matthew's gospel is particularly good at making Jesus sound like the Messiah the Jews had been waiting for. He refers back to Isaiah a lot.'

'So there's one example of a prophet *with* honour in his own country!'

'Yes.' Robert smiled. 'At least three prophets, actually. But it's the first Isaiah we all know best, Isaiah of Jerusalem. As distinct from Isaiah of Babylon, in the exile, and the other Isaiah after their return.'

It was surprisingly interesting, Suzy thought. 'So why did you get into all this?'

'I wanted to be a writer originally. I think Mary wanted to be a writer's wife. But we had rather a rocky patch early on, and I never really got started. A little later on, Mary and I were estranged for a short while. I started reading about the Church, and about theology, and it went from there.'

Suzy looked into her empty cup. So Mr and Mrs Perfect had had their problems, even if she hadn't been screwing George Pattinson. This was a turn-up. It would teach her to pigeonhole people. It had even taken her mind off Jake for a few minutes. She looked at the kitchen clock. Half past three. Another hour and a half to wait till the time he said he'd be home. It was too long for a boy of thirteen to be out in a car. Or was she being over-protective? Then she thought of the pile-up on the motorway at Easter, and jumped up, wanting to do something, anything, rather than sit.

'I'm just going to put a load of washing in. It's great now the machine's fixed.'

Robert smiled. He recognized her need for sudden bustle. Waiting for the results of Mary's cancer tests, he had decorated the spare room in frenzy.

'Make yourself some more coffee,' she added.

She needs someone to be here, he thought. And I'm glad it's me. He got up to put the kettle on, feeling strange but not uncomfortable about doing things in Suzy's kitchen. He heard her upstairs, every move audible in the modern house with its wooden floors. Odd, he thought, that there was so much parquet in Tarn Acres.

Then the telephone bell shrieked through the house. Suzy was on the landing with the washing basket, but she threw it down and hurtled into her bedroom, picking up the phone after the third ring. Robert could hear her through the open door.

'Hello . . . hello . . .'

The silence seemed to last forever. Then Suzy said, 'But how did you find him? Yes. Yes please. Oh, but should you be driving?'

There was another pause; then he heard Suzy say, in a purposefully calm voice, 'I'm sorry, of course. That's great. Thank you so much.' Then she came scrambling down the stairs, the washing forgotten, and stood in front of Robert, torturing one of her longer lengths of hair distractedly, grinning at the same time.

'What a relief! Though it's a bit weird. That was Stevie Nesbit. He was on his way home with two friends from Lancaster when they found Jake. They're bringing him back.'

'Where was he?'

'Sitting in a bus shelter. On his own.'

29

Whit Sunday afternoon and evening

Dearly beloved, forasmuch as all men are conceived and born in sin . . .
From the Public Baptism of Infants

In the living room of his sister Joanne's house in Carlisle, Matthew Bell was yelling at his parents.

'So what's going on, Mam? I was staying over at Russell's and we got up late. Then there were things I had to do. But you started sending me weird messages, and when I called Dad he said you'd buggered off over here.'

'Calm down, Matt,' Frank said, aware that his authority was wearing very thin, but scared that his son-in-law might get back from the rugby club before they'd got this all sorted out. His daughter was sitting white-faced on the sofa.

'Calm down? You can fucking talk, Dad!'

'Matthew! Watch your language.' For the first time since her son had arrived in a fury, Monica sounded like herself again. 'It's quite simple. I left you a message saying that Dad and I had some things to discuss, and that in the meantime, I was at our Joanne's. I said you were welcome to come over, but not to behave like this! I didn't want to say more than that on the phone.'

'Well, it sounded weird to me. So what's going on?'

Wearily, Monica told him. Yvonne Wait was dead, and the police were involved. His father had been at the scene and had no alibi. For once, Frank had seemed to realize the seriousness of things, and she was gratified now that he had come straight over in the car to find her. He'd said, 'I swear to you, Monica, all I did was open the church doors and leave the ladder.'

'Where did you leave it?'

'I laid it down in the aisle.'

'You didn't prop it up against the pillars?'

'No! I knew Suzy Spencer had a few blokes coming to help her, so I reckoned they could prop up the ladder when they needed to. I was in a bit of a hurry to get away.'

'So what about all this showing off, saying you'd deal with Yvonne?'

Frank looked a bit shifty. 'I was planning to go and see her last night. I was working it out all day while I was in Hexham.'

'So why was Jeff Simpson congratulating you?'

'He jumped to conclusions, that's all.'

Matthew Bell had listened to all this, barely able to control his anger. He'd had enough on his mind, after the events of Saturday night, without having to put up with his parents throwing wobblers all over the place. Then, slowly, it struck him that his father might really be in trouble. His face went white and blank, like his sister's.

'Shit,' he said finally. 'What are you going to do, Dad? Go to the police?' He had his own reasons for dreading that particular option. Shit and shit again, he thought. Everything happened at once.

'No!' His mother sounded sharper. Better. Matthew felt relief. If Mum was back in control, things might be OK. She said, 'Your father would be mad to go the police. They'll come to him in time. The best thing for us all to do is sort out a story and stick to it.'

'It's the truth, love. I swear it.'

'It may be the truth.' Monica looked at Frank with disgust. 'I don't know any more about your truths. But whether it is or not, it needs to be consistent.'

What Frank said sounded perfectly plausible – but she'd always suspected that he'd been up to something with that cow when she was in hospital all those years ago. He'd had a smooth answer then as well. This was the same – only worse. She just couldn't be sure. Would the police think Frank was capable of killing? He was certainly capable of adultery. She glanced at Joanne, who was huddled and grey, inside a shapeless sweatshirt, head cocked to listen for her husband's key in the lock. It had been a mistake to come here. Her daughter wasn't ready yet to be a matriarch.

'We'd better go home and leave you in peace, Joanne,' Monica said. She felt she could cope again now. 'Thanks for putting up with this. You've gone through enough today for your father.' She spat the word out, and Frank squirmed. 'We'll talk you through what you need to say, Frank, before the police get to you. And in the meantime, we'll all stick together on this one. And that means you too, Matthew. You'll have to grow up. The last thing we need now is you drawing attention to this family by driving around like a madman.'

Matthew turned silently away from his parents and stared out of the window at Joanne's neat square of green lawn. His mother could be sharp with everyone else but she had never spoken to him, her favourite child, like this before. Fuck, he thought. Why had this happened today of all days?

Still, Jake Spencer knew better than to talk, though who would have thought that Jake would go all scaredy on him and demand to get out of the car? Good thing he'd done the important job before all these bonkers calls from Mum. So now his poor old dad was the one who was running scared. It was almost funny.

'All right, Mam,' he said, not arguing. Monica was surprised for a moment by his chirpy agreement. Matthew was too like his father. They had spoilt him, she admitted to herself. She'd had a rough pregnancy with Matthew, and because he was her baby and only son she'd let him get away with too much. When all this was over, she would make sure he knuckled down to something. Otherwise he would grow up like Jeff Simpson, cushioned by a family business he could waste. It was time for the Bells to pull themselves together.

Half an hour later when Joanne's husband came rolling back he found his in-laws sitting calmly drinking tea in his living room.

'Mam had lost some invoices in her accounts package on the computer,' Joanne explained blandly. 'But we've managed to sort everything out now with my software. Would you like a cuppa?'

'We'll be leaving shortly,' said Monica.

Good, thought Joanne's husband. He wasn't going to ask too many questions about his in-laws' business dealings. He hadn't said a word when his mother-in-law had turned up white-faced at eight o'clock on a Sunday morning. Whatever it was, he didn't want to know. He just wanted his house back and for them all to go.

Matthew silently agreed. He wanted to get home. With any luck, Jake Spencer would have caught the Sunday bus that ran between Carlisle and Tarnfield, and gone straight to Tarn Acres where he would keep schtum, especially to his nosy mum. She thought she was really trendy, that Suzy Spencer, 'cos she worked in telly. But she didn't know anything really. Matthew smiled to himself.

I'll catch Jake somewhere, he thought, and see to it that he keeps his mouth shut. Whatever it takes.

That morning, Jeff Simpson had been furious with his wife. The short period of domestic glasnost caused by Yvonne's death had been overtaken by his anger at finding Jane on the phone to her downmarket Strickland relatives.

Jeff usually tried to forget his wife's origins, and he was pretty sure she did too. So he couldn't understand why she sidled into the breakfast room, where he was chewing rubbery scrambled eggs, and said in her most wheedling little girl voice: 'Jeffrey, I'm sorry, darling, but I'm going to have to take Vera to Carlisle in the Volvo. Tom's been hurt in a road accident.'

'So what's this got to do with us? You, rather.'

'Vera doesn't drive and she doesn't want to get a taxi. As she said, I am family.' Jane looked edgy, and rubbed her hands up and down her black wool-mix trousers. Jeff noticed they were pilled and bobbly at the side. The fact that his wife was wearing worn clothes upset him. He felt even more annoyed with her.

'Family? He's not my family! Good God, woman, he's only your cousin. And let's face it, he's not the sort of person we'd invite for lunch. His daughter's a tart and his wife looks like a sack of potatoes. I bloody well hope this isn't going to be the start of some sort of reunion!'

'No, darling, of course not. But when it comes down to it, Vera says she needs me.'

'Oh, bugger off then and go. But don't be out all day. I hope you haven't forgotten that the Ridleys are popping in for a cup of tea this afternoon. You can bring a cake back on your way home from Carlisle. Now that bitch Wait is dead, we want to make sure she said nothing to Malcolm Ridley before she copped it. You'd better not be late.'

'Of course I won't be, sweetheart.' Jane had hurried away.

Jeff had turned back to the *Sunday Telegraph*, distinctly put out, not helped by his hangover. An hour later he stomped off to the Plough where, in his view, Frank Bell had behaved like a bloody maniac. What had been the harm in suggesting that Frank might have been responsible for seeing Yvonne off? Whoever killed her had done everyone else a service. They all wanted her dead. Sulkily, Jeff then trudged home and opened a bottle of red wine, and when Jane still didn't appear, he cut himself a slice of Stilton and took a handful of Carr's water biscuits. At least these were made in Carlisle, not like that bloody 'own brand' rubbish that Jane had bought on one of her economy drives. And where was Russell? He'd been in bed when his father had left for the pub, and now there was no sign of him. Selfish little sod.

Jeff hated having to do things for himself in the kitchen because the room was dark and old-fashioned, not the sort of set-up he wanted for his wife. By keeping away from it as much as possible, he could ignore it – except of course for the increasing number of meals which Jane served up at the kitchen table. He usually sat with his back to the ancient Aga and shabby units, but this time he sat in her chair so that he could reach the chocolate biscuits without getting up. It was a frigging pain, he thought, Strickland getting himself injured. He hoped Jane wasn't going to get involved in regular trips to Carlisle – there was the petrol to think about for a start, and the unfortunate contact with Vera, who was common as muck.

Jeff pushed the remainder of the *Sunday Telegraph* to one side and groped for his favourite chocolate digestives. As he did, his eye caught something lilac on the dresser. It was a screwed-up letter and matching envelope, and at once he knew the writing. That bitch Yvonne must have written to him, and Jane must have opened it!

But why didn't she say? She certainly hadn't been furious with him when she left to go sick visiting – if anything it was the other way around. He levered himself up and grabbed the flimsy paper in his hand.

It was Yvonne's writing all right, but with a sudden shiver of shock he saw that it was addressed to his son. Surely Russ wouldn't be dipping his wick in there? Jeff held the letter up to the light that came in from the gloomy windows, overgrown with ivy. He had a momentary qualm about reading Russ's mail but he needed to know about this.

He could tell from the first lines that it wasn't a love letter. He read it through twice, and then sat down heavily and let the implications sink in. The bitch, the absolute bitch, he thought. But he knew intuitively that what she was saying was right.

He crumpled the letter up, then smoothed it out again, and ripped it into pieces, dumping it in the bin with the remains of last night's celebratory dinner. Thank God Yvonne was dead, but not before she'd caused even more trouble. A quick smashed skull had been too good for her.

And where was Jane in all this? Had she read the letter?

Probably not. If she had, she would have destroyed it. So it was most likely Russ who opened it, read it, screwed it up and dropped it in disgust.

Jeff Simpson was not a sensitive man. It never occurred to him to wonder about his son's state of mind after this bolt from the blue. All he wanted to do was confront his wife. He regretted ripping the letter up now. It would be a lot easier to demand an explanation if he showed Jane the poisonous words. He groped in the bin and pulled out some of the bigger pieces of lilac paper, but they could hardly be stuck together again. As he was doing so, he heard her key in the lock and her squeaky voice calling to him.

'Jeff? I'm back, darling. I'm just unloading the car. I'm sorry it took so long. Vera wanted to stay and Sharon wanted a lift to her boyfriend's afterwards and the time just dragged on. But I did manage to stop at Tesco's and get some groceries and gateau . . . Jeff, what's the matter?'

As she stepped down from the narrow hall into the dark kitchen, she saw her husband was advancing on her with a bin liner full of stinking rubbish in his hands. His eyes were bulging.

'Did you see a letter to Russ? From Yvonne Wait? On purple paper?'

'What? Yes, I did see a letter for Russell. But I didn't know it was from Yvonne.'

'Did you have any idea what it said?'

'No, of course not. She must have sent it before she died. I can't imagine why Yvonne would write to Russ. Did she want him to join All Saints Bible group?'

'Don't be so frigging ridiculous!'

Jane flinched. They stood, silently staring at each other. Jane could be very po-faced and it was just possible she was bluffing, Jeff thought. It was just possible that she'd seen the letter, read it and then screwed it up before Russell received it. If so, then she would have every reason for wanting Yvonne dead. Her motives would have been as strong as his own!

'So you don't know what she wrote?'

'Of course I don't, Jeff. If I did I'd tell you. Other than something about the church, I can't imagine what she'd want to ask Russell.'

'She didn't want to ask him anything. She wanted to tell him something.'

'What? And why are you so worked up about it?'

'Because she knew far too much about the past, Jane, about *your* past. She quotes medical records that she could get her hands on. Does that ring any bells with you?'

'No, no, why should it?' Jane was growing paler now, as if a horrible thought was slowly crawling across her face.

'Christ! You're as stupid as your son. God knows where he is now, with this piece of information.'

'What information, Jeff?'

'That he's yours. But not mine. Don't look so bloody horrified. The Wait woman might have been a cow, but she was smart and she knew what she was talking about, unlike you. You've been found out.'

Jeff was advancing on her now, brandishing bits of soiled letter, the bin liner full of garbage leaking its damp, smelly contents on to the once bright red check table-cloth.

'Is Russell's father who she says he is, Jane?'

'I don't know what you mean. Who are you talking about?'

'You know damn well who I'm talking about. Say it.'

'It's rubbish, Jeff. It's not true. It's not –'

The front doorbell jangled across them. 'Hello!' boomed a cheery masculine voice. 'Anyone at home? You'd left the front door open. It's us, the Ridleys.'

Jane looked at Jeff, her face white and her eyes round.

'Malcolm, Carol, lovely to see you. Come on in,' Jeff shouted, and brushed past his wife, who jumped out of his way. She leant her hands on the kitchen table, put her head down and took a deep breath, but a moment later she turned around and followed her husband into the hall.

Preserving the proprieties at Tarnfield House was always her main concern.

'Hello, Carol dear!' She kissed her friend. 'I'm just putting the kettle on. Do go and make yourselves at home in the drawing room. Now, would you like Darjeeling, or Earl Grey?'

30

Whit Sunday night

Of a truth I perceive that God is no respecter of persons.
From the Epistle for the Monday in Whitsun Week, Acts 10:34

'But I think you should get over here, Nigel. I can't get much out of him and he might open up to you.'

Suzy felt as if she was talking through clenched teeth. It really pained her to have to tell her husband that Jake had disappeared for the afternoon, coming home truculent and cowed. It hadn't seemed so bad at first. All the people had overawed him, and Stevie's friends were sufficiently exotic to give his homecoming an air of the surreal. Plus, there was the added interest of Stevie's return as a hero.

Alan had come over to Tarn Acres straight away. Suzy could see that Robert was worried they were going to indulge in a passionate embrace in front of everyone, but Alan maintained his tweedy countryman persona, beaming and inviting them down to Church Cottage for the predictable 'G&Ts'. Suzy and Robert declined. When they'd gone, she'd left Molly with Robert, and knocked on the door of Jake's bedroom, where he'd retreated.

Trying to be calm, she asked him for an explanation.

'I just went out with Matt for a spin,' Jake said, avoiding eye contact. 'Then he had to go to his sister's in Carlisle. So I said I'd get the bus home. That's all, Mum. Don't fuss.'

'And don't you be so rude! I've just had half of Tarnfield in here *fussing* about you!'

'But I knew you wouldn't mind me getting a lift off

those people, 'cos we know Stevie from the church. And anyway, he said he'd call you. So that was OK.'

'But Jake, it wasn't OK, was it? You shouldn't have gone out with Matt in the first place. You took advantage of me going to All Saints. And you presumed on Mrs Piefield's time. Plus, you know I don't like us being under an obligation to neighbours.'

She could hear her voice rising, but knew that a shouting match would be counter-productive. This was the first time she had seriously fallen out with Jake. She had been lucky, she knew that, and she didn't want to jeopardize their relationship, especially as his father lived seventy miles away, too far to be of any immediate help, but too near to be disregarded – and always ready to criticize her parenting skills.

She said, 'All right. You go downstairs and make a cup of tea for Robert Clark. He's been very supportive while I've been worried. I'm going to make a phone call.'

So here she was, almost begging Nigel to come over. She could hear the answering tension in her husband's voice. Didn't she remember that he was going to a sales conference in Barcelona? He was off at crack of dawn tomorrow morning and wouldn't be back till Friday. He would come round first thing Saturday. In fact, he'd take the children to Newcastle. His voice was loaded with patient generosity. In the meantime she should keep calm and not overreact.

Suzy felt hot with irritation. She regretted calling him, but she had no option. He was Jake's dad. And this was about Jake, not about her pride.

'OK, Nigel. But I thought you should know. Perhaps you can talk to him about it.'

She put down the phone feeling small, and left the privacy of her bedroom. Robert was still downstairs and she could hear the children talking to him. Jake sounded better. Having to make an effort for someone he liked was pulling him back into shape.

'I've just been telling Jake about the new Apple Mac software at the college,' Robert said. 'I wondered if he might like to come over to Norbridge tomorrow evening and have a go on one of the computers?'

'I'd like to do that, Mum.' It was a statement, not a request. Suzy felt suddenly angry.

'Is that all you can think about, Jake? Going out and having more fun after the anxiety you've caused?' Jake reddened and turned away from her, sloppily pouring tea into two mugs which looked less than clean. Robert caught her eye and held her glance for a second.

She took a deep breath and started again. 'OK, of course you can go, Jake. It's kind of Robert to offer. But you must realize that you got me really worried. Matt Bell is a nightmare in that boy racer car. I wouldn't be surprised if he killed someone one day.'

Jake spilt the tea. He looked at his mother and for a nanosecond she saw fear in his face. Then he reached for the kitchen roll and said, in a deeper voice that sounded surprisingly adult, 'I won't be going out with him again. Don't worry.'

Suzy leant her arms on the table and sat down heavily. She felt tearful with relief.

'Good. Would you like a glass of wine, Rob?' she said unsteadily. 'And Jake, you need to tidy your room. It was a mess when I went up there this afternoon. Why don't you choose one of your DVDs for us all to watch tonight?' And on the spur of the moment she added, 'Would you like to stay this evening, Rob?'

'Well, a glass of wine would be great. But then, I'd better get home. The Briars will be feeling neglected. I'll call for Jake at about five o'clock tomorrow if that's OK?'

Suzy felt a twinge of disappointment. But Robert had been at Tarn Acres all day. She poured two glasses of red wine, and they drank them slowly at the kitchen table, hardly speaking as Molly played happily with Flowerbabe. Then they heard the sound of Jake's music upstairs. It was loud enough to say 'back to normal' without being too aggressive.

'What do you think really happened?' Robert asked softly.

'I don't know. But I do know one thing. If I ask him directly, I'll never find out.' Suzy frowned. There had definitely been fear on Jake's face. What had Matt Bell said or done which had alarmed him? Was it the fast driving, or something else? Why had he got out of the car and gone to get the bus? If she waited, maybe Jake would tell her. Or maybe he might even tell Robert. The thought pleased her. And surely he would talk to Nigel? But something stopped her mentioning that Jake's father was coming over next week.

After Robert had gone she put a pizza in the oven. Will he have supper with us tomorrow night? she wondered. Then she pulled herself up. Robert Clark was intruding far too much into her thoughts, and he had been right to go. This had been a ghastly weekend, but now must be family time.

She turned to find Jake hovering behind her, looking nervous at what she might say when they were alone. She needed to reassure him now. She tousled his hair and gave him a quick maternal kiss on the forehead. For the first time in a while he didn't flinch or say 'Yuk.' She felt a rush of love, but patted him on the arm and went over to see how Molly was getting on, being careful not to give her feelings away. Teenage boys hated demonstrations of affection – except from teenage girls.

But something had happened to upset her son, and it was something to do with Matthew Bell. I'll find out, Suzy said to herself, if it kills me. And then she realized what she had thought, and shuddered.

'So what exactly was this all about?' Alan had adopted the voice of a kindly headmaster at a decent public school. Sammi and Wendy had tactfully left.

'And where's the car?' he added less hammily, suddenly remembering. 'It was a rotten night to go rushing out. There's been one bad accident we know of . . .'

'The car's in Lancaster, totally unscathed. I managed to get there without any difficulties. I may have lost my licence but everyone knows that was really bad luck. I can cope with most cars.'

'But it was a bloody foolhardy thing to do, going off into the night like that.'

'And it was bloody awful of you to talk about me the way you did to Robert Clark! What did you call me? Faithless, irrational . . .'

'You know I was only playing to his prejudices.'

'Thanks! Look, from what I overheard, Robert Clark thinks the same person who killed Yvonne, killed Phyllis Drysdale. But I have no motive for killing Phyllis, do I?'

'Exactly!' Alan chortled, a self-satisfied laugh.

'But think about it, Alan. Who *would* have had a motive for killing Phyllis? No one! It's inconceivable, isn't it? She was an elderly lady who irritated some people but no one really hated her. She had no enemies. So the motive must be really well hidden. Which means it could have been anyone. Me.' He paused theatrically. 'Or even you.'

'What, me? Have a motive for harming Phyllis Drysdale? Don't be ridiculous.'

'But somebody did! And you certainly had a motive for killing Yvonne. Maybe Phyllis had something on you too. Maybe your past isn't any cleaner and brighter than mine. At least I never tried to hide anything. But you did.'

'Stevie!'

'So that's why I came home,' Stevie continued. 'You see, Alan, I love you just as much as you love me. And if either of us could be fingered for these crimes, then I want us to be together. Even if you do think I'm flighty and idiotic. So here I am.' He moved to stand beside his lover.

Alan was silent. Finally, he said gruffly, 'Thank you, Stevie.'

'You're welcome,' Stevie answered in his best camp voice. 'Another gin?'

'Yes, thank you. We should drink to you coming home.'

They raised their glasses, and once again Alan felt total happiness. It was wonderful that Stevie was home. It had been awful without him, worrying about what might have happened to him while he was driving the car down the country lanes, mad with anger in the stormy weather.

'To our future together,' said Stevie, sounding more confident than he had since coming to Tarnfield five years earlier. 'By the way,' he added, 'you said something about an accident?'

'Oh, yes. Tom Strickland was knocked over by a hit-and-run driver last night. I was worried in case it was you, in the car.'

'Me!' But Stevie stopped in mid-huff and his face creased. 'It's funny you should mention that. There was no traffic when I left last night. But I took a wrong turning up towards Tarn Ford, and a car overtook me going at a hell of a speed.'

'Who was it?'

'I'm damned if I know. The headlights were at full beam. Why anyone would be racing to the ford, I don't know.'

'Should you tell the police?'

'You must be joking. I'm going to keep clear of them as long as I can. Anyway, it was probably nothing. Here's your drink, Al. Then what about an early night?'

Stevie ran his hand down his partner's thigh. He was aware that in the last five minutes their relationship had subtly changed. While he had been driving to Lancaster through the rain, concentrating on the road, he had suddenly realized that despite his 'victim mentality', he was no more likely to be accused than anyone else. Even Alan.

Everyone had hated Yvonne Wait.

They're suspects in this lovely little village, he told himself with vengeful amusement. All those heterosexual churchgoers! They're all possible murderers. Every one of them!

31

Whit Sunday to Monday

God so loved the world, that he gave his only begotten Son.
From the Gospel for the Monday in Whitsun Week, John 3:16

Kevin Jones always dreaded his mother-in-law coming for Sunday tea. She was a dragon. She still ran the farm, though Janice's brother was nominally in charge, and she'd made it clear she thought Janice would have done better if she'd taken her advice and married someone from a local agricultural dynasty.

Kevin had been annoyed with himself for accepting the money Janice's mother had offered as a down payment on the house in Tarn Acres. It was the smallest house in the crescent as well. If she'd been going to give them a hand-out, and if he'd been going to swallow his pride and take it, then why shouldn't it have been for a bigger house? Something like Suzy Spencer's. Or the Arthurs'. Why two women should rattle round in a four-bedroom house like that, he had no idea.

His crush on Daisy had all but evaporated. Now, if anything, he felt irritated with her. She hadn't shown as much commitment to Nick's Vision as he'd hoped. He was annoyed that she had compromised with Suzy Spencer over the Whitsun Festival. There had been a brief moment when he had been trapped into offering to help to put up the decorations himself, but Yvonne's death had soon put the kybosh on the whole stupid idea. Good.

Like a lot of men, Kevin easily transferred blame to the former object of his affections. Daisy had clearly been out to ensnare him in order to make Nick Melling jealous and to provoke him into asking her out. That was what he had told Janice and that was what he now believed. It never occurred to him that perhaps his wife guessed the truth and as a Christian she had decided to forgive him.

He squared up to his mother-in-law across the kitchen-diner table.

'I fully support Melling in all this. The church needs to change with the times, Grandma.' He hated calling her that, but it was better than 'Mam'. His mother-in-law was tight-faced with disapproval.

'That's all very well, Kevin,' she said, 'but it's no good moving on if you don't take people with you. Oh yes, this young man will get people into the church. People in Tarnfield will need to go to All Saints in order to get their children into church schools. But young families aren't the ones with the money or the time. And anyway, it's wrong to put people's backs up. A lot of us have done a great deal for All Saints in the past.'

'With all due respect,' Kevin said, meaning nothing of the sort, 'it just wasn't enough. Attendances have been going down for years and we need new blood. A show of Christianity isn't enough, all this middle class stuff with choirs and flowers. It puts most people off. And it wasn't even a very good choir. Or top class flowers.'

'But it gave a lot of committed people a lot of pleasure.'

'Committed? Yes, to their own gratification. Not to the Lord.'

'Or to Nick Melling,' the older woman said drily. Janice kept her head down. She thought her mother was probably right and that there was a strong dose of vanity in Nick Melling's Vision. But she loved her husband, too. He really believed in Nick, and these changes at the church had filled him with confidence. Kevin was unsure of himself deep down, aware of being the poor white boy from the back streets of Bradford. No wonder her mother terrified him. In a way she was glad he was fighting back.

She listened to them bickering, one eye on the baby asleep on the sofa, the other on Zoe who was playing in front of the TV. Half aware of the debate, she was sensitive to the determination in Kevin's voice. He really wasn't giving way. Kevin was raising his voice now, asserting that God might have included the deaths of Phyllis and Yvonne in his plan so the church in Tarnfield could make progress.

Like everyone in the village Janice knew that the police were looking into Yvonne's death and that there wouldn't be a funeral for some time. There was a chance they were viewing it as a possible crime. If my husband is so convinced that Yvonne had to go, she thought, is it possible that he gave her a helping hand? It wouldn't take much to twitch a ladder. After all, he'd told Suzy Spencer he was willing to go and help.

The room felt cold. Where had Kevin been on Saturday morning? He'd taken the car to go for some shopping in Norbridge. Then later, he'd walked down to Lo-cost for something he'd forgotten. Tinned custard, was it? Or pasta sauce? Something like that. She couldn't account for where he'd been for a great deal of the time.

Oh Kevin, she thought. Could you have done it?

She looked at him. He was red-faced now, saying loudly, 'You really don't understand, Grandma. It doesn't matter how much people did for the *church*. It's real commitment to the *Lord* that counts.'

'And what about the commitment of young couples who just want their children in the best schools? Is that "real" commitment?'

'Well, at least they're not stuck-in-the-mud old fogeys like Phyllis Drysdale. Or self-serving cows like Yvonne Wait!'

Oh dear, thought Janice.

In their bungalow a few miles to the east, Joan Pattinson passed the phone over to her husband. Why had Vera Strickland called now, when George was awake, ready for his Sunday tea watching hymn singing on the telly? In the past, George had been too sophisticated for things like this, but now he seemed to take comfort from it. When the phone rang she had sighed, put down her cup and saucer, and picked it up. She didn't like George tackling phone calls himself. The last time he had picked up the phone, it had been Mrs Spencer with news of Phyllis Drysdale's death. That had had a very strange effect on him.

'George, it's Vera Strickland,' she said calmly. 'Tom's had a bit of an accident. But he's OK.'

Another one! The Bishop had telephoned them that morning to inform them of Yvonne's Wait's death 'just as a courtesy'. Joan had intercepted that call, thank goodness. The Bishop had stressed that there would be no need for George to be in any way involved. He just graciously wished to avoid the Pattinsons' hearing of the accident through gossip, or, heaven forbid, on the local TV or news. George should know that Nick Melling was well on top of the situation. Best to let things be.

But was that best? From the start of George's break-down, Joan had been inclined to comply with everything the Bishop had suggested, even when it caused George so much distress. But now she was beginning to wonder. She still met people from Tarnfield occasionally in Tesco's or in the Lanes shopping centre in Carlisle. And since Phyllis's death she had heard that there was a growing rift in All Saints. Sometimes she wondered if it might do George more good to have something to occupy him, which gave him a link with the past. She knew that he had been deeply damaged by their sudden departure from All Saints, even though that had seemed the right thing at the time. The Bishop had been obsessed with avoiding gossip.

On the other hand, though, she had never been sure exactly what people in Tarnfield really believed about George's illness. It was a dilemma. By going back, he risked facing criticism from people who thought they understood what it was all about. But by staying away, he could cause more misguided speculation. She sighed. If only George's parishioners could be told the truth. It was a lot stranger than anything they'd imagined, she was certain of that. But the Bishop had been appalled at the suggestion.

She turned back to her husband and the phone call. George was listening intently. 'Good heavens, Vera, this really is terrible!' he was saying. But to his wife's surprise there was a growing trace of the old confidence in his voice.

'And they have no idea who did it? Horrific! There are all sorts of maniacs on the roads these days.' George was listening again to Vera's repeated description of Tom's multiple injuries. Joan strained to hear.

Then to her astonishment her husband replied, 'But if you want me to visit Tom, of course I will. You realize of course that I haven't been out for some time. But Joan will drive me during the week.'

He put down the phone and smiled at his wife with a look she thought was slyly triumphant.

'Someone in Tarnfield needs me,' he said. He closed his eyes, and put his head back, but just when Joan thought he was dropping off to sleep, he opened them again and said, 'I never forgave myself for not seeing Phyllis straight away, you know. I put her off and put her off, and she died before she could tell me what was on her mind. I'm not going to let that happen with Strickland.'

To his wife's amazement he drank his tea straight down, and leaned forward to turn up the TV set. He smiled again when he heard the hymn the ardent congregation was singing. It was 'Make Me a Channel of Your Peace'.

'Nick Melling doesn't have a monopoly on it,' George said with a hint of his old confidence.

'A monopoly on what?'

'The Holy Spirit,' George said, and chuckled. Joan stood up to go in the kitchen for more cake. She wanted to hide the tears of relief in her eyes.

Nancy Arthur woke up on Monday to hear Daisy coming down the stairs. Her footsteps sounded light and carefree, and a moment later Nancy was sure she could hear Daisy

242

singing to herself in the kitchen before putting the radio on. Good, Nancy thought. Daisy had spent much of Sunday asleep, after Saturday's visit from the acting vicar.

Nancy shook her head as she heaved herself out of bed. She didn't like Nick Melling. He was snobbish and ungracious, she thought. Nancy reminded herself that she had little experience of what she called 'the Brideshead type', but if they were all as noblesse oblige as he was, she was grateful that she'd escaped! The worry was that Daisy seemed so besotted with him. But after his stilted attempts to talk to her, Daisy had seemed even more distressed.

As if finding a dead body wasn't enough, Nancy thought, Nick had made her daughter feel tainted. He was far too egotistical. Nancy knew little about the Anglican Church. She was a practical person who lived in the present and, for her own reasons, she wanted nothing to do with religion. How ME could square with any kind of loving God, she didn't know. But she did believe that people who set themselves up as spiritual guides needed to be experts on human nature too, with all the messiness that involved. She very much doubted whether Nick Melling had either the stomach or the sweetness to really love his fellow man.

'Daisy?' she called.

'Morning, Mum. Would you like your coffee?'

'Thanks, petal. And some of my special bread.' Nancy's newest toy from her catalogue was a breadmaker. She liked the bread made with egg, yellow and soft. It reminded her of her childhood in Leeds. She was lucky to be able to afford new gadgets like that and she had noticed Babs Piefield's jealous glance. Nancy would have preferred not to excite envy, and that was one of the reasons – though not the main one – that she kept Babs out of her kitchen as much as possible. But it would have been silly to deprive herself so as not to provoke her neighbour.

'Coming up, Mum,' sang out Daisy.

Nancy pulled herself into the kitchen. 'You seem brighter this morning?' It was always a relief when Daisy was happy. She'd been her daddy's girl and his death had knocked her sideways. Nancy had never really been sure of her.

'I am. What happened to Yvonne was awful and I will never forget it. But these things happen, don't they, Mum?'

'I suppose so.' Nancy frowned. It didn't seem right that a violent death could be dealt with so easily. And Daisy had been deeply depressed the day before. After Nick had left on Saturday afternoon, she had refused to talk, and had turned her face away when Nancy had dragged herself up the stairs.

But now she was back to normal. Of course Nick hadn't been their only visitor over the weekend. Babs had been there on and off, coming back on Sunday evening to tell them how Jake Spencer had disappeared for the day with Matthew Bell, and how cross Suzy Spencer had been.

'She tried not to show it,' Babs said smugly, 'but she was really put out.'

Babs told them about Tom Strickland, too. She'd heard about it at Lo-cost, which was open on Sundays. Daisy had livened up then, saying she'd be back at work on Tuesday, when her next shift was scheduled. She liked working at Lo-cost. It was undemanding and it was in Tarnfield, which was becoming more and more the centre of Daisy's world. Nancy sighed. It wasn't what she wanted for her clever daughter.

'Anyway,' Daisy was saying, 'I need to know how Nick is going to cope. He just wasn't himself when he came to see me on Saturday.'

He was exactly himself, Nancy thought, cold and insincere. But she couldn't say that to her daughter. Daisy got fixed ideas. If Nancy tried to pour cold water on them, she risked Daisy withdrawing as she had on Saturday night.

'Have you heard from any of your college friends in London lately?' Nancy asked carefully. She saw Daisy's back stiffen as she bent to get butter from the fridge she used for dairy products.

'Well, no, not for a while.' Daisy laughed, a tinkling

sound. 'Honestly, Mum, you can be quite obvious, you know. Anyway, they're all over the place now.'

'But what about that nice lad you were keen on? Daniel, was it?'

'Mum! That was in the second year. And anyway . . .' Daisy said nothing more, but hustled around the coffee percolator. Nancy had a shrewd idea what had been wrong with Daniel. He hadn't shared Daisy's growing interest in Christianity. But he had been a nice boy, much more suitable than this Sebastian Flyte character of a vicar.

Nancy deeply regretted sending Daisy to Sunday School. She hadn't sent her sons, but her ME was already encroaching when Daisy was a child, and she had thought it would do no harm and help keep her daughter occupied. Anyway, Daisy's father had been quite keen that she should go. He had got more conservative as he got older, and liked the idea of being involved in the church, as many people do, in middle age. Nancy wasn't the sort to create a rift over something like that. She rarely thought about her own background. It had been overtaken by Tarnfield, the shop and her husband. She had been more than happy to please him. And Daisy had enjoyed Sunday School, but not too much. During her teen years, when so many youngsters become fanatical, she had been relatively relaxed about religion. It was at university that she had become so serious about it, after her father died.

'I was just wondering,' Nancy went on, 'about us having a holiday. We could go down to London and stay with your Auntie Cora.'

'No!' Daisy's voice was sharp. 'You know how I feel about Auntie Cora's family. And anyway, there's a lot going on in Tarnfield.'

'But Daisy, there have been two deaths here. And a hit-and-run accident. You know how fond you were of Phyllis. And although Yvonne Wait wasn't a very nice woman, it was still a nasty way to go. Don't you think it might be a good idea to get away, meet other people, do a show, go to the shops?'

'I said no, Mum.' Daisy's voice was petulant. 'I'm happy

here at the moment. And Nick will have to decide what he's going to do now Yvonne is dead and Tom's in hospital. He'll need my support.'

Will he really? Nancy wondered, as she turned away to sit down heavily at the kitchen table. Daisy was singing again and, to her dismay, her mother realized it was one of those modern songs about Jesus. Oh dear, Nancy thought.

32

The Tuesday after Trinity Sunday

*We beseech thee, that thou wouldest keep us stedfast in
this faith.*
From the Collect for Trinity Sunday

The good weather came late after a few false starts, as it so
often does in the North. But once it arrived, every hedge
seemed to drip with blossom. The Tuesday of the spring
half-term week was almost hot.

Robert took his mid-morning cup of coffee into the back
garden. It was looking a bit of a mess. He'd hardly touched
it since Easter. He sat down gingerly at the wooden bench
Mary had loved so much, by the picnic table, up against
the north-facing wall of the house where the ivy grew. The
laburnum she had planted was covered in ragged blossom
and the clematis and Russian vine were out, though this
year they looked stringy.

The flowers reminded him of Phyllis, and she in turn
reminded him of Nick Melling. It was odd, he thought,
that a snob like Nick was in cahoots with someone like
Kevin Jones, but the partnership seemed to excite them
both. Yet although it would normally have outraged
Robert, this crisis over forms of worship seemed much less
important than the unexplained deaths of the two women.
Yes, it had annoyed him that Melling had refused to use
any of the traditional Trinity hymns like 'Holy Holy Holy'
or St Patrick's Breastplate that Sunday, but as he was
disbanding the choir it was hardly a surprise. Yet Robert

felt distant from the controversy and much more worried about the bigger picture.

He reviewed the events of the last two months. Two women had died in the church, a man had been knocked down, the vicar had instigated huge upheavals, and two boys had taken a mystery tour. Robert had seen enough cases of bullying, child abuse, domestic violence and downright wickedness in his work at the college to be under no illusions about rural life. But although bad things happened in villages as much as in the darkest slums, they didn't happen all at once like this. It was too much of a coincidence. There had to be some sort of unlikely connection.

He'd taken Jake Spencer to the college the week before and let him use the computers in the IT section, as he'd promised. Robert wasn't much of a talker and they had been silent in the car on the way there, and chatted a bit about Apple Macs on the way back. Jake had said one intriguing thing. He'd mentioned that Matthew Bell had the latest computer game – but that Jake hadn't been asked to try it.

'So you're not really a good friend of Matthew's?' Robert asked.

'No. S'pose not.'

'Did he have his other mates with him as well as you when you went off?'

'No. The others were paint-balling again.'

The boy turned to look out of the window. Jake had been used, Robert thought, but he wasn't sure why. He wondered why Matt had called for him and taken him out on his own. Was it because he was younger and more malleable? Was it because his dad wasn't around? In either case, Robert suspected Matthew Bell had made a mistake in his choice of sidekick. Jake was young, but he wasn't timid. And Suzy seemed to exert a fair bit of authority. Robert glanced at Jake. He was biting his cuticle. At some point, Robert thought, he would tell his mother what had really been going on.

Now, sitting in the garden, Robert was surprised to find

himself thinking that the brief talk with Jake reminded him of conversations with his wife – the waiting for a revelation, the care not to probe or prod, the suspicion that all wasn't well and the overwhelming sense of responsibility. He had cared for Mary deeply, but he was beginning to understand that much of that love was about protecting her and that for a great deal of the time he had been walking on eggshells.

He thought of something Suzy had said to him. 'After your first baby, you can't believe you've got enough love for another. You almost have the second one for the first child's benefit. It's just "Jake's new brother or sister". But before long, you have more than enough love for the next.'

Perhaps romance was like that as well, he wondered. You think you've exhausted it, and then someone else comes along. Could that happen to him? It seemed impossible. His wife had drained him, he thought as he finished the dregs of his coffee. He'd better take the cup into the kitchen and wash it up. Mary hated dirty dishes lying about.

He stood up to go inside, but instead he walked over to have a closer look at the struggling wisteria. He really had to get to grips with the garden. For more than a year, all he had wanted was to keep things going as they always had been. It was unimaginable that things could be different. But they were, of course. For a start, the old front fence had gone, where Suzy had run into it. Frank Bell had replaced it with a twisted weave effect. Robert had had no idea what sort of fence Mary would have liked these days. And it didn't matter. That had been the first time he had made a decision about the garden on his own.

And now, suddenly in the sunshine, he looked back on his marriage and it seemed to be really in the past, like his schooldays or his years at university. He could see it as a section of time with a beginning and an end, and a character. He had genuinely never thought about remarrying because he had still felt married.

But he didn't any more. It was over despite his huge

efforts. It had taken enormous striving to keep the relationship with Mary going, with its complex secrets. For years before she died, he had no energy left for anything else. And then her death had been as exhausting as her life. For the last fifteen months he had still been living for Mary, running on empty but still free-wheeling. Now, it wasn't just he who was exhausted. The relationship with his wife had run its course.

And did love have to be so enervating? Did it have to be such a one-way street? Say someone was prepared to care for him as he had cared for Mary? The idea was a novelty. It amused him. He was still thinking about it when he went back into the house.

He had left the used coffee mug on the wooden table outside.

On the same day, Suzy dropped Jake at another music workshop, this time in Carlisle. Then she drove home with Molly, played with her for a while, and started working on a brief for Tynedale TV. But she couldn't concentrate. The sunlight seemed warm and yellow for the first time that year and the dust motes swirled in it. The computer screen was smeared in the bright light, however hard she rubbed it with her the sleeve of her jumper, which felt itchy. In a fit of irritation, she changed into a T-shirt and felt the heat on her bare arms. She thought, I'll go over to Lo-cost, just to get out. It would be a nice walk. In the sun, she could smell pollen. Molly trotted along with Flowerbabe the doll, not wearing her hooded jacket for the first time that year.

She bumped into Monica Bell at Lo-cost. Normally Monica would have been bursting to talk. But she seemed a bit distracted, and Suzy felt awkward. After the initial hello, there wasn't the usual rush of chat. Monica clearly knew nothing about her son's jaunt with Jake, so Suzy didn't push it. It would be better if Jake's decision not to repeat the experience resolved the whole matter. He would never forgive her if she waded in with Matt Bell's mother.

'I gather Daisy called you, after she found Yvonne?' Monica said eventually. It was as if she were annoyed about it.

'Yes. We were planning to meet half an hour later. Poor Daisy. It was awful.'

'But it was so typical of Yvonne to try and take over the decorating, wasn't it? No one asked her to go up a ladder, did they? Stupid thing to do.'

'Well, that's true.' Suzy was surprised at Monica's tone. Then the conversation stalled. Suzy asked about the ladder, and Monica said the police had taken it away. She was edgy, which wasn't surprising, Suzy thought. For the first time, she wondered about Frank. When had he taken the ladder to All Saints? Monica looked agitated so Suzy changed the subject.

'Do you know how Tom Strickland is?'

'Oh, Tom's OK. Frank called in to see him yesterday and apparently George Pattinson himself turned up at the hospital. He's been to see Tom a few times.'

'George Pattinson? I thought he'd gone to ground.'

'No, it seems he's up and about again.'

There was a silence, but then Suzy thought, I ought to take this opportunity to find out what's happening at the church. She had missed Trinity Sunday at All Saints because Nigel had come over to talk to Jake, though he'd got nowhere. The day had been rather a strain.

'So what d'you think about Nick Melling's proposals, Monica?'

'Oh, it's terrible. What a time to choose! We got a leaflet through the door. Just a scruffy piece of paper! I bet it was delivered by Kevin Jones. I don't think that's a very decent way to treat me and Frank after years of working at All Saints. But what can you do?'

'Write to the Bishop, I suppose.'

But Suzy could tell that Monica didn't want to get involved in a fight with Nick. Far from it being a bad time to make swingeing changes, it was probably an intelligent move. Everyone was winded by Yvonne's death, and probably too shocked to fight back. Nick was pretty crafty, Suzy thought. Or so self-obsessed, he'd hit on lucky timing through sheer insensitivity.

'Will you be staying at All Saints?' she asked.

'I don't think so. I like traditional things. I think in the end I'll be looking for another church, though this is our parish, where we live!'

Then Monica's mobile rang and she grabbed it with relief, rushing off to talk loudly to a plasterboard supplier in Darlington. Suzy felt slightly put out. She watched her hurry to the Bells' pick-up in the Lo-cost car park, and saw her stop to speak to Jane Simpson who had come hurrying out of Tarnfield House. They put their heads together.

Strange, Suzy thought. She hadn't realized the two other women were so pally. They were probably talking about the church. But at the back of Suzy's mind, something tugged. Of course. She had wondered whether the Bells and the Simpsons were friendly when she had been to the wood yard and heard Frank and Monica quarrelling. What had Frank said? 'Don't ring the Simpsons about it . . .'

About what? She turned away from Monica and Jane with a sense of being excluded, and felt the warmth on her face. The door of Lo-cost was open, and Daisy waved to her from the check-out. Life was going on, and the sun was out.

After lunch, she took Molly to the long-awaited birthday party of her latest best friend. One or two people mentioned the death in the church a week earlier. Some had heard the item on the local radio news, but the report had sounded bald and matter-of-fact. Most parents were more concerned about the chicken pox cases that had been reported in Norbridge. On the way home, Suzy felt a heightened sense of normality, as if a light had been turned on in a scary cellar.

But when she got back, she found that words wouldn't come as she tried to use the keyboard. Fighting national obesity wasn't something she could pontificate about. She had enough trouble with her own excess pounds. She looked at the grime on her kitchen window. I must spring-clean, she thought, and then smiled. She hadn't used the word for years. It reminded her of her grandma, and her own early childhood, a lifetime away – when her gran used washing soda, scouring powder and loose tea. The thought of Phyllis's bungalow came back, with its little pile of coupons and elastic bands, and the stained old-fashioned tea cosy. Who would inherit the bungalow now? Would it have gone to Yvonne if she were alive? And who would get the Georgian house and Yvonne's beautiful things? It was all in limbo while the police investigated. But there had been no sign of any more activity.

Suzy chewed her pencil, which she was supposed to be using for jotting down thoughts for her memo to the producer at Tynedale TV. She drew a doodle of the helle-bore leaves she thought she had seen by Yvonne's body. But had she been mistaken? It all seemed so long ago, though it was little over a week earlier. Since then, Tom Strickland had been run over, and Jake had caused her all that anxiety going off with Matt Bell. And Nick Melling had dropped his bombshell about reforming the church. All this in a place like Tarnfield, where people thought nothing ever happened. What a joke. But she couldn't tell any of her neighbours how she felt. They would be offended.

Except perhaps Robert, whom she'd last spoken to when he'd dropped Jake off the week before. She had missed seeing him at church on Sunday. It had been strange with Nigel back in the house for the day. The visit had not been a great success.

Jake's chat with his father had descended from a poten-tially useful heart-to-heart, into a lot of horseplay in the garden which established their male bond but did nothing to uncover what Jake had been doing with Matthew Bell the previous week. Still, it made Nigel feel good. He told Suzy he thought it had just been a one-off prank, and made her feel silly for fussing. He'd taken them to lunch at a smart pub in Norbridge, and then left as soon as possible for Newcastle. To her surprise, Suzy had found Nigel easier to talk to, but more remote. He's like a cousin or a colleague, she thought. How could I ever have loved him enough to marry him?

Having forged a completely new life in Tarnfield, she could look back and see her old life quite differently. Nigel had been OK in another environment, surrounded by similar friends and constrained by common conventions. But he seemed quite wrong for her now. Real love didn't depend on a context, she thought. It would work anywhere. The idea made her think of Robert and Mary, willingly defined by The Briars. Was that what Robert had really wanted?

On a whim, she called his number.

'I can't stop thinking about Yvonne. Have the police come back to you?'

'Not yet.' He sounded reassuring. 'There's a sense of calm in the village, isn't there? You wouldn't think there'd been a violent death.'

'Maybe it's the sunshine.'

'Or the fact that Yvonne is hardly lamented.'

Suzy thought again about Monica Bell, how she had sounded irritated rather than shocked by Yvonne's death. And how she had seemed so wary with her, but keen to talk to Jane Simpson.

'Have the Simpsons and the Bells always been good friends?' she asked Robert.

'No, not at all,' he said. 'I always thought that Frank was rather contemptuous of Jeff's lack of drive, and Jane and Monica are like chalk and cheese.'

Suzy laughed. 'But I met Monica this morning and she couldn't wait to leave me and rush to talk to Jane. Or maybe the weather just means everyone is out and about chatting for the first time.'

'Yes. Makes you want to go striding out over the fells.'

Suzy thought for a moment. 'I was going to take the children for a walk tomorrow, on the Scar. Why don't you come with us?'

'Oh!' Robert sounded surprised. There was a long pause, and then he said, 'Why not?' He had nothing planned and it meant he could avoid feeling guilty about the garden. 'I'd enjoy that. I like Jake.'

'Only Jake?'

'And the rest of the family, of course!'

Suzy laughed. It had been an attempt at flirting and there was something lighter in Robert's tone. 'You sound cheery for someone whose vicar is virtually giving him the elbow!'

'Well, I've been worrying for months about Melling doing this. Now I know where I am. But he can't hurt Phyllis any more, and I'm more concerned about Yvonne and the hellebore leaves than Melling and his reforms.'

'Maybe we can talk about it tomorrow? The weather forecast's good. We're taking a picnic and leaving at about eleven thirty. Shall we see you at the car park?'

Robert stopped himself agreeing too quickly. Suzy waited for his answer, aware she was holding her breath. When he said yes, she exhaled. She was really pleased that he'd agreed.

And the day improved. That night, Rachel called Suzy to say she was coming up for the weekend.

'Hey, you sound better!' she said.

'I feel better too,' Suzy said. 'Not so spooked.'

'But you still think there's funny goings-on at Cold Comfort Farm?'

'It's not all like that, Rache. I know it seems a bit over the top when you're not here . . .'

'A bit? It sounds completely bonkers to me. Dead women and messages in leaves! Are you sure this isn't just an excuse to get together with your gorgeous widower?'

'He isn't gorgeous. And he sure as hell isn't mine.'

'Not yet!'

'Oh, get lost!'

But the thought lingered, and Suzy went to bed that night looking forward to the next day more than she had to any day since they had first come to Tarnfield. Even her dreams were full of well-being.

33

Wednesday and Thursday after Trinity Sunday

Beloved, let us love one another: for love is of God.
From the Epistle for the First Sunday after Trinity, 1 John 4:7

The next morning she packed up the picnic things and they all set off in the car. Jake had perked up with the news that Robert was joining them. He'd been pretending that he didn't want to go out with his mum and sister, but he was secretly looking forward to running about on the fell top. He'd brought a kite that had complicated strings and streamers, and reckoned Robert would be good at getting it to work. Suzy doubted whether it would fly in the light breeze but it gave the outing a focus.

Robert was waiting for them at the car park. It was another beautiful day, with blue sky as far as the eye could see, the fells like a soft sage duvet with pockets of heat lurking in sheltered spots like in an unmade bed. The leaves were fully out now, giving the impression of privacy where there had been bleak spindly skeletons in winter. Suzy felt as if she was in a bubble where things were safe and warm.

'Hi! Where shall we go?'

'If we walk over on the footpath to the Tarn Valley there's a wonderful view over the Scar down to the river. Do you know it?'

'No. This is our first trip into the deep countryside.'

The footpath looked like a parting on a green scalp, and led more or less straight to the edge where a fuzzy fringe of low stunted trees clung to the ridge of the Scar. Thirty feet below them the Tarn began to flatten and swell out, growing from a rushing stream into a mellow, broader river. Tarnfield was three miles to the west. To the east the hills rose up, still round and upholstered with gorse and heather but showing signs that the rocky outcrops which marked the start of the North Pennines might push through like brown jagged teeth. Suzy put the groundsheet down in a sheltered spot and Jake and Molly immediately clambered back up to the ridge and tried to get the kite up.

'It isn't too steep, is it?' Robert asked.

'No, it's just nice.' The path went down to their left in a series of bumpy steps to the bottom of the valley. It was darker and muddier down there, but where they had put the groundsheet it was dry and the ground was covered with springy grass.

'Where does it get really sheer?' Suzy asked.

'Just a few hundred yards further along the river. The water slices through the Scar to get to the plain. Then it merges with the Eden at Brampton this side of Carlisle.'

'It's lovely. I can't believe it's so empty.'

'You hardly ever see anyone here. Mary and I used to come out a lot for walks on a Sunday.'

He looked away, lost in thought. Suzy felt a tiny constriction in her chest, and realized it was jealousy. How strange and annoying, she thought. Why should I envy him his memories? But she had wanted this family day out to be something special for Robert, not just a pale replacement of the past. That's arrogant of me, she thought, wanting to make a difference.

'Have some wine, Rob. It's just half a bottle. It's in the cool box and we can make it last.'

'Thanks.' Robert pulled himself back from the thought of that last awful row he had had with Mary, out here on the hills on a day like this when he had warned her that she was playing with fire. They had yelled at each other, free from the ever-present feeling in Tarnfield that they were on display. Even when there was no one around, Robert still sensed Mary's father and mother in The Briars sometimes. But on the fells they had really let rip.

'Here it is. Sancerre. Yvonne Wait's favourite.' Suzy laughed and handed him the glass.

'God yes, Yvonne. That's always lurking, isn't it? I've been struggling with it over and over, but I can't make head or tail of it. What was it you were thinking about the Bells and Simpsons?'

She told him about her visit to the wood yard and how she'd overheard Frank and Monica arguing about talking to Jeff and Jane.

'And why are the sons so close?' Suzy asked.

'They both come from families where there's money, but not really much attention. Matthew's spoilt materially but his mum and dad have always been wrapped up in the business. And Jeff has never been that close to Russell.'

'How old was he when Russell was born?'

'In his fifties. Russell was sweet-natured as a boy, but he seemed to go downhill later. His dad was too old to be very interested. Jeff was middle-aged at thirty. Jane and Jeff had been married for years with no children and then Russ came along.'

'That can happen. People's hormones change in the menopause.'

'Well, for Jane it was all in the nick of time. Jeff was a bit of a lady's man in those days – don't laugh. So when Jane failed to produce a son people thought he would dump her. Then along came Russell.'

'Very handy!' For a second Suzy wanted to ask him why he and Mary had no children, but she didn't. It was a shame, she thought. He was good with Jake and Molly. She smiled at him, a smile from nowhere, which was nothing to do with what they'd been saying and was everything to do with the sunshine. They could hear the children whooping above them. Suzy sipped her wine and waited for the slightly light-headed effect. It was good not having to talk.

After a few minutes she said, 'How's Tom Strickland?'

'He's OK, I hear. Hasn't Sharon been reporting back to you?'

'I haven't seen her much lately. I don't need her at the moment. I haven't been to work for about six weeks.'

'D'you like being a full-time mum?'

'All mums are full-time mums.'

'OK, OK. But you know what I mean.'

'Well, in answer to your question, it's not exactly been a normal time, has it? First of all I was working like crazy to try and get the Whitsun Festival off the ground, and then there was Yvonne's death, and Jake's little trip. There was Tom's accident, too.'

'Yes. I suppose I should go and see him.'

'Oh.' Suzy sat up. She'd been lolling on the groundsheet, face towards the sun. 'One thing Monica Bell did say to me when I met her outside Lo-cost was that George Pattinson had been to see Tom on Monday.' She glanced sideways to see Robert's reaction.

'Really?'

'Yes. Sounds like he might be on the mend. George Pattinson, I mean. And what about you?'

'On the mend?' Robert sounded a little surprised.

'No, idiot. Going to see Tom Strickland.'

'Oh, that. I was thinking of going tomorrow.' They laughed, but Suzy thought, it wasn't so odd to ask Robert if he was recovering too. She couldn't imagine losing a partner you loved, but then she couldn't really imagine loving a partner. She sighed. Nigel would be coming on Friday to take the kids to Newcastle again. This little oasis would be over. She passed Robert a packet of crisps.

They heard Jake yelling in excitement as the kite caught the summer breeze and lifted above the children's heads. 'Hey, Mum, Robert, come and look at this!' Suzy stuffed her plastic cup into the heather and scrabbled to her feet. Robert looked up at her. She was always moaning about being a few pounds overweight but looked slim to him, and she was quick too. There was something spontaneous and joyful about the way she leapt up, keen to see what was happening.

'Come on, Rob!' she said, bringing him in.

They scrambled up the hill to the brow where Molly was standing transfixed, holding the kite's controls. 'Look, Mummy, it's trying to escape!' she shouted.

'Here. I want to show it to Mum. Look, Mum, you can make it dance!' Jake went to grab the line from Molly and in his enthusiasm he dropped it. The wooden reel fell to the ground, bounced, then skittered along. The kite lifted, and then dived. All of them scurried after it, running recklessly along the cliff top. With a superhuman pounce, Jake managed to catch the toggle and he turned, followed by Molly, to run back up the hill, the kite still swooping and soaring.

Suzy couldn't stop. She dug her heels in and skidded down. Grabbing at bits of gorse and stray branches she slid until she stopped, gasping and laughing, a few yards from where the path, steeper now, wound down the Scar into the valley. Above them a bare sandstone rock jutted out, the start of the Scar proper. Robert was right behind her. He couldn't stop either. I'm going to crash, he thought. He tried to stop himself, arms flailing, but he thumped into her and they both slid into a stunted oak.

'Sorry!' he gasped, pulling himself away.

'It's OK,' she laughed. Suddenly it seemed very still around them. The few trees on the ridge opened out here into a tiny clearing, with smooth green grass. A lark sang above them. The children were still laughing and calling, but their voices seemed miles away. The sunshine dappled through the few leaves on the tough little trees. Robert looked up at the pure blue sky.

'It's lovely here,' he said. 'Just a few yards away from the path and it's gorgeous. I never came here before.'

'It's a find.' Suzy stretched her arms out. 'It's beautiful. Makes you happy to be alive.' Without thinking too much, she grabbed Robert by the shoulders and kissed him on the cheek. 'Great!' she said. 'Come on, the kids will wonder where we are.'

He watched her scrambling back up the path, hands and knees in the dirt. It was the first time in two years he had been touched by a woman who didn't pity him. She had smelt fresh and active and she had been unembarrassed. His face tingled.

In the distance they could hear another engine burst into life in the car park.

'That's the first car we've heard for ages,' Suzy said.

'You can often come here and see no one else,' Robert answered.

But someone else had seen them. The car executed a sharp three-point turn in the car park before heading back to the village. It jerked and took the corners a little bit too sharply. Everything about its movements seemed angry. It flew past the turning to The Briars and was soon lost among Tarnfield's shops and houses.

Robert was quieter in the afternoon, but Jake and Molly wanted lots of attention until the kite finally gave up, and was bundled up for home in a tangled heap. They ate their picnic in fits and starts, dozed in the sunshine, and then made for the car.

'It's been a lovely day,' Suzy said at the car park.

'Yes. Thanks for asking me,' Robert replied.

'We should do it again sometime?'

'Yes, why not?'

As he drove home, a few yards behind the Spencers, he felt Suzy's kiss on his face. She had said they should be happy to be alive. It seemed the greatest disloyalty of all, but it was true. He was.

The next day, Robert drove to Carlisle to visit Tom Strickland in hospital. Tom looked shrunken and even grumpier with his blue striped pyjamas hanging over his bony frame. He wasn't in bed when Robert arrived, but sitting in a high-backed armchair at the end of the ward, watching racing on the TV. Typically, he failed to say anything at all welcoming, but then announced he was getting back into bed.

'They're letting me out on Saturday,' he said. 'I've had a fractured rib, punctured lung, bruising, and cuts on my arm and my head. Plus signs of hypothermy whatsit – but I'm OK now. Vera will have to do some work on me and the district nurse will have to come round, but I'm not staying here eating this muck. It was some sort of curry today. Curry! Who wants that crap?' He shuffled towards his bed.

Robert followed him. 'Well, you've had quite a lot of cards, Tom,' he said. He was rather surprised. There was an enormous flowery thing to 'My Dear Husband' which had to be Vera's astonishing contribution, and there was a card from the Bells, and the Arthurs, and another from Alan and Stevie, pushed to the back. Robert was touched to see that Suzy, Jake and Molly had sent a home-made one too. And then his eye was caught by the message inside a simple notelet with no 'get well' on the front. In block capitals it just said, 'ISAIAH 5:11.' Robert inhaled sharply.

'That's a funny message,' he said conversationally.

'What? Oh that.'

'Who's it from?'

'I dunno. Melling, I suppose. It's a Bible reference, isn't it? I haven't looked it up. Can't be bothered. It was a messy card, though. All these bits of flower fell out. Typical Melling! He's a bit of a nancy boy, if you ask me.'

'Flowers? You mean bits of flower inside?'

'Yeah. Stupid.'

'Have you still got the flowers? What were they like?'

'Nah, of course not. What d'you think I am? Another shirt-lifter? There's enough dirt around here without keeping bits of dried marigolds. I don't want to get a ruddy superbug.' Tom heaved himself laboriously into bed, wiped his nose on the back of his hand and rubbed it on the covers.

'No. No, of course not,' Robert said soothingly.

Isaiah 5:11. He had to remember that. He tried to make conversation with Tom for the next fifteen minutes, but all he could think about was the card. He had to check out the Bible reference. And talk to Suzy about it. Marigolds. What could they mean? Tom's eyes were more closed than open now. After a decent time, Robert thought, he ought to go. Then suddenly the older man's eyelids shot open, and his head swivelled round like a tortoise.

'Oh good,' he said unkindly. 'Here's someone I really want to see.'

Robert turned to see George Pattinson, followed by his wife, coming into the ward. Despite everything, the former parish priest had presence. He had lost weight but his big head with its crest of silver hair, and his tall frame supported on a black stick, gave him an air of significance.

Oh no, Robert thought. I'll have to speak to him.

George Pattinson saw Robert but did not break his stride down the ward. 'Tom,' he said, his round deep voice sounding confident again. 'Here I am again, as I promised. How are you? And Robert! Good to see you!'

Robert stood up. 'How are you, George?' he said civilly.

'Better! Surprisingly better. Robert, we should talk.'

'I don't think so,' Robert said quietly. He turned to Tom, who was watching with beady eyes. 'Glad to hear you're coming home, Tom. I'll see you in Tarnfield. Goodbye, George.'

Robert walked out of the ward and through the hospital into the car park. It was no longer sunny. Grey clouds were coating the sky like stale batter. So George Pattinson was recovering! He was fine, and Mary was dead. Robert felt angry, and rammed his key into the car door. Then he stopped himself. Wasn't it only yesterday that he had felt glad to be alive? He remembered that he had never felt suicidal when Mary was dying, but he had felt that life was something just to be endured. Last spring and summer had been seasons to bear, sometimes ironically beautiful but never a source of pleasure. Yesterday had changed all that. He liked being alive. Did that mean he was a hypocrite too? No better than George?

He knew his urge to go and see Suzy wasn't just because of Tom's odd note. Seeing George Pattinson for the first time in a year had unsettled him and he wanted to be with someone who wasn't part of his past. He sat in the driving seat and thought about it. The note with the Isaiah reference surely had to have come from the person they had started to call the flower arranger. Perhaps the same person had knocked Tom down? But why? There was only Suzy whom Robert could talk to. He put his foot down, and headed for Tarnfield.

34

The Thursday after Trinity Sunday, continued

Almighty God, unto whom all hearts be open, all desires
known, and from whom no secrets are hid . . .
From the Collect for Purity at Holy Communion

In the dark shabby over-furnished grandeur of Tarnfield
House, Jane Simpson followed her husband's unresponsive back out of the kitchen. She trailed him through the
long dim hall, where pink and golden sunlight filtered
from a Gothic stained glass window above the stairs, and
into the stuffy, paper-strewn little room at the back of the
house that he called his office.

Jeff had hardly emerged during the last five days, except
to go to the golf club or the Plough. He had communicated
with his wife through barks and the odd note left on the
kitchen table. He had come to bed after her, and risen
silently while she was still in an uncomfortable doze.
There had been no sexual activity between them for years,
though there had been the inevitable bumping or brushing
and the occasional chat in the night. Now Jeff lay immobile
at the farthest edge of the bed, ignoring any attempts from
Jane to speak to him.

During the day, in front of other people it was just as
before. The Simpsons had fewer social engagements than
they liked others to think. But in the last four or five days
there had been tea with the Ridleys, and the golf club
lunch at the weekend loomed. But between the two of
them there had been no conversation.

On Thursday morning, Jane pounced on her husband when he wandered into the kitchen to make some coffee. She had been waiting in there, knowing that if he heard the slightest noise he would avoid the room. But she'd trapped him by silence. He'd mooched in, and stopped when he saw her. But he said nothing and turned around, put his mug noisily into the sink, and stomped out. She'd been on his heels.

'Jeff,' she said twice in a wheedling voice. Then she stood on the threshold of his office and watched as he sank heavily on to his chair and turned to the screen on his desk. He ignored her.

'Jeff darling, Russell is coming back tonight. He called earlier when you went out to get the paper. He sounded awful. Jeff, what are you going to do?'

Her husband turned round and looked her up and down in disgust. 'What am I going to do? I don't know. I'm still thinking about it.'

'But what about Russ?'

'Why should I give a fuck about him?'

'But he's your son, Jeff. How can you believe that awful woman?'

'Oh, come off it, Jane! We were childless for twenty years and then a baby comes along. Don't think I haven't thought about it before. Russell hasn't got one Simpson feature. And he's useless.'

'How could you say that!'

'It's easy. He's a waster and a loser. A total waste of space. He's thick like you.'

There was a silence. Jane Simpson stopped peering up coyly from under her eyelids. For the first time, she looked at her husband levelly.

'I see.' She sounded cold now. 'So you really think that any son of *yours* would have been brainy and capable? Like you?'

Jeff ignored the heavy sarcasm. 'So you admit it. He's not mine, is he?'

'What do you think? I tried to talk to you about it but you just wouldn't listen. When nothing happened year after year, I went to the doctor's and then I went to Newcastle for tests.'

'Without my permission?'

'What was I supposed to do? Have you refusing to get treatment, then buggering off with someone else – saying it was my fault? Not that that would have done you much good . . .'

Suddenly Jane laughed nastily. 'You know, it's quite funny. I was absolutely fine, and it was you who couldn't function. But I got all the stick for it.'

Jeff couldn't resist. He asked, 'How can you be so sure it was my problem?'

'Because if you must know, it was wham bam, right up the spout the first and only time with someone else. And you and your bloody mother were so relieved you never asked any questions. No one would ever have known he wasn't yours, except for Russ's blood group. That's how Yvonne found out, isn't it? Through the hospital, when he had his tonsils out.'

'I suppose so.'

'But no one knows who Russ's father is. I'm the only one who knows that.'

'Yvonne mentioned a name.'

'She was guessing.'

'Or your boyfriend told her.'

Jane opened her mouth and closed it again. That possibility hadn't occurred to her. The man who'd fathered Russ could never have known for certain. But he might have guessed. And if he'd had a relationship with Yvonne – like half of the men in Tarnfield – he might have talked.

'You can't be sure,' she said quickly. 'Not without a DNA test or whatever it is. And why would you do that?' Her eyes narrowed. 'Be honest. I just solved your problem for you. Did you want your precious mother to know you were firing blanks?'

She paused, growing more confident as she thought it through. 'You didn't complain at the time, did you? But you knew, all right. That's why you weren't even a good father, were you? Maybe Russ has turned out badly because he was brought up by you!'

'You bitch! I did everything for that boy.'

'Except give him the time of day. I should have walked out when I found out he was on the way. We might have been poor but we wouldn't have been used!'

'Well, it's not too late. You can bugger off now.'

'Fine. If you want a divorce, go ahead. I'll take you for all you've got, which isn't much, let's face it.'

'What?'

'I had a reason for playing away. You didn't, you dirty bastard. Don't think I didn't know that you were screwing everyone you could get your hands on. Including Yvonne Wait. Well, the worm's turning now, Jeffrey. I'd get alimony, and you know it. Then I'd make you sell this dump and I'd get a decent bungalow.'

It was the first time Jane Simpson had thought about a future without Jeff. For forty years her whole life had been focused on being a Simpson of Tarnfield House. She looked up at the yellowing ceiling with the flaking paint, and then down the corridor to the dirty fanlight and encrusted door. It suddenly seemed too much. Why should she fight day after day with the dust and grime in this cavernous hall and these mouldering rooms?

She turned, and left her husband at the desk with his mouth open. Over her shoulder she said calmly, 'It's you who's the loser and the waster. And the coward. Even Frank Bell had the guts to tackle Yvonne Wait.'

'How do you know?' Jeff yelled, goaded. 'How do you know it wasn't me?'

He stood up sharply and ran down the hall after her, his cumbersome belly shaking in his tight cream-coloured jumper with the gold golf club crest on the chest. He staggered forward and grabbed the banisters.

'How do you bloody well know it was him? It could have been me!' he called again. But Jane had shut the kitchen door in his face. He leant there, wheezing. A minute later his wife opened the door and looked out. He was still leaning on the newel post, breathless.

'Janey,' he gasped, 'I think it's my heart. Oh God . . .' He slid to his knees and rested his head on the bottom stairs. His eyes rolled. His wife grabbed the phone from the antique hall-stand. With one hand she punched 999. With the other she stroked his shoulders.

'Ambulance,' she said tersely into the phone. 'And make it fast.'

'And so you see,' Babs Piefield said breathlessly to Suzy, 'I really can't sit with Nancy on Saturday because I've got to go and pick up Tom Strickland. Now her husband is in hospital, Jane Simpson can't possibly go.'

'Well, I'll do anything I can to help,' Suzy said. 'Don't worry about it, Babs. If you want me to keep Nancy company on Saturday, I will.'

'Oh, thank you, Suzy. I know Nancy will appreciate it. And I really want to help everyone as best I can . . .'

Suzy raised an eyebrow. It would have been unbearable for Babs to give up the chance of going to fetch Tom Strickland. Not only would the trip mean she'd be a local heroine but she would also get first-hand information about Tom's accident *and* the changes proposed at All Saints!

'But I always sit with Nancy on Wednesdays and Saturday afternoons when Daisy is on her late shift,' Babs was explaining. 'I know she really depends on me, and this week it's worse than usual because Nancy's got an awful cold. If you *could* pop over . . .'

Suzy was mildly surprised. On the few occasions she'd spoken to Mrs Arthur when she ventured into the garden, she had seemed quite self-sufficient and hardly in need of a nursemaid. But Babs was clearly agitated about neglecting her, so the easiest thing was to agree. Rachel was coming to stay for the weekend but she wouldn't mind popping in to the Arthurs' for an hour, Suzy thought. She liked seeing inside people's houses and she wasn't really one for the great outdoors.

'Well, thanks again.' Babs backed down the hall. As she

did so she caught sight of Robert in the living room. 'Oh, hello. You're here again,' she said pointedly. She couldn't resist giving Suzy an old-fashioned look, but commuted it into a forced smile before hurrying out.

Robert was playing a noisy word game on the floor with Molly while managing at the same time to look over Jake's shoulder at the computer screen. He'd come straight round to Tarn Acres from the hospital, but had been hijacked by the kids before he could tell Suzy about the note by Tom's bed.

Suzy said, 'Molly, give Robert a break. You can watch kids' TV now. And Jake, I need you to go down to Lo-cost for me. If Rob's staying for tea we need more spaghetti.' Jake grumbled as he got down from the desk, but Suzy could see that he was pleased.

'Does this mean I get some help with my course work?' he asked.

'Maybe.' Suzy smiled at Robert. 'I haven't even asked you if you want to stay?'

'That's all right. I do.'

'Great.' Suzy watched Jake amble into the hall, and Molly tune in to the TV.

'OK, now we've got a second, tell me what you found at the hospital.'

'It was a get well card. No, it was just a notelet. And in it was the message: Isaiah 5:11.'

'You're joking!'

'No, I'm not. Get the Bible. What does that verse say?'

Suzy leafed through Jake's Good News Bible. 'I don't believe it. It says, *You are doomed! You get up early in the morning to start drinking, and you spend long evenings getting drunk . . .*'

'That's it!' Robert was so excited he stood up, and Molly tore her eyes from the TV to look at him. He sat down again, but without thinking he grabbed Suzy's hand. 'It's the flower arranger. That must be the person who knocked Tom down. Tom said there were dried flowers in the envelope.'

'Really? What were they?'

'He said marigolds. Where's *The Language of Flowers*?' He had brought it round after Molly had asked about it, the evening he'd taken Jake to the college. It had been good of him to think of something for Molly too.

Suzy grabbed it from the shelf. 'Yes! Look, Robert. African marigolds mean vulgar minds. You couldn't get more vulgar than Tom Strickland.'

'Exactly! That proves it, doesn't it? First Phyllis, with a reed. That means indiscretion and has a direct reference to Isaiah. Then Yvonne with the hellebore message, all about Isaiah. Now Tom, who survived but who got his message in the post. It's conclusive. We've got to tell the police.'

'But we can't be the only people to have realized what's going on.'

'We were the only people to see the hellebore. I agree that it could have just been over-imagination on our part. But now there are these flowers, and the note to Tom Strickland.'

'You're right.' Suzy bit her lip. 'But I felt such a fool last time I tried to explain all this to the cops.'

'So we need to talk it through with someone else. We need an objective view . . .'

'Look, my best friend Rachel is coming this weekend. It's not long to wait. Come over on Saturday night for supper and let's see what she thinks.'

But would it be soon enough? And even if Suzy trusted her best friend, why would Rachel's opinion be worth listening to? Yet Robert could see that Suzy was unsure now about telling the police. It did all seem far-fetched. The change in the weather from the grim grey of winter to the bright normality of the sunshine, plus the way the police had treated her as an idiot when she had tried to talk, had undermined her confidence in her earlier judgement. Well, maybe Rachel would help restore it, he thought. He became aware that Suzy was holding his arm, waiting for his reply.

'OK,' he said.

The front door slammed and Jake came ambling into the room. As if guilty, Suzy jumped away.

271

'Here's the spag,' Jake mumbled, and chucked the packet on to the kitchen counter. Then he turned away and shambled out. They heard him banging up the stairs. His body language had signalled discomfort. He was at the stage when a happy, open face could look cherubic one minute and Gothic the next. Suzy said nothing, but she had noted his change of mood.

But twenty minutes later, when he joined them at the table, he seemed happier.

'What time is Dad coming to pick us up tomorrow?' he asked.

'In the morning. About eleven.'

'Great,' he said. Suzy shot a worried glance at Robert. Until then Jake had shown no enthusiasm for going to Nigel's. I hope he doesn't suddenly feel resentful of Robert, she thought. But at the first whiff of bolognese sauce Jake was cheerful and chatty again. As they waited for their pasta, Molly came bouncing over and put the kitten into Robert's lap.

'She likes you. D'you like kittens?' Molly said, as it fought to get away.

Jake guffawed. 'I like kittens. But I couldn't eat a whole one.'

'Jake,' Molly whined, 'you're horrible.' Her brother cackled, the cat fled, Robert sucked a scratched finger, and the smell of singed tomatoes filled the kitchen. Apologetically, Suzy caught Robert's eye. But he was smiling. Whatever had upset Jake earlier was over and normal service was resumed.

Jake ate his meal, forcing himself to think ahead. He loved his dad but he hadn't really wanted to go to Newcastle that weekend. Like a lot of children, he was totally pragmatic about his parents' separation and he'd hoped that Robert might offer him another trip to the college computers on Friday. But now he was glad he was getting out of Tarnfield. On his trip to Lo-cost to get the spaghetti, he'd been accosted by Matthew Bell.

'Oi, you. Spencer.'

'What?'

272

'Come 'ere. Listen. If you say owt to your nosy mam about our trip to Carlisle, you're for it. OK?'

'I'm not going to split.'

'Fucking better not. You just keep yer mouth shut. Or else.'

'I've said I'll keep quiet.'

'I won't be around next week. Me mam's sending me to me sister's. I've got exams to take in Carlisle. But see them lads over there?' Matthew gestured towards two of his older gang. 'They've got their eyes on you. If you say anything, they'll be round at your house. Your mam an' your sister 'ad better watch out. Understand?' He put his hand on Jake's arm. Jake shook it off, and walked away.

Secrets were OK, Jake thought. You were supposed to have them from your parents. But this one made him feel really uncomfortable. It was scary. He bitterly regretted going out with Matthew Bell. The trip had been tense and he knew he had been manipulated. At times he felt really scared about what they had done. At least going to his dad's at Newcastle gave him a weekend's respite, and then Matthew would be away for a week. I'll just have to keep my head down, he thought, and hope this all goes away somehow. He remembered Matthew Bell's balled fists waved in front of his face, and gagged. Then he attacked his spaghetti bolognese with ferocity.

35

The weekend of the First Sunday after Trinity

Be ye sure that the Lord he is God: it is he that hath made us and not we ourselves.
From the Jubilate Deo, *Psalm 100, sung at Morning Prayer*

The next morning, the Friday of half-term week, Suzy saw the children off with Nigel in his new posh car, made up the bed in the spare room, and then drove into Carlisle to meet Rachel from the train. She parked in the Lanes multi-storey car park. It was another beautiful day. The city's biscuit brown buildings stood out against a pure blue sky. Rachel's train wasn't arriving till three o'clock and Suzy had some knickers and socks to buy, but the job took no time. She bought a sandwich in Marks & Spencer's, prowled round the shops, walked round the pretty old town hall with the steps up the outside, and went and sat on the wall by the cathedral.

When she had finished eating, she wandered into the cathedral close with its beautiful eighteenth-century houses, still in the same dark sandstone, with the medieval archway leading into the city. There was a clear sense of the ancient layout. She put her head inside the huge wooden cathedral door. There were two or three people working inside, primping at flower arrangements and sorting service books for the weekend, and one woman was polishing, so the scent of beeswax drifted over the dark shiny wood. There were a couple of tourists talking softly with a smiling verger figure in a robe. It had a warm, accessible air.

Suzy sat down at the back and thought about when she had tiptoed into All Saints at Tarnfield. There had been the sense of care and communal effort there too. She shut her eyes and remembered how suddenly Mary Clark had appeared at the end of the pew, with George Pattinson a few yards behind. Yet at the time she had had no sense of disturbing them. Surely if they'd been having a tryst in the church, she would have seen them jumping apart or something, as she had jumped away from Robert the day before? She tried hard to recreate the scene, but she remembered nothing except a sense of being welcomed. Yet she knew that everything pointed to George and Mary having an affair. Whatever Robert said, Yvonne Wait had asserted it, categorically.

And to some extent Suzy wanted it to be true. She was sick of Mary being Mrs Perfect, and she was jealous too. She thought about Robert in his shirtsleeves and jeans, waiting for them in the car park at the Scar. He had looked quite young, and he had the sort of build she liked. She'd had enough of Nigel's self-conscious style and gym-lean figure.

She knew she was getting dependent on Robert because he was her only friend in Tarnfield. And she missed the physical closeness of Nigel – not Nigel as such, but as a man and a companion. The empty space in the bed was getting bigger. But there was no point in getting remotely fond of Robert if he was still in love with his wife. Or even if he was prepared to move on, but with Mary's blessing. That wouldn't feel right. Suzy knew that she couldn't bear to come second, even to a memory. If she and Robert were to have a relationship, she didn't just want to be different from his wife – she had to be better. It wasn't a very nice thing to acknowledge, but it was human nature. Her nature, anyway. She was made that way.

But all the cards were stacked in Mary's favour. People always edited their memories and she was sure Robert was no different. However hard you tried, it was nearly impossible to really recall the sense of fear or apprehension, or worry or suspicion once it was over. You just remembered how events turned out, not how you anticipated them. So Mary was bound to become even more perfect in retrospect.

She got up and walked past the department stores to the Citadel, the big Victorian sandstone towers which gave the city its tough Border appearance the moment you got off the train, and then she strolled down to the station. It was festooned with flowers now, but it still squatted, strong and square as if expecting a regiment of Border reivers or Jacobite rebels to get off the 0930 from Euston. I wonder what Rachel will think of me, she thought, looking down at her old denim jacket, baggy trousers and trainers. The train pulled in, sleek and growling, smelling of brake fluid and metal and hot plastic, and suddenly after the tense waiting there was the drama of people disembarking. As always, Suzy couldn't see anyone specific in the bustle of people and bags and kids and luggage, so Rachel appeared right in front of her while she was still peering short-sightedly into the distance.

'My God, it's freezing up here,' Rachel was saying, wrapping her woollen jacket round her tiny body. Suzy pulled her close in a hug.

As always, it was as if they'd last met over a cappuccino the day before. As Suzy skirted the roundabout at the Sands, and took the road to the east, Rachel was still talking about the stupidity of the latest director on *Living Lies*.

'But it's beautiful here.' Rachel stopped gossiping for a second to pay respect to the scenery and then started again. She only paused a little later to say, 'So this is terrifying Tarnfield,' as Suzy slowed down into the village. It helped, Suzy thought, to find that all the same things were bugging Rachel as had bugged her in the past, that no one's life was perfect and that the world beyond Tarnfield was full of frustrations too. The commissioning editor was incapable of honesty, the producer had been promoted beyond her ability, the director was a fuck-wit, and the programme was only saved by the team, who were wonderful but thoroughly exploited.

'But nobody cares what we think,' Rachel said cheerily. 'Wow, your house is quite nice. The street's tiny, Suzy, not like Hampstead Garden Suburb at all.'

An hour later she allowed Suzy to drag her out into the fresh air wearing a jacket and pullover over a twin set, with a pair of borrowed lace-ups, but the country walk was really only a pretext for Rachel to see The Briars.

'So this is where he lives! Not bad. It would be worth a couple of million in Clapham.'

'And even more in Barbados! Anyway, nice as it is, it's a bit too big to look after, if you ask me. Still, it's not a stately home like Tarnfield House.'

They walked back past the Simpsons' early Victorian pile, which duly impressed Rachel, but she pointed out that the windows needed replacing and the huge door was warped. Suzy was surprised. She hadn't realized how much the place had deteriorated since she had moved to Tarnfield. Rachel raved about Yvonne's Georgian town house and expressed admiration for Alan Robie's efforts at Church Cottage. Then they passed All Saints, skirted the Green and ambled into the Plough for a quick drink, where Rachel caused great amusement by asking for Kir Royale and settling for something sparkly with a dash of sweet dark cordial.

'How's Jeff Simpson?' Suzy asked the barman.

'Out of intensive care, I hear,' he replied. 'Funny how Lady Jane's got two of them to look after now.' He smiled cheekily, and moved off to tell a group of darts players about the woman from London demanding blackcurrant fizz.

'So what about your murder mystery?' Rachel demanded.

'Shush!' Suzy lowered her head. 'It's not a murder mystery and anyway we shouldn't talk about it in here.'

'Suzy, those are contradictory statements. So when am I going to get to meet the lovely Robert?'

Suzy squirmed even more. 'Tomorrow, over supper, but

till then we've got loads of time to talk. Oh, and I want you to help me with a neighbourhood thing.' She explained about sitting with Nancy.

'It's like being in *The Archers*.' Rachel giggled. 'But it's OK by me. And then it's dinner with the gorgeous man?'

'Yes! But keep your voice down,' Suzy hissed.

'My God, what's got into you? You never used to worry abut what people thought.'

'Well, I do now!'

Rachel laughed out loud. 'Time you came back to London for a long weekend. Bring the widower! Now, what about another of these delicious Ribena cocktails. The barman's quite cute too!'

Suzy watched her friend sashay to the bar. She was right. It had been too easy to get sucked into the Tarnfield value system. What did it matter what Babs Piefield or Jane Simpson thought? And Yvonne Wait? But Yvonne had been different, Suzy reminded herself. She had been dangerous.

That night, over a bottle of wine, she told Rachel all about it. Her friend's good sense soon asserted itself. Rachel could be a laugh but above all she was sensible.

'I think you might be right about something sinister going on. But that's not your problem. Your big worry's Jake. You need to find out what he was up to. It could have been drugs, Suzy. They're rife everywhere, perhaps even more so here where the kids have less to do.'

'I know. I thought of that but I decided that if he said he wasn't going to get involved with that gang again, I'd let it go.'

'But even if that's what Jake says, he might not be able to avoid this awful Bell kid. This is a small place.'

'True.' Suzy sighed. 'You're right. I'll tackle Jake when he comes back from Nigel's.'

That decision made things easier. Once Tarnfield matters were out of the way, they could go on talking till past midnight. The great thing about long-term friends, Suzy thought, was that you got beyond posturing.

'It's funny,' she said; 'when Nigel left I thought that my

sex life would be over, for a few years at any rate. I was stuck here in Tarnfield with a bit of freelance work, mostly with other women or gay men. So who was I going to meet?'

'And then . . .?'

'Oh, I don't know.'

'So you're confirming that you've met someone? Is it the widower? Am I right?'

Suzy's instinct was to laugh it off but she knew her friend would see through her. She was surprised to feel heat creeping over her neck. 'I'm not stupid enough to compete with a dead woman who had an affair with the vicar!'

'Well, there was that film director from Granada. The one you said couldn't find the clitoris, but caught your sore toe every time!'

Suzy threw a cushion at her. Rachel stopped laughing. 'But seriously, Suzy, I hope you don't fancy someone who's in love with the past. I can see you blushing.'

'Bollocks. It must be a hot flush. C'mon, it's time for bed.'

Nearly a fortnight after his bombshell had hit the congregation at All Saints, Nick Melling sat with Kevin Jones in the vicarage to take stock.

'I'm surprised how calmly everyone's taken it.'

'Me too, Nick, me too. But then again what could they do?' Kevin chuckled happily. But Nick was really rather disappointed. He had progressed from dreading any confrontation to working himself up to being pilloried and loathed, and it was mildly frustrating to find his martyrdom *de trop*.

'Have you heard from Daisy at all?' he enquired.

'No, not a dicky bird,' Kevin grunted. 'I don't know if she's really up for it, Nick. I mean, she's got a lot of friends and neighbours in the old guard.'

Nick didn't mention that Daisy had come round after dark the evening before. He'd kept her on the doorstep.

He was worried about being compromised. Daisy had seemed supportive. She asked him twice about the Bible study group.

'The Bible is so important, Nick. We really do have to start studying it again. I'm sure I can persuade some of my old school friends to join us. Some have got young families now and I know they're just the sort of people you want. I could do a lot to help.'

He really didn't want any form of Bible study to prepare for. It was so much effort. And however hard you tried, people brought their own ideas along.

'Thank you so much, Daisy. But you work full-time. And have your mother to look after.' That gave him a thought. 'Perhaps if you just got your mum to come to church that would be a beginning.' What a bright move! It would give her something evangelical to do while keeping her out of his hair.

'My mum. Yes.' Daisy had looked at him anxiously. 'You haven't ever talked to her about the church, have you?'

'Good heavens no.' Nick felt a shiver of anxiety. 'Do you think I should?'

'No!' Daisy almost yelped. 'No, don't do that, Nick. My mum's too ill to go to church.'

'Well, of course I could bring the sacrament to your house.' Nick wasn't really keen on this idea. It was a lot of effort for one communicant.

'No! Mum's not confirmed. Or baptized.' Daisy's voice sounded suddenly loud. 'But I promise, Nick, really, I'll try and get Mum to think about it.' Then her head dropped as if defeated. She turned to walk away, drooping slightly. It was really too much, Nick thought. As if he didn't have enough to do reorganizing the parish and leading them in a new direction, without having to worry about individuals like Nancy Arthur.

He had gone back inside to work on his new service sheet. He had been worried over whether he ought to lead the intercessions as well as do the sermon. That was one of the things he had asked Kevin Jones to meet him to discuss.

'What do you think?' he asked, safe in the knowledge that Kevin would agree with anything he suggested.

'I dunno,' Kevin said. 'I suppose if someone else leads the praying there's a danger of, y'know, off-message ideas.'

'Absolutely!' Nick sighed. He was going to have to take on everything himself. He wrote NM in the margins next to 'Prayers', and glanced over at Kevin, who was scratching his bottom. What a pity he was so unappealing, Nick suddenly thought disloyally. Still, Kevin was the cross he had to bear. If only there had been someone in the parish he could really relate to, someone with an attractive manner who talked the same language – modern argot laced with intelligent insight. Kevin coughed and massaged his fleshy ear luxuriantly.

There was a ring on the vicarage doorbell. Sighing again, Nick rose to answer it. It would probably be Daisy, back for another try at penetrating his defences. Despite the warm weather it was cool and dark in the hall, and he put the bright overhead light on. When he opened the door, the person on the doorstep was fully illuminated.

Nick almost stepped back in surprise. In front of him was one of the most handsome young men he had ever seen. He was dressed in a black leather jacket, his long legs in slim-fitting black trousers and his blond highlights shining in the harsh electric light.

He had a soft, educated voice. 'Nick Melling?' he said. 'I wonder if I could have a word with you? I want some personal advice, and it's hard to know where to get it in Tarnfield on a Friday night. We haven't met, though you know my mother.

'My name is Russell Simpson.'

36

The weekend of the First Sunday after Trinity, continued

Have pity upon us miserable sinners, who now are visited with great sickness.
From the Prayer in the time of any common Plague

On Saturday afternoon, their hangovers dulled by smoked salmon, scrambled eggs and about a gallon of tea, Suzy and Rachel ventured out and turned towards the Arthurs' house.

'If this woman has got ME and a heavy cold and doesn't want to get out of bed, how do we get in?' Rachel asked.

'Babs Piefield put her key through my letterbox this morning,' Suzy explained.

Actually, Babs had rung the doorbell three times first, but Suzy hadn't answered. She'd been wearing her pyjamas and much-used dressing gown, and had felt as if walking down the hallway might dislodge her head. And she hadn't wanted to listen to Babs rabbiting on.

Suzy struggled with the lock. Then the key turned and the door swung inwards. The Arthurs' house was completely quiet. Like all the houses in Tarn Acres it had parquet floors, but these were covered with expensive oriental rugs. The wallpaper was dark blue and there were several heavy original paintings in twisted gilt frames. As in Suzy's house, the kitchen opened straight from the hall, open-plan style, but there was a separate front room to the right.

'I feel really awkward,' Rachel whispered.

'Me too. Hello . . . Nancy?' Suzy called.

From the room to the right there was the sound of someone waking, the sharp gasp of breath and the rustle of bedding. Suzy knocked on the half-open door. 'Hello,' she said again. 'Mrs Arthur?'

'I'll wait,' Rachel said. She slipped down the hallway.

A disembodied voice, confused with sleep, answered from inside the downstairs bedroom. 'Who is it?'

'It's me, Suzy Spencer. Babs Piefield asked me to call.'

There was an audible sigh. 'Oh dear,' groaned Nancy Arthur. 'Just hang on a minute . . .'

While she waited, Suzy peered at the expensive paintings in the hall.

Then Nancy called: 'Come in.' Unlike the hall, the bedroom was light and feminine, modern, decorated in white and pink, with a huge double bed facing a television. Nancy Arthur was a big woman but everything around her was to scale. She had pulled a pink dressing gown round her shoulders.

'Why are you here?' she asked. 'And how did you get in?'

'I'm sorry we startled you. Babs gave me her key. She needed to go and pick up Tom Strickland from hospital so she asked me and my friend to sit with you instead.'

Nancy relaxed. She raised her eyes. 'That's typical of Babs. What a commotion! I'm quite capable of staying by myself. To be honest, it's almost a relief . . .'

'I'm sorry. We'll go . . .'

'No, please, I didn't mean to be unpleasant to you. It's just that Babs fusses so much. She wants to be needed, you know.' Nancy blew her nose into a large pink tissue.

'But this is embarrassing for us! Look, now we're here is there anything we could do for you? Make a cup of tea?'

'I don't usually like people having to look after me. I always leave a tray ready for Babs so she doesn't need to do anything more than boil water. But if there are three of us . . . Oh dear, I'd get up if it wasn't for this awful cold . . .' Nancy heaved in the bed like a small earthquake.

'We can do that.' Suzy called out: 'Put the kettle on, Rache.'

'Well, if you don't mind.' Nancy looked agitated. 'Does Daisy know you're here?'

'I don't know.'

'Oh dear! Perhaps we should call her?'

There was no need. They heard the sound of a car pulling up sharply. Within minutes there was the rasp of another key in the lock, and Daisy came huffing in, scattering jackets and bags.

'Mum . . . are you OK? Who's that woman in the kitchen?'

'It's Mrs Spencer and her friend, dear. They've come instead of Babs.'

'So there are two of them? I saw Babs driving out of the village when I was checking the lemonade delivery. I was really surprised because she always sits with you on Saturdays.' Daisy started plumping up Nancy's pillows and straightening the bed around her mother.

'She asked us to come instead,' Suzy said apologetically. She was unused to Daisy in aggressive mode, but this was the first time she had come between her and her mother. Perhaps it was understandable, Suzy thought. Daisy was her mother's keeper, after all.

'She should have told me first!'

'Well, it doesn't matter, dear,' Mrs Arthur said placatingly. 'Let's have some tea.'

'But you know having visitors always wears you out.' Daisy turned to Suzy. 'Mum can get very easily tired.' She motioned with her head towards the bedroom door. Suzy and Rachel followed her.

'I'm sorry, Suzy,' Daisy whispered in the doorway. 'I know it seems rude but Mum sometimes exhausts herself. It would have been much better to let her have a rest this afternoon. It's very hard for other people to understand Mum's illness. I sometimes think Babs hasn't a clue about the stress she can cause.'

'That's OK. We'll go now.'

'Thank you.' Daisy gave them a quick, unhappy social smile. She shut the door swiftly behind them.

Suzy waited until they had climbed up the Arthurs' drive, past the rockery that distinguished Nancy's front garden, and into the street. Then she put her hand on her friend's arm.

'I'm sorry, Rachel. I've never seen Daisy like that. She couldn't wait to get rid of us. I can't think what was wrong.'

'Oh, I can.'

'What?'

'Don't you realize?' Rachel looked at her. 'Oh, never mind. I could be wrong.' Then her eyeline flickered past Suzy's head.

'Hey!' she said excitedly. 'Isn't that a car at your house? Suzy, it looks like you're having a visit from Jude Law in his prime! This isn't the gorgeous widower, is it?'

'Sadly, no.' Suzy squinted at the apparition walking down her path. 'I don't know who he is.' She frowned and hurried towards her own house.

The beautiful young man came towards her. 'Mrs Spencer? Jake's mum? Could we go inside? I've got something I must tell you.'

Five minutes later, Russell Simpson was sitting on Suzy's sofa with the kitten on his lap. Suzy hadn't taken her jacket off. She was sitting opposite him, leaning forward, desperate to hear what he had to say.

'So what's this about?' She felt slightly sick.

'I'm a mate of Matt Bell's. At least I *was* a mate of Matt Bell's. I need to talk to you in confidence, Mrs Spencer.'

Russell squirmed a little on the sofa and then settled down. 'I have to tell you all this so you understand. About two weeks ago I found out something about my family.' Suzy tried not to push him, though she was desperate to know what this had to do with Jake.

'I found a letter addressed to me.' He stopped. Suzy was in an agony of suspense, but bit her lip. 'The letter said that the person I thought was my dad, wasn't my dad.

285

And when I think about it now, I've heard rumours, and heard funny remarks in the past. But this was the first time I saw it written down as a fact.' He swallowed. 'The letter said that the man who really was my father was someone else.'

'Who?' Suzy knew he wanted her to ask, and that she ought to try and be sympathetic to this. But all she wanted to know was where Jake came in. Russell Spencer leant forward to re-engage her eyes.

'You know him, Mrs Spencer. My dad.'

Suzy looked at the handsome face in front of her. 'I know your natural father?'

'Yes. Everyone does.' Russell Simpson smiled and, as with one photo transparency over another, Suzy saw the resemblance.

'Oh yes!' she said.

'You can see it, can't you? I know you can! I'm a Strickland. Like my mum.' He paused for effect. 'And like my dad too!'

'Tom Strickland is your father?'

He nodded, and smiled. He was quite gorgeous. Even in her anxiety to move the story on and find out what it had to do with Jake, Suzy couldn't help staring. Russell had Tom's big, muscular frame and a slim version of the beautiful face Sharon Strickland had under the puppy fat.

'Matt and I got pissed that Saturday after I found out. We took Matt's car. I was furious. I wanted to have it out with old Tom. We knew he usually went drinking at the Scar Inn. So we went up there to find him. He was staggering all over the road as usual. Matt was going too fast and . . . well, he hit him.'

'So it was you! But where does Jake come in?'

Russell carried on, slowly and patiently. 'When we got back there was mud and blood and bits of Tom's old raincoat on the front of Matthew's car. We knew the police were all around the place because Yvonne Wait had been killed in the church. Matt wanted to go back and drive the car through Tarn Ford to get the muck off. We went as fast as we could. But the ford was too full to drive into.'

He took a breath, and went on, 'So on Sunday Matthew had to get it to a car wash. I wanted to go back to Newcastle to avoid my mum and dad. So we decided Matt should pick up Jake and take him to Carlisle. Matt gets allergies. He's allergic to the car wash stuff. So he needed help.'

'And Jake was young and easily impressed, and you thought you could bully him . . .'

'Yes. Jake had been gagging to get in the car with Matt.'

'And why have you had a sudden turn of conscience?'

'Because Matt said he was going to see to it that Jake never talked. He was going to scare him a bit. That was going too far.'

'What? I don't bloody believe it!' Suzy jumped up, disgust in her voice. 'Well, you can tell Matthew Bell that if he lays a finger on my son – no, if he even *thinks* of laying a finger on my son, I will have him strung up by the balls, if we can find any, and left to swing until he screams for mercy.'

There was a silence. Suzy sat down again. In a way she had to admire Russell Simpson. No one had made him come to see her. 'I suppose I should thank you. Except that you got Jake into this mess in the first place.'

'In a way he got himself into it, Mrs Spencer. He's been hanging around Matthew since Easter.'

Suzy looked at the floor. It was true. Jake had been longing for a trip in Matthew's car. But what should she have done? Should she have let him go? Had she been too strict? Had she failed because he couldn't talk to her like he could to his dad? How bad was it for Jake to have an absentee father?

'And what about your dad?' she asked.

Russell laughed disarmingly. 'I've got used to the idea of Tom Strickland. I'd rather have been born than not. And now I know I'm a Tarnfield boy really. I like village life. I mean, the first thing I decided to do about this mess was to see the vicar. I used to be a choirboy for George Pattinson, you know.'

Suzy looked up. 'You didn't tell Nick Melling any of this?'

'Shit, no. I called at the vicarage last night but the new chap looked at me as if I was something the cat brought in.'

'You and me both! What about going over to see George Pattinson? People say he's much better now.'

'I might do that. Thanks, Mrs Spencer. And friend.' He unwrapped his long body. He had Jane Simpson's legs, Suzy thought, and he turned his brilliant smile on Rachel who looked like a rabbit trapped in headlights. I bet he has that effect on all women, Suzy thought.

Rachel motioned to Russell to follow her out and left Suzy sitting stunned on the sofa. Suzy heard him saying goodbye. He sounded innocently cheerful, not at all as she had imagined the famous Russell Simpson, playboy of the parish. She was aware her hand was shaking and that the tea Rachel had made and pressed into her hand was spilt on the coffee table. It was relief. So Jake had been bullied, and by helping with the car wash he'd been caught up in what was possibly a crime. But it wasn't drugs. And he had learnt his lesson.

Rachel came back into the living room, open-mouthed. 'Well, what a charmer! You can tell me the full implications later. So what's next on this roller-coaster weekend? Shouldn't we be cooking? Or at least opening some wine!'

'I suppose we should. Look at the time!' Suzy stood up. 'But I still need to get my head around what Russell has told me. And maybe ring Jake at Nigel's. Oh . . . and there's something else . . .'

'What?'

'Well, this has changed everything. I think Robert's going to be disappointed to find that Tom Strickland's accident was nothing to do with the phantom flower arranger.'

'Why should that disappoint him?'

'Well, perhaps it means that we've been imagining the whole thing from the start!'

37

The weekend of the First Sunday after Trinity, continued

O Eternal God, our heavenly father, who alone makest men
to be of one mind in a house . . .
From the Thanksgiving for restoring Public Peace at Home

Matthew Bell dragged his backpack out from under the bed and started to ram it full of half-dirty clothes. He was mad as hell. He didn't want to go to Joanne's for a fortnight while he resat his exams. In fact, he didn't want to resit his exams. He'd done no revision and he had no interest in them. What he wanted to do was go travelling.

It wasn't fair. Other lads he knew had gone to Australia and New Zealand. One even had a relative who'd got him into the States. 'The United States of America,' he said aloud, rolling the consonants and deepening the vowel sounds. His mum would've let him go, but his dad said no. And even his mum had said he ought to do some wimpy gap year scheme. But that wasn't what Matthew wanted. He had visions of taking a car and motoring coolly through the desert, music blaring. Shit, shit, shit, he said to himself.

He'd told his mother that morning that he wanted to get out of Tarnfield.

'Well, you can,' she'd said. 'To our Joanne's in Carlisle. Pack tonight and I'll take you first thing in the morning. You're not having the car. You can get the bus to Norbridge

College from Carlisle. There's plenty of public transport from there.'

And then Russ had turned up, which should have been great, but instead Russ gave him an earful about stupid little Jake Spencer. Matthew didn't know what had come over Russ. He'd gone all mature and sorry. And he'd blabbed to Suzy Spencer, that big-headed cow who thought she was someone 'cos she'd once met Judy from *The Richard and Judy Show*. So seeing to Jake wasn't on the agenda – more was the pity.

Still, there were things Russell didn't know about. Matthew savagely yanked his desk chair towards him and switched on his computer. He wasn't that brainy when it came to IT, but he wasn't just into games and porn. He switched on his email. He didn't use it much but he'd had the sense to get addresses for most of his cronies. Jake Spencer had been really proud to give his. Good, here it was.

Matthew bashed his bony fingers on to Create Mail. I'll rattle him, he thought angrily. *Spencer*, he wrote, *You tell your smart-arsed mam that my car was clean when we went to Carlisle. And if she tells my mam or enyone else, I'll get all of you. Your sis as well. Gess who?*

That made him feel better. 'Matthew?' he heard his mother yelling. 'Get down here now for tea. And then we're having a family conference. So you're grounded.'

Shit, shit and double shit, he thought. Maybe it was just as well that he was going to Carlisle. Who knows, he might get out to a pub and find some totty. And it was nice to think he'd be leaving the fear of hell behind him. Hellfire, he thought. It would be nice to put a bomb through the Spencers' window. That would keep them quiet.

'Coming, Mam,' he said, and then went downstairs.

In the Mid Cumbria Hospital, Jane Simpson sat by her husband's bed. He was out of intensive care now. His heart attack had been mild, but he'd need more surgery in time.

'A wake-up call,' the consultant had said. 'But it was a good thing your wife was there.'

'I didn't want to see you drop dead,' Jane had said drily. She rather liked being a hospital visitor. And to her surprise, Russell had turned up at Jeff's private ward. He hadn't said much, but he'd come. When she'd called to tell him about Jeff's heart attack, he hadn't mentioned the lilac letter. But he'd said, 'Poor Dad. I suppose all this is getting to all of us.'

Jane rarely thought about other people's motives, but she was more sensitive to her son's feelings than to anyone else's. When Russell had been a little boy, before the money troubles and worries about the future had soured his relationship with his father, they'd had the odd moment of companionship. But Jeff was always too wrapped up confirming his place in the world to have much time for a child.

Even so, Russell had been a little darling before he went to boarding school. She remembered when he was in the nativity play at All Saints, when George Pattinson had come back to the village as vicar. Russ had been so sweet. He'd always been a good-looking boy.

'Hello, Dad,' he said when he came into Jeff's room. That was really nice of him. It was her old Russell talking. She'd glanced warily at him a few times, but he'd said nothing about Tom Strickland. And then, after visiting time was over, he'd taken her to the hotel opposite the hospital for coffee. She had waited, tense, for the subject of his parentage to come up. But he had merely patted her on the hand and said, 'Dad looks a bit brighter than I thought he would.' They had chatted about the hospital. Jane was careful to say nothing that might provoke any outpouring. But Russell had been the model of restraint.

Then, as they went to their separate cars, he said, 'Mum, I went to see George Pattinson on my way here. It's been ages since I saw anyone from Tarnfield. Except that chav Matthew Bell.'

'Good. That's nice,' Jane said. 'What did he say?'

'He asked me to go and see Tom, so I did.' Russell's face

looked different, Jane thought. Clearer, somehow. She couldn't quite put her finger on it. And then she thought, my son looks *happy*.

Russell said, 'Mum, Tom knew it was me with Matthew in the car that hit him. He's always known about me, hasn't he? I told him it was an accident. He said it was his own fault. He shouldn't have got rat-arsed and tried to walk back in the dark.'

When she got home, Jane allowed herself a huge wave of relief. Things were changing for the better. With luck she could persuade Jeff to get out of this mausoleum and into a nice bungalow. Perhaps they could buy Phyllis's place and do it up. The thought made her laugh into her sweet sherry. Russell didn't hate her. Jeff was grateful to her. Above all, Yvonne Wait was dead.

She poured herself another drink. It went down smoothly like silk and tasted wonderful.

Saturday night at Suzy's house was anything but smooth. Robert and Rachel had hit it off surprisingly well, but, after a few drinks and some dips as starters, Suzy could hear them bickering in a friendly way about politics as she was sorting out the roast chicken and watercress salad.

She sat down with them and told Robert about Russ Simpson.

'So that's what happened! It doesn't explain the card with the Isaiah reference though.'

'Isn't it possible you misread it? And you never actually saw the petals.'

'It's possible I got it wrong, I suppose.' Robert's forehead wrinkled; then he shrugged and smiled. 'Still, I'm really pleased Russ came and confessed. But will he tell the police?'

'I don't know,' Suzy had said. 'Perhaps that will depend on George Pattinson. I suggested that Russell went to see him. He seemed to want to talk to someone and he obviously respects George.' Robert had said nothing, but a frown had creased the bridge of his nose.

'So there you go,' Rachel had said chirpily. 'Another rational explanation. Don't you think something straight-forward like that might be behind all of this?'

'You mean the reed through Phyllis's hand and the hellebore leaves?'

'Yes! I mean, isn't it possible that you imagined too much into them? In fact neither of you saw the reed at all, did you? It was just that Strickland chap who told you.'

'But the hellebore definitely said something. And there was Yvonne's hair as well.'

'She could have had it cut professionally. That may seem odd but it's not as odd as some murderer cutting it off to match a Bible reading.'

'You weren't there, Rachel. There was definitely a mes-sage, wasn't there, Suzy?'

Suzy came over to the table with the meat. 'It's organic and free range,' she said. Now Rachel was here, it was a lot more difficult to imagine what it had been like two weeks ago. The new season with its bright sunshine and fresh blossom, and the arrival of her friend from the world outside, had helped her put much of her anxiety behind. But Robert was adamant.

'Don't change the subject. You saw those leaves, Suzy, didn't you? They meant something, didn't they?'

Suzy sat down. She wasn't sure what to say. At the time she had been convinced that the hellebore leaves had been placed in a pattern. But now all she could see in her mind's eye was Daisy's feet slipping all over them, and the sound of her voice saying 'It's awful, it's awful' over and over again.

'Rob, I really don't know any more. I just can't see what it could mean or where it could lead. I wouldn't be sur-prised if someone pulled Yvonne off the ladder but it could have been anyone. So many people hated her. And why write Bible messages? And as for Phyllis – well, we only have Tom's word for the reed.'

'But it was you who started me thinking. Why have you changed your mind? Again!'

'Because the explanation for Tom Strickland's accident is

so mundane. The truth is, it was just about two lads tearing round the countryside looking for trouble. It's obvious, in a way. I mean, putting motives aside, we should have thought of Matthew Bell as the hit-and-run driver straight away.'

'And the card?'

'The notelet was just a spiteful anonymous letter.'

'So there you are,' said Rachel, laughing. 'It's the perfect rural story, the sort of thing we Londoners always think goes on in villages. A dark stormy night, a drunken dirty old local, joyriders, incest –'

'Incest?' said Robert sharply.

'Yeah. That's a village problem, an incest thing, isn't it? They're all supposed to be at it in the country.' Rachel laughed. 'You know, this boy Russell whose father was really his second cousin.'

'That's hardly incest,' Suzy said, glancing at Robert who was staring at the floor.

'OK, OK, but you know what I mean.' Rachel laughed louder. 'If you say so, I'll pass on the incest. But I think you'll find this whole thing is a lot more about confusion than conspiracy. It always is.' She grinned at them. 'Still, at least it got you guys talking about a trip to the British Museum.' She looked over her specs at Suzy and turned the full force of her smile on Robert.

'The Lachish frieze,' she said. 'C'mon, how about it, Rob?' Robert was still looking down. Rachel could be a bit too enthusiastic, Suzy thought. She hoped Robert hadn't been scared off.

'What do you think, Robert? D'you fancy a trip to London?' Suzy asked, tentatively. She waited, aware Robert was taking a long time to answer. Then he downed his wine.

'Why not?' he said abruptly, as he had when she asked him to go on the walk to the Scar. 'When do you have in mind?'

She said quickly, 'Nigel's supposed to be taking the kids again the first week of the summer holidays. He's finally promised them a trip to Oasis.' Molly had been campaigning to go to the theme park near Kendal for months.

'That's the last weekend in July, isn't it?'

'Yes. Can you do it?' She was sure he would have nothing else in his diary.

'OK,' he said, 'you're on.' Suzy felt the red wine fire her up. This wasn't just something to look forward to. It was a way of getting him out of Tarnfield, away from the nightmare of who might have hurt Phyllis, or pulled Yvonne off a ladder. As Rachel said, sometimes the cock-up theory made most sense. The flower arranger? It seemed like a crazy theory now.

'And now,' Rachel said, 'let me tell you about my new idea for a documentary for Channel Four . . .'

Before long, she had Robert talking and the difficult time was over. Robert rarely had awkward moods, Suzy thought gratefully. After years of tiptoeing round Nigel's ego, it was so relaxing to be with someone who didn't make taking offence into an art form.

She tried to remember when Robert was ever less than easy-going. He could be a bit prickly whenever George Pattinson was mentioned. And he'd been uncomfortable when Rachel had been joking about incest – but then, it must be infuriating when townies came up with every cliché in the book about village life. But apart from those early days when she had talked about Yvonne's inheritance, she couldn't remember Robert getting impatient, not even when she had suggested that George and Mary were having an affair.

It was what she liked most about him. He never judged or blamed. He was equable. Best of all, he never indulged in the most masculine of traits, giving advice. It was a semantic problem, Suzy thought. Men thought 'advice' meant 'instruction'. She laughed to herself. Robert wasn't like that. And she hadn't taken his advice! He was still convinced 'the flower arranger' was on the loose.

Whereas she just wanted to forget about it.

It was late when Robert left Tarn Acres. He had kept his car at home because he actively wanted to drink. He had felt the need to relax with Suzy, and he had been wary of her friend and needed some Dutch courage. He tried to remember the last time he had met someone new, never mind someone as different as Rachel Cohen. Urban, Jewish, working in TV, she was unlike anyone he came across in his everyday life.

He had been disarmed by her invitation to London and it had taken him a few minutes to decide what to do. It was years since he had been to the capital, or anywhere outside the county for that matter. So much of his life had been about preserving Mary's security. Even after her death he had still been wary, nervous, always on edge in case anyone else had come near to the truth.

He shivered although it was June, and darkness had only just dropped like a chiffon scarf over the clear sky. Now, he had to take risks. It was either that or be marooned on the shores of old age waiting for the tide to take him away.

But Robert had discovered that he wanted to be back in the swim.

On Sunday, on a day of hazy sunshine, Suzy drove Rachel into the Lake District where she bought two cashmere sweaters, and they took a boat trip on Derwentwater, before Suzy dropped her back at the station. When Rachel had been waved off, Suzy went home in time to be there when the children came back from Nigel's.

She sat on Jake's bed and told him about Russell's confession. He avoided her eyes.

'Did you know why Matthew Bell wanted to go to the car wash?' she asked.

Jake snuffled. 'It was awful, Mum. I thought they'd killed someone or something. I helped Matthew, but then I felt sick. That's why I made him drop me off.'

Jake had cried a little bit, like a child, and then told her he was getting up. She waited anxiously to see what he was going to do. She followed him downstairs and watched him delete something from the computer. It was an email from Matthew Bell.

When he was asleep, breathing noisily, she went to bed herself, exhausted at midnight. She fell straight to sleep, feeling better than she had done for a while. Then at two o'clock in the morning she sat bolt upright in bed.

She had been dreaming about the Lachish frieze again. The new dream had bumped around the old dream she had had months before about the dreadlocked Assyrians and the broken reed. But this time Yvonne Wait lay dead on the church floor surrounded by lilies. And out of her blue lips came the words with Rachel's voice.

'Mary's insisting. Mary's insist-ing. Mary's incesting. Mary's incest thing.'

Suzy felt panic rising and choked it back with her fist. Then she snapped on the light. Around her the room looked normal. But she knew that everything had changed.

38

The Monday after the first Sunday after Trinity

Marvel not, my brethren, if the world hate you.
From the Epistle for the Second Sunday after Trinity, 1 John 3:13

Suzy sat at the computer. It was five in the morning. She had to contact Robert but she didn't know what to say. She got up and stood by the window. Dawn was breaking over the fields behind the house. In the distance the clock on All Saints' tower chimed the hour. Birds were singing in Tarn Acres gardens. A pinkish sunlight polished the green fells in the distance; somewhere a delivery van hooted.

She reheated the kettle and poured fresh hot water on her coffee. Then she sat down again. *Dear Robert*, she put, *I had a dream last night*. It sounded over the top. I've heard that before: Martin Luther King.

Dear Robert, she started again, *I understand now*. But did she?

By six o'clock she had still failed to write anything she could send. Her relationship with Robert might be ruined by the wrong words. He seemed so even-tempered, but surely there'd be a point at which he would blow?

In half an hour Molly would wake up, and then the chance would be gone. Suzy put some bread in the toaster. It popped up, and she spread some butter on it. It tasted dry and scratchy. She looked back at the screen. It was hopeless.

Then she picked up the phone, looked at it for a second, and punched in the number for The Briars. It rang twice before Robert answered. He sounded terse and breathless.

'Hello. Robert Clark.'

'I'm sorry, Robert. It's Suzy. I have to talk to you.'

'The children?' he said hoarsely. She was surprised but pleased at his reaction.

'No. I mean, they're fine. It's something else. I'm sorry it's so early but I couldn't sleep.'

He sounded more relaxed. 'Have you been worrying about the reed again? You agree with me now that the flower arranger really *is* on the loose?' He was self-mocking. But he wasn't mocking her.

'No. It's something else.' She breathed deeply. 'D'you remember when Yvonne Wait was talking to you in the hall at the Bells'? After Phyllis died? And I was on the landing?'

'Yes . . .' There was caution in his voice now.

'Did she say something about incest?'

He didn't reply. Suzy waited, aware that in the nervous gap between them she was chewing the same bit of toast over and over, her jaws working. It's nervousness which makes Daisy Arthur chew the cud all the time, she thought. I'm doing the same. I need to push him.

'Robert, tell me. Please. The word Yvonne used wasn't "insisting", was it? It was "incest thing", wasn't it? Mary's incest thing.'

The silence stretched like over-chewed gum, thick between the teeth. Then he said, 'Yes. That's what she said. And I suppose you want to know why?'

'If you want to tell me?'

He paused forever. 'Yes, I think I do. I nearly did once before. Let's talk, but not here. I'd like to get out of this bloody village. Would you have supper with me?'

'I'll get Sharon to babysit. Or if she's looking after her dad I'll ask Daisy.'

'Walk towards All Saints at seven o'clock. I'll pick you up.'

When Suzy put the phone down she was trembling. She had got it right. So what could he be going to say? That

Mary was his mother? She laughed out loud. Then, to her own surprise her next thought was what to wear. She giggled, telling herself this wasn't a date. But suddenly the coffee smelt fresh and the sunshine sparkled like soapsuds in the stainless steel sink. When Molly came down, bumping Flowerbabe the doll on every stair, Suzy picked her up and danced a polka round the kitchen, rather than tuning to the news.

When she'd put out the cereal and juice, she powered the computer down. And then the reservations clicked in. What was Robert really going to tell her? She pulled her dressing gown around her, and turned back to Molly.

Breakfast dragged. Jake was infuriatingly full of beans, a new person. Suzy tried not to smother him, but even now her instinct was to cuddle him as if he was five years old and to quiz him all the time about why he'd fallen in with Matthew Bell. But she bit her tongue, and he went off on the school bus at eight thirty, wandering down the road with two or three other boys from the outlying farms that he'd recently discovered took the bus from Tarnfield to Norbridge. He was better now she wasn't driving him everywhere.

It was no good working on the obesity brief. Instead, she got out the Good News Bible and turned to Isaiah. She started at the beginning. It was almost comical in places. Doom! You're all doomed! *The city which was faithful is now behaving like a whore!* Sexist or what! *At one time it was filled with righteous people, but now only murderers remain.* It sounded like Tarnfield. *Your leaders are rebels and friends of thieves, accepting gifts and bribes.* Was there any truth in the rumours about Jeff Simpson and his lousy business ethics? Or Frank, with his surprisingly large, well-fitted house? It was easy to see how the Bible could be applied to anyone at any time. It was just about human nature, which stayed depressingly the same.

Yet that's not true, she told herself. Education must make a difference. No one today would be influenced by this stuff, would they?

But Isaiah had to be significant for a reason. Why else

would several writers have their work collected under the name of the original Isaiah of Jerusalem? And why was he so important to Christians? It seemed to her that Isaiah was the first person who instructed the Hebrews to behave not by rules but by conscience, telling them that being the earliest monotheists wasn't enough. But didn't Christ also introduce personal responsibility and the notion of goodness for its own sake into the cause-and-effect religion of the time? Just like Isaiah? It was certainly a vital link.

At midday she emailed Robert, asking him if he had any commentaries on Isaiah which he could lend her, and suggesting he brought them with him that evening. The message made her feel better. It made their meeting seem friendlier, less of a summit conference about Mary.

At seven o'clock, in a summer skirt and sandals for the first time that year, Suzy walked self-consciously towards the church. Robert's car drew alongside and she got in feeling she was playing at being a secret agent. He looked different, in cord trousers and a sweatshirt – smarter but tenser.

'I think we got away with that,' he said, pulling away from the kerb.

'Does it matter?'

'It depends whether you want everyone having a view on what you do.'

The idea of people passing an opinion niggled. It was the downside of village life. But once they were on the M6 Suzy felt elated, as if they'd escaped on a holiday, or were having an illicit affair. She'd only done that once, in her twenties, with the film director who always hit her sore toe but nothing else, and it had ended in tears. She reminded herself that this time she was separated from her husband, and Robert was widowed. It didn't matter what people thought.

But that wasn't true. It always mattered what other people thought – if you were a normal human being.

Robert pulled up at a country pub on the road above Keswick. The mountains formed a fretsaw panel against the clear sky and the valley swooped below them. It smelt of summer. They sat in the garden with menus and ordered drinks. It was warm and quiet. A blackbird sang suddenly and almost painfully.

'OK,' Robert said. 'This is it. Are you ready? I am.' He had never expected to talk to anyone about all this. Suzy understood. She smiled and nodded, as if cueing him to talk in an interview. It was best if he kept it as factual as possible.

He started with himself. He was a northern grammar school boy who'd made it to university. Afterwards he'd done a teacher training course, but he'd always wanted to be a writer. He'd had the usual run of girlfriends; then he met Mary when she was secretary at the school where he worked in Liverpool. He liked strong women. She'd been a powerhouse. He'd admired her efficiency as well as her looks, but one day he had caught her crying softly after a problem with one of the more aggressive boys. Beneath her crispness there was massive insecurity. After a few months, he had prised the story out of her. Mary had been a clever girl, destined for college. But in her teens she had fallen in love. Her boyfriend said they should keep quiet about it because her parents might disapprove. He was from a poorer branch of the same family, and Mary's parents would have nothing to do with his mother and father. So theirs had been a secret romance.

'All this happened in Tarnfield?' Suzy asked. Robert nodded.

Mary had committed everything to the relationship, seeing her boyfriend as her passport to the world. There had never been anyone else for her. Then she found she was pregnant. She waited months before facing the facts; then she told her father, whom she adored. His reaction was horror. Despite the extent of the pregnancy, he insisted that the relationship end and that Mary had an abortion. But his motive wasn't snobbery. The real reason couldn't be divulged, so Mary's operation had to be secret. It was illegal and done locally, and it was botched. It was a late termination and Mary ended up with a scar which ran down her belly.

'How terrible!' Suzy said.

She meant it. But underneath she was thinking, how appealing to a knight errant! She stopped, feeling disgusted with herself. But she could see how someone like Robert would be drawn to Mary Pattinson, whose character was such a fascinating combination of the vulnerable with the tough.

'And who was the boyfriend?' she asked, as if she needed to.

'It was the boy she thought was her second cousin. George Pattinson. But Mary's father had had an affair with George's mother years earlier, when she was barely out of her teens. George was the result. Mary's grandfather had married the woman off to a distant, impoverished cousin so his precious son could go on to be a doctor. Mary and George were half brother and sister.'

'That's appalling – at least the bits I can follow are! But tell me the important things. What happened to Mary?'

'She went to pieces. She lost her baby, her boyfriend and her confidence in her father, all at the same time.'

'And George?'

'Oh, he was OK. He took after his natural father, Mary's dad. He was pretty bright. He went to Oxford. He became a teacher. And then some years later, he decided to go into the Church. I suspect by that time he'd met Joan and that Mary was just a memory. But to her, he was still her one true love. She was completely broken by it all. Phyllis was her rock at that time. She helped her do a secretarial correspondence course and eventually encouraged her to get away to Liverpool. But Mary never had any real confidence ever again. Funnily enough she was hopeless outside Tarnfield.'

'I can sort of understand that. It's so unspeakably awful, to lose your virginity to your half brother and to get pregnant too. You'd cling to whatever security you had, even if it was the father who'd got you into that mess. God, how awful.'

And they talk about dysfunctional families today, Suzy thought. The waitress came over and asked for their order, but they needed to look at the menus. It was hard to think about food, but Suzy was glad of the borrowed time. Poor, poor Mary, she thought. But she felt jealousy as well as sympathy. It was irrational and pointless but it hurt like hell.

'And you mended it?' she asked. He looked blankly at her. 'You mended the broken heart?'

'I've never thought of it that way. I just did everything I could to make her life better. She'd been through hell.'

'And she couldn't have kids after this?'

'We never put it to the test. She didn't want to.'

'So why on earth did you move back to Tarnfield?'

He said that it had seemed the right idea at the time. Mary felt that the world despised her. Despite everything, Tarnfield was the centre of her life. She bore no resentment towards her father – how could she? She agreed that he had done the only thing possible in arranging the abortion. She had hero-worshipped him and she had grieved terribly when he died a few years afterwards and the family home was sold. She and Robert were still living in Liverpool at the time.

Then, a few years later Phyllis had phoned out of the blue to tell them that The Briars was on the market again. Mary had cried with relief. She wanted to go home, so Robert had ploughed in all their resources.

'And we moved to Tarnfield only to find that George had just got the living as the vicar!' Robert laughed a little grimly. Had he been taken for a mug? Suzy wondered.

'How did you feel about that? D'you think Phyllis knew when she phoned you?'

'Maybe. You know, I didn't mind. I had lived for so long with the shadow of George in our home that it was almost a relief. To be honest, it was as if it was meant to be: the final catharsis for Mary. I thought our relationship was strong enough to cope. I was a bit of a fool.'

'So they had an affair?'

'No! That's where everyone got it wrong.'

Mary had promised that there would be no revival of a romance and Robert had believed her. He still did. And he knew that, as a priest, George had strong principles, not to mention his commitment to Joan and his children.

Robert shrugged. 'But Mary and George got closer and closer, and met more and more often, until I was squeezed out. George was undoubtedly the love of Mary's life.'

'But it wasn't mutual?'

'I don't think so. George had had so many more chances to broaden his life. His love for Joan was genuine, I'm sure. It was a mess, really. Mary was the loser.'

'And what about you?'

'It hurt like hell. I knew she never got over him. She was a disappointed person, whatever I did.'

'So in the church that day when I turned up, she and George were meeting, just to talk. You're right, it wasn't sexual. I didn't have any sense of them touching.'

'But that wasn't the point. She'd promised me to see less of him. Promised!' He winced involuntarily and looked down at his plate.

Ouch. And how jealous that makes me feel in turn, Suzy thought. 'And then she died and George went to pieces?'

'I suppose so. I think guilt got to him then.'

But none of this explained Yvonne Wait's hold over Robert. If Mary and George were half siblings, why not just come out with it? It was hardly a crime, especially these days, and if they weren't sexually involved who would care?

'But why did this mean Yvonne could threaten you?'

'She told everyone Mary and George were having an affair. It couldn't be disproved. If she had dropped another bombshell, that they were siblings too, and that there had been a pregnancy, it would have been a real scandal. Maybe Yvonne's father was party to the abortion – doctors, dentists, they were all the elite then. Yvonne certainly knew everything. She's got a real tap into the past.'

But it wasn't just the past, Suzy thought. Yvonne would have not only her father's old records, which must have been a mine of information, but new information too.

Being in administration in a hospital must have been the job from heaven for someone like her.

'Did she use medical records from the hospital to threaten other people?'

'I think so. How else would she know about Stevie's HIV test? And I wouldn't be surprised if she was the person who wrote to Russell Simpson telling him Tom Strickland was his father.'

'So everyone wanted her dead!'

'Me included. Yvonne thought I should sell her The Briars. I refused. Then she wanted the bungalow, so she tried to blackmail me into ignoring any will Phyllis might have made.'

'And did you give in to her? Did you ignore Phyllis's will?'

'No. I didn't have to. I searched the house for the will, and found nothing. There was no document. In the end, Phyllis was a Drysdale from Tarnfield. If Yvonne was family, however distant, she was family, and she should get everything.'

But what if Mary had lived, and been threatened by Yvonne? What would Robert have done then? Suzy wondered, after the story he had told her, just how far he would have gone to protect his wife's reputation. It was only the timing that stopped him being a suspect too.

'Excuse me,' she said. 'I need to go to the loo.' Robert looked at her anxiously.

'Don't take too long,' he said. 'There's no bidet here! Or at least not in the Gents!'

In the Ladies she stood with her hands on either side of the sink and looked at her face in the mirror. She looked flushed, excited even. The story of Robert's marriage both intrigued and appalled her. He was such a loving person, but he had spent his love on someone else. If she were to pursue her feelings, would their relationship always be a competition she couldn't win?

She went back to the table to change the subject. They talked about Isaiah over their dessert. It was a good conversation.

On the way out, in the car park, lulled by the wine and the soft lilac Lakeland dusk like smoke on the hills, she said, 'So you really loved Mary, didn't you?'

'Oh yes! But I often wondered if she really loved me.'

Interesting, she thought. Madly, it was on the tip of her tongue to say, 'Well, sod Mary. Move on.' But it was too much, too soon, for both of them, and anyway it sounded like a challenge rather than a declaration. Instead, she raised her eyebrow and looked out of the window.

Robert glanced at her. I wonder what it would be like, he thought, to make love to someone and feel equal passion returned, rather than to someone who has another person in her head? Fighting for Mary's attention had had its erotic side, but not for very long. He had come to terms with being second best, and eventually that had been good enough. But, at least to start with, it had caused him great pain. So could he impose that on someone else? No, there was no way. If he were to love again it would have to be mutual, strong and equal. Mary would have to move over and make room in his heart.

He shook his head to clear it. The motorway was coming up.

'We haven't talked about the flower arranger very much,' Suzy said as they approached Tarnfield.

'One thing at a time, I suppose. D'you still want me to come to Rachel's in London and see the Lachish frieze?'

Suzy had put that to the back of her mind. But now, aping him, she paused, then said, 'Why not? I'm sure you'd be really interested. And by the way, Robert, what started your own interest in theology? You were a mature student, weren't you?'

'Yes. I wanted to beat George at his own game.' Robert laughed. 'The books I brought for you on Isaiah are in the glove compartment. And thanks for listening.'

'Thanks for talking. Goodnight, Robert.'

'Goodnight.'

He dropped her on the corner. She got out and his car turned away. She watched the red lights glow like rubies through the navy night.

39

Trinity season

Be vigilant; because your adversary the devil, as a roaring
lion, walketh about seeking whom he may devour.
From the Epistle for the Third Sunday after Trinity, 1 Peter 5:8

The following Monday, Molly came down with chicken
pox. Suzy ached for her, watching her toss and turn, desperate to scratch. The scabs came off in the bed and dried
in the summer heat, pricking her tender pink skin. After
three weeks she emerged a longer, thinner child and Suzy
realized her baby was gone.

Jake had been taking his first serious tests at school.
Robert gave him some extra classes in English and called
at the house with comics and Lucozade for Molly. Suzy
didn't invite him in: chicken pox in children could cause
shingles in adults. It was best to keep everyone away. She
and Robert phoned and emailed – sensible, restrained
messages about Molly's health. She didn't go to church,
and somewhere in that miserable month she realized that
Nick Melling hadn't called to ask after her or her daughter.
She got her gossip from Babs Piefield. And Daisy popped
round a few times to see how Molly was, but always
stood on the doorstep, terrified of passing infection to
her mother.

Suzy had bought herself a new Bible, the Revised Standard Version, and spent a lot of time reading about Isaiah.
She sampled a commentary which was fairly academic
though accessible for the general reader; then she read a
book about *Isaiah of Jerusalem* – hardly a page-turner,

but she had the book in her hand when Daisy knocked at the door.

'Light reading!' joked Suzy.

'It's really interesting,' Daisy replied, seriously. 'You will be coming back to All Saints when Molly's better, won't you?' she asked anxiously.

'I don't know, Daisy. To be honest I think I've had enough of all that.'

'Nick will be so disappointed.'

'Oh, I don't think so.'

Robert had left her *The Language of Flowers*, with its little Edwardian-style illustrations, and also brought her an old book on flower arranging which had belonged to Mary. Suzy browsed though it, sitting by Molly's bed as the little girl dozed one silent, sunny afternoon in the front bedroom, surrounded by soft toys and the soporific sense of a child's sickroom.

Suzy recognized some of the flower arrangements. Mary was the sort of woman who cooked by recipes and followed manuals, her work always perfect. Suzy was much more slapdash and achieved the occasional stunning success after dozens of messes.

But she admired Mary's thoroughness. She spotted the illustrations of the azaleas and rhododendrons, with glossy camellia foliage, which Mary had used for the Trinity Sunday decorations two years ago, just after her illness had been diagnosed. And there was a dahlia and chrysanthemum display, using leaves of globe artichoke and the ubiquitous hellebore. She caught the name 'zinnias' and recognized them from some of Mary's work. Wondering what they were, she turned to the end of the book and read that their bright colours came originally from South America. Native English flowers were softer and vaguer in tone. Suzy liked the calm of it all; she was missing all this.

Molly muttered and shifted in her sleep; Suzy put down the flower-arranging book sharply. A piece of headed paper fell out of the final pages she had just disturbed. She recognized Phyllis Drysdale's handwriting straight away on the back. It was a note she had written to Mary years before, reminding her she was reading the lesson in church that Sunday because someone else was away. It made Suzy feel sad and creepy in equal measure.

She turned it over and looked at the printed heading. It was from a college in London, and below it was an invitation to a reunion. Someone else had written in blunt black letters, *Are you going, Phyllis? I'm thinking about it.* It was signed, *George P.* Interesting. They must have gone to the same college.

So he had been a postgraduate and Phyllis an undergraduate at the same place. Perhaps they had kept in touch for years and Phyllis had known all along that he was coming back to Tarnfield when she suggested Robert and Mary bought The Briars. Now both women were dead and Suzy would never know.

It made her think again about the deaths in church. The police seemed to have come up with nothing and village life went on, as varied and as unchanging simultaneously as the River Tarn, always in the same bed but with different water.

But the idea of a second link between Phyllis and George Pattinson intrigued her. She thought about Phyllis's note to George. *An old colleague has some very disturbing information about someone.* She had assumed it meant a colleague of Phyllis's. But say it meant a mutual colleague? Someone they both knew? Then it would be much easier to pin down the source of the information, the original broken reed.

She picked up *The Language of Flowers.* It was all very sweet, but it was hardly an academic tome of any real importance, unlike the commentaries on the Old Testament. She and Robert had really been getting mixed messages. It was as if the flower arranger had been playing a game with them: Isaiah for the serious messages, flowers to get them involved. It showed contempt and compulsion in equal measure, as if he was laughing at them by swinging from the sublime to the ridiculous. Perhaps he thought flower arranging was silly – but useful for communication. Suzy saw him as macho and arrogant, using a girlie thing like flowers to get to her. It was suddenly personal and suddenly real all over again.

But who would think of connecting flowers and prophets? Was it someone who had stumbled on a way of scaring people, rather than planning it that way from the start? Perhaps the flower arranger had terrorized Phyllis with a reed, then overheard Tom Strickland, seen Robert and Suzy's response, and realized the potential. It had to be someone who had been within earshot when Tom talked. But that meant the same few suspects as always. Who could it be? And why?

Suzy stood up and looked down the road from the window at the front of the house where Molly's little bedroom was. She had tried to comply with Rachel's instructions when she boarded the train: 'Forget about it, Suzy. You've got enough to do, worrying about your kids.'

But she couldn't forget it. Jake's problems seemed more or less ironed out. Molly was recovering, and before she had been ill she had acquired yet another new best friend. Suzy's family was OK now – so she had time to worry about other things. And the idea that the flower arranger was playing with her frightened her. Of course, nothing had happened for weeks. But nothing had happened for the weeks between Easter and Whitsun. It didn't mean they were safe.

At the beginning of the summer holidays Nigel was planning to take the children away to Spain. Suzy felt a physical twist in her stomach at the thought of being without them for a fortnight. But she was glad they would get away. And she had to get back to work. There was the possibility of holiday relief shifts in several TV newsrooms. Maybe if something more permanent came up as a result, she could move away from Tarnfield and leave all this behind.

And then what would happen about Robert? She wasn't sure. She knew she had fallen for him, but perhaps that was because there was nobody else. If she went back to work, meeting like-minded people in a busier environment, surely she would forget him?

July had been very hot to start with. Stevie Nesbit liked the warm weather. But Alan didn't: he hated the constant bright reflection on his glasses and the way he had a tendency to sweat. He remembered as a child thinking that Trinity was the longest and most tedious of the Church's seasons. The green altar frontals in his home parish always had a dusty, well-worn look, which wasn't surprising. He had always looked forward to the summer holidays, then found them stuffy and constraining in the big Edwardian house his parents had rented, filled with dark furniture and threatening family portraits. He only felt that summer had really blossomed when he took the two buses to Tarnfield and his Auntie May's. Then they could go walking, up on the top of the world. He remembered pacing over the fells, following in Auntie May's footsteps until they had reached Tarnfield Scar, and an almost magical grove where the little oak trees had been clinging to the thin layer of shaley earth. He'd only been there once since. His brow creased.

'Shall we go for a walk, Stevie?'

'Oh, do we have to? It's so nice sitting here with a glass of wine.'

That was true. But he noticed Stevie was staring into space again. He was probably thinking about Nick Melling, Alan thought. Stevie felt snubbed. Without even telling him, Nick had cancelled the Whitsun service where Stevie had been going to play the keyboard. Not that Stevie would have been in any fit state to play, the day after finding Yvonne's body, but he should have had some sort of acknowledgement, Alan thought. Stevie had been prepared to get really involved in the church again, despite that awful day. Alan remembered it vividly – Yvonne's cropped hair and staring eyes, and the scattering of dark green serrated leaves around her body. But Melling had ignored Stevie, not even visiting to comfort him.

Alan sighed. Stevie had gone back into the house.

'What are you doing?' Alan called through the french windows.

'I'm just putting some flowers in a jug. Come and see.'

Alan got up and went into the lounge. Stevie was arranging some flowers for the centre of their dark oval Victorian table.

'Look,' he said, 'aren't they lovely? I've been reading up about flowers recently. It's really interesting. There's love-in-a-mist – that's Nigella! And sea holly with clematis. It's all from the garden. Except this one.'

'Where did you get that, Stevie?'

'Oh that? I sneaked in and got it from the church ages ago. It's just dried hellebore!'

Alan looked at him in horror.

Frank took his gin-and-tonic down to the mahogany bench at the bottom of the garden. He hoped Monica would join him. He looked at her broad bottom as she bent to dead-head the Queen Elizabeth roses they'd planted when they first built the house. The roses were lovely but their big sugar-pink blossoms didn't last long. Still, they could be easily removed. Things had got better recently, he thought. Yvonne's death seemed light years away. The police had accepted everything he said about the ladder, and Monica had slowly started treating him decently again.

She came and sat next to him, took off her sun hat and flopped it on the table. He'd put another glass there for her and she raised it to her lips.

'Matthew seemed to enjoy staying with Joanne, didn't he?' he said cautiously.

'Well, he must've. He's still there. Is it a girl, d'you think?'

'I reckon so. A girlfriend would do him the world of good. He doesn't seem to be seeing so much of Russ Simpson, does he?'

'No. That's no bad thing either.'

Frank stretched out and put his arm round his wife. It

was the first intimate contact he had risked since that awful Sunday at Joanne's. 'Now things have calmed down, we ought to think about a holiday.'

'I'd rather spend the money on the house.'

'OK, love. What would you like?'

'Well, maybe a water feature in the garden?'

'That would be lovely!'

Trust Monica to push the right button every time, Frank thought. He would really like a water feature too. Some sort of waterfall, perhaps, leading to a pond. He said, 'We could have all sorts of plants too. Lilies. And reeds. As long as they're not broken reeds of course. We've had enough of them!'

Instead of laughing with him, his wife looked horrified. She stood up sharply and marched back into the house. Oh, for goodness' sake, Frank thought. What the hell have I said now?

Monica looked back at him from the conservatory at the back of the house. Frank ought to watch his mouth, she thought. It would be awful if he made remarks like that to anyone else. It didn't take rocket science to work out that Phyllis's death and Yvonne's death were connected.

On the bench, Frank felt that he could kick himself. Of course, he shouldn't have mentioned reeds. Tom Strickland had told him in confidence about the mess to Phyllis's hand. But then why did it give Monica such a shock?

He felt suspicion creep over him like the clematis on the sunny side of the house. Could she have things on her conscience too? A sense of fear grew with the shadows in the Bells' garden.

40

Trinity season, continued

*. . . thou being our ruler and guide, we may so pass through
things temporal, that we finally lose not the things eternal.*
From the Collect for the Fourth Sunday after Trinity

The end of the term was suddenly round the corner. Suzy
hadn't allowed herself to think about it much, but she
was still hoping she and Robert would go to London to
see the Lachish frieze. She needed some adult company.
But the trip was fraught with difficulties. She wasn't sure
how committed Robert was, and arrangements with the
kids could be very difficult. Nigel wasn't that reliable
and she had heard nothing more about the proposed holiday in Spain.

Then suddenly one evening he phoned her, confirming.
He would be at a conference in Harrogate until the weekend, but would pick the children up on the following
Friday, the start of the summer holidays, and take them
away. Then she would be free to do whatever she wanted
for a fortnight.

Coincidentally, Molly seemed suddenly much better and
Jake announced that he had passed all his exams – even
English. A holiday mood prevailed. The kids started pack-
ing in advance for their Spanish trip.

Nervously, Suzy called Robert who confirmed that he
was still interested in going to London. He seemed a little
bit distant but she put it down to their lack of contact.

'Why not?' he said, yet again.

Suzy allowed herself a sense of anticipation, but, the day

after she bought the tickets for herself and Robert to travel to London, Nigel called to say he couldn't pick the children up until Saturday morning. 'I've got to stand in for my boss and give a paper,' he said shortly. 'There's nothing I can do about it.' Suzy stopped herself asking what would have happened if it had been the other way around, but this was likely to wreck everything.

'It's OK, Mum.' Jake had overheard. 'Go on Friday like you've planned. We can stay by ourselves that night.'

'No, you can't. You're too little.'

Suzy called Sharon Strickland, who was rather awkward about saying no to babysitting. 'I might be goin' out that night,' she said. Suzy felt embarrassed for asking. Briefly, she wondered why Sharon was being so coy.

When Daisy knocked on her way back from Lo-cost with some sweets for Molly, Suzy tried her too. 'Molly's totally over chicken pox,' she said. 'She's really OK now. There'd be no chance of infection.'

'I don't think I should, Suzy. You know how I love Molly. But I've got to think of Mum. Of course I'd do it if it was an emergency.'

Jake was lurking, listening again. 'It's OK, Mum,' he said. 'I can look after us.'

'No! I've told you, it's not a good idea. You're too young for the responsibility!'

'Pants!' he said, before skulking back upstairs.

In desperation, Suzy went to ask Babs Piefield.

'Well . . .' Babs took her time. 'It will mean staying at your house overnight.' There was a long pause. 'But I'll do it,' she said, after milking the silence.

The next weekend, just to please Daisy for being so kind to Molly, Suzy went to church, alone. Molly wasn't quite ready for the manic activity of Sunday School yet and Jake wanted to work on the computer. She had noticed that he never went out on his own now. Instead he waited for his new friends to call for him. He was clearly scared of bumping into Matthew Bell. But Matthew hadn't been seen around Tarnfield for weeks.

The church felt different. Nick was waiting at the altar steps, beaming, while Kevin Jones ushered people into their pews. Suzy recognized nobody. The service order was printed out on a laminated sheet. Children ran about. The singing was very thin and awkward, with Nick on guitar. It bore hardly any resemblance to the Church of England services Suzy had known. But the most obvious change was that everything was channelled through Nick. He led the choruses, said the prayers, and preached an uninspiring sermon.

On the way out, Daisy stopped her. 'Thanks for coming, Suzy,' she said. 'Are you glad to be back?'

'To tell you the truth, Daisy, it's not for me. I like a grown-up relationship with God.'

Daisy's brow crinkled. 'What about Molly?'

'Oh, she loved Sunday School with you. But I'm not sure I want her getting involved again.'

Perhaps it had been rather a mean thing to say, but the service had upset Suzy. The empty space in the choir pews where Robert and the others had sat, and the ugly plant where Phyllis's flowers had been, depressed her. She had done a quick head count. There were fewer people at the church that morning than there had been six months earlier. This wasn't about a revival. It was about Nick Melling's ego.

On the Sunday afternoon she took the kids into Carlisle to buy some more summer clothes for their holiday. In the Lanes shopping centre she was astonished to find herself looking at boys' shorts in a sale, next to Joan Pattinson.

'For our grandson,' Joan explained.

'Don't you object to Sunday trading?'

'No, though I haven't told George I'm here!' She smiled mischievously, like the old Joan, forbearing and good-humoured, the practical woman behind the larger-than-life cleric. 'It's about time I started taking an interest in our grandchildren again. But I've been so caught up in George's illness.'

'You look well,' Suzy said.

'I am well. We're both a lot better. You know, I think it was a turning point at Easter when you came to see us. And how are you?'

'Preparing for the holidays. The kids are off to Spain with their dad and I'm having a culture trip to a friend's in London.'

'Oh, London.' Joan sighed. 'We used to pop down quite a lot. We stayed with an old chum from our teacher training college days, in Islington.'

'That's where my friend lives!'

'Really? Well, if you get the chance, go and see Michael. He lives off Gibson Square. I'm afraid we haven't been in touch since . . . well . . . since George's illness.'

For a few seconds, she looked grey and haunted again. 'I know Phyllis kept in touch with him but since her death, we haven't made contact.' She groped in her bag for a pen and a scrap of paper. 'Here's his address. He'd love to meet someone from Tarnfield.'

'Thanks.' Suzy stuffed it in her pocket guiltily, knowing she would never follow it up. To her surprise, Joan pecked her on the cheek before moving off down the aisle in search of a bigger size in shorts.

Suzy was glad Joan Pattinson was happier. She knew Robert was angry on Mary's behalf, thinking George had paid so little and Mary so much for their bittersweet relationship. But that wasn't true. It had led to George having a breakdown through guilt, and Joan suffering terribly in turn. Deep down, Suzy thought Mary could have made her life turn around, with Robert's help. She could only feel pleased that the Pattinsons' lives were improving again. And it was salutary to think of Joan and George having friends in Islington. She had thought of them as purely Tarnfield people, but of course they had had lives beyond the village. Didn't everyone?

On the Friday she met Robert at the station. They were both awkward with each other and he looked anxious, she thought. The train left at half past one. Jane Simpson, who was dropping Russell off, saw them on the platform. She

318

raised her eyebrows, but on the train Russell came and sat with them.

'I'm going to Preston today to see the campus. There's a course in agriculture and marketing at the West Lancashire Uni that I might apply for.'

'Great!' Suzy smiled at him.

'Going to London, are you?' he asked. 'So are you guys an item?'

They both said 'No' at the same time. Russell laughed.

'So you are, then. Don't worry; your secret's safe with me.' He laughed again. 'In fact most secrets are safe now Yvonne Wait's dead! I saw her go into the church really early on the day she died, you know. I bet she delivered that letter for me on her way there! I was on my way home after an all-night party in Ponteland. Those were the days!'

'You won't be going to too many gigs if you're taking agriculture seriously,' Robert said.

'Too right! By the way, did you know my dad's got to have a triple bypass op? Mum's trying to persuade him to give up Tarnfield House. It's too much for them now.'

Then suddenly, with a lack of inhibition that was quite touching, Russell fell asleep, his head on one side. He looked like the angelic choirboy his mother had been so proud of, Robert thought.

They watched the hills rise steeply beside them as the train nosed its way through some of the most dramatic scenery in England: valleys so deep, the hills rose like green and grey pillows in the bed beside them; then the track dropped down to Morecambe Bay and the wide sweep of the Lancashire plain. As more strangers boarded and Russell slept on, Tarnfield slipped behind them, and they felt less constrained without having to speak. It was easy to talk, but just as pleasant to be silent, watching the warm lush world out of the window.

Russell woke suddenly, cleanly with no snorting or dribbling, as the train pulled into Preston.

'Well, here we are,' he said brightly. 'Bysie-bye.'

He grabbed his designer travel bag, moving away easily

down the lurching aisle, and waved chirpily to them from the doorway.

'He's gone very camp,' Suzy commented.

'I think there's always been an element of that in Russell.'

'But does it go with his new rural image?'

'Why not? Look at A. E. Housman. Or Alan Robie, for that matter. You can't stereotype country people, you know.'

'Ha! Tell me about it!'

Rachel met them at the station in London and they took a cab to her Georgian flat off Liverpool Road. It was months since Suzy had been out of Tarnfield. She stood on Rachel's tiny balcony and listened to the rumble of traffic. So many people – and troughs of geraniums with no flower arranger.

'We're having a Jewish supper,' Rachel said as the darkness thickened outside. 'It's sunset. Well, I'm not doing it perfectly of course, because it would be wasted on you guys. But . . .' she lit the candles on the table and they flowered into flame, the acrid smell of the match making Suzy's nostrils twitch, '. . . here's the challah bread – that's really soft and yellow and made with egg – and the chopped liver, with roast chicken to follow.'

Robert joined them. He was sleeping in the spare room and Suzy was sharing with Rachel. He wore a crisp blue shirt and jeans. His hair was ruffled.

'L'chaim!' Rachel said raising her glass. 'Great to have you here.'

'Great to be here,' Robert said. 'I've never had anything kosher before.'

'Not even with your Red Sea walking neighbours?' Rachel laughed. 'They haven't asked you round? No? Well, I'm not surprised.'

Suzy stopped, with her knife in mid-air. 'What? Rachel, explain.'

'Oh, you must know who I mean, Suzy. That woman we

went to see. Nancy something. Didn't I tell you at the time? I meant to. I was sure she was Jewish.'

'Really?'

'I should know! Of course, some people keep it hidden.' Rachel shrugged. 'But that's their problem. More wine?'

'Thanks.' Suzy sipped. 'What makes you so sure?'

'Two fridges: one for meat, one for milk. And a Passover night plate in the crockery cupboard. I saw it when I was making tea. We call it a Seder plate. It's for all the relevant fruit and spices.'

'How interesting! We'll have to ask Daisy about it when we get back.'

'I shouldn't.' Rachel got up to fetch the next course. 'I have a feeling she might not thank you for it. Being Jewish isn't universally popular. More chopped liver, anyone?'

Suzy nodded, but yet again something was tugging in her head, something that Daisy had said. But the moment passed and the wine flowed and it was one o'clock before they realized it.

In the bedroom, Rachel whispered, 'Robert looks tastier this time.'

'In what way?'

'I think being out of that village suits him. He's done his hair differently. Come on, Suzy, admit it, he's attractive.'

'Well, he has got a rather nice variegated holly bush!'

Suzy snuggled down on the sofa bed. It was surprisingly comfortable. She was safe in London. She had called Jake and all was well at home. The kids would be with their dad by Saturday lunchtime. She closed her eyes. Tomorrow looked as if it would be a really great day.

But three hundred miles to the north, someone was wide awake, and thinking about Suzy Spencer. The weather was on the turn, too. Over the Scar, thick grey clouds no bigger than a man's hand were starting to gather.

41

The Week of the Feast of St James

St James, leaving his father and all that he had,
without delay was obedient.
From the Collect for St James the Apostle, 25 July

In the morning they set off for the British Museum, which was striking in itself with the glass dome stretching above them and the air of a Mediterranean courtyard in the heart of London. The frieze wasn't a disappointment, either. Suzy was astonished at the realism of the figures carved in relief on the flat, honey-coloured stone.

They had a late lunch in a gastro-pub on Barnsbury Road, and strolled back, slightly light-headed.

'I've got tickets for the theatre as a treat,' Rachel said.

'Wonderful!' Robert felt quite different here. Mary had always worried so much about leaving Tarnfield. She always feared she might bump into someone who knew her from the past. Or maybe she hated being too far from George. He blamed himself for going along with it. He should have made her expand rather than let her contract into herself.

'Oh,' Suzy said, rummaging in her jacket pockets. 'Look, here's that address Joan Pattinson gave me. It's somewhere round here, isn't it?'

Rachel scanned it. 'Yep, just round the corner. You're not going to drop in, are you?'

'No, of course not. We don't have time . . .'

But something was niggling her. This was a chance which had dropped into her lap. If he was an old college friend of the Pattinsons, mightn't he also be an old college friend of Phyllis's? Hadn't Joan said they had lost contact since Phyllis died? In the kitchen, over a mug of coffee, Suzy pulled another piece of paper from her handbag.

'I've been carrying this round since George Pattinson gave it to me. It's Phyllis's note to him. I just wonder . . .'

'What?' said Robert.

'If we found a mutual friend, we could ask if he knew what Phyllis's original worry was all about!'

Rachel looked over her glasses. 'So you want to go and see this old man who lives around the corner? And pump him?'

'Do you think that's wise?' said Robert.

'Look, I know how you feel about the Pattinsons. Don't worry, I'll go myself. I'll only be half an hour. It'll be my good deed for the day.'

'OK,' said Rachel. 'There's no rush, if you really want to. We'll wait for you, won't we, Robert? We can have a good old chat about politics!'

It was a dry, high, grey afternoon, but warm enough for people to be clustered outside pubs on the pavements, wearing skimpy vest tops and T-shirts. Suzy had forgotten there were so many twenty-something people in the world, having a normal time. Her fears seemed like murky over-complex dreams. She felt a surge of optimism. Perhaps the Pattinsons' friend, who must be Phyllis's friend, too, could supply some key fact that would make everything click into place like a stiff door lock which suddenly gives.

Walking through the Georgian streets to Gibson Square, Suzy was reminded of Yvonne Wait and all the misery that she caused in pursuit of property. This place was beautiful in a totally different way. And the houses were four times more expensive, at least. If you needed property as greedily as Yvonne, you could never be satisfied. It could never be worth it, making everyone hate you just for a house or a field. What had Yvonne really been about? Power, probably. Property was power and money was power.

She looked at the flat number on the paper. Joan's writing was big and clear. I'm sure the old chap won't be at home, Suzy thought. But when she rang the bell, a fruity voice bleeped metallically only inches away through the intercom, and immediately invited her in. When she arrived at his flat the front door was open. She entered, following the sonorous voice. She wasn't too surprised to find that the Pattinsons' friend from college was a clergyman.

In Tarnfield, Jake put down the telephone, and went into the garden. Molly trotted behind him. It had been his father, calling to say he was delayed at his conference in Harrogate, and would collect them on Sunday morning.

That's all right, Jake said. We've got a babysitter. He didn't mention that Babs Piefield had already gone because she needed to sit with Nancy Arthur, and that they would be alone that night if Nigel didn't come for another twenty-four hours. But it didn't matter, Jake thought. He wouldn't go and ask Babs to come back. He was still embarrassed about asking her to mind Molly when he went off with Matthew Bell. He could look after Molly for one night. It would be easy.

We'll be fine, Jake thought. I'm virtually a grown-up.

'C'mon, Molly,' he said. 'I'll make your tea.'

'You should call Mummy. You're being disobedient. She'll go mad when she finds out.'

'No she won't. She'll be pleased. And it's exciting being here by ourselves. I'll look after you.'

'I don't want you to, Jake. What if that Matthew Bell comes round? I'm scared of him.'

That was a fair point. Jake had deleted Matthew's email but the message had been burned into his brain. That day, he had been bothered to see the Bellmobile circling the house for the first time in weeks. He knew Molly had seen it too, through the window. He remembered what Matthew Bell had said about his mother. And his sister.

'He won't touch us.' But the words sounded loud and hollow. Jake realized he was sweating. He looked up. Big grey clouds were rolling in from the east. The sky was matted with them.

'Let's go in and get some Coca Cola.' Inside, he opened the fridge and almost put his head in, it was so refreshingly cool. 'Here you are, Molly.'

'But what about Mummy? She'll ring Daddy, won't she, to see if we're safe in Newcastle. And he'll tell her.'

'She won't do that for hours yet. We can watch films and eat ice cream.'

'I don't want to.' Suddenly, in the distance, there was a roll of thunder. Molly screamed, more for effect than in fear, but when she saw how it alarmed her brother, she screamed again for real. 'There's going to be a storm. Jake, I'm frightened, I really am.'

'OK, OK. What do you expect me to do about it?'

'You've got to get us a babysitter, Jake. That's what Mummy would say. Anyone will do. Ring people up.'

'All right.' Jake gave his sister a hug. 'Don't worry, I'll find someone.' He thought for a minute. 'It's an emergency, isn't it?'

'Yes!' Thunder rippled through the sky and cracked above their heads. Outside, darkness had come early.

'OK,' Jake said, and started to punch a number into the phone.

In his London flat, the elderly vicar was holding court to the rather nice young woman who had turned up out of the blue.

'George Pattinson? Oh yes,' the self-consciously mellifluous voice went on. 'Super chap! And Joan is marvellous. Such a tragedy about his breakdown. But I was so sorry to hear that Phyllis passed away. I saw her earlier this year, you know. Quite by chance! I lecture on Roman art. It's a sideline of mine. Came out of lecturing in theology, a fascination with the ancient world . . .'

'Theology?'

'Absolutely. Anyway, you were asking about Phyllis? I bumped into her at a college reunion in March. I was giving the talk. Though I must say, I thought she looked her age.' Suzy watched him preen a little, running his hands through his sparse white hair. He seemed to have lost his thread.

'Did you tell Phyllis something that upset her?' she prompted quietly. 'She left a note which nobody could understand. It referred to meeting a mutual colleague, someone George Pattinson knew too. Could that have been you?'

'Oh, very possibly. Phyllis was doing teacher training as an ordinary student. George and I were postgraduates, of course.' He laughed in rather a superior way.

'What was it you told her?' Suzy held her breath.

'Well, I'm not sure I should repeat it. Confidentiality, you know. Of course Phyllis was a teacher so that was all right . . .'

'Please . . .' Suzy breathed. She didn't have time for his complex ethics system. 'Phyllis died before she could tell anyone. Even George. It might be important.'

'So George was never told? He was probably too ill to cope. It's not nice when things like this happen,' he said. 'Such a pity. That sort of person can be dangerous, you know.' He shook his head.

'Can't you give me some sort of clue?' Suzy's eyes were pleading. In response he shut his own. Then suddenly he snapped them open.

'All right,' he said, his voice brisk now. 'But I'm not giving names or pack drill!'

Suzy allowed herself to breathe, and to listen.

It had been very sad, the prissy old man went on. He had come across a talented student, surprisingly intelligent, at the university where he now lectured in theology. That was one of the problems with theology. It didn't just attract those who wished to study. It attracted people with blind faith, too. Then they spent the whole course trying to prove their point. He didn't want to name names, he stressed again. But this had been a mature student who came from Cumbria, who'd seemed a little unhinged and who'd been sent down from the university, and then returned to the original parish. He'd only made the connection a few months ago, and then when he'd bumped into Phyllis, it seemed a good idea to mention it to her.

That was all he thought he could say, really.

A mature student of theology. Like Robert Clark? Suzy had never asked Robert where he had studied. It could have easily been 'distance learning' at a London college, with summer schools and occasional visits.

'May I use your loo?' Suzy asked.

In the bathroom, she looked at her white face in the mirror. What had Russell Simpson said when they met him on the train? He had seen Yvonne Wait going into the church, really early on Saturday morning. So Robert could have killed Yvonne *before* he met Suzy for coffee. Suzy had assumed Yvonne had gone along to All Saints at mid-morning. But if she was there at eight o'clock, or even nine, Robert could have pulled her off the ladder and then ambled home to meet Suzy.

And he did have a real motive to kill Yvonne. She could damage his wife's reputation, and she was going to inherit Phyllis's bungalow. Suzy had thought about this as she'd walked through the Islington square, crammed with Georgian houses more beautiful than any in Tarnfield. What made the village special was the environment. It would be just like Yvonne to develop Phyllis's house, ruining the view from The Briars, spoiling the home that was a shrine to Mary Clark.

She had to make the old man tell her the name of the mature student. He couldn't be a broken reed any more, talking one minute then clamming up the next! He had to tell her the truth, and stand by it.

She went back into the dining room. The elderly clergyman was talking as she pushed the door open.

'I really shouldn't be discussing these things!'

'But you have to. People's lives are hanging on this! Look, if you can't tell me directly, just talk about this student's good points, things that everyone knew . . .'

'Oh dear, this is such a tricky one. I suppose I could . . . you know, this student was very thorough, but failed the second year exams because of an obsession with Old Testament prophecies. In the end, the college had to say goodbye to her, sadly.'

'To her?' Suzy felt her head spinning.

'Yes, she tried very hard. But as I said to Phyllis, someone like that really ought to be watched in a parish. In my opinion she was mentally disturbed. Such a pity because she worked so hard. Like all students, spare cash was always an issue.' He chuckled. 'I remember she even worked part-time in the local hairdresser's!'

'Oh God,' Suzy said.

Fifteen minutes later she scrambled up the stairs into the flat. Robert and Rachel were sitting, sipping wine and laughing.

'It all fits,' she said to their uncomprehending faces. 'It's really strange, but it all fits. I know who it is. But we've got to go home.'

In Tarnfield, Jake opened the front door. 'Thanks so much for coming,' he said. 'Molly's scared of the storm and Dad isn't picking us up till tomorrow. Molly's not infectious any more, are you, Moll?'

'No, I'm fine.' His sister gave a squeal of delight and ran clattering down the hallway. 'I'm not scared any more either.' She flung herself at the visitor, arms round her waist.

'I'm OK now you're here, Daisy.'

42

Trinity season, continued

From battle and murder and sudden death, Good Lord,
deliver us.
From the Litany

Robert crunched the gears in Rachel's little car and said, 'Oh, shit.' Beside him, Suzy was trying yet again to raise Nigel on her mobile phone.

'I can't understand it. He's not at the flat and he's not answering his mobile. He should have picked up the kids and let me know this afternoon.'

'Perhaps he's taken them out?'

'Maybe. They don't fly until Monday. But I wish I knew where they were.'

She sat forward, grim-faced. Robert crunched the gears and said 'Shit' again. Suzy couldn't concentrate. She was navigating from Rachel's tatty road maps, but Robert had taken on the driving of the first leg because he said he knew the way to the motorway. To her surprise, he said he had a sister who lived in Hendon.

'You never mentioned her?'

'Mary didn't like her so we hardly met,' he said. 'I'd like to get in touch with her again.'

'What's stopping you?'

I don't know any more, he thought. Jenny had come to Mary's funeral and invited him to stay with her in London. But he hadn't been away from Tarnfield overnight until this weekend, which seemed astonishing now. It was surprising how easy it had been. Even coping with the North

Circular seemed achievable, though he could feel Suzy's tension at every red light.

'We have to get to the police,' she said again. 'I've got a feeling in my bones that something's going to happen.'

'Why?'

'Because I was sharp with Daisy last week at All Saints. She wanted me back in Nick's fold and I told her I wouldn't go. And worse, I said Molly wouldn't go back to Sunday School either. I shouldn't have done that. It was spiteful.'

'You're not a spiteful person,' Robert said.

'I can be sharp-tongued sometimes. I wish to God I hadn't done it to Daisy.'

'Other people's certainty can be pretty provocative.'

They sat in silence as the car bowled along the motorway.

'It's going to take us hours in this thing,' Robert murmured.

'I know. But it was good of Rachel to lend it to us and saves fussing over cabs and things at the other end. I just want to get back.'

'The kids will be all right, Suzy.'

'But I won't be happy till I hear from Nigel.'

She tried ringing again; then she stuffed the phone into her bag in frustration. She had called the house too, but there had been no reply.

Rachel had made a flask of coffee for them, while they packed. They shared the driving, passing each other plastic-tasting liquid and drinking it from a mug with a straw. The drink was the only comforting thing on the journey. The motorway had been busy at first with people going out for summer evenings, but after the Midlands it grew quieter and by Knutsford, the sky was darkening.

'Looks like a storm,' Robert said.

They had been quiet on the first leg of the journey. But tension couldn't make the car go faster. When they reached the North, they began to talk urgently, putting the pieces in place.

'If Phyllis had already told Daisy that she knew she'd

been chucked out of uni, Daisy would be terrified of Nick Melling finding out. And there's the allegation of instability.'

'Perhaps he would have asked her to stop working with the children. That would have really upset her.'

'So she goes into the church and threatens Phyllis with the reed. And maybe she leaves her, and Phyllis dies later.'

'Could Daisy be so callous?' Robert asked.

'I think so.' Suzy remembered the evening they had spent making Whitsun decorations. 'Daisy was absolutely uncompromising about religion.' She had a sudden insight. 'She bullies her mother, too. I think Nancy's terrified of her. And she said she did English at uni, then changed. It must have been to theology.'

'I bet Yvonne was blackmailing Daisy. Perhaps Nancy filled in some hospital form saying she was Jewish.'

'Yes! That would be it! Why should being Jewish worry someone like Nancy? But Daisy relates to her father and her Christian half. She thinks Jesus is the only way to God. If she can't persuade her own mother to believe, it doesn't look good, does it!'

'Do you think Nancy knows?'

'Not conclusively. But she must know Daisy is disturbed. Monica told me that the Arthurs still owned the land behind Lo-cost. I bet Yvonne was blackmailing Daisy about her mother's background, to get the land.'

'So Daisy killed her. But why leave the hellebore?'

'Because the reed worked so well.'

Robert thought about it. Daisy may have used the reed to ram her point home, and realized later how much it would affect people who knew their Bible. The Isaiah references were clever, and to Daisy they would clinch her case. She had found the time to cut Yvonne's hair, and it was luck Yvonne was wearing her anklet. The hellebore was just an extra special touch.

'I see. There would be no point in these people getting their come-uppance if no one knew why. And much of Isaiah is about how to behave before God.'

'And Tom Strickland's accident was a God-given opportunity.'

'Yes. It's a warning too. Anyone who stands in the way of her and Nick Melling and the one route to salvation gets hurt.' Suzy shuddered. 'I shouldn't have been rude to her. I can't help feeling I'm next on the list.' She jabbed at the phone again. 'Where the hell is Nigel?'

The rain came at Lancaster, great fat drops splattering against the windscreen. It was fierce but sporadic. There was some sickly sun as they drove towards Shap Fell, but at the top the sky was gunmetal grey and the crack of thunder came from the east.

'I wish it would get on with it,' Suzy said fretfully. But the sky just went on darkening, and, as they turned off the M6, night and the coming downpour mingled in inky blots of cloud.

By comparison, the street lights of Tarnfield looked welcoming.

43

Trinity season, continued

O ye Lightnings and Clouds, bless ye the Lord: praise him
and magnify him for ever.
From the Benedicite Omnia Opera, *Morning Prayer*

The first thing Suzy realized when she entered the house
was that the luggage was still there. She nearly fell over it
in the blackness of the hallway.

'Oh my God, Robert. The kids' stuff is still here.'

She flung open the living-room door. Empty. Then she
pounded up the stairs.

'Jake's here,' she yelled. Robert went up two at a time
behind her. She was shaking her son, and shouting.

'Stop, Suzy. He's completely out.' Jake opened his eyes,
showing the whites, then shut them determinedly. Suzy let
go of his shoulder and he slumped back into his duvet. She
shook him again.

Robert went back on to the landing. He opened all the
doors as he went, looking for Molly's bedroom. He could
sense at once that she wasn't there and snapped on the
light. Suzy was right behind him.

'Oh my God!' she said. 'Where's Moll?' Frantically she
pulled open the fitted wardrobe; then she crashed into the
bathroom, ripping at the shower curtain. 'Where is she?'
she screamed.

'Stop, Suzy. She's not here. But look at this.'

Suzy went stiff and silent with fear. She looked down
where Robert was pointing. On Molly's cupboard the

books and toys had been moved and there were some small, wilting flowers.

'A daisy chain.'

'Yes, but it says something.' Robert leaned forward. 'Get me a pen.' He peered at the flowers. 'Actually, it's quite clear. She's left them on paper and written the reference herself. It's Isaiah 57.5.'

'I'll get the Bible. And call the police.'

'Get the Bible first. This is Daisy's message to us. Remember, Daisy loved Molly. She won't want to harm a little girl.'

Suzy was already back. At first her hands were shaking too much to turn the pages. But she forced herself to be steady.

'It's weird: *You who burn with lust among the oaks, under every green tree.* Oh, listen to this – *who slay your children in the valleys, under the clefts of rocks.* Robert, what is she saying?'

'I don't know. We don't have many oak trees around here.'

'But we do!' Suzy grabbed his arm. 'That day on the Scar, when we stumbled down over the edge of the fell. They were little oaks, weren't they? And we left the children playing on the hill. I kissed you, remember? That car we heard . . . maybe she saw us but we didn't see her!'

'We can go to the Scar and call the police on the way.'

Lightning laddered the sky. Robert kangaroo-hopped the car down Tarn Acres, crashing the gears again. He swore. The fuel indicator was on empty. Suzy was fumbling in the dark with her phone when suddenly it rang out. She punched the keypad.

'It's Nigel,' she said to Robert. 'Where the fuck are you!' she said to the phone. Robert could hear his enraged voice at the other end; then Suzy clicked it off. 'It's my fault of course for leaving the kids. Oh God, oh God,' she moaned to herself. Her phone made a sad little bleating noise. 'Shit. My battery's flat. Can't we go any faster?'

There was no sign of Daisy's car at the Scar.

'So we're wrong.'

'And we're out of petrol,' Robert said. He let the car freewheel into the car park and bump to a halt on the dry-stone wall. An enormous drumroll of thunder rumbled overhead and Suzy felt the first drops. 'It's hailstones,' she said. 'But it's July!' The world had gone mad. Robert was standing on the wall, waving his arms.

'I can see a car. It's hers. She's driven right over the fell to the edge of the path. Let's go.'

He started to run. Suzy felt the pain in her chest and her knees giving as she ran, the hummocky ground tripping her up and the sharp pins of ice-cold hail pricking her face. Robert was ahead of her.

When he was ten yards from Daisy's car, Suzy heard her gun the engine. The car jumped, then moved slowly towards the edge. For a moment it stopped, caught on one of the first rocks that meant the start of the uphill country. Robert lurched forward, hurling himself on the back of the car. It coughed and roared, then pounced forward, only to stop again in a rut beside the path. Suzy caught up and hammered on the window. Then she wrenched open the back door. Daisy was crouched over the steering wheel and Molly, fast asleep through all this, was strapped in the back. Daisy turned to look at Suzy, her face blank and her eyes staring.

Suzy fell forward on her daughter, hearing her own screams. Inside her head she was dead calm but the shriek-ing went on. She unbuckled the seat belt. Her fingers worked well. She watched them as if they belonged to someone else. Somewhere she could hear Robert yelling at her to hurry up. Daisy was pushing at her with her right hand, poking at her eyes and steering with her left towards the edge. Suzy tugged at Molly who shot out of the seat, and they tumbled backwards.

Robert was pulling her and holding the door open. She heard him scream with pain as the rear wheel went over his foot; then they both fell back into the gorse.

Daisy's car went on, bounding over the rocks. It tilted forward; then, in silent slow motion, it tipped over the edge. They heard nothing for an age but the whistling of the wind. Then there was a crash. Robert stood up. He felt no pain, but his legs could hardly carry him. He stumbled to the lip of the Scar.

'It's burning,' he said, but Suzy couldn't hear him. 'The car's burning!' he yelled. She was lying in the soaking gorse, holding Molly. He staggered back, put his arms round both of them and leant on Suzy who stumbled back, guiding them through the freak storm towards Rachel's dented, empty car.

They stood looking at it, drained and in shock. They couldn't leave. The hail had become rain. Through it, headlights loomed and a car pulled up alongside. A girl in the passenger seat opened the back door.

'Gerrin'!' ordered Sharon Strickland. 'Is Molly OK?' Suzy saw that the driver was Matthew Bell.

But wasn't he the enemy?

No, she said to herself slowly. Daisy was the enemy. The woman she thought was her friend and neighbour. What was going on here? She shut her eyes and fell on to the car's back seat, still clutching her daughter whose breathing went on, steady and shallow. There were saliva trails down her chin. Her fists were balled like a baby's.

'Molly's drugged,' she whispered. Her voice sounded cracked, a hundred years old.

Sharon was still talking. 'We saw the kids in the garden by themselves this afternoon. We drove past a few times. We knew their dad was supposed to have come for them, like you said when you asked me to babysit. The front door was open when we drove past just now. Then we saw you in this car and followed it. We went past at first in case you'd just come up here for . . . you know, but then Matt said it was more likely summat was up.'

Suzy couldn't take it in. Robert was beside her, making strange high-pitched gasping noises and holding his foot. Then he said, *'The Lord will cause his majestic voice to be heard and the descending blow of his arm to be seen in furious anger and a flame of devouring fire, with a cloudburst and tempest and hailstones.* Hailstones, Suzy. It's Isaiah 30.30.'

'What does that mean?'

'It means it's over.'

'Sharon, ring the police on your mobile,' Suzy said, her voice coming back. 'There's a car over the edge of the Scar. It's on fire. Then let's get Jake. And take us to the hospital.' She heard herself crying like the track of a very blurred and dreamlike film. In her arms, Molly wriggled and murmured, and then carried on sleeping.

A week later, Frank and Monica Bell went out for a meal at the Plough. It was a rare event, but Frank felt that he wanted to talk to his wife in more formal surroundings. He ordered prawn cocktail and steak and kidney pie, and Monica chose the melon and Dover sole.

After a few glasses of wine and some chat about Daisy's death and the conclusions drawn by everyone in the village, Frank said, 'Can I ask you something? Did you really think I might have killed Yvonne Wait?'

'I could ask you the same question!'

'Well, it did occur to me, but not until just a few weeks ago. You're a bit of a tigress, Monica, where your family's concerned.'

She took it as a compliment. 'And what about you, Frank? You can get very angry. I know you went out very early that Saturday. What really happened?'

Frank squirmed. 'I left the ladder and Yvonne came in. We were both in the church. I told her to keep her mouth shut about the parquet, but she told me to get lost. When it came down to it, I lost my bottle. I meant to go back that night to have another go at her.'

'But she was dead. So who did you suspect? Not counting me!'

'Not Daisy, that's for sure! I thought it was Jeff. Or Jane. They're both tougher than I am when it comes down to it.'

Monica was glad. She had admired the new, strong Frank who'd offered to rip up Yvonne's floorboards, but it was the old softie she really loved. Her son seemed back on track, too. There'd been a time when she had worried about what he was hiding.

'I wondered what was making Matthew so twitchy, too,' she said, 'but now he's calmed down, thanks to Sharon. Who'd have thought he would meet her in a pub in Carlisle. Oh well, the Stricklands aren't all bad.'

'No. Russell's pulled his socks up, hasn't he!' Like most people in Tarnfield, Frank had guessed who Russell's real father was years ago.

'Let's hope Matt does the same. Maybe this girl will be the making of him. I realize now I've always indulged him, maybe because I had such a hard time carrying him!' Monica smiled, reminiscing. 'All that morning sickness and nausea. You know, Frank,' she said, looking at him levelly, 'even now I've got a really keen nose for odours. I can always tell when someone's been smoking. I can smell cigarettes a mile away.'

Frank said nothing, but put his head down and studied the menu with complete concentration. Then he said, 'I just wanted to say thank you, Monica. You're the only woman in the world for me.'

Monica said nothing but she blushed, and smiled quietly into her lemon cheesecake.

44

Trinity into Advent

Almighty God, give us grace that we may cast away the works of darkness and put upon us the armour of light.
From the Collect for the First Sunday in Advent

Three months later, the Reverend Linda Finch said, 'Come in, please,' and motioned Suzy Spencer towards the sofa. Suzy sat down and reviewed the front room of the vicarage under its new occupancy. There was a log fire in the grate and there were new bright-coloured curtains and a throw over the settee. Joan Pattinson's lamps were back and the furniture gleamed. There was the smell of hot coffee.

'You had a terrible time in the summer,' Linda went on. 'Now the inquest is finally over, I wanted you to make the choice to come to me, rather than have me just turn up on your doorstep. That's why I wrote to you. You must have very mixed feelings about the church.'

'No, not at all! It's straight cynicism, actually.'

The priest laughed. 'I don't blame you. Now the Bishop has moved on, I think I can safely say that we mishandled things. We were very lucky that Daisy's death was treated as a straightforward suicide, or we could have been dragged through the press. Poor Nick was totally inexperienced. You sometimes get priests with no ability to empathize. And he completely took in the Bishop.'

'Nick was very credible. I do see that.'

'Yes. He's coping now in a more urban parish with extra support. We should have got counselling for him. And for

George too, after his breakdown. He's helping me out now with the team ministry. He speaks very highly of you.'

There was a silence. I'm not going to make it easy for her, Suzy thought. She hadn't been back to any church since Daisy's death. But she had stayed in Tarnfield because she needed to come to terms with things, and because it was home for all three of them.

On one of the golden days of autumn when the inquest into Daisy's death was over, she and Jake had walked over Tarnfield Scar. Jake had suddenly grown up as boys do. Suzy had found that she liked his easy company. He had done his best to cope and to sort things out in his head, she thought, and he had worked out what had happened for himself. The police had gone out to the Scar and retrieved the car wreck and Daisy's body, and the following day she and the children had been questioned. But Jake could remember little about it, and Molly had been dead to the world. Later, there was no forensic evidence that Daisy had drugged them, and it had been arguable that she'd taken Molly for a drive and lost control of the car. Suzy was more than happy to play down the drama.

Nigel had delayed the holiday in Spain for a few days, but then the police let the children go away. It was the best thing. By the time they came back, the official procedure was under way. But with no real proof, it was just a matter of conjecture about what Daisy had done. The police closed the inquiry into Yvonne's death. And life went on.

Who would have guessed that Daisy would turn out to be dangerous? Suzy often thought. She had been to see a counsellor who had talked to her – and to Jake – about Daisy's psychosis as an individual. There were people who were obsessed with religion, just as others were obsessed with drugs, she learned. And Rachel had talked to her about it a lot. She knew several Jewish friends who had converted to Christianity – and occasionally vice versa – without such terrible traumas. But on the whole it had left Suzy feeling that religion caused little but trouble. Like Nancy Arthur, who had come out of this with great sorrow and dignity, Suzy thought proselytizing religion had nothing to commend it.

'And how are your children?' Linda Finch asked.

'Fine. Amazingly fine.' Robert had said it was because they were the product of a happy, stable home. Suzy had raised her eyebrows, but loved him for saying it.

'We failed Daisy too,' Linda said. 'I realize that. She needed our help.'

'And my daughter nearly died. Daisy thought she'd be better dead than with a mother who denied Nick Melling's mission.'

'That's not Christianity at all.'

'But what could you have said? Isn't it in your New Testament, that if you're not for me, you're against me? Isn't that the Christianity Nick Melling preached? Didn't he relate it to himself?'

Linda Finch leant forward. 'That's Matthew chapter 12. But in Mark chapter 9 Jesus says, "He that is not against us is for us." I like that much better.'

Fair point, Suzy thought. She nodded. But she was still unconvinced.

'And how's Mr Clark?' Linda asked.

'I haven't seen him since August,' Suzy said. 'He had his foot strapped up; then he went to his sister's to recuperate. We met for one weekend.' She remembered that strange meeting at Robert's sister's house as if it were a dream. 'He's missed the autumn term. But he's coming back for Christmas. We've been emailing.' She felt her face reddening. It was the fire, she thought.

'Look,' Linda poured more coffee, 'I know you've got your doubts. You're an intelligent woman. I respect that. But we need people like you. In Mark's gospel someone says, "Lord I believe; help thou mine unbelief." We're all struggling fellow travellers.'

Suzy grimaced. The last time she had heard that phrase it had been used by Daisy, with exactly the opposite meaning.

Linda was saying, 'But you enjoyed being part of All

Saints before. Why not think about joining us again? I need someone to do the Christmas flowers –'

'You must be joking!'

'No, I'm not. Please think about it.'

Suzy put her cup down. 'You get full marks for trying,' she said. 'What about Monica?'

'She's got her hands full now Sharon and Matthew are getting married and going off backpacking.'

'Jane?'

'The Simpsons are moving to Norbridge over Christmas.'

'Or Janice Jones?'

'You probably know that Kevin's got a job with computers in Dubai now. He told me he wanted more financial independence from his mother-in-law, especially as Janice is pregnant again. So they won't be around.'

'Who else is there?'

'Steve Nesbit. He says he'd be your assistant. He's very good. But he doesn't want the responsibility of being in charge. I just thought you might consider it.'

'No way,' said Suzy.

'Please think about it. We're a broad church. We want everyone who wants us! Jesus had twelve dedicated disciples but innumerable followers. There's room for everyone. It's up to you, and to God, how long the journey of faith takes you. Not every priest is a spiritual dictator like Nick Melling, you know.'

'Thank you,' Suzy said, 'But I don't think it's for me.' Unbelievable! Where did these people get their persistence?

'Please . . .' said Linda Finch.

A few weeks later, Suzy parked the car at Carlisle station. Robert looked fatter and walked with a stick, but it was great to see him. They had kept in touch, sometimes quite intensely, but there was a queasy uncertainty about their meeting. She helped him into the car and told him the latest village news as they drove down to Tarnfield.

'I'll try not to knock down the fence,' she laughed as they pulled up. He had sent her the keys in advance and she had put on the heating and the lamps. Although it was only four o'clock, the dusk was coming in and little flurries of snow blew on and off outside.

'How about a bottle of wine?' Robert said. 'Makes a change from all that coffee and biscuits we got through.'

'Great! It's good to see you back home.'

'It's good to see you too. But I don't know about "back home".'

'Oh, come on, Robert. You love The Briars. It was the centre of the world for you and Mary.'

'But it was a small, confined world. And Mary's dead.'

'But you loved her so much!'

'That was another time. I was another person. Down at my sister's I realized that the real me was very different from the man who became Mary's protector. And it's owing to you. I've written and told you I love you, Suzy. It's completely different this time.'

'And better?' It was a difficult question, but she had to ask it. She hadn't worked in daytime TV for nothing.

He looked at her evenly. 'And better. Yes. Much better.'

He took a sip of his drink and looked out of the big bay window. 'What about you? You seem to have reservations?'

'You've answered them. Of course I love you. I did even before you helped me get Molly back, but that clinched it. You're not my type but I think you're wonderful.' She walked over to him and put her arms round him. 'I like old farts a lot more these days, but not with tweed hats. They have to go!'

'It's a deal!'

She smiled and stared out at the grey and white garden. The snow was sticking now, and the slow change and silence were mesmerizing. It looked like a monochrome photograph, absolutely still but for the tiny gentle flakes, no wind now to stop them slowly coating the foliage like icing sugar. The roof of Phyllis's bungalow was completely white.

Robert held her and whispered, 'Suzy, I'm like Ruth the Moabitess.'

'What, you're a transvestite?'

'No, you idiot! I mean, I don't have to stay in Tarnfield. I'll go where you go and your people will be my people. That's what Ruth said to her mother-in-law in the Old Testament. I'll go wherever you want. We can leave The Briars behind.'

'Maybe. But not yet. And I don't want it to be up to me. Make up your mind for yourself. You adapted to Mary. I don't want you to adapt to me.'

He stroked her hand. 'Thank you,' he said.

There was a moment's silence. 'Anyway,' she went on, 'if I do the Christmas flower arrangements at All Saints I need to get my hands on your variegated holly bush!'

Robert didn't know whether to laugh or kiss her. So he did both. Then Suzy pushed him away, and looked at him seriously.

'Pick up your glass,' she said. 'To the future.'

'To *our* future,' he answered.

That Christmas, as well as all the usual decorations, there was one simple arrangement of cream-tinged holly with lilies at the back of All Saints Church. A tiny card on it read: *In Memory of Phyllis Drysdale. Much missed flower arranger. From Suzy Spencer.*

A note on the Church's seasons

The Church of England's calendar starts with the season of Advent, beginning officially on the nearest Sunday, before or after, to St Andrew's Day (30 November) – in effect the fourth Sunday before Christmas – and ending on Christmas Eve.

The twelve days of Christmas, celebrating the birth of Jesus, come to a climax with the feast of Epiphany on 6 January. This marks the arrival of the wise men bringing their gifts to Bethlehem, when the Christ-child's arrival was first made known to non-Jewish people. In some countries, people give presents at Epiphany rather than at Christmas.

For the rest of the year, major Church festivals are linked to the date of Easter. This falls on the first Sunday after the first full moon after the spring equinox (20 March). Easter could fall at any time from 22 March to 25 April.

Before Easter comes the forty-six-day season of Lent (the forty days Jesus spent in the wilderness, plus six Sundays), starting with Ash Wednesday and ending just before Easter. The name 'Lent' is from an old English word meaning spring – literally, when daylight hours lengthen. Depending on the date of Easter, Ash Wednesday can be as early as the first week of February and as late as the second week of March. Lent is a period of repentance, prayer, fasting and reflection. There will probably be no flowers in church.

The fourth Sunday in Lent is Mothering Sunday and the fifth is Passion Sunday. Then comes Palm Sunday, when the Church remembers Christ's triumphal entry to Jerusalem on an ass. This is the start of Holy Week, leading up to Good Friday (perhaps originally 'God's Friday') – the bleakest day of the year as the Church commemorates the crucifixion of Jesus. Then, after Easter Eve (sometimes known as Holy Saturday), is Easter Day, the joyful celebration of Christ's resurrection from the dead. The name 'Easter' could come from the pagan god Eostre whose feast was celebrated in April, or it might be from the Anglo-Saxon *ostre*, to rise.

The Sunday after Easter is known as Low Sunday, though no one seems to know why. Perhaps there's a feeling of come-down after the joy of Easter. The fifth Sunday after Easter is Rogation Sunday (from the Latin *rogare*, to ask), when there are special prayers for God's blessing on the crops. Some churches observe the tradition of 'beating the bounds' on Rogation Sunday, processing round the parish boundary. The following Thursday is Ascension Day, marking the ascension of Christ into heaven.

A week and a half after Ascension Day is Whit Sunday (or Whitsun). This feast commemorates the coming of the Holy Spirit to the disciples on the Jewish harvest festival of Pentecost, and many churches refer to Pentecost rather than Whit. 'Pentecost' is from the Greek word for fiftieth; the original Jewish celebration was on the fiftieth day after the second day of Passover, while the Christian Whitsun/Pentecost falls on the fiftieth day of the Easter season. The name Whitsun probably comes from White Sunday, after the ancient custom of wearing white robes at and after baptism.

Because of the movable date of Easter, Whit Sunday could come any time in the period from 10 May to 13 June. Whit Monday is a public holiday in most European countries. In Britain it has been replaced by the Spring Bank Holiday on the last Monday in May, though many people still refer to it as the Whitsun holiday.

The Sunday after Whit is Trinity Sunday, when the Church reflects on its fundamental doctrine of God as three persons in one God: Father, Son and Holy Spirit. The long season of Trinity continues until the start of Advent, punctuated by occasional saints' days on fixed dates such as Michaelmas (St Michael and All Angels) on 29 September. Most churches hold a Harvest Festival in late September or early October. The Church also commemorates All Saints – or All Hallows – on 1 November, though popular ways of marking Hallowe'en the previous day have lost any connection with the Church's teaching.

Acknowledgements

All quotations at the heads of chapters are from The Book of Common Prayer.

I would like to thank my agent Vanessa Holt for all her help and advice. Thanks too to Barbara Carthew for teaching me the little I know about real church flower arranging, and for helping me with research for this book, and also for her personal support. And I'd like to thank all my old friends who were so kind during the unhappy winter of 2003/4 – Jane Mawer, Jane Joscelyne, and Vreni and Andy Stephen and many more.

I want to thank my friend Lesley Beames, former TV researcher, now magistrate, who was the first to read this, and my sister-in-law Gill Chivers of Ontario for helping make it more readable in North America. Thanks also to my friends Claire Kilvington and Lynn Miles, for reading the manuscript and for their suggestions. Sadly Lynn died before the book was published but her enthusiasm inspired me (and everyone else) and she will be sadly missed.

I would like to thank journalist and writer Victoria Kingston for her friendship and for making me persevere! I owe her a great deal for her unfailing professional support and interest, and for introducing me to the very kind novelist Peter Lovesey who in turn introduced me to Vanessa Holt.

Thanks also to my great friend Peter Elman for his help with twists of the plot, and to my colleague Harriet Gilbert of the MA in Creative Writing at City University for her encouragement and sterling advice to 'get on with it and write another murder mystery'.

My faith in the accepting Anglican Church has been revived by the Reverend Michael Learmouth and his wife Bridget of St Andrew's, Thornhill Square, Islington, who run a warm and welcoming parish where I and my partner Richard Parker are now so happy.

And I would especially like to thank Richard for his help, on every aspect of this book but especially with all things theological. The character of Robert Clark bears some resemblance to Richard Parker . . . and yes, dear reader, I married him!

Lis Howell
September 2006